D0868121

CULLIGAN'S WAY

Marvin Levine

Contents

Paperback ISBN: 979-8-9851999-4-9

Cover Design by www.coveredbymelinda.com

CULLIGAN'S WAY

CHAPTER 1

Tim sat on the edge of the exam table waiting for his test result, his hand held tight over his bouncing knee in a futile attempt to calm his nerves. He'd been waiting over half an hour in the small room, watching the walls. One had glass framed cabinets filled with various liquid chemicals. On another hung a crooked picture of a stock beach scene in a cheap frame. The place smelled antiseptic, and something else the disinfectant tried to mask — maybe some disease of the prior patient. At least it was better than the hour he spent waiting in the front of this Doc-in-a-Box where a room full of masked patients coughed and wheezed.

Tim stared at the faded beach scene print and daydreamed about his long ago home in South Carolina. This spring would be ten years since he fled Culligan's Way, right after his high school graduation. He recollected his annual call to his older sister, Sally, last month right before Christmas. Randy was back with Molly again, but then got arrested for another DUI. Mom had another episode. Connie may have to go back to rehab. Dad still ruled the coast. In other words, par for the course in Pawleys Island. Tim had told her he was fine, in good health, etc. etc. He missed Sally, the only one in the family he could talk to. She asked him again if he thought he might make it down to the Way next year. He told her the same thing he did every year. Not a chance.

Tim heard a knock on the door and a young man in a white lab coat and N95 mask entered the room. To Tim, he appeared to be even younger than he was, and had similar features to himself — straight auburn hair, blue eyes, and a few freckles on his cheek visible above the mask. What he didn't have was any form of bedside manner.

"You're Tim Culligan?" he asked, not looking up from his clipboard, making no attempt to shake hands or otherwise greet Tim.

"Yes, sir." Sir came out reluctantly. Old Southern habits die hard.

"I'm Mark Baker, the PA on call." He finally took his eyes off his clipboard and looked at his patient. "You have Covid, Tim. The Delta variant is widespread throughout the city right now."

"Aw fuck." Tim shut his eyes, hearing the confirmation of his worst fear. When he reopened them and looked at Baker, the PA's eyes were as indifferent as the raw, blustery wind howling down Manhattan's canyons.

"You should get through it alright. Do you have any underlying conditions?"

"Yes! I have asthma. That's not good." Obviously, he hadn't checked the form Tim filled out, stating his condition.

"Hmm," Baker replied, now checking his clipboard again. "Yes, I see." He mumbled something unintelligible.

Tim could have sworn Baker muttered, "sucks for you," but couldn't be sure.

Baker's eyes again met Tim's. "Well, Tim, there's nothing much we can do for you. Make sure you have plenty of inhaler, get rest and drink as much fluid as you can. Don't go to the hospital except as a last resort. Most Covid patients checking into hospitals right now are leaving in bags." He said it as if he were saying, 'looks like it may start snowing.'

Blood drained from Tim's face. Fuck this guy. He couldn't wait to get out of there.

Baker made a few notes on his clipboard again. He glanced back to Tim. "That's all. Good luck. See the nurse on the way out. If you would excuse me." Baker didn't wait for a reply, he just walked out of the room.

Tim sat there dumbfounded as a wave of nausea washed over him.

******

Two months later, Tim stared out the sixth-floor window of his tiny Upper West Side studio apartment and contemplated his dismal situation. He survived Covid, barely. He couldn't remember how many times he laid in bed, racked in pain, trying to catch his breath, thinking, this is it, I can't go on, I need to call 911. But each time he thought he had reached rock bottom, he remembered what that damn PA told him about Covid patients in hospitals leaving in body bags. He never made that dreaded call.

By the end of the first month, he felt somewhat better, but still had difficulty breathing, on top of his normal asthma attacks. A visit to an actual doctor confirmed he had scarring in both lungs and would face a long recovery — months, or even years. Tim had no strength, no stamina, and hadn't worked since the week before they diagnosed him.

Ellen, the owner of the dance studio he had worked in ever since he arrived in New York, had been patient and sympathetic. But when she called last week and asked when he'd be able to return, he couldn't say anything positive. Soon his financial assets would dwindle to nothing. Thank goodness for his friend and coworker, Brian, and a few of the girls at the studio. They had checked in on him and brought groceries. Otherwise, he might have starved to death.

Tim heard a knock on his door. Brian had told him he needed to stop by. "Come in, it's unlocked," he said, his voice still hoarse.

Brian entered the room, holding an envelope. "How's it hanging, buddy? Making any progress?" He took a seat next to Tim on his dilapidated, threadbare couch.

"No, not really. What do you have there?" Tim stared at the envelope and could see it had the studio's logo.

"Here," Brian said, handing it to Tim with a sheepish grin, "it's from Ellen."

Tim knew it would be bad news. Brian was never good at hiding his emotions. When he opened the envelope, he saw a letter and a check. A quick glance revealed a payroll check for $500. Tim received the last funds he was due, including all accumulated vacation time, two weeks ago. He knew immediately what it meant. He bit his lip and opened the letter.

Tim,

I am so sorry to have to write you this letter. You have been such a positive member of our team for the past ten years. We all send you our very best wishes for your recovery. However, until you can regain your strength again, I have no choice but to end our business relationship. Enclosed is a small severance check. I know it's not much, but it's the best I could do. Please let me know when you are well enough to return. Until then, we all wish you the very best.

Ellen

Tim looked up at Brian. "Well, that's it. I'm out."

"I'm so sorry, Tim. What are you going to do?"

"I don't have a fucking clue," Tim said caustically. He gazed out the window again, fighting back the tear forming in the corner of his eye. "I don't know how I can stay in New York. I'm almost broke now. A five-hundred-dollar severance and unemployment won't dig me out of this hole."

"Do you think you might go back to South Carolina? What about your family? I've never heard you talk about them."

Tim scoffed. "Yeah, for good reason, too. That's an absolute last resort."

Brian paused and watched as his friend looked back out the window. "Sounds like you're pretty close to that now. Tell me about them. Maybe I can offer some encouragement."

Tim turned back to Brian after he wiped the tear away. "Yeah, sure. Why not?" Sarcasm leached out of Tim. "So, let's see. When I came out as queer, my father practically disowned me. My brother should be in prison for the rest of his life, for what he did to me, and others. Instead, he walks all over my parents. My mother is bi-polar *and* schizophrenic. You never knew what side of crazy she'd wake up on. And my younger sister is a drug addict who spends more time in rehab than at home. I talk to my older sister Sally once a year. At least she's on a more normal plane. What a cast of characters, down there in good old Culligan's Way."

"It's been ten years, Tim. Maybe things have changed."

Tim chuckled at his friend's optimism. "Changed?" Tim said, as if he didn't know what the word meant. "Let me tell you something, buddy. Things don't ever change in the South. Shit, they still fly the goddamn Confederate flag on top of the statehouse."

Brian pondered Tim's acerbic remark. "Wait a minute, no — you're wrong. I remember reading last year they took down that flag. So there, things *can* change in South Carolina. All I'm saying is I think you should give your family a call. They might surprise you."

Tim tried to take a deep breath. His chest ached. It always ached. He felt like he was heading down a rabbit hole with no idea where he'd come out. Or a black hole, where nothing ever came out. "I'll think about it, Brian. I'll think about it."

CHAPTER 2

Three days later, Tim reached the end of his rope. The bills were piling up and he had no way to pay them. He wasn't strong enough to work anywhere. He couldn't even do phone solicitations, too much talking wore him out. Something had to give. After the conversation with Brian, Tim thought more and more about his family—the cast of lunatics, bigots, drunks, and fools he'd sworn he would never again have anything to do with. It was exactly ten years ago this May, one day after graduating high school — humiliated once again at his graduation party at Culligan's Way — that he'd cashed out his savings account, boarded a bus out of Pawleys Island to Myrtle Beach, then caught a Greyhound to New York City to start his new life.

Now, for the first time since that fateful summer day, Tim thought seriously about the possibility of going back. He contemplated more what he remembered about his family, what Sally had told him had happened in the last ten years, and what they might be like now.

It had all begun with his father, of course. Judge Rudolph Culligan, a driving force in Georgetown County justice and politics for over thirty years. The judge — Rudy to his friends and confidants, simply sir to Tim and everyone else — ruled Culligan's Way with an iron fist, the same way he ruled his courtroom. The Charleston Post Courier ranked Rudy the second most conservative and punitive judge in South Carolina, according to Sally, and rumor had it he was none too pleased about being runner-up to anybody.

Rudy was a devout Catholic who insisted anyone living in his home attend Mass each Sunday, attend Sunday dinner at the Way, and never utter a cuss word in his presence. In Tim's childhood, the phrase "washing your mouth out with soap" had been applied literally and liberally in the Culligan household by Rudy, and by Tim's mother occasionally. Tim remembered how awestruck he'd been at the vulgar language all around him upon arriving in New York. He'd adjusted pretty quickly.

Rudy had no patience or temperament for many portions of the population — lawbreakers foremost, but not too far behind were Democrats, liberals, Yankees, anyone not heterosexual by nature, and feminists — in no particular order. He insisted he was colorblind and had no bias towards race, religion, or national origin. A statistical study of his thirty years of rulings might suggest otherwise.

Tim hated him as much as any other human on earth. Except for his brother. Tim considered his older brother Randall — Randy to everyone except their father — the most loathsome creature God had ever placed on the planet. No two men could be more opposite from each other, and Tim often wondered how it was conceivable they shared the same DNA. Randy was four years older than Tim, but light-years less intelligent, compassionate, considerate, and respectable. In Tim's humble opinion, his brother was a drunk, a misogynist, a homophobe, and a sadist rolled into one despicable human being. At least, that was what Tim remembered.

It was Randy, more than anyone else, who had made life so intolerable for him in Culligan's Way. Tim's last four years there, his high school years, had been a living hell. But for

Randy, who'd barely made it out of high school himself, those four years were where he'd honed his skills to become a malignant narcissist and turned his parents into his enablers.

Randy was responsible for what had happened at the graduation party. The fury Tim felt that night, the last night he had seen or spoken to his brother, still burned hot a decade later. He never asked Sally about Randy on their infrequent phone calls. Every once in a while, she'd throw in an unsolicited tidbit or two.

Randy had served some time for his umpteenth DUI, and eventually, even Rudy couldn't save him. He was engaged to Molly Elmwood twice, but never married.

Tim remembered Molly from Waccamaw High; she was just a year older than him. A nice girl, even if she was a little on the slutty side. She'd understood how he was different. Few kids had. According to Sally, Molly and Randy seemed to have an ongoing love-hate relationship. Rudy disapproved.

Randy lived part time at the Way and partly at a fish camp on the Waccamaw river, where he stayed drunk with his buddies and left the real world to everyone else. Tim would have to check with Sally to see if this was still the case. The thought of living in the same house with his brother, even in the spacious home of Culligan's Way, might just be a deal-breaker — even if there'd be a deal to begin with.

Then there was mother — Ruth Jennings Culligan. What memories did Tim recall most vividly? The bi-polar rants when she went off her meds, the off-the-chart OCD with the cleanliness of Culligan's Way, and the iron grip she held managing the home. More than anyone else, Culligan's Way *was* Ruth Culligan

— the embodiment of a woman who was both a pillar of strength and bat-shit crazy.

But if Tim *were* to be allowed to come back home, it would be Ruth who would allow it. She made no secret of the fact that while Rudy may consider himself the head of the family and the household — that was his right — Ruth was the neck, and the neck turns the head. Rudy knew his place. He loved his wife despite her many flaws. Their marriage of now thirty-five years, twenty-five at the Way, had survived her mental instabilities, including two hospitalizations Tim knew of, infidelity, and attempted murder. In fact, there were ties to all the above.

Well known in Pawleys Island lore; in 2002, Ruth caught Rudy in a sordid affair with a local waitress. She subsequently mixed a teaspoon of rat poison into his pimento cheese, which nearly killed him and left him with partial paralysis on the left side of his face. Ever since, Rudy had a droopy left eye, a flabby left cheek, and difficulty hearing out of his left ear. A constant, convenient reminder, in Ruth's estimation. Ruth agreed to a guilty plea by reason of insanity. Rudy bargained a stint at the Charleston Arlington Mental Health Institute instead of prison time. After that, he kept his cock out of the local pussy pool, or at least he kept any shenanigans out of Ruth's sight.

The second incarceration, five years later, had more to do with a seventeen-year-old, out-of-control Randy. Tim had witnessed that whole repugnant affair. If Ruth had spent any more holidays in Charleston in the last ten years, Sally hadn't mentioned them.

But Ruth had her bright side as well. On her meds, she was a loving mother. She took care of the help, including their extended families. She defended the Culligan name with fierce determination. Any negative news about them in the media would cause a behind-the-scenes threat to the offending outlet's advertising being pulled.

After one such negative story aired on WCXM Channel 12 out of Myrtle Beach, relating to Ruth's second stay at Charleston Arlington, the news outlet found themselves on the short end of their two highest-grossing revenue sources, the Juan Rivera law office, and Coastal Chevy / GMC. Rudy had gone to law school with Juan, and the president of Coastal Chevy played eighteen holes with Rudy every Saturday afternoon at the Caledonia Country Club in Pawleys. The following week, Channel 12 aired a retraction of their previous story and a glam piece on their morning talk show, showering the Culligans with praise for the many contributions they had made to the community. The neck always turns the head.

Tim paused his recollections and smiled as he thought about the power and influence his family had wielded over the entire South Carolina coast north of Charleston. And that was just what *he* had experienced, plus the little Sally had shared. A ray of hope shone on Tim; he actually looked forward to hearing more of the stories from the past ten years he had shut himself away from.

Finally, there was Connie, the younger sister — the rebel. Four years Tim's junior, Connie had been only fourteen when he'd left but was already a hell raiser. Tim thought he'd witnessed Connie have her mouth washed with soap (or attempted) more times than any of the other three combined. She obstinately refused to follow Rudy and Ruth's strict rules.

She paid a high price for her stubbornness, but to his recollection, she never fully bent to their will. And that was when she was only fourteen. From what Tim had gleaned from Sally, Connie had been in and out of rehab several times and had a serious narcotics problem, but she still somehow lived at the Way. Tim couldn't wait to hear more about her.

In short, the women in his family would be his salvation. They had stood by him and defended him when the brutal harassment from his father and brother had been too much to bear. Tim would either be allowed to return to Culligan's Way because of them or not. He put his financial papers aside and girded himself for the call to his sister. Sally — the normal one. The only one in the family with a conventional life.

Sally was the second child of the Culligan clan, two years younger than Randy and two years older than himself. She had been married to Steve Hobart for eight years now, and Tim always regretted not having made a return trip for her wedding. The two years between his flight and their nuptials had been just too short a time for him to come to grips with. Sally and Steve had two kids, Joey and Amber, aged what — he guessed four and two? Or five and three? Tim wasn't great on birthdays.

Sally maintained a steady job as an Assistant Manager at the Pawleys Island Publix, and Steve was an accountant. They lived in one of the nicer subdivisions in Pawleys, close to where Rudy played his golf. Tim made sure he and Sally talked every Christmas. If he remembered, he sometimes called on her birthday in June, but he didn't think he had last year.

Tim tried to picture what he remembered of Sally; petite, just five foot one, chestnut brown hair and flaming amber eyes. She didn't have the good looks Tim and Connie had inherited from their mother. She had a slight horse's face, courtesy of her father. But she more than made up for it in attitude. He recalled from his school days, any comments made to Sally about her looks resembling Mr. Ed resulted in a swift kick to the offender's nuts. That assertiveness she got from Ruth. Tim grinned to himself again. He really missed his sister.

He was ready to reach out. A call in late March would definitely raise the alarm. Oh well, it would be what it would be. Tim took a deep breath and dialed the number.

CHAPTER 3

Sally sat in her living room on the oversized chair where she liked to do her reading. It was also where she contemplated and stewed over the conflicts in her life — something she was currently embroiled in. She sipped Chardonnay late Sunday afternoon and considered the latest crisis that erupted at the Way.

Sally and her family had returned from her childhood home two hours earlier after another dinner descended into a family food fight. Why did she go there today? Their visits for Sunday dinner had been decreasing steadily over the past several years — now down to maybe once per month. They would be even less if not for her mother's incessant nagging.

"It was bad enough," Ruth had remarked on more than one occasion, "that her family had forsaken weekly Mass at the Holy Grace of Christ Catholic Church." This was true for several reasons, her parents being only one of them. But distancing themselves from the time-honored Sunday dinner burned at Ruth's core.

Today's dinner had devolved like so many others she had witnessed over the years. Center stage was the latest controversy surrounding Randy and Molly. Apparently, Rudy explained to everyone, Molly had filed charges last week against Randy for harassment, violation of his restraining order, and molestation.

The enormous great room fell silent. The whole family stopped eating, sensing another Culligan meltdown. Sally sat glaring at her brother from across the ten-seat walnut dining table. Fucking Randy! she thought. And my kids are here to hear it all.

Evidently, Randy, on the tail end of his latest two-week drunk, felt Molly owed him a face-to-face meeting. Restraining order be damned. Rudy demanded to know if he had laid a hand on Molly.

As his perceived property, Randy felt entitled. "Yeah, sure. It was consensual. She asked me to come over."

Everyone at the table rolled their eyes. Lie followed by more lies. Randy expected Rudy to have the charges dropped. After all, he'd done it many times before.

But today, Rudy was having none of it and told his elder son, in no uncertain terms, he wasn't getting involved this time and that Randy was on his own. "Find your own daggom lawyer," Rudy bellowed. "And you can pay for him as well. I'm *done* with you!"

Randy became belligerent, and dinner descended into chaos. It was still brewing twenty minutes later when Sally had heard and seen enough. She grabbed the kids and told her mother on the way out, "Thanks again, Mom, for such a lovely time!"

Joey asked in the car on the drive back, "Mommy, what's molesting?"

Steve gave her one of those looks again. *Your* family. She'd seen it a million times.

"Well, sweetie," Sally tip-toed, turning around to face her five-year-old. "It's when a man is not nice to a woman. Let's just leave it at that, shall we? It wasn't polite conversation to have at a family dinner." As if today was the first time impolite banter passed through the ears of her children in that house.

Now, finishing her second glass of wine, her composure regained, Sally thought again just how badly screwed up her family was, and had always been. Her cell rang and when she saw Tim's name displayed, her eyes popped wide open.

"Tim! What a surprise! Is everything alright?" Sally's radar went up immediately. Something had to be wrong. Tim never called this time of year.

"Hi Sal. No, I can't say everything is alright." Tim paused. Sally waited, holding her breath. He sure didn't sound alright. "I've had Covid, Sal. A pretty severe case."

"Oh, Tim. I am so sorry."

"Yeah, I get that a lot."

"How bad is it? Were you in the hospital? What about your asthma?" Sally set her wineglass down and fully focused on the conversation.

"No, it didn't get that bad. But I have scarring in my lungs, and it's been difficult to breathe easily. I'm sure the asthma complicated things."

It sounded to Sally that Tim was already out of breath. "Oh, Tim. How are you managing things up there?" A long silence followed. Sally heard only labored breathing. She waited, not sure if he was going to reply.

"I'm not, Sal. I'm not at all. In fact, I'm at the end of my rope. That's why I'm calling. I'm — I'm thinking of coming back to the Way. To recuperate."

Sally gasped. "Oh my God. Oh my God! You're serious!" Steve came around the corner to see what the commotion was about. Sally mouthed to him, "It's Tim," then waved him away. "Have you talked to Mom yet?"

Tim scoffed. "Are you kidding? No. I needed to talk with you first. Tell me, what's going on over there these days?"

Sally chuckled. "What's going on? It's the same old insane asylum it's always been. Sunday dinner today — no exception. But before we talk about them, I need to hear more details. When did you get sick? What did your doctor say?" Sally settled in. This was going to be a long call. The thought of Tim returning to South Carolina made her giddy. She forced herself to listen as Tim recounted the diagnosis and the painful two and a half months he had spent since. Twice he had to catch his breath. By the time he finished, Sally was on the verge of tears.

"So, that's where I'm at. Minimum six months and up to five years for complete recovery. It sucks."

Sally shook her head and told him again she was sorry. She collected her thoughts. "And I assume you're still…" after all these years, she still had trouble saying the word.

"Queer. Yes, Sal. Nothing's changed there."

Sally nodded. She knew how difficult it was for Tim to talk about his orientation. She certainly would not be the one to judge. "Ok, so now you want to hear about what's going on at the Way — and the rest of the family."

"And you too, Sal."

"Oh, I'm fine. So are Steve and the kids. I *insist* on normalcy around here." She heard Tim snicker at this.

"Let's start with Dad. Still the most powerful man on the coast, I assume?"

"Oh, I'm sure he'd like to think that."

"Has he, you know, mellowed at all in his attitudes?"

Sally scoffed again. "If you're asking me if he's developed a sudden affinity towards Yankees or Liberals — that would be a definite *no*. But, around the Way, I think he's a little more tolerant. Maybe he's just resigned to admit his perceived failures regarding Connie and Randy."

"Still lost souls, I assume?"

"Connie yes. Randy has no soul. Nor does he have Dad defending him anymore. He made that clear at this afternoon's dinner."

"Can't wait to hear all about that."

"Let's save that one, shall we? Molly's involved again."

"Oh, Ok — and Mom? I assume she still runs the place. She staying on her meds?"

"She does. Yeah, I think so. I mean, she hasn't gone back to Charleston in a while."

"It was just the two times, right?"

"Two times?" Sally snorted. "No, Tim, she's been there four times. I can't remember what I've told you. The last time was three years ago. Again, long story. Best to tell when you're here."

"You're right, Sal. So the question is, *can* I come back? I don't have anywhere else to turn. Will you ask them?"

"Of course I will. I am *sure* Mom would love to have you stay. Dad and Connie will fall in line, no doubt. Randy — well, you know Randy. He's a loose cannon. I can't predict…"

"Does he still stay there? Last you mentioned, he spends most of his time at the fish camp on the river."

"He does when he's on his drunks. In between, he still stays at the Way and does his handyman jobs. Usually every few weeks. But after today, I don't know. I sensed a real shift in Dad. Let me do some checking and I'll get back to you soon. I still can't believe this, Tim. The thought of you back home just gives me goosebumps. I love you and miss you. You know that, right?" Now Sally could hear Tim cry.

"I do, and I love you too, Sal. Call me when you know something."

"I will, Tim, soon. Bye now." Sally ended the call and took a deep breath. This was big. The biggest thing in a long time. Her little brother, in trouble, maybe coming home. She shrieked with delight and got up to get another glass of wine. "Steve," she shouted to her husband, "you will never believe what just happened."

******

The next day after her shift, Sally made a surprise visit to Culligan's Way. She arrived before 5:30 PM, knowing it would give her at least twenty minutes with her mother before Rudy returned home. Sally thought Connie might be there; you never knew with her. She was pretty sure Randy would be elsewhere minding his own business. Depending on how things went, she left instructions with Steve for dinner — she may or may not stay. As Sally approached Culligan's Way and pulled into the left side of the expansive open carport under the main level, she still couldn't believe what she was about to do, and the implications it held for her and the entire family. She went up the wide staircase at the center front of the house, then took off her shoes and placed them in the basket by the massive oak front door (no one wore outside shoes inside the Way).

Sally knocked and let herself in. "Hello, it's me."

As expected, Ruth and Annabelle, the family's dedicated housekeeper and cook, were busy in the kitchen preparing tonight's dinner. Ruth looked up from the sink set in the gigantic granite laid island, "Sally! I didn't expect you here again so soon." Sally knew her mother, with her sixth sense, would immediately suspect some significant event, and not just because of the unexpected and unannounced visit. "Something's up, I can tell. Come, let's sit. Annabelle, you can take over from here."

"Good evening, Annabelle," Sally said.

Mom was all business. She removed her apron and hustled over from the kitchen to the great room's sectional couches, which formed a perimeter around the 80-inch TV mounted over the wide white-brick fireplace.

"Evening, Ms. Sally," Annabelle replied, then went back to her tasks. She wouldn't be taking part in the ensuing conversation, but Sally knew she'd hear every word. Annabelle Simpson had been around the Way for nearly fifteen years. She'd been Ruth's alter-ego ever since. Ruth owed Annabelle her life *and* her freedom from jail more times than either would care to remember. The great-great-granddaughter of a Carolina rice plantation slave, Annabelle knew more about the local area, and the Culligans than anyone else around.

Ruth turned her attention to her elder daughter. "So, what's going on? Tell me."

Before she began, Sally marveled again at her mother. When properly, but not overly medicated, Ruth flaunted strength and energy. At 57, she was in exceptional physical condition (lots of beach walks certainly helped) and although her face showed signs of typical middle-aged wrinkles, she was still astonishingly beautiful — her high cheekbones and illuminating blue eyes magnetically attracted those around her. She even had all of her auburn hair, set in broad curls, with no need for dyes.

Sally smiled at her mother. She knew exactly how Ruth would react. "I heard from Tim yesterday."

Ruth's mouth opened immediately, as her right hand went to cover it. According to Ruth, no respectable woman should ever be seen with her mouth open wide. You never knew what might fly in.

"He's sick, Mom. He had Covid earlier this year." Sally watched her Mom switch from anticipation of news of her lost son, to worry. The wrinkles showed it all.

"Covid, oh dear. Is he all right?" Ruth sat with her hands neatly on her lap, her closed mouth now pursed with worry.

"Well, yes, and no. He told me he had a pretty severe case of it in January. Stayed in bed all month, but never needed to go to the hospital. After he recovered from the pneumonia that came with it, he still had difficulty breathing. His asthma complicated things. He told me it's like a weight constantly on his chest. His doctor told him he had scarring throughout his lungs, and it would take months, or even years, to recover. He lost his job and sounded quite desolate. Long story short, Mom, he asked me if he could come back here, to the Way, to recuperate."

Ruth's hand immediately returned to her reopened mouth. This time, she gasped. "Oh my Lord!" she cried out. "Oh my, oh my!" Ruth turned and looked across the great room, back to the kitchen, towards Annabelle, who also had her hand over her mouth. "Did you hear that, Annabelle? Our Tim wants to come home."

Annabelle vigorously nodded her head. She was speechless.

"Tell me more." Ruth turned her attention back to Sally. "Tell me everything. I want to know."

"There isn't too much to tell, Mom. He's had a rough go of it." Sally conveyed what she had learned from Tim, ending with his concern about living again at the Way with their father and Randy.

"Phooey!" Ruth spit out, then scoffed, as if they were nothing but a mere nuisance. "Your father will be no trouble at all. I'll see to that. As for Randy, from what I've learned, he'll be finding himself new lodging any time now. You heard what went down yesterday. From what your father seems to think, Randy's crossed the line this time. When did Tim say he would come down? We have to get the house ready for him. What room should we put him in, Annabelle?" Ruth steamrolled through her train of thoughts at a mile a minute.

Sally sat back and watched. Ruth seemed even more excited than she would have guessed. No telling how much she had thought about and missed Tim over the years. She certainly never let on. After the first year when Tim left, his name simply ceased to be part of the family discussion. What Sally didn't know was not a day had passed where Ruth didn't think about her younger son — and prayed for him. Same with Annabelle.

"We shall have a *party!*" declared Ruth. "A welcome home party. When do you think he'll be back, Sally?"

"Mom, I just heard about it myself. He's made no plans yet. If all goes well, I'll call him tonight and ask him. I'm glad you're excited about seeing him again. So am I. When does Dad get home these days?"

Ruth gave Sally an odd look as if to say, what wouldn't go well? I run Culligan's Way the way *I* want to. "He'll be home in about twenty minutes. Will you stay for dinner, dear?"

"Wouldn't miss it for the world, Mom."

Ruth barely heard her. She was already on the way back to the kitchen to talk about party plans with Annabelle. "I'm thinking a blue and yellow color scheme, Annabelle. What do you think?"

CHAPTER 4

Twenty minutes later, right on schedule, Rudy pulled his Lexus sedan into the right side of the carport. His interest piqued when he noticed Sally's Ford Escape. Something's up, he thought, and it's probably not good. Rudy lumbered up the stairs, his six-foot-three, 260-pound frame struggling with a combination of an unhealthy diet, lack of exercise, and the general poor attitude he held at the time for any number of reasons. He could only imagine what new revelation lay in store to sour his temperament even more.

Ruth greeted her husband as he entered the home with a kiss and a smile. Now he knew something no good was in the works. "How was your day, dear?" Ruth asked him.

"Another day locking up the degenerates of Georgetown County," he growled. "Why is Sally here?"

"Nice to see you so soon again, Dad, especially after yesterday's show," Sally retorted. She turned to Ruth and asked, "Do you want to tell him, or can I?"

"You can tell him. You brought us the news."

Rudy stood by the kitchen island surrounded by the three women, all sporting wide grins. "Tell me what?" demanded Rudy. "What's going on?"

"I heard from Tim last night," Sally said straight out. "He's sick. He's coming home." After the earlier conversation, she purposely did not say he *wants* to come home. Sally watched Rudy's face for the first reaction. Initially, it was one of confusion. His salt and pepper mustache did a bit of a dip and his weathered eyes squinted slightly.

"Tim? I don't know a Tim. Tim who?" Rudy knew full well but had his own point to make.

"Tim *Culligan,* Dad — your son!" She looked furtively at Ruth and Annabelle, who both sported looks of concern. Ruth crossed her arms but stayed silent for now.

"I have only one son, my darling daughter — and he's a worthless drunk."

This was all Ruth needed to intervene. She marched around the island and stood directly in front of her husband. The twelve-inch height difference meant nothing to her. "You listen to me, you overweight bag of poop! Our son, Tim, is in trouble. He's had Covid and has lung problems now. He's coming home to recuperate. Am I making myself clear, or do I need to Roto-Rooter the crap that's clogging your ears?"

Rudy turned silently and strode across the great room to the bar, where he proceeded to pour his standard nightly cocktail of Woodford Reserve bourbon on the rocks. Tonight he added an extra ounce. Now it all made sense to him. Although he was slightly intrigued, this still wasn't good news.

All three women stared at his back, waiting for his response.

With his drink made, and the first sip of whiskey flooding his senses, Rudy turned back around and rejoined the women. "If I remember correctly, our son Timothy high-tailed it out of here right after the graduation party we graciously threw for him. Left before dawn without telling a soul. No forwarding address, no contact information. Tell me again, Sally, where he fled to? New York City, was it?" He paused, waiting for an answer.

"That's right," Sally answered, narrowing her eyes.

"And you know this only because he had contacted you, after how long a time?" Rudy knew this came across as a cross-examination, and he knew Sally hated to be questioned like this. Too bad, he thought. She brought it here. He saw his wife standing by quietly — defense counsel ready to object.

Sally gulped. "He first called me right before my wedding, to wish me the best and apologize for not being there."

"Yes, so let me see. That was eight years ago, two years after he disappeared without a trace."

"It wasn't without a trace, Dad. He texted me the day after he left. To let me know where he was headed and why. You never saw that text, but I still have it on my phone. Copied it over each time I got a new one. You've never seen it. None of you have."

Rudy could see Sally's temperature rising and knew her legendary temper could flare at a moment's notice. He sipped more bourbon, interested to see where the discussion might lead.

Sally punched up her text library. "Here it is, and I quote. Sal, I'm so sorry to have to do this. I am on a bus headed to New York City to begin a new life. To find a life where people will treat me with respect for who I am. I will never again be humiliated the way I was last night. I hope we can keep in touch. Love Tim."

Sally looked up to see the other's expressions. Jolted back to that fateful day, Ruth and Annabelle seemed shocked. Rudy's outside appearance remained calm.

"You remember what he's talking about, don't you? You remember what happened that night?" No one said a word. No one could say it. Even though they all knew, no one ever spoke about it. It was the most skeleton of all closet skeletons — and this family had them in spades. Fury forced its way into Sally's throat. "They *raped him!* They *raped* my little brother! That bastard brother of mine had it arranged. I know it. You all know it."

"That was never proven, Sally," Rudy interrupted. "And you know it. The alleged victim disappeared, so no charges were brought. The alleged perpetrator and witnesses never admitted to anything, and without a victim, there was never any proof."

"Bullshit!" Sally swore, violating the first rule of the Culligan household.

"I'll not have you swear in…."

But she cut Rudy off. "I don't give a damn! You old fool. I talked with Molly after it happened. She told me what Randy did, who he put up to do it, how much he paid him, and who the witnesses were. I talked to all of them. They all admitted to it in private but would never in public. Some were sorry it happened. Some weren't." Sally had lost control.

Rudy glanced at Ruth and could tell she wasn't far behind. "*Molly* told you! Humph." Rudy sneered at his daughter. "Molly Elmwood is the biggest liar in this county. Nothing she says is credible. Nothing she has said has ever held up in court."

"*That's enough!*" screamed Ruth at the top of her lungs as she turned her ire at her husband. "Our long-lost son is sick. He has reached out to us to help him recuperate. *We* are going to welcome him home. And *you* are going to make sure your *worthless drunk,* as you call him — generously, I might add — of a son, is nowhere to be seen when Tim arrives home. Do I make myself clear, *Your Honor*?"

Rudy scowled at this last quip. He knew when Ruth used the sarcastic 'Your Honor' to address him, he had about as much judicial authority in the house as the squirrels in the backyard.

"I'll take it under advisement," Rudy said, trying to save some dignity after another losing debate with his wife. "What's for dinner? I'm starving." The discussion was over. "Sally, are you staying?"

"You know, Dad, I was going to, but you somehow spoiled my appetite — again." She went back to the couch and grabbed her purse. "I'll call you later, Mom. Goodnight, Annabelle." She sneered at Rudy on the way out, then slammed the front door for good measure.

CHAPTER 5

Two days later, on Wednesday afternoon, Rudy sat in his chambers with Georgetown County Sheriff Leroy Keating. The Sheriff matched the Judge's large frame pound for pound, except much more of his was muscle. Leroy was one of the few black men Rudy respected; there were a smattering of lawyers and businesspeople as well, but he was the only one Rudy confided in. The two had been friends and colleagues going back almost twenty years. Both had many election victories under their belt, and the distinction of sending countless numbers of convicted criminals to the Williamsburg State Penitentiary, forty-five miles inland from Georgetown. Too many of them were black, in Leroy's opinion, but he knew his job was to arrest the lawbreakers, not convict them.

Leroy tried to pay an informal visit to Rudy's chambers at least once a week. Normally he'd stick his head in when he knew Rudy had some time off the docket. Today, it was Rudy who requested Leroy to come and see him. That meant the Judge needed a favor. Just as well, Leroy also had a serious matter he needed to discuss with Rudy.

"Come in and have a seat, Leroy," Rudy rose to greet his sheriff, "and close the door behind you, please."

Leroy nodded; this discussion absolutely needed privacy. He closed the door and removed his Sheriff's hat. "I'm glad you called, Rudy. I was going to come by later, anyway. We have a situation on our hands."

"We have several situations on our hands, I'm afraid," Rudy said with a grumble.

Leroy took a seat in one of the three oversized leather armchairs which molded around his king-sized frame. Rudy knew how to make his guests feel at least physically comfortable. "Go ahead, you go first," Leroy said.

"Very well. So, on Monday evening, I find Sally waiting for me as I walk in the door. She informs me *Tim* is coming home to recover from Covid."

This caught Leroy off guard. "Tim! Wow, how long has it been? Is he bad off?"

"Almost ten years, with no contact. Sounds like he has lung issues from Covid. Lost his job, no money. Ruth was thrilled. Me, not so much."

"If I remember, wasn't he the gay one?"

Rudy smirked. "No, queer, yeah — lucky me."

"Isn't that the same thing?" Leroy asked innocently. He didn't hold the same biases Rudy did, but wasn't exactly up to speed on the latest LGBTQ+ definitions.

"Apparently not."

Leroy waited for an explanation.

Rudy shrugged. "What? You want me to explain it to you?"

"At the moment, I would love nothing more than to have you explain it to me." Leroy smiled. He knew how much the subject put Rudy off.

Rudy gave Leroy a sideways glance. "Well, for your education, Sheriff Keating, as it was explained to me a decade ago, queer can mean different things. In Tim's case, it's the same as gay, except for the sexual part."

Leroy sported a confused look on his face. "I don't get it. He's gay, but he doesn't have sex with men. Who does he have sex with?"

Rudy became exasperated. "You know, Leroy, I would love to sit here, taking up our valuable time discussing the intricacies of my son's sexual orientation. But I must move on to actual issues I need your help to resolve."

Leroy smiled back. He prized getting under Rudy's skin. Just a little, though. You don't want to poke that bear too hard.

Rudy continued, "Ruth is throwing a welcome home party for Tim this Saturday night at the Way. We're expecting you and Doris to attend."

"Appreciate that. We'd love to see Tim again. That's not what you wanted to see me about, though, is it?"

"No, not that specifically. My problem is the other son."

"Ah yes, the true rogue of the family. The one currently facing more charges from his ex. Does Randy know about Tim's return yet?" Leroy now felt he knew the direction of the discussion.

"Not that I'm aware of, but he might. Connie knows, and the two of them can still be thick like thieves. After what happened last week, knowing Randy and what had gone on between him and Tim before, I don't want him anywhere near the Way when Tim gets home — which looks to be Friday afternoon. Sally's picking him up in Myrtle Beach then. So — "

"So, you want me to bring Randy in and put him on ice to smooth the transition? Is that what you're asking?"

"You can be quite the perceptive sheriff, Leroy. It's one of your strong suits."

Leroy snorted. "High praise coming from the likes of you. Rudy, you know the protocols. Just because Molly filed charges doesn't mean I can arrest the kid. I need some kind of probable cause."

"Of course. Well, you have the restraining order violation."

"Allegedly. Randy said he was called and invited. You know the issues with Molly's credibility."

"And Randy's! I had it out with him at dinner last Sunday. I'm not defending him anymore. I won't get involved. But I can't risk having him around this weekend. What can you do about it?"

Now the head of the county's law enforcement knew exactly where things stood. He recognized he had to come up with some reason to lock Randy up, per Rudy's request. It was simply how things were done in this neck of the woods. That plus other issues of indebtedness Leroy owed to Rudy. By comparison, this was a small favor to ask. Leroy pursed a smile and slowly nodded his head. "Don't worry about it, Judge. I'll take care of it. But I've got to get to the other concern I have to dump in your lap today. And you won't like it at all."

Rudy brought his fingertips together and slowly exhaled. "Let me guess — Greeley Construction." The two stared each other down. Leroy understood he had to walk on eggshells regarding the ongoing investigation into the largest construction firm on the coast.

"Yes," he replied softly but firmly. "Greeley. I just received an update from Meacham with new information. Information that doesn't put you in a good light, Judge."

Rudy sat across from his sheriff, stone-faced and expressionless. Leroy knew Detective Tony Meacham, the county's lead detective for the past five years, had been a pain in Rudy's ass ever since they butted heads over the Buckingham murder case. Rudy had dismissed the case of the (white) Mark Buckingham accused of running the (black) Tiffany Johnson off the road and into the Murrells Inlet creek, killing her and her unborn baby, which on autopsy, turned out to be Mark's. The evidence was overwhelming, but also circumstantial. Rudy dismissed key pieces of evidence on technicalities, and the jury hung. Tony, who had accumulated much of the evidence and believed to this day that Mark was guilty, had held a grudge against Rudy ever since. The two coexisted professionally but kept their distance otherwise. Now, Meacham was snooping around again in areas Rudy did not appreciate.

"Well now, that doesn't surprise me, given your detective's passionate dislike for me. What does he have?"

"Tell me this, Rudy, what relationship do you have with DHEC?"

Rudy stayed silent for a second. Leroy knew this hit a nerve. When Rudy replied, it was tentative. "The Department of Health and Environmental Control? I don't currently have any relationship with them. I seem to recall a case or two a few years back. Why do you ask?"

"A case from 2016 involving another construction company and marsh lot permits," Leroy jogged Rudy's memory for him.

"Sounds familiar."

"A case you ruled in favor of the company."

"Perhaps so. Spit it out, Leroy. What are you getting at?"

"What I'm getting at, Judge, is there is speculation you're involved in directing unauthorized zoning changes at DHEC, to the advantage of Greeley."

"Humph," Rudy scoffed loudly. "Total bullshit. What proof does your detective have?" Rudy's ban on profanity did not include the privacy of his chambers.

"Rudy, you know I'm walking a tightrope here. There's no direct proof other than what the guys at DHEC are telling Tony. If it's true, we could have a major crisis on our hands. DHEC can push it up to the Governor if they want to. Get the tree-huggers and the press involved and now you got a PR crisis on top of a legal one. Is that what you really want?"

Rudy had reached the end of his patience and his allotted time with Leroy. "What I want, Leroy, is for you to do your job. If there's a crime, then arrest the perp. I'm telling you; your detective is pissing into the wind. And if he doesn't aim better, he's going to end up a stinking mess, including everyone around him." Rudy stood up. "Keep me up to date."

Leroy understood the meeting was over. He rose and put his hat back on. "Have a good day, Judge. And congratulations on the return of your son. I hope he recovers soon." Leroy knew his politics well.

"Thank you, Leroy. And don't forget about Randy — that asshole!"

CHAPTER 6

On Friday morning, Paula Ryder dreaded doing this month's inventory at the Pawleys Island Publix pharmacy. She had a sinking feeling the counts were going to be short again, like they were last month. At that inventory, three painkillers — OxyContin, Tramadol, and Percocet were all between 50 and 100 pills short. Someone had to be skimming, and if they were caught, it would be the end of their employment there, or at any pharmacy.

When Paula informed the Pharmacy Manager, Linda Kale, about the first shortage, after triple checking the prescription receipts against the pill usage, Linda told her to keep it on the down low. Both of them would take extra precautions, monitoring the other pharmacy technicians for any signs of skimming pills. They didn't want to alert the general management yet.

Paula began her monthly exercise by entering the data of prescription demand for each drug in their inventory, then the quantity of each drug brought into inventory. She then compared the inventory pill count from last month and took the current pill count for each corresponding drug. She entered the amounts in her inventory spreadsheet and checked the theoretical to the actual counts. They almost always matched within a couple of pills, easily explained by a miscount of one or two. Anything more than a dozen would raise a red flag, especially with painkillers.

As Paula went through her list alphabetically, all seemed in order, until she got to the first painkiller, Endocet, an oxycodone derivative. It wasn't short last month, but now she was coming up 75 pills short. Alarm bells went off in her head. She looked again at the data. Twenty scripts written for 600 pills. Last month's inventory had 250 pills left. With the next order of 500 pills added, there should have been 150 pills left. But there were only 75. Paula made the notation and moved on. When she got to OxyContin, things got worse — 125 pills short. Same with the Percocet and Tramadol.

The four painkiller drugs were 475 pills short this month. On the black market, these could go for over $10,000. There was a thief amongst them, and things were getting worse. Paula finished her inventory and printed out the results. The meeting with the higher-ups would not be pleasant.

******

"It looks like we have a thief skimming pills," Paula told Linda, along with Assistant General Manager Sally Hobart. They were sitting in Sally's office with the spreadsheet printout laid across her desk. The meeting was hastily called when Paula told Linda about the new inventory results. Linda cursed and told her they had to go to management right away. They couldn't sweep it under the rug anymore. It would be bad enough they didn't take any action last month when it first came to light.

The two pharmacists sat in the cramped office across from Sally's desk with solemn faces. It was one more headache Sally had to deal with this morning. She was already struggling with a late supply of seafood from their primary vendor, which would mean running out of almost all fish by the end of the weekend. Then she had to leave early today, by 12:30 PM, to drive to the airport and pick up Tim. Now this? Not only would she and

Linda be in hot water, but the police would need to be called in and, well, nothing good ever happened when the cops came to Publix. It would be far better if they catch the perpetrator internally.

"So, you have a shortage of 475 pills from this month's inventory." Sally began the investigation with the facts laid out in front of her. "And last month, everything was fine?"

Paula and Linda looked at each other with grim faces. Linda had no choice but to admit the truth. "Actually, Sally, there was a shortage last month as well."

Sally was dumbstruck. "*What!* Are you kidding me? How many?"

"250 pills short last month. Three of the painkillers. This month there were four."

Sally closed her eyes and forced herself not to lose her temper. They had warned her before about emotional outbursts when things didn't go as planned — she knew it was one of her weak areas. "And you didn't tell anyone about it then? Why *not*?" She said it without emotion until 'not'.

Linda immediately went on the defensive. "Sally, we thought we could nip it in the bud. We've been watching the other techs closely whenever they filled a painkiller script to see if anyone might have been skimming."

"And did you? Did you find anyone skimming pills?"

Linda and Paula exchanged looks and shook their collective heads. "We did not."

Sally couldn't keep a lid on her emotions anymore. "Well, that's just fucking great!" she spit out. "We have a thief stealing narcotics! Bud is going to freak out when he hears this." Bud

Wright, the General Manager, was a no-nonsense ex-navy who ran his store like the ship he once captained.

"I'm sorry, Sally. I'm so sorry," replied Linda, nervously fiddling with her hands on her lap. "It's my fault. I should have told you last month, but I told Paula to keep it under wraps. I shouldn't have done that." Sally could see she was on the verge of tears.

Sally sat back in her chair and thought it through. This was a first for her. She'd dealt with shoplifters before. Between the security cameras and the barcode scan detection warning system, it was hard to get away with much shoplifting these days. But skimming and sneaking out pills was trickier from a detection point of view. "Ok, Linda," she said with more calm. "Tell me exactly what the two of you have done in the last month to catch the thief."

"Like I said, Sally, whenever a painkiller script came in, we would discreetly watch it being filled and try to see if anyone pocketed a few pills. We saw nothing. To skim that many, the person would have to have done it multiple times. I would have sworn we'd have seen something."

"Assuming it's an internal job," Sally countered.

"What else could it be?" Linda asked with confusion. "We seal off the pharmacy from the rest of the store after hours. "Only Paula and I have keys, and I guess you and the other managers do as well."

"Just Bud, Lori, Ginger and I are the only ones with keys." Sally thought for a second how unlikely it was that any of the Publix managers would break into the pharmacy after hours to steal drugs.

"And if anyone broke into the store after hours, you would know about it, right?" Linda countered. "And there's no way they could get into the barricade without a key. So what are we saying here, that one of the three of us, or the other three, is guilty? Can't be."

"I agree, Linda. But I can't rule anything out. For now, you'd better bring the narcotics supply into the safe after hours. I'll talk to Bud and get a plan together. I'll let him decide when to get the police involved. For now, this stays between us, understood? I don't want any of the other pharmacy techs to suspect anything. They're still the most likely suspects. Keep a close eye on them. I have to leave early today and won't be back until Monday morning. If Bud wants something done before then, he'll let you know. Questions?"

Paula and Linda silently shook their heads.

"Alright then, let's keep our eyes and ears open. If anything else comes up, you can call my cell. That's all then." Sally stood up to show the meeting was over.

"Thank you, Sally," Linda replied. "We will. I'm so sorry this happened. I know we'll get it resolved soon."

The two left her office without another word. Sally walked two doors down and knocked on the door. "Come in," barked her General Manager.

Sally opened the door as Bud looked up from his desk. He didn't look happy. But then, he never looked happy. "Boss, we have a situation."

CHAPTER 7

Tim stood outside his apartment door, overwhelmed with melancholy, and looked inside for the last time. Ten years of his life; ten years that had real meaning, that defined him as an individual, were gone. He didn't know if he would ever return to New York, even though he had every intention of doing so. He would put up with his despicable family just long enough to recover his strength and make a triumphant return, then walk into Ellen's studio and declare, "I have returned; let's get on with it!" Or he wouldn't. He might never recover. He might be an invalid for the rest of his life, indebted to his parents to support him. Stuck on that island forever.

Tim took as deep a breath as he could muster and closed the door to his former existence. The next four hours, until he landed in Myrtle Beach, were going to be physically excruciating. After that, the emotional toll of returning to Pawleys Island and reuniting with his family might be insufferable. "Do this," he said to himself again. "Just do it."

Tim descended the elevator with his one small suitcase and dropped the letter in the outgoing mail. It explained in the briefest of terms why he was leaving town. He would forward the remaining unpaid rent at a future unspecified date and plan for the furniture and other belongings he left behind.

Tim walked out the front door into a breezy, early spring morning. The sun was coming up over Central Park. A wave of encouragement washed over him as he breathed in warm fresh air. It was too bad — he loved springtime in the city. But this year, reality was different. It would work out. It had to work out.

His Uber arrived shortly. Tim hopped into the back seat and put his mask on, then settled in for the drive to Newark to catch his nonstop flight on Spirit. One way, cheap — only $59. He had almost no money left. Tim focused on his breathing. It would be four long hours before he could take his mask off, assuming no flight delays. He'd worn a mask only a few times since he had recovered; to the doctor's office, twice to the market. Never more than half an hour. Breathing was hard enough without one. He checked again to make sure he had his inhaler. Now he just needed to focus, and not panic.

The skyline drifted by as Tim headed south on the Henry Hudson Parkway before they dipped under the river through the Lincoln Tunnel. Then he looked back at the city from New Jersey and felt absolutely nothing. New York was gone, South Carolina loomed, but he wasn't ready to deal with all of that just yet. Instead, he felt like he was in an abyss; a dark void where nothing existed — no feeling, no emotion, no cares — just numbness. He couldn't cry, he couldn't laugh, and he couldn't think. Tim closed his eyes and let the emptiness overtake him.

******

Sally got out of Pawleys later than she wanted, giving her only thirty minutes to get to the airport before Tim's flight landed at 12:30 PM. As expected, the meeting with Bud did not go well. He was, to put it bluntly, furious. Furious to have a thief stealing narcotics from his store, for not being informed of the first breach a month ago, and for the seafood shipment debacle — at least he had already known about that.

Then, when Sally told him she had to leave for the weekend, which she had already pre-approved, Bud went ballistic. Sally tuned him out and let him rant.

He finished with, "and you tell that Pharmacy Manager of yours her job is on the line if she doesn't sort this out soon. And your own job security might not be far behind."

"Yes, sir," was all Sally said. She had to choke down the temptation to rebuke him with the fact that the pharmacy manager had a name — Linda. And that she, in fact, reported directly to him, not her, plus he had no grounds to threaten anyone's job security. At least not yet.

Sally put her Publix problems out of her mind as she left Pawleys Island and headed towards Myrtle Beach. She had to focus on Tim and what awaited them this weekend. So much was about to happen, the most consequential of which would go down within the next hour. That's when they planned to have Randy arrested and sent to spend the weekend in the county jail.

So far, the plan had unfolded seamlessly. After her visit and announcement at the Way on Monday night, a course of action materialized, with her mother, of course, at the helm. They hatched the plan by Tuesday evening. Connie, the only one who could reliably reach Randy, would let him know of Tim's planned return on Friday and of the welcome home party planned for Saturday. They did not inform her of the surprise arrest planned for her brother. The two were still close, and they could not trust Connie with such sensitive information.

As far as Randy went, everyone knew he wouldn't miss the chance to ruin things for Tim. Her father arranged logistics with Sheriff Keating, and after confirmation that Randy was at

Culligan's Way, they would arrest him for violation of his restraining order, as well as any other charges the Judge and the Sheriff deemed worthy, then spend at least 48 hours in the Georgetown County pen.

Sally received confirmation last night that Randy had indeed returned to the Way and was at this hour sleeping off a hangover, curtesy of Rudy's bourbon supply. Mom would text her when the arrest had happened, scheduled for 1:00 PM, thirty minutes after Tim's flight was supposed to arrive. Once the coast was clear, Tim would reunite with Ruth and Annabelle, (maybe Connie) and settle in to begin his recuperation. The women would then focus their efforts on preparing for the party Saturday night. Sally told Tim on their last call two days ago that Ruth and Annabelle were preparing the party of all parties to celebrate his return. Tim groaned and muttered, "Wonderful."

After the party Saturday, the family would attend Sunday Mass, minus locked-up Randy, not that *he'd* been inside a church in like — forever, followed by a grand feast for Sunday dinner. When Tim heard about his expected attendance at Holy Grace, he groaned even louder. This time, instead of saying "Wonderful," her brother said with reservation, "Sal, I'm not religious anymore. You know how the church feels about my orientation. It would be sacrilege for me to go."

Sally had expected his response and assured him there would not be any long-term commitment needed. The folks just wanted the return of their prodigal son to be announced and celebrated in their place of worship. "Surely you can suffer this one *indignity*," she had said, lacing the last word with sarcasm. "Steve and I and the kids will be there as well."

His mocking reply — "Wonderful!"

Sally entered the southern outskirts of Myrtle Beach, past the Market Common, and the approach to the airport. Fortunately, traffic was light on this Friday. The worst of the summer tourist traffic was still a couple months off. As she exited Highway 17 at the airport entrance, she pondered the most troublesome part of the coming transition.

When they released Randy from his weekend stint later on Sunday, he'd be sure to confront Dad and Tim at the Way as soon as possible. Dad would inform him he couldn't stay at the home any further and would need to find permanent lodging elsewhere — immediately. That, and a stern warning to leave Tim alone. After the fireworks from the previous Sunday, this Sunday was sure to be a bonfire. But her father seemed unfazed and determined to see this through. She and her family planned to be back home after dinner, well before Randy returned. That would be one shit show she didn't need to see.

Sally pulled into airport parking and found a spot in the short-term lot, right on time. She still couldn't believe her long lost little brother would step out of an airplane any minute, arriving home. He didn't know just how warm a welcome awaited him. The guest list for tomorrow's party had topped one-hundred, and Mom was sure there'd be drop-ins as well. When the Culligans threw a party, everyone knew about it. It was Sally's job to prepare Tim for what to expect, knowing he'd be overwhelmed, but in a good way. With Randy out of the picture, nothing stood between them and the grandest welcome home seen in Pawleys since probably the end of the Second World War.

Sally waited near the baggage claim area at the base of the escalator. A sign showed his Spirit flight had landed, and baggage appeared on the carousel. People were milling around, looking for their bags. Sally's heart beat hard as the anticipation built within her. "Where is he, where is he?" she said to herself, thinking, what is he going to look like? That's what she really wanted to know. One by one, passengers descended the escalator.

The plane had to be emptied by now. Where is Tim? Sally's never deep patience wore thin. She got concerned. Did he miss his flight? Did something happen to him? Or maybe…., but there he was. His tousled auburn hair gave him away immediately. He caught Sally's eye and nodded slightly. Sally bounced on her heels, watching him descend the escalator. When he reached the ground level, Tim removed his mask and smiled weakly. Sally rushed up and buried him in her arms.

"Hello Sal," Tim barely whispered in her ear, putting two frail arms around her.

"Oh, Tim," she said, breaking her embrace. He was so thin; she thought she might snap him in two. She inspected him. The first thought in her mind was she was looking at a ghost. His eyes were gaunt, his cheeks sunk in. This was not the Tim she remembered. "I hope you're hungry. Mom's going to take a lot of joy fattening you up."

Tim grinned back. He still had that toothy smile, and his eyes brightened a little. That was a glimpse of what Sally remembered. He answered, "I'm starving."

CHAPTER 8

At that same moment, Randy Culligan sprawled his lanky body out on the sectional sofa in the Way's great room. The TV was on, some true crime documentary, and Randy had just opened his second beer of the day. Connie slouched her skinny body on an adjacent couch, totally stoned. Ruth and Annabelle were busy in the kitchen preparing for the party, ignoring both of them. Ruth knew a visit from Sheriff Keating and company could come at any minute — Rudy assured her it would be between 12:30 PM and 1:00 PM. As Ruth rolled out another pie crust, her sixth out of eight planned, she anxiously glanced between the clock and the road.

At 12:45 PM, her nervous wait ended when she saw Leroy's brown and gold Georgetown County Sheriff's SUV pull into the carport, followed by another patrol cruiser. Leroy and three of his deputies exited the two vehicles. Two of the deputies climbed the steps to the front entrance. The third made his way around back to the beach entrance. Ruth met them at the door.

"He's right over there." Ruth pointed a thumb in the Randy's direction, then let him inside the house. On this occasion, she ignored her 'no shoes inside the house' rule. Didn't matter, the cleaners would mop the gleaming oak planks spotless before the party kicked off. Randy looked up, first with disregard, then with sudden alarm as he saw the Sheriff and two deputies make their way to the living area.

"What the fuck!" Randy jumped to his feet, panic stricken.

"Randall Culligan," began Leroy, "you are under arrest for the violation of your restraining order against Molly Elmwood and for sexual assault to the same. You have the right to remain silent..."

Ruth saw Randy cast one accusing eye towards her, then bolt for the back door. Leroy's third deputy met him there as soon as Randy opened it and quickly corralled Randy, forcing him back inside. "This is *bullshit,* and you know it, Sheriff. I told you she invited me over. Who put you up to this? Who? Was it you, you bitch?" Randy glared at his mother.

By now, the two other deputies had Randy in an armlock and were cuffing him. Connie watched with slight amusement. Annabelle stayed in the back of the kitchen. Ruth turned towards her son to offer a few parting words. But first she let Leroy finish his speech, which he did a couple of inches from Randy's face. "Anything you say, can and will be used against you in a court of law."

Randy's face turned red in fury, but he let Leroy finish reading the rights. "It's because of Tim, isn't it?" Randy screamed at the top of his lungs. "That chickenshit faggot is coming home, and you need me out of the picture! That's what this is all about, isn't it? *Isn't it?"*

Ruth heard enough. She spoke to Randy with icy certainty. "Think what you will, Randall. Your days here are done. I'm *done* with you. Your father is *done* with you. We have all *had it* with your uncouth conduct and your complete lack of decency and respect." Ruth's tone and pitch continued to rise to where she was shrieking. "I want you out of this house, and I don't ever want to see you back in here unless you learn how to act like a human being." Ruth kept a firm grip on the wooden roller in her right hand, fighting the urge to raise it in her anger.

Randy stayed silent for just a second, looking around the room as everyone else stood frozen, waiting to see if Ruth had finished. When allowed to retort, Randy screamed, "Fuck you, you old hag…" He probably would have kept the stream of invectives pouring out of his mouth, except for the rolling pin making a beeline toward the center of his head. Had he not been so hungover, or slightly quicker on the uptake, he might have been able to duck, however — he didn't. He turned his head just enough, so the pin hit him above his left eye instead of between the eyes. Blood spurted everywhere, and all hell broke loose.

"You crazy fucking bitch!" Randy tried unsuccessfully to wipe the blood from the open wound, now pouring into his left eye — a hard thing to do with his hands cuffed behind his back.

Simultaneously, Leroy called to his deputies, "Get him the hell out of the house!"

Annabelle rushed to retrieve the blood-stained rolling pin before inserting herself between Ruth and Randy.

Connie sat up from the couch, sensing something important had just happened. "Jesus, Mom! Why d'ya have to do that?"

Randy never let up. "You saw that Sheriff! Arrest that crazy bitch for assault and battery! You saw it with your own eyes. Don't tell me you didn't." Then back at Ruth, "They're gonna haul your ass back to Charleston, you fucking lunatic!"

Annabelle faced Ruth and refused to let her make a move around her to get another free shot at her eldest son. "Ruth, honey, it's over now. It's over," she said in her most soothing voice. This was hardly her first pony ride in the Ruth crazy circus. During the infamous fight between Ruth and Randy that sent the Way's matriarch to Charleston Arlington in 2006, Ruth reached the cutlery set and went at Randy with a 10-inch carving knife. Annabelle and Rudy had wrestled it away that time before Randy met an even bloodier fate.

As the two deputies hauled Randy out the back door, Leroy barked orders for them to get a bandage on the prisoner before they put him in the patrol car. He turned back to Ruth before leaving the household, her eyes were still glazed with hysteria. Annabelle held her closely. "Mrs. Culligan, please get some rest. I believe Tim will arrive fairly soon. And don't worry about Randy; he won't be going anywhere for a while. I'll have a talk with Rudy this afternoon."

Ruth blinked and allowed a sliver of sanity back into her mind. She wrestled free from Annabelle's hold around her waist. "I'll be fine, Sheriff. Thank you for all your help today. I apologize for making a scene."

"Come on, Ms. Ruth," urged Annabelle. "Let Sheriff Keating do his job. We need you to be at your best when Tim arrives."

Ruth looked around the room as Leroy left, then closed the front door behind him. The shock of the sudden descent into violence stunned Ruth. She knew her vulnerability to such episodes remained, even under the current regimen of Risperdal she had been on for the past three years. And she knew Randy could always bring out the worst in her. Ruth's eyes met Connie's across the living room.

Connie knew better than to poke at her Mom in her current state. She rose from the couch. "Do you need any help, Mom? Can I get you anything?"

Annabelle beat her to it. "Get your mother a glass of water, if you will, please. Come on upstairs, Ms. Ruth. I think a Valium will do you good." She held Ruth by the arm and placed her other arm around her waist. Connie made her way to the kitchen to pour a glass of water, then the three of them proceeded upstairs.

"When will our Tim be home?" Ruth asked, still a bit dazed.

"Should be within the next hour. I'm going to call Sally as soon as we get you situated."

The three women made their way into the upstairs master bedroom. Connie helped her mother lie down on the king-size bed, while Annabelle went to the bathroom to retrieve the bottle of Valium they kept for just such occasions. Once she returned and Ruth had taken her pill, they removed her house slippers and propped the pillow under her head. Ruth seemed to relax. Connie and Annabelle looked at each other and shrugged.

"I'll wake you before Tim arrives," Annabelle said. "I'm sure you'll be in better spirits by then."

"Thank you, Annabelle. Thank you kindly." Ruth paused a second as the other two made their way out of the bedroom. But before Connie reached the doorway, Ruth had one last bit of advice. "Connie, darling."

"Yes, Mom, what is it?"

"Do me one favor, please."

"Sure Mom, anything."

"You tell that brother of yours if I ever see him in this house again, I'm going to kill him." Ruth gave Connie one last wry smile, then turned over to begin her nap. Connie and

Annabelle looked at each other nervously. They both knew Ruth had never kidded about anything.

CHAPTER 9

Sally and Tim were both in a great mood as they made their way south on Highway 17 towards Pawleys Island. Even though Tim could feel exhaustion setting in from his long trip, the mix of excitement and apprehension of the homecoming boiled inside him like an emotional Molotov cocktail. He felt honest encouragement from what Sally had told him so far — about how much his mother had missed him, as well as Annabelle, and even Connie. Sally exuded enthusiasm over how she and the family, excluding Randy, would welcome him back into the fold, how much the warm beach climate would suit his rehabilitation, and how the community would rally around him.

"Things have changed in Pawleys over the last ten years."

There were more stores on Hwy. 17 than Tim remembered — and a lot more traffic. "How so? You mean it's not the same old sleepy beach town no one ever heard of?"

Tim grinned as Sally looked at her brother again. She'd been looking at him at least as much as she'd been watching the road. "Oh, well, you know," she qualified her answer, "it's still that. They keep pretty strict building codes, so it doesn't get too commercial. But there's a lot more residential property here. Lots of retirement people from the North."

Tim nodded some more, then chuckled. "Yankee transplants," he said, then snickered some more. "And I'll bet Dad loves that! Tell me again what I'm to expect from the strictest, most conservative judge in South Carolina? The man who held Yankees and liberals in the same regard as thieves and arsonists. Or at least that's what I remember from ten years ago."

"Well, he's not real thrilled about the preponderance of New York accents he hears on the streets these days. But like I told you on the phone, he's mellowed somewhat as he's aged. He's not one to stand in the way of progress here. I told you about what happened with Randy last Sunday."

It had heartened Tim to hear how his older brother would be absent for his return and the party, and with any amount of luck, for some time after that.

"Dad will be fine with you. I mean, don't expect him to invite you to the club for a round of golf. But Mom keeps him in check at the Way. Just don't start any political discussions. And for God's sake, whatever you do, do *not* mention Donald Trump."

This time, Tim laughed out loud. "Of course not. I'm sure Trump was Dad's answer to all that ails this country."

"Well, he was, until that little insurrection thing on January 6. Ever since then, Dad's been pretty disappointed with anything coming out of Washington. Best to stay off any political discussions."

"No problems there, and I'm glad he turned against Randy." They were leaving Murrells Inlet, about twenty minutes from Culligan's Way, when Sally's cell rang.

"Hello?" Sally had the phone on hands free, so Tim could also listen to the call.

"Hello, Sally. Annabelle. How close are you to home?" Tim could sense the unease that tinged in her voice.

"We just passed Brookgreen Gardens, Annabelle. Everything ok there?"

Tim felt trepidation crawl up this throat. He didn't think Annabelle would call to chat.

"Well, seems we had us a minor incident with your Mom and Randy, I'm afraid. Things didn't go quite as planned with his arrest." Tim saw Sally close her eyes for a second and curse to herself,

"Ok, care to elaborate?"

"I'd rather not, Ms. Sally. But Randy is gone, and Ms. Ruth is resting comfortably right now. She had to take one of her special pills. She be fine by the time y'all get here. We are so looking forward to seeing Tim."

"As is he, Annabelle. Why, you should see the look on his face right now." Sally grinned and cast her eyes sideways to her brother, who looked astounded.

"That's right, Annabelle. Can't wait," said Tim, also giving his sister a sideways glance.

"I hope you're hungry, Tim. Got your favorite sandwich for lunch, just a waiting on you."

Tim knew what she was talking about, alright. "Ham and pimento cheese with sweet pickles!" he shouted out with glee. "Am I right?"

"You are absolutely correct, young man. With barbeque chips and sweet tea. I remember alright."

Tim closed his eyes and envisioned his much-loved lunch. And he hadn't had real Southern sweet tea in the whole of the ten years since he'd left. Some things just don't migrate well. "Yes, you do, Annabelle. Yes, you do. I'm tasting it right now."

"Ok, then. Like I said, Ms. Ruth should be woke up by then. I need to get back to trying to get the blood out of this here rolling pin. We still got two more pie shells to roll out. See ya soon."

The call ended with Sally and Tim looking at each other with their mouths gaped wide open.

******

It was getting very real for Tim now that they were in the Pawleys Island town limit. He knew the memories would hit him when he arrived in his hometown. He just didn't realize how hard they would hit him. When they took a left onto the North Causeway and drove across the bridge over Pawleys Island Creek, the marsh view opened wide to the south and Tim gasped at the sheer beauty he remembered so well. In early April, the marsh grass colors had yet to reach their deep summer green but were still a gorgeous mix of golden yellow and pale sage. The creek shone bright blue, and he recognized a small group of snow-white egrets flying overhead. Now that he was home, it felt like he had never left. It was as if a decade of time had vanished — that it was only yesterday he had left the island in such a tizzy.

The town may have developed more, but the island hadn't. Off the causeway, they took a right turn onto Myrtle Ave, the lone road extending the length of Pawleys Island. Two miles further south lay Culligan's Way. Sally smiled, seeing the sheer wonder in her brother's eyes when they passed the familiar landmarks on the road to home. First in sight was the iconic Pawleys Island chapel, standing out in its white simplicity against the marsh, as it has for the past 72 years.

The next minute, they passed the Pelican Inn. Tim felt the lump in his throat as he recalled the two summers he had bussed tables in the inn's dining room. Thoughts of Molly Elmwood flooded his senses. Molly waited tables both summers. They shared so much together; his first beer, his first cigarette, the moonlit night he lost his virginity on the beach behind the inn. He closed his eyes and could see her bright blue eyes, wavy blonde curls, and the dimple in her cheek. It was a time before she was involved with Randy — the time Tim came to realize and understand who and what he was. He'd forgotten how much Molly meant to him, and how much it had hurt when he found out about her relationship with his hated brother. Nostalgia washed over Tim. When would he see Molly again? What would she be like now? Tim hoped he'd see her soon.

Now they passed the Pritchard Street landing and headed down Springs Avenue, the last stretch — the most isolated and quiet section of the island. This end of Pawleys was nothing but a narrow strip of barrier island, just wide enough to hold a house on the beach. Across the street, short piers and docks bracketed the east side of Pawleys Creek and surrounding marsh. The creek went south another mile before emptying into Pawleys Inlet, then the Atlantic Ocean. The scenery was quintessential Lowcountry. Nothing in New York could match the sheer natural beauty of the only place he knew growing up. Many times, lonely in his cramped, noisy apartment, he recollected those memories of the island's raw splendor. Now that he was back, it felt absolutely surreal.

Sally pulled into the massive carport and parked between the giant wooden pillars that held the Way fifteen feet above the street level, protecting the house from even the worst hurricane surge.

Tim gulped as he glanced up at the namesake sign posted above the front door. Culligan's Way, painted a deep bronze in bold lettering against an azure background, assorted seagulls surrounding the name. It was oval with a thick rope frame. It appeared the sign had weathered some since he last remembered seeing it. He wondered how much everyone else had aged as well.

Sally put her hand on Tim's shoulder and asked, "Are you ready?"

"I suppose so. Let the show begin."

As soon as he opened the passenger door, he could hear Ruth screaming with delight as she ran down the front steps. "My baby's home! My baby's home!"

By the time he stood outside, opened his arms and whispered, "Hi Mom," Ruth had him buried in her arms. She hugged him so tight Tim thought she'd break his back.

Sally moved around the car and gave Annabelle a hug while she waited for Ruth to break hers. Ruth couldn't stop crying, which turned out to be contagious as all five of them shed open tears, including Connie, who stood waiting in line for her hug with a brother she hadn't seen or heard from since she was an early teen.

Finally, Ruth broke her embrace and assessed her son at arm's length. "My goodness gracious, Timothy, you look like a chicken on a hunger strike. Annabelle, just look at our Tim! Isn't he a just a sight!"

"A sight that needs some serious fattening up." Annabelle smiled as she came in came for her hug. "It's so good to have you home, Tim." She kissed Tim on the cheek, then stepped aside to make room for Connie to embrace her brother.

"Good to be home, Annabelle, and so good to see you too." Tim turned to her sister. "And who might you be, young lady? You seem to resemble a spry squirt I remember." To Tim's surprise, he noticed he had slipped back into the Southern accent he hadn't spoken in ten years. Tears weren't the only thing contagious that afternoon.

"I'm all grown up now, Timmy." Connie didn't forget her pet name for her brother.

Tim took a harder look at her. Connie was the closest in looks to himself, with a reddish tinge to her long straight brown hair and the freckles on her high cheekbones. But something was different about her now. She wasn't just 'grown up' — she looked at least ten years older than the twenty-four years she was. Her blue eyes seemed to glaze over, and her skin appeared gaunt and pale. Sally had described her ongoing challenges with addiction, and Tim knew well enough to stay clear of that discussion until some later date.

With the welcome hugs concluded, Ruth was ready to begin the fattening process. "Come y'all, let's get Tim to his favorite lunch and put some meat on his bones." The five of them made their way up the stairs. Tim had to pause halfway to catch his breath. The women all took notice of this, along with his quiet voice. Seeing him in this state brought home the reality of the reason he was here in the first place — to recover from long-haul Covid.

When Tim entered the home, more memories flooded his senses. The great room and open kitchen looked even more spacious than he remembered. The space on the main level had to be at least four times the size of his entire apartment. On the right he first noticed the remodeled kitchen. The old brown cabinets and black Formica countertops from a decade ago were now a sleek driftwood grey with shimmering charcoal granite on the counterspace and island. Further to the right of the kitchen were the huge walk-in pantry and laundry room.

The rest of the great room looked pretty much as he remembered. In back of the island, with a view out the back French doors sat the walnut dining table — the scene of so many meals and Sunday feasts. Sadly, also the place of too many family arguments, mostly thanks to Randy. To the left of the foyer was the wide split staircase leading to the bedrooms on the second floor, then the master bedroom on the third floor. Tim imagined he would be sleeping back in his old bedroom, the one next to Connie's. Randy also had a bedroom on the second floor and Sally's was probably now a guest room.

Further to the left of the stairs was the entertainment area / living room. The old set of couches were now a humongous cream leather sectional couch forming a horseshoe around the white brick fireplace. The TV mounted above had to be twice the size he remembered. In the far-left corner was Rudy's wet bar with leather bar stools and a generous display of booze on the wall. The back left of the great room was a sitting area with bookshelves loaded with hardcovers and paperbacks. Tim made a mental note to see what new titles were stocked. He imagined Ruth still read a good deal.

Finally, Tim took in the grand back view to the ocean. He walked to the back of the great room and opened the French doors. He had looked forward to this moment ever since he first thought about coming home. The wide blue Atlantic, fronted by the Way's walkover and dunes, and a sky with only whispers of clouds filled his eyes. The surf's gentle roar sounded like music to his ears, and the salt air hung long in his nose. *This* was the home he longed for. *This* was where his recuperation would happen. Tim forgot all about his family troubles, financial problems, and his poor health. He took a seat in one of the multitude of swings and rockers on the wide wraparound back deck and took in the deepest breath it seemed he had taken all year. He smiled and congratulated himself, realizing he had indeed made the right decision to come home.

Ruth, Sally, and Connie joined him on the deck. They couldn't stop staring at him. Tim smiled back. Although Connie had aged, his Mom looked as vibrant at fifty-seven as she had at forty-seven. He'd forgotten how much he resembled her. The same auburn hair, he thought, and not a streak of grey in it. The same bright blue eyes, high cheekbones, and thin lips. No-one else in the family carried this much of a resemblance to him. Why had he waited so long to come home? Why had he resisted so much? He felt more love on this deck right now than he had ever felt in his life. Of course, he knew the answer why. These were the women who loved him. They weren't the reason he left. The men in the family would show up soon enough. But until then, Tim relished the comfort and security of arriving back home, back at the Way. Culligan's Way. Now his way.

"Lunch is ready, Tim!" Annabelle yelled from the kitchen.

And now my favorite lunch I haven't had since I left, Tim thought as he rose out of the rocker. Life never felt sweeter.

CHAPTER 10

Rudy was having another awful afternoon as his blooming headache attested to. Stewing in his chambers, he just got off the phone with his elder son — a conversation which quickly descended into a profanity laced shouting match. His one freaking phone call, thought Rudy. What sane person wouldn't use it to call their lawyer? Not Randy. Once more, Randy assumed he had enough personal slickness to sway Rudy into releasing him from his barred confinement. When he discovered his own father had instigated his detention, the guttural language flowed non-stop.

After Rudy heard his son's version of the rolling pin incident, he groaned, then put the phone on mute while Randy finished spouting. One more knot to untie, Rudy mused. When he checked the phone again, Randy had finally hung up. "Good riddance," Rudy said out loud, then paged his secretary to have Sheriff Keating come see him as soon as possible.

When his phone rang shortly after, Rudy expected it to be Leroy, but the number flashed as unknown.

"Hello, Judge." When Rudy heard Molly's unmistakably familiar soft Carolina accent on the other end, his headache quickly deepened. "Do you have a minute?"

Rudy instantly compartmentalized his concerns about Randy, Leroy, and Ruth, and his mind flashed to several possibilities of why she'd be calling. "What do you want, Molly? I'm rather busy right now. Is this about Randy?"

"Oh no, Judge. Although I appreciate you locking that asshole up for the weekend. No, this is about something much more important." Molly paused for effect.

"And what would that be, Miss Elmwood? Spit it out."

"Greeley Construction, Rudy." This came out much more caustic. Rudy figured as much.

"What about Greeley, Molly?"

"What about it? Oh, maybe about how I'm on to your little scheme. How you're bribing DHEC to approve marsh lots Greeley wants to build on. And how much kickback money you're going to receive from Greeley once they approved those lots."

Rudy rolled his eyes. The knots kept growing tighter, same with the headache. "You don't know what you're talking about, Molly. And you're getting into something way over your head. Do you have any proof to back up this fabrication?"

"I have all the proof I need. It's called pillow talk."

Rudy pinched the bridge of his nose. He reached inside his desk drawer for a couple of Extra-strength Tylenol. "Of course! I'm not surprised the biggest whore in Georgetown County is sleeping with Jack Greeley. Care to go into more details? Or better yet, just tell me what you want. I have more important things to do than waste my time listening to your dribble." Rudy realized he now had to add Jack's name to his list of knots to untie this afternoon. He had only forty-five minutes before his 4:00 PM hearing, followed by the reunion with his younger son at home. One more headache piled on top of all the others.

"I'll make it simple for you, Rudy." Molly's caustic tone became even more bitter. "One hundred thousand in cash, hand delivered to me at Tim's party tomorrow night, or I'm going to the press to spill the beans on you and Greeley."

"Hah! Ho! Oh, that's rich," Rudy bellowed. He wondered how Molly even knew about Tim's homecoming. She'd obviously gotten wind of Randy's arrest. Molly had her sources. He had to give her credit for that. "And while you're waiting at the party empty-handed, I'll give Sheriff Keating the honor of arresting you for attempted extortion. Then you can join your ex-fiancé in our lovely facility here for the rest of the weekend."

"Don't blow smoke up my ass," hissed Molly. "It's very unbecoming of a judge. I want the cash tomorrow night, or you'll be in all the papers from Charleston to Wilmington on Monday morning." Molly ended the call before Rudy replied.

Now Rudy had another dumpster fire he needed to put out. He knew he was, in fact, blowing smoke to Molly. He couldn't have her arrested at the party — any evidence he could offer Leroy was only hearsay. Besides which, doing so would only open yet another can of worms. No, there were other ways to put pressure on Molly. Some legitimate, others — not so much. Two things were certain, though. There would be no cash payments made to Molly and there was no way the press would receive any fresh stories about him, Greeley Construction, or DHEC any time in the foreseeable future. Rudy would just need to pull a few extra strings this time. He made some notes on a legal pad, then paged his secretary again.

"Janice, where's Keating? Did you get in touch with him?"

"I did, Judge," Janice answered. "He told me to give him about thirty minutes. I told him you had a 4:00 PM hearing. He should be here before then."

"Thanks, Janice." Rudy switched off the pager and picked up his personal cell phone. Muttering, "fucking piece of shit," he dialed Jack Greeley's cell number.

******

After cooling his heels for a couple hours in one of Leroy's holding cells, Randy Culligan appeared before Judge John Kramer for his arraignment. Kramer was the second most senior judge in the county to Rudy and usually fell in line with Rudy in the ruling of cases coming before him — that being swift and severe justice. Kramer also knew how to grant a favor to his senior judicial partner when the need arose, as it did this afternoon.

Leroy sat in the front row as a somewhat more sober, yet still disheveled, Randy walked in with his public defender. Since he used his one allotted phone call to plead with his father instead of calling a lawyer, Randy had to settle for a feeble rookie who was no match for the county's DA, Gina Slocum.

Kramer immediately noticed the large bandage over Randy's left eye. "What happened you to your head there, Mr. Culligan?"

"My bat-shit crazy mother threw a…"

Kramer slammed his gavel down before Randy could finish. "I'll not have that language in my courtroom. Do you understand?"

Randy grumbled. "Yes, sir."

"So, let's try this again. What happened to your head?"

"My mother threw a rolling pin at me, and it hit me above my eye. The Sheriff was there, he saw it." A smattering of giggles broke out in the courtroom. Leroy saw Kramer roll his eyes.

"Sheriff Keating," Kramer addressed Leroy, "Is this true?"

Leroy stood and said with the straightest face, "No, Your Honor. The injury occurred while the defendant tried to resist arrest. Things got a little rough for a second." Leroy looked directly at Randy, who stood there speechless.

"I see then. Ms. Slocum, what are you seeking?"

Gina stood and stated, "Your Honor, we request denial of Mr. Culligan's bail at this point because the defendant's release may cause unforeseen harm to a certain event at the defendant's home residence over the weekend. Don't forget, y'all are invited to the party to celebrate Tim Culligan's return home," Gina assured Judge Kramer and the other staffers present. They all smiled and nodded with approval.

Randy seethed at his assigned defender to get him out on bail, but the defender simply shrugged. "My hands are tied, Randy. I'm sorry."

Leroy heard Randy shoot back to him, "How 'bout I tie your hands behind *your* back and dump you in the river?"

Kramer sent Randy back to his cell and told him if he could secure an attorney by Monday, he'd think about setting bail. Leroy chuckled all the way back to his office.

A few minutes later, his door knocked, and Leroy looked up from his desk to see his detective enter the office. "Hey Tony, come on in. You just missed a doozy of an arraignment with the Culligan kid. What's up?"

Tony Meacham strode into Leroy's office and took a seat. He had a mischievous smile on his face along with a twinkle in his blue eyes. His wavy brown hair always seemed to partially cover his left eye, giving him a boyish look, which contrasted with the otherwise chiseled features of his nose and cheeks. "Wanted to bring you up to speed on this Greeley Construction / marsh lot problem," he began. "I just got off the phone with my contact at DHEC, and things are getting stickier."

Leroy knew the background already and had been rebuffed when he tried to warn Rudy on Wednesday. According to Tony, it started with Jack Greeley's vision of turning much of the Lowcountry's vast marshland into prime real estate lots. The housing market had boomed in coastal South Carolina during the past three years and properties values with water views had skyrocketed. Oceanfront properties were extremely limited and out of reach for all but the obscenely rich. But the marsh front — well, the Lowcountry had tons of that. And all of it protected from development unless they followed very strict protocols. These all went through SCDHEC — The South Carolina Department of Health and Environmental Control. Greeley had built at least a dozen subdivisions with marsh lot views from North Myrtle Beach to Georgetown in the past ten years. But the approval process for new marsh front development was long and drawn out, not to mention expensive. And it seemed to be getting worse, at least from a developer's point of view.

To a growing number of environmentally conscious residents, building new marsh front property was an aberration of the pristine beauty the marshland offered, plus an environmental burden the sensitive natural buffer could no longer afford. These groups had launched several bills in the South Carolina legislature and the federal EPA to expand the remaining marshland protection zones and to make areas open to residential development extremely difficult to gain approval. It all hinged on DHEC. They had the last word on which subdivisions, and lots, were approved or not. And their reputation was one of caution.

Greeley had plans for twenty more developments on the marsh front, totaling over 150 new homes. The revenue from these would exceed one-hundred million dollars, twenty percent of which would find its way into Jack Greeley's pocket. And currently, DHEC blocked every single one of them. That was, according to Tony's sources, until recently when approval was received for one subdivision. Tony had a source in an environmental activist group who monitored the marsh front zoning like a hawk. This source had another source within DHEC who told him marsh zoning maps were being surreptitiously changed.

A minor scuffle broke out yesterday at the changed site in Murrells Inlet, where the environmentalist source chained himself to a five-hundred-year-old live oak being readied to be taken down. The literal tree-hugger got hauled off to the Horry County jail, charged with a misdemeanor, and released on $1,000 bail. A reporter for WCXM news out of Myrtle Beach was there to report it. Once released, he called his DHEC source to find out who, why, and how the zoning maps were being changed. He also placed a call to Detective Meacham on what he suspected was going on. When Tony pressed the source in DHEC, who did some checking, he was informed that yes, indeed some maps were updated, but there lacked a proper trail on who approved the changes. Yesterday, a section of wetlands was on the books. Then today, a new map appeared as residential, as if the old map never existed. The source didn't know who might have done the changes, could have been one of several engineers on staff, but he got an anonymous tip a few days earlier. Check out Judge Culligan. No further details supplied.

So Tony had gone straight to Leroy and asked permission to trace Rudy's personal cell phone records. That's what Leroy wanted to give Rudy the heads up on Wednesday, but Rudy cut him off before he could tell him. So he gave his detective permission. Now Tony was back with new intel.

"I got the results of Rudy's cell records here. In the past three weeks, he made ten calls to three different numbers at DHEC's main office in Columbia. My source in DHEC confirmed Rudy has been in conversation with people there, primarily the department's head, Robert Huntsman."

"So he lied to me on Wednesday," Leroy said dismissively. "Well now, doesn't that suck for our judge?" he told his detective as he stood up from his desk. "I was just getting my notes together before I walk over to the courthouse and pay him a visit. Besides his son's problems and his own, he also has to contend with his crazy wife's antics."

"Ruth Culligan?" Tony, like everyone else in the justice system, knew of Ruth's colorful history. "What'd she do now?"

"Well, if you go by Randy's cell and notice a large bandage over his left eye, you'll get an idea."

Tony chortled as he and Leroy left the office. "I'll have to take a look. If anything else comes up, I'll let you know."

"Thanks, Tony, same here."

As he walked across the courtyard to Rudy's chambers, Leroy smiled to himself, recollecting how the dumbfounded, likely hungover Randy barely made a move to avoid the wooden projectile from smashing him in the face. If it wasn't blatant aggravated assault, Leroy would have said it was the most hilarious thing he'd seen all year. But then, as he thought back to the Greeley mess, his mood soured, and he felt a knot the size of a grapefruit form in the pit of his stomach. This conversation would not be pleasant.

CHAPTER 11

Tim woke early Saturday morning after sleeping for fifteen straight hours and for a second, didn't know where he was. It wasn't his cramped apartment in New York where he woke the previous morning, that was for sure. In the few seconds he spent in a hazy semi-consciousness, the morning sunlight shining bright into his ocean facing bedroom, he thought he might have died and gone to heaven. Then he recognized his night dresser from his childhood and realized he was in Culligan's Way, sleeping in the same bed he had slept in every night from the time he was eight until he left at eighteen. Tim sat up in his queen-size bed with the four pineapple carved walnut posts, on a mattress far more comfortable than what he had been on the past decade, stretched his arms over his head and recollected the events of the previous day.

By the time he had finished his lunch on the porch yesterday — two ham and pimento cheese sandwiches, with sides of sweet pickles, pickled okra, Annabelle's homemade potato salad, and fudge brownies for dessert — Tim had just enough energy left to cross the walkover and take in the ocean. It brought back waves of memories. From building sandcastles as a youngster, to surfboarding as a young teen, to bonfires in the sand, toasting marshmallows. And it brought back the memories of long solitary walks north to the pier, or south to the inlet, where Tim had sorted himself out. Came to understand who he was, what he was — not why, or how by any means — but an understanding that put him at peace. Even if that meant anything but peace from the assorted miscreants around him with far less broad mindsets.

After ten minutes on the beach, Tim was exhausted. He made his way back to the ocean side porch, remembering Ruth's golden rule to wash and dry your sandy feet off at the spigot before entering the Way. Amazing the things that come back to you like that. The rest of the 'rules of the house' would also fall into line for Tim — shoes off in the house, dirty clothes in the hamper, wet towels hung — more would come back to him soon enough. Tim made his excuses to the ladies and was asleep as soon as his head hit the pillow.

Now, at 8:00 AM Saturday morning, he could hear the rustling downstairs and smelled coffee and bacon from his upstairs bedroom. His stomach rumbled. Tim grinned when he realized he would be eating so much better than he had been. Annabelle was a master in the kitchen, and Mom was no slouch herself. If their goal was to fatten him up, he wouldn't be putting up much of a fight.

As he dressed, his stomach turned for a different reason. He'd slept through the evening and missed the reunion with his father. But Rudy would be downstairs eating breakfast now. "Oh well," Tim grumbled out loud. "Let's get this over with."

Tim stepped down the staircase in his stocking feet towards the heavenly smells of the bustling kitchen. Connie and Rudy were at the breakfast table. Ruth and Annabelle were busy at the island. "Good morning, everyone," Tim said, softer than he meant to. All four looked up at the sight of Tim grinning his shy smile.

"There you are!" said Ruth. "Heaven's sake, you got a good night's sleep. Come down and have some breakfast. I can't remember how you liked your eggs, scrambled or fried?"

Tim kept his grin up as he reached the floor level. "Scrambled is fine, Mom." His smile subsided as he made his first eye contact with his father. Rudy made no move as he stared at his son.

"Scramble Tim a couple of eggs quick, Annabelle. Come on over to the table, Tim. We have biscuits, country ham, and bacon ready."

Ruth hustled over to the table and went behind Rudy, who still hadn't said a word or made a move. He just kept a keen eye on Tim. This changed when Ruth smacked her husband upside the back of his head. "Get up!" Tim heard his mother hiss in Rudy's right ear. Rudy got the message and rose from the table, then went around to greet Tim. For a second, the two stood a few feet apart, the three women watching. Tim stopped, unsure if he should speak first or not. The old feeling of intimidation flooded back through him.

"Hello, Tim," Rudy said. "Welcome home." But he made no move to embrace him. He just stood there, stone still.

"Hello, Dad. Thank you for letting me come home. I truly appreciate it."

Rudy glanced over at Ruth, then back to Tim. He cleared his throat then said, "Yes, well, please make yourself at home. I understand you have a long recovery ahead of you." Then, having cleared himself of the pleasantries required of him, Rudy added, "If you would excuse me, I need to head out of town for the day.

I'll be back before the party tonight. Perhaps we can talk more then."

"Yes, sir, that would be great," Tim responded, relieved the initial meeting appeared to be brief and over with.

Rudy nodded, showing he approved Tim's respectful reply, then left for the master bedroom.

Tim made his way over to the breakfast table, all smiles. "This looks fantastic. Thank you so much for everything." He helped himself to the homemade biscuits, going straight for the fig preserves Ruth only brought out for special occasions, noted by both Rudy and Connie ten minutes earlier.

"Don't get too used to the special treatment, Tim," offered Connie. "We'll be back to Culligan slop in no time at all." She winked over at Annabelle.

Annabelle brought over the skillet with fresh scrambled eggs and placed them on Tim's plate. "There ain't been no slop around here, Miss Connie, since the last help Ms. Ruth hushed outta' here fifteen years ago. Remember her, Ms. Ruth; what was her name?"

"Annie," answered Ruth. "Annie Dougherty."

"Woman didn't know grits from Shinola. Ain't been no slop around here ever since Ms. Ruth put me in charge of this here kitchen."

"And we all appreciate it, Annabelle. Every single day. We're going to have Tim here fattened like a plump pig in no time at all."

Tim nodded his approval as he stuffed his mouth full of biscuits and ham. "So," he continued after swallowing, "where is Dad going today? He seemed to be in a rush." Everyone at the table turned to Ruth. After what they experienced last night, they knew something was not well with the Culligan patriarch.

"I don't rightly know. He came home in quite the mood yesterday. Just as well you slept through. Your father's been under a lot of stress of late. I'm sure Sally told you about your brother."

"She has, and I appreciate it. Is that it? What about a certain rolling pin?"

Ruth stiffened. "Why, I don't know what you're talking about. Annabelle, is there something wrong with one of our rolling pins?"

"Nothing I know about. They was sure put to work yesterday." Connie giggled while Tim grinned. "Eight pies we made, Ms. Ruth. And they will be the hit of the party — fo' sure."

Tim felt he should move on. "Tell me more about this party tonight. Who all can I expect to be here?"

"It's more like who won't be here," quipped Connie. "It's all anyone on the island's been talking about the last three days."

"I believe we're going to have a full house," answered Ruth. "Probably an overflow. The weather looks like it will cooperate.

"Aren't you a little concerned about Covid spread, Mom? I mean, I'll be alright, but — what's it been like down here?"

The three women glanced at each other, not sure how to answer the sensitive question. "Well," Ruth began, "the older folk are vaccinated. Me and your father have, Annabelle has, and Sally I know has with her work. Other than that, people just need to take responsibility for their actions. As it's always been."

Tim expected nothing different — that's the way it has always been in Culligan's Way. Survival of the fittest.

******

Later that afternoon, Sally was in the middle of draping blue and yellow bunting over the front entrance when her cell rang. "Shit," she cursed when she saw Bud's name appear on the screen. She stepped down from the ladder and, with reluctance, answered. "Yeah, Bud, what's going on?"

"Sally," her boss barked over the phone, "I'm calling the managers in for an emergency meeting. IT just finished reviewing the security footage from the last two months and we found our thief."

"Really?" she said, surprised. "So then, why do you need us to come in?"

"The thief had the goddamn keys to get into the building and the key to the pharmacy, Sally. We need to sort this out as soon as possible."

"Ok, so have you been able to identify him?"

"Her. No, we could not identify her. I'm hoping one of the managers can. How soon can you get here?"

Sally looked at her watch, shaking her head in disbelief. The drug thief is a she? 2:15 PM, well, there goes the rest of the afternoon. "I'll be there in about twenty minutes."

"Make it ten," retorted Bud, then ended the call. Sally sighed and wondered why she ever agreed to work for such an asshole.

"Mom, gotta go," she shouted across the great room to Ruth. "Crisis at work. Sorry. See you at the party." Then Sally gathered her purse and headed out the door.

Fifteen minutes later, a gathering of the five Publix managers settled in Bud's office around his computer. Lori Winehart and Ginger Spearman were already there, as well as Linda. When Sally entered, they all gave her a 'what took you so long' look. Sally shrugged and took a seat. Bud had the security tape cued to the first of the two break-ins.

"Here's the first break-in. Tuesday March 2, 2:30AM." IT had already split the screen between the back door entrance and the pharmacy camera. The five managers watched as a figure in a red sweatshirt, hoody pulled tight over their face, used two keys to enter the back door. "She knew to use the first key to disable the security alarm, then the second to unlock the door. Can't make out the face from this angle."

They watched the thief enter the back door, then a minute later, come into view of the pharmacy camera. She kept her head down, hiding from the camera, while she opened the pharmacy barricade. Then she disappeared between the rows of shelves filled with drugs. Out of sight from the camera, the thief set to work finding what she was looking for. The managers watched, waiting for any sign of the thief making a visible appearance. Bud kept his finger on the mouse. When the thief finished taking the pills which went missing from the first month's theft, she left the pharmacy and locked the gate. It was then, just before she exited the camera's viewing span, that she looked back and, for a brief instant, stared into the camera. Bud froze the screen. Everyone looked at the image of the young female thief looking straight at them.

"That's her," said Bud. "Anyone recognize her? She anyone of your techs, Linda?"

Linda shook her head. "No, not any of ours."

"Anyone else? Anybody recognize this woman?"

Bud looked at each of his other managers. Lori and Ginger shook their heads. When he looked at Sally, he got a much different reaction.

Her eyes were wide open and when she removed her hand from over her mouth, she said, "I do. That's Molly Elmwood."

CHAPTER 12

Harvey Klinger had been on edge since Thursday, when he tried to save that live oak in Salt Cove. First, he was out $1000 after posting bail — he expected that. But then, when he watched the 5:00 PM news on WCXM, the bastards left out his story of the Murrells Inlet live oak protest. The entire purpose of the exercise was to get on the news. That bitch reporter, Heidi, promised him the story would make the cut that night. The cameraman shot the scene of the cops with the bolt cutters, breaking the chain with which he had secured himself to the massive tree, all the while him blasting Greeley Construction for destroying the precious natural habitat. That beautiful five-hundred-year-old tree was now nothing but a stack of sawed up logs — removed to make room for the latest Greeley Construction marsh front monstrosity. Now he had nothing to show for his efforts.

Harvey had been active in the Grand Strand environmental protection circles for several years. It often felt like a long death march, seeing his beloved shoreline and wetlands overtaken by commercial and residential development. There were a few minor victories. Expanding the Waccamaw National Wildlife Refuge was one. They defeated attempts to nibble back portions of the Huntington Beach State Park. But these weren't big wins. The Grand Strand continued to expand. More and more snowbirds wishing to escape the frigid and overtaxed North and avoid the overpriced coastal real estate that extended from Hilton Head all the way to Miami were moving into the Grand Strand. The land between Garden City and North Myrtle Beach was already a lost cause. Nonstop commercial and residential developments had choked off any of the previous natural habitats. That left the undeveloped marshlands of Murrells Inlet and on south — Huntington Beach State Park, Litchfield, Pawleys Island and Georgetown as the only remaining natural wetlands on the Grand Strand.

Harvey and his cohorts had contacts at DHEC and knew every inch of undeveloped marshland in the area. They fought and, if not won, at least put up roadblocks to every proposed expansion that the construction companies sought to build on. Public enemy number one was Greeley. Harvey smelled something rotten when he discovered the approval of the Salt Cove development in Murrells Inlet for residential construction. Development of that section of wetlands had been blocked for years because of the sensitivity of the area known for its nesting sites for a variety of osprey and bald eagles. When he first noticed surveyors out on the property, he contacted his source at DHEC, and they could not provide a satisfactory answer why.

That's when he got Molly involved. He needed an inside mole to gather intelligence. A pretty mole — with charms. Molly had sympathy for the environment cause and their friendship went back many years. He never quite understood her attraction to Randy Culligan, but that was a different matter. They had a simple plan. Seduce Jack Greeley and find out how he got Salt Cove approved.

The seduction turned out to be ridiculously easy. Molly went to a Murrells Inlet bar they knew he frequented, and two winks of her baby blues and a pert smile later, they were in the Brookhaven Inn just down the street. One week later, laid three times, Jack was putty in her hands, and talked about how he wanted to divorce his wife of twenty-five years to be with her.

On their fourth rendezvous, when Molly gave Jack some pseudo assurances of a potential future together, she pried for inside business information. "What are your next big plans?" she had asked him, lying in bed.

Jack bragged about how easy it was to get Salt Cove approved.

Molly asked, "Weren't those wetlands protected?"

Jack looked at her naked in bed, distracted by her firm breasts and hard nipples. "Well, they were," he had started, squeezing her tits, more concerned about a second round. "But I have some good contacts at DHEC." Jack dove in to suckle the nipples. Molly let him enjoy himself. When he came up for air, he offered the real tidbit. "Your ex's father has been a great help as well."

"Judge Culligan? How so?"

Jack caught himself before he went out even further on a dangerous limb. "Why are you so interested in this, Molly?"

Whereby Molly switched gears. "Come here, Jackie poo, and fuck me some more."

After Jack spent himself again, his tongue loosened more. He talked about the grandiose plans he had for the next ten years of residential developments, now that DHEC would no longer be a roadblock with Judge Culligan smoothing over the rough patches. The profits his company would earn in the future would dwarf what it cost him in kickbacks.

"What about the poor eagles and osprey?" Molly asked.

"Fuck them." Jack said, callous to the bone.

Molly smiled to herself and thought, fuck *you*, you cheating bastard. I got it all recorded.

Harvey giggled with delight when Molly relayed the story to him. That's when they hatched their next plan. Harvey would contact the Georgetown County Sheriff's office and put some shade out about DHEC and Judge Culligan. He had some dealings with Tony Meacham a few years back when he provided clandestine information about a Myrtle Beach drug ring. He also knew Tony was no friend of Rudy. Let it brew a couple of days, then have Molly squeeze Judge Culligan with the news and the extortion bid.

That was yesterday. This morning Tony called him with news he was hot on the trail of Judge Culligan. He would appreciate any further insight from Greeley's end. Harvey doubted this would happen. Jack called Molly on Friday afternoon and blasted her out, explaining that he got a call from Rudy, exposing the fact that Molly's charms had duped him. Rudy also wanted to know what the *fuck* was Jack thinking, shacking up with the likes of her. Molly told Jack he needed to go back to his wife, or better yet, go straight to hell.

Now, on Saturday afternoon, the two of them sat in Harvey's apartment and plotted their next move. "Don't spend much time at that party, Molly," Harvey implored his friend. "I don't trust anyone of that bunch."

"I've got other business there as well. You don't have to worry about me. I can take care of myself." Molly passed the joint they were sharing back to her friend. She had two more hours to relax before dressing for the main event.

Harvey didn't feel as well assured — and the pot wasn't helping. "And didn't you say the Sheriff is going to be there? Half the damn courthouse as well?"

"Harvey, you know as well as I do, Rudy was just blowing smoke. There is no way the law is going to make a move on me based on hearsay."

"I hope not. I've already paid for one bail bond this week. What about the money? Think the Judge will pony up?"

"Mmm, don't know. I doubt it, though. If Rudy is anything, he's cheap. I'll make him plenty concerned about seeing himself in the papers, though. You remember how much he hates bad press?"

"And what about that? Are you still going to the media if he refuses to pay? What are you going to tell them? Jack Greeley told me this in between lays?"

Molly smirked back at Harvey. "Of course not, darling. I'm going to tell them an even better story."

Harvey sat back on his aging, overstuffed couch and smiled. He knew this was going to be worth listening to. "Go ahead, I'm all ears."

"Yes, so it seems a few weeks ago, Randy hacked into Rudy's cell phone and found these incriminating texts between him and Jack Greeley, and also contacts within DHEC, concerning the matter of zoning maps at the proposed Salt Cove development in Murrells Inlet. Randy came up with a plan of his own, bless his heart. He would blackmail his father for $100,000 cash or else he'd turn over the texts he had copied to the press. Once Rudy paid him the cash, he'd bribe his way back into my heart. When he showed up unannounced at my place the next week with this crazy plan, I told him to get lost. Poor soul is in jail now. Might be a while longer if the story comes out."

Molly winked at Harvey, who nodded with approval. "And these made-up texts are where?"

Molly held up her own cell. "Right here, as sent from Randy's phone."

Harvey gave her a quizzical look. "I don't get it. You just said you told him to get lost. He's in jail because he broke his restraining order and forced himself on you. Isn't he?"

Molly grinned and shook her head. "Oh, darling, you can be so gullible, just like the rest of them. No, once I had the goods on Jack, that's when I called Randy and invited him over. He got drunk, then passed out. I made up some texts on his phone, sent them to me, then deleted them off his. When he woke up, I kicked his sorry ass out and called the Sheriff."

Harvey laughed some more. "Shrewd, you little hussy, you are shrewd. And if Rudy doesn't pay, the texts go to the press?"

Molly grinned back at Harvey. "That's right. By Monday morning, I'll have Greeley, Rudy, *and* DHEC all wallowing in their own shit."

CHAPTER 13

The Pawleys Island party event of the year got off to a rocky start. It began when Rudy called Ruth at two in the afternoon to tell her he was running late and might not make it for the start of the party at six.

"Where in tarnation are you?" demanded Ruth

"Ruth, honey, the less you know, the better. I'll be there as soon as I can."

Ruth was not pleased. Nor was she happy with the caterer, who had just called to inform her the trays of mini quiches and ham and cheese crostinis would not arrive with the rest of the food. They would be there by 6:30 PM and they would give these trays to her at cost.

"Phooey!" Ruth complained to Annabelle. "Takes twenty dollars off a $1500 bill. She's about to lose a lot more than that off her tip."

By 4:00 PM, Culligan's Way resembled a beehive in full motion. Caterers were coming and going in a steady stream. Ruth and Annabelle were busy baking the eight homemade pies they would serve (two apple, two peach, two pecan, a lemon, and a chocolate cream). Homemade pies were a tradition for Culligan parties going back to when Annabelle arrived on the scene in 2005. What started as a friendly competition between the two women over who could bake the best homemade pie, grew to a collaboration of efforts and the now widely and highly regarded dessert centerpieces of their bashes. Although there were other catered desserts set up around the kitchen island, the pies were always the main attraction.

Once Sally returned from her disturbing impromptu meeting at Publix, she, Connie, and Tim put the finishing touches on the decorations. The cleaning crew finished their work, and the Way was a spotless gem. Bartenders arrived to begin their preparation. The setup was completed by 5:00 PM, and the family returned to their bedrooms to prepare themselves for the party.

Tim looked at himself in the full-length mirror. He had now been home just over twenty-four hours, yet he felt like he'd been back for a week. He dressed casually in jeans and a white button-down shirt, another from his high school wardrobe, kept meticulously in his closet for the past decade. It now hung loosely on his slim frame. He examined himself in the mirror with concern. Was he really up for this party? How would the other people he had had no contact with in over ten years view him? With empathy, most likely. They would all know of his condition and the reason he had returned. But what would they really think of him?

Tim knew all too well about the duplicity of the South. How many times would he hear 'bless your heart' tonight, when behind the eyes of the well-meaning guests would be doubts about his orientation, his abandonment of his family, his complicity living with liberal Yankees, or maybe just the fact that he's a spoiled rich kid who spit out the silver spoon thrust in his mouth. The cynical would think these things, Tim knew, but not everyone. Think positively — his mantra now. Enjoy yourself, have fun, be kind, and whatever you do, do not get into any kind of argument with these people. Tim's wide grin reflected back towards himself. He was ready for — whatever.

Heading downstairs, Tim could smell the sweet pies fresh out of the oven and hear the clinking of glasses being readied at the bar. He looked over towards Ruth and Annabelle. Ruth would switch her role in a minute from party overseer to social debutante. Annabelle would switch her role from party preparer to party server.

At the official starting time of 6:00 PM, Tim already recognized a few early arrivals. He had not seen his father yet. He shook off the disappointment he felt earlier from Rudy's sudden exit at breakfast and his failure to return early and have a 'talk' with him. Some things just don't change.

But the house looked stunning. Welcome Home Tim signs covered both front and back entrances along with an assortment of 'We missed you!' and 'We love you, Tim' placards. Colorful blue and yellow balloons and streamers filled the great room. Tim thought it looked more like a baby shower than a welcome home party, but he would not be sharing this with Ruth or anyone else.

Party lights strung around the front porch and the entire back deck. The servers and bartenders were at the ready with mountains of food and wide assortments of beverages. The display of eight pies sat front and center on the kitchen island, surrounded by an extensive selection of party trays and other catered desserts. A carving station with an enormous ham the size of a beach ball, sat in one corner along with the expected condiments. Tim took it all in and wondered how long it would be before the story of Randy and the soon to be fabled rolling pin would make the rounds. He had inspected the pin that morning and, although thoroughly scrubbed, still had a faint red tinge at the point of contact.

Sally's family arrived shortly before six and in a manner of minutes, guests began streaming through the front door. Tim knew his obligation to greet each guest as they entered. He and Ruth straddled the entranceway and began the formalities. The first guests were Dr. and Mrs. John Marcum, Tim's pediatrician, and the only doctor he knew before he left. Tim suddenly realized that expecting seeing long lost faces paled to the actual sight of them. He caught himself flooded with long ago memories of Marcum's office — getting shots, treating a broken wrist, or strep throat. Tim smiled warmly as he welcomed them.

"It's so good to see you again, Dr. and Mrs. Marcum."

"We're so glad you're back, Tim." Marcum shook his hand and did a quick up and down visual exam. "I don't want to hold up the welcome line, but please see me later this evening. I've seen a lot of Covid come through here, and I want to see you regain your health as soon as possible."

"Yes, sir, I'll do that." Tim expected as much, actually looked forward to what his old doctor might tell him.

"Bless your heart, Tim," Julie Marcum said as she hugged his neck. "I know Ruth here is going to take good care of you. It's so good to see you again."

"Yes, Ma'am," Tim replied, his southern accent firmly back in place now. That's the first 'Blessed', he thought — maybe she meant this one — or not. "I believe I've gained two pounds on the first day back." Tim grinned back at the doctor's wife, then looked up and saw a line of five more couples waiting their turn on the front porch. This was just the beginning. Tim knew it would be a long night. Thank goodness he slept some that afternoon.

The next guests were the neighbors, Paul and Rhonda Glasgow, followed by the Wilsons who were friends of Sally, the Greens — friends from Ruth's bridge club, then Father Mulroney from Holy Grace, then the Babcocks from the courthouse (Marty Babcock was Rudy's designated bailiff on most of his hearings and trials), and on and on. By the time Tim explained to Marty he didn't know where Rudy was or when he would return, the line outside had stretched to the street.

For the next thirty minutes, the routine continued. Seemed every man wanted to test Tim's grip strength, which wasn't much, and was getting weaker — Tim supposed this was the male version of them judging his recovery — and every woman felt compelled to bless his freaking heart. Finally, the crowd waiting to enter the Way thinned, and Tim got Ruth's permission to break away from the front door. He marveled at the burgeoning crowd. All the food and drink stations were in action, and they had even violated a couple of pies.

He talked with the guests he had a genuine interest in. Tim made a special effort to chat with Jerry Robinson, his gay high-school teacher, who taught him chemistry, but also the trials and tribulations of being non-hetero in the South. He and his husband Gary, married for seven years now, wanted to know all about his life in New York, something Tim could have talked for hours about, but seemed distant to him tonight. He bantered some with Colleen Reynolds, who ran the only dance studio between Myrtle Beach and Charleston, in Georgetown. She had helped to turn Tim towards his career path.

Tim brimmed with confidence and comfort, seeing so much of his past come together in one place and time, all to wish him well. He circled back around to the kitchen to check on Annabelle, then made his way to the front door and saw cars lined up far down the avenue. Still no sign of his father. Tim wondered if Rudy was purposely avoiding the party, sending a signal of his discomfort and displeasure with the event. Tim didn't think even he would stoop that low. After all, he was a politician as much as a judge — and politicians *never* missed an opportunity to be seen with their electorate. No, it had to be something else, and something important enough to be this late.

As Tim mused about his father's whereabouts, then about his brother stewing in a Georgetown jail cell, he almost missed the young lady, dressed to kill in a short miniskirt and low hung blouse, walk up the stairs smiling at Tim the whole way. When their eyes met at the top step, Tim's heart skipped a beat. His face broke out in an enormous grin as he opened his arms to greet her.

"Hello, Molly."

"Hello, Tim," Molly replied as she pulled him into a warm embrace.

CHAPTER 14

Tim assumed Molly would come to the party, but couldn't be certain. Twice in the last day when her name came up, there seemed to be some iciness in the air, which he couldn't quite put his finger on. But here she was, and she looked gorgeous. Her blond curls hung below her shoulders, her blue eyes sparkled, and her bright smile with the dimple in her cheek looked as charming as ever. But beneath the glossy exterior, the makeup and eye shadow, Tim sensed something else. Something aging her, pulling her down. Maybe it was the early crow's feet which cracked through the makeup, or some wrinkles around her mouth which certainly weren't there ten years ago. Or perhaps it was an overall unspoken level of anxiety which he sensed permeated from his friend. Tim brushed it off as normal aging, like everyone else in the room — all ten years older than he had last seen them.

"Quite a spread your folks have here," Molly remarked as they walked together into the great room.

"Yes, Mom pulled all the strings for this one. Here, can we sit for a minute? I need to get off my feet." Tim escorted Molly to one edge of the sectional. He could feel the eyes of guests nearby on both of them.

Molly sat and held Tim's hands in hers. "Tell me, Tim, are you going to make a full recovery? Are you going to be home for a while?"

Tim was lost in her blue eyes. He felt the passion for Molly rush to his loins, just like the night behind the Pelican Inn so long-ago. He blushed. "They say I will, but it could take several years. But I feel I'm in a good place now. The right place for me." He broke the grip of Molly's hands and relaxed back on the couch.

"I do hope so. So much has happened. I really want to take some time to get to know you again. But, well, there are some things — "

Just then one of the female guests came behind the couch, then bent over slightly and whispered in Molly's ear, "Skank" loud enough for Tim to hear. By the time he looked up, the guest had turned and mixed back with the crowd, and Tim couldn't recognize her. He turned to Molly in disgust.

"That was uncalled for!"

Molly's face flushed, but Tim noticed she didn't look all that surprised. "Listen, Tim — there are a lot of people at this party who don't think too highly of me, ok?"

Tim shook his head, confused.

"I needed to come and see you and take care of some other business, but I can't stay here long."

Tim continued to shake his head. "I don't understand. Does this have to do with Randy? I can assure you the people here aren't taking his side of the story about what happened the other day."

Molly gave him that look, like she was about to say, 'Bless your heart,' but said instead, "It's not that." Molly looked around and spotted Connie near the kitchen island. Turning back to Tim, she continued, "Listen, I need to take care of something first. Then I'm going to have to leave."

"Leave! But you just got here."

"Please, Tim. I can explain later. Later tonight, in fact. Can you meet me privately, say at midnight, when the party will have died down? Meet me out by the dock? There are some things you need to know."

"I don't understand. What's going on?"

Molly looked around, her eyes darting from side to side. "I can't explain it now." She rose, and Tim rose with her. "Tonight? Midnight at the dock. Promise me you'll meet me there, then?" Molly implored Tim, grabbing his hands.

He couldn't refuse. He could never refuse Molly. "Sure, midnight at the dock."

"Thanks, I'll see you then." Molly turned and walked away, heading towards Connie.

Tim watched as Molly followed Connie up the stairs. Then he looked around the sectional and saw Sally watching the two. She looked like she had daggers in her eyes. Tim walked over to her, and she broke into a semi-smile when she saw Tim approach.

"Enjoying your party, little brother?"

Tim thought her face looked flush with color, probably from the wine. "I am. What's going on with Molly and Connie?" Tim quickly changed the subject.

Sally's expression changed back to a sour look. "I don't know. But know this, Tim. Do *not* trust Molly Elmwood."

"And why not?"

"Look, I don't want to throw cold water on your party tonight. But I just found out some things about our Miss Molly that will not go down well for her. I don't want you to get involved, ok? I mean, I know she was your friend. Just don't get too close to her."

Tim eyed Sally with even more confusion. This certainly wasn't what he had expected tonight. "She's still my friend. What did you find out about her?"

"I can't go into it now. I suspect you'll find out soon enough, though. Oh look," Sally turned her attention to the front entrance, "Dad's back. How about that? The old man didn't blow you off completely."

Tim watched as Rudy entered the house and immediately went to the bar. Several men gathered around him as the Judge quickly downed his first bourbon. "Where do you think he's been all day?" Tim asked.

"Well, I'm sure he's been busy protecting the good people of Georgetown County from the near-do-wells of the world," Sally sneered, then scoffed. "Either that, or he was off at some motel getting laid."

"He doesn't still screw around?" asked Tim, somewhat shocked. "Does he?"

Sally giggled. "Nobody knows what the Judge does when he's not in the courtroom or on the golf course. I'm sure he has his hands in lots of people's pies, even if his dick isn't in any of them."

Tim marveled at his sister's coarseness. All those years keeping their mouths clean sure didn't have any lasting effect. "Has Mom caught him again, I mean, since that rat poison thing? I see he still has that left eye droop."

Sally snickered between sips of her Chardonnay. "Well, let's see now. There were rumors he had an affair with a court reporter back in 2013. Nothing proven, except the young lady soon found that a transfer to Greenville best suited her health.

Then, another rumor with a TV reporter out of Myrtle Beach. This was in, let's see, 2016. That one got snuffed out fast."

"What do you mean, 'snuffed out'?" Tim's mind flashed to some young lady laid out from rat poison.

"Well, let's just say a certain Ruth Culligan paid a visit to WBPK and allegedly threatened to do the same thing she did to WCXM, remember, with the advertisers, unless this reporter vamoosed. Which she did within the week."

Tim's eyes popped. "And did she do anything to Dad?"

"We never knew. I'm sure she did something, but apparently, whatever it was didn't leave a lasting physical scar."

"I see. And what about Mom? You mentioned on the phone she had been back to Charleston twice more than the two times I had known about. What were they about?"

Sally started to answer, but then became distracted when she saw Leroy and his wife over by the bar. "Tim, we have lots of time to catch up more. But I have to have a conversation with Sheriff Keating over there. If you would excuse me."

Sally left Tim standing by the back door. He watched as his sister greeted the county's sheriff and then almost immediately get into a heated discussion with him. *What the hell is going on around here?* Tim thought, watching the argument play out.

Suddenly, someone bumped Tim from the side and he felt liquid saturate his shirt. Looking down, he realized a guest had spilled their glass of red wine on his white shirt. It was Mary Ellen Gathings, another neighbor from down the street.

"Oh my gosh, Tim, I am so sorry!" Her face turned the same shade as the Pinot Noir that soaked his shirt. "Oh my, look what I've done! And to the party's host."

Tim saw how shaken his guest was and put her at ease. "It's fine, it's fine, Mrs. Gathings. Really. I have plenty of other shirts upstairs to change into. Please don't worry about it. If you would excuse me." Tim wondered how drunk the neighbor was. Did she slur her words slightly? Didn't matter. Before he started up the stairs, he glanced back to see Walter Gathings having a stern discussion with his wife, who was most definitely drunk. And she had just embarrassed her husband once again.

Upstairs, just before Tim entered his bedroom to choose another shirt, he heard another heated argument in the bedroom next door — Connie's bedroom. Connie and Molly were having it out. Now what? Tim thought, as he quietly stepped to just outside of his sister's bedroom door.

CHAPTER 15

"You are so full of shit, Molly!" Tim heard Connie loud and clear. "You can't screw me over like this."

"I'm not screwing you, Connie. It's simply supply and demand. Right now demand is sky high. So, the price goes up with it."

"You jacked the price up triple from last month. Who the hell do you think you are? Who do you think got you that key in the first place?"

Key to what? Tim mouthed silently. He hung on every word.

"You got paid for those keys, you spoiled bitch. You know that. Now you're simply a customer and I'm a supplier. Don't forget, I'm the one risking my ass breaking into Publix."

Tim couldn't believe what he was hearing. Molly, breaking into Publix, from keys she got from Connie?

After a moment of silence, Connie said, "I need ten Oxyies to get me through next week. How much?"

Oh shit, now it was out in the open. His sister, the drug addict. And his friend was her supplier. Breaking into Publix? Does Sally know about this?

"Two hundred for ten Oxyies. That's the best I can do."

Silence in the bedroom. Tim guessed Connie was trying to decide if she really needed the deal. It certainly answered one question — Connie was still an addict.

Finally, his sister replied. "I only have a hundred."

"Then I guess I'll sell you five."

"Molly, please, five won't get me through next week. I can't get any more cash until then."

"Well then, don't buy any from me. Get them from your other sources."

"They dried up."

"Like I said, supply and demand. You want the pills or not? I have business with the Judge and then I need to get out of this shit show."

"Fine," Connie replied, defeated — addicted. "Give me the five."

Tim sensed the impromptu meeting would end soon, and he didn't want to be caught eavesdropping. He quietly slipped into his bedroom, leaving the door open a crack so he'd know when the coast was clear. A minute later, Tim watched as both women strode past his bedroom door and proceeded downstairs. His head swirled as he searched his closet for another clean shirt, picking out a blue striped Ralph Lauren button down. He tried to think through what he had learned in just the last fifteen minutes. Molly had to take care of something — now he knew. She had to sell his sister drugs, which she had stolen — from his other sister! How fucked up was that? But she also had business with his father — no idea what that's about. And Molly needed to see him out at the dock at midnight tonight. That'll be one interesting conversation.

Tim steadied himself as he strode down the stairs to rejoin the party. He marveled again at the crowd gathered in his honor. Never in his wildest dreams would he have imagined this scene three months ago. The party was at full throttle, the great room and back deck crowded with guests. Tim thought he had greeted most of them. He paused several steps up from the main floor, scanning for Molly and Sally. He caught them both engaged in what seemed like intense conversations. Molly was standing with Rudy over in a far corner of the great room. Rudy had a bourbon in his hand and a frown on his face. Molly looked intense — and mean.

Over by the kitchen island, Sally continued her conversation with Sheriff Keating.

Did she know about the drug theft already? Or was it something else? Tim wanted to know about both exchanges, but wasn't about to interrupt either of them. Instead, he got himself a bottled water and headed toward the back door, then outside to the deck. It was a beautiful, balmy April evening. Tim soaked in the fragrant nighttime sea breeze.

Lots of questions, no answers — yet. The guest of honor didn't spend long in his own thoughts, however. Dr. Stan Greenberg, the family's long-standing dentist, saw his opportunity to welcome him and ask how he was doing. Tim smiled and told his story one more time.

******

After another twenty minutes on the deck, Tim went back inside and found Sally. She had broken away from Leroy and was sipping wine in the corner, talking with Steve. Her face brightened when she saw Tim approach.

"How you holding up there, little brother? I'm glad to see you're drinking water and not wine or whiskey." Sally put her hand on Tim's shoulder.

He got the feeling Sally had more than her share of wine as he watched her rock on her feet. "I'm fine, really. Enjoying seeing all the people from the past. I believe they're happy to see me. Do you think they are, truly?"

"Truly?" Sally retorted, ending on a higher note, like she didn't think the word had real meaning. "Do you truly believe anyone in the South tells you the complete truth about anything? This isn't New York, Tim."

Ok, Tim thought, now I know she's drunk.

"I mean, I wish we lived in a land where people tell you exactly what they think. In the North, if someone thinks you're full of shit, they say 'you're full of shit'. Am I right, Steve?"

Steve raised his eyebrows at Sally. "You're correct, darling. But being completely candid isn't always a great thing either, you know. Filters have a purpose."

"Oh right, of course." Sally reached over to pet Steve's arm, almost spilling her Chardonnay. "Tell me, Tim. How many times tonight has some woman said to you, 'Bless your heart'?"

Tim grinned. "Plenty. And I know what you're thinking. But I feel I can read people pretty well, and I think the empathy is genuine — mostly."

"Hmm, well, maybe, some of them. But I saw others looking at you out of the corners of their eyes, whispering things to their husbands or friends. You know you're considered close to royalty in these parts. And the best part about royalty, for the peasants that is, is to gossip about the royalty. And there's been a ton of that tonight. Don't let it go to your head."

You mean like the wine has gone to your head, dear sister?

"Steve, darling, be a dear and get me another glass of Chardonnay."

Steve narrowed his eyes, looked furtively at Sally, then shrugged. Tim knew Sally wasn't one to cross when she was sober, and definitely not when she was drunk. Besides which, it wasn't like she'd be driving home tonight. "I'll be back soon," said Steve. "I want to have a word with Marty Daniels over there. Give you a chance to bond some more with Tim." Steve took her glass and headed over to the bar.

"I've got another update on your Miss Molly," Sally said in confidence to Tim, her eyes juicy with her own gossip. "When you were out on the deck, she made a hell of a scene with Dad. The two were arguing and soon everyone within earshot stopped what they were doing and watched. I only caught a little of it, except the ending when she told Dad to go fuck himself in no uncertain terms. Mom went over and told that hussy to get out of her house and don't ever think about coming back. Molly didn't hang around."

Tim took another swig of his water and nodded his head. "Something is definitely up with her. I don't know what it's about with Dad." Tim paused, momentarily unsure if he should share the secret he had just learned with his sister. But his love of gossip got the better of him. "However, I have some other shocking news to tell you."

Sally grinned at Tim. He knew she loved to chin-wag as much as he did. "Shocking, you say — tell me."

"Well, let me ask you this. Have you had any recent problems with your pharmacy?"

This instantly wiped the smile off Sally's face. She grabbed Tim by his arm and glared at him. "What do you know? Tell me now!" This reply was absolutely guttural. Her amber eyes burned into Tim's, assuring him of the discovery of the drug theft.

Tim leaned into Sally so he could lower his voice. "So, I take it you know there have been narcotics missing — stolen."

"Yes! How do you know? Did Molly *tell* you?"

"No, she didn't tell me, but when I went upstairs to change my shirt after wine got spilled on it, Molly and Connie were having an argument in Connie's bedroom. I eavesdropped from outside the door. Apparently, Connie wanted to buy some Oxyies — OxyContin pills, I assume — from Molly and was upset Molly had jacked the price up on her. I heard Molly say how she was risking her ass breaking into Publix, and that Connie had been paid for the keys."

Sally erupted. "What! *Connie* gave *Molly* a key!" Sally's face turned to fury as she scanned around the room for her younger sister. "Why that little *cunt!* She must have sneaked the keys out of my purse and made copies. Where is she? This is the last straw for that strung out piece of *shit!*"

"So, wait." Tim tried to catch up to what Sally knew and didn't know. "You knew Molly broke into Publix?"

"Yes, just this afternoon." Sally turned back to Tim, who saw his sister in a light he had never seen. "I saw her on the security tape. They reported the theft yesterday, right before I left to pick you up. The boss called us in earlier today when he saw the video. I ID'ed Molly as the perp." Sally scanned the room, fuming. "Where is she, *goddamn it!* There she is!" Sally pointed to Connie on the other side of the room near the foyer and marched directly towards her. Tim followed behind, with a pit in his stomach, foreseeing the confrontation between his two sisters about to explode.

Connie saw Sally approach from about ten feet away, not understanding her little secret was out of the bag. But judging by the look on her sister's face, Connie had to know something was out of whack.

Sally went right into Connie and shoved her hard with both hands on the top of her chest, knocking Connie to the floor. "You goddamn piece of shit! You stole my keys, didn't you? Stole my keys so your *whore* friend could get you drugs!" The sudden eruption caught everyone in the vicinity off guard. Tim arrived and grabbed Sally by her shoulders so she wouldn't dive in after Connie.

Steve heard her wife's scream and cursed as he set the glass of wine Sally wouldn't get to drink down on the bar and hurried over to the commotion. Rudy and Ruth arrived seconds later.

By now, Connie had recovered a bit from the initial shock and started verbally hitting back. As she rose to her feet, seeing Sally pinned back by Tim, she hurled her own invectives. "What are you talking about, you crazy bitch? I stole nothing from you!" The two glared at each other in silence long enough for Ruth to butt in and put an end to the brief catfight.

"I don't know what is going on between you two, but I want it stopped this instant! Do you hear me?" Everyone in the room heard her, because by now, the entire party had fallen silent, with all eyes on the turmoil. Ruth inserted herself between her two daughters and held them both at arm's length.

"Mom." Sally gulped, trying to get back some control over her emotions. "This woman is a thief! She's in cahoots with Molly and stole narcotics from Publix." Sally turned her ire back to Connie. "You're going to jail, little miss drug addict — you and your whore friend both." Sally's voice rose in anger again. Ruth, Rudy, and Steve all had heard enough.

"Come on, Sally," Steve said sternly. "Say goodnight — we're leaving — now!"

Sally looked around at all the shocked faces directed at herself and realized the scene she had caused. Embarrassment flooded through her. "I'm sorry, Mom, Dad — Tim. I need to leave now. I'm sure I'll see you all tomorrow." Steve escorted his wife out of the front door.

Meanwhile, Connie quickly made herself scarce and ran up the stairs to her bedroom. She wasn't waiting for anyone to come and console her. Two minutes after Sally and Steve left, Connie hightailed it down the stairs and headed for the front door.

"Connie, a word with you…" Rudy spoke directly to her as she passed by him without stopping.

"Skip it, Dad," she answered curtly, and rushed out of the house.

CHAPTER 16

After a few uneasy minutes, the party settled back down. Leroy joined Rudy, Ruth, and Tim out on the back deck to sort the mayhem out.

"So, what about this alleged drug theft from Publix?" Rudy started out. "What do you know, Leroy?"

All three made a captive audience. Tim had known Leroy from his time here before, but only as a friend and colleague to his dad. He always regarded Leroy as fair and no nonsense — and he came across now as exactly that.

"So, my office received a call from Bud Wright, GM at the Pawleys Publix earlier this afternoon, probably around 3:00 PM, that they had video evidence of a narcotic theft from their pharmacy. He told me Sally had identified the person involved as Molly Elmwood. Since there was no crime in progress, the theft happened two weeks ago and apparently another one the month before, we told Bud we could come out on Monday and begin an investigation. About half an hour ago, I had a conversation with Sally about the incident and she didn't know how Molly could have broken into the store or the pharmacy. She was more miffed because I wouldn't arrest her on the spot here at the party."

"Ok, makes sense," answered Rudy. "So how does Connie suddenly get caught up in this?"

Everyone looked at each other. Tim knew he had no choice but to spill what he knew. "That would have come from me," he said with reluctance. Now he had everyone's undivided attention. "After you and Sally were having your discussion, someone bumped into me and spilled red wine on my shirt. When

I went upstairs to change, Connie and Molly were arguing in her bedroom about drugs. It sounded like Molly was trying to gouge Connie, selling her OxyContin pills she had stolen from Publix. I heard Molly tell Connie she paid her for the keys, which Sally assumed Connie stole from her purse." Tim saw Rudy shake his head and pinch the bridge of his nose and Ruth cover her open mouth with her hand. Leroy silently nodded his head. "So, that's what I told Sally a few minutes ago, and well, looks like I stirred up a hornet's nest."

"You didn't, Tim," corrected Leroy. "Those two women are the ones who are going to get stung. Is that why you were getting into it with Molly earlier, Rudy?"

"Huh?" Rudy broke his train of thought. "Molly? No, I didn't know of any drug theft until just now. She's got other problems with me I can't go into at this moment. Leroy, I don't know what to tell you here. You have your job to do. But I wouldn't expect we'll be seeing much of Connie or Molly anytime soon."

Tim thought briefly about the planned meeting with Molly on the dock later, but decided he'd already caused enough strife for one night and kept his mouth shut.

"Leroy, please enjoy the rest of the party. Ruth, darling, we need to talk about Connie."

Ruth fired back, "That's not all we need to talk about."
******

It was getting close to 9:15 PM, and the party was winding down. Tim reversed the welcome greeting routine with a well-wishing farewell tour. One by one, couples and smaller groups bid Tim their goodbyes, and the crowd began to thin. Tim took a few minutes to catch up with Annabelle.

"So, how does this rank in the standings of Culligan bashes?" he asked.

Annabelle gave Tim a reassuring smile. "Oh, is up there, Mr. Tim. Is definitely near the top."

"I didn't know Sally could be so short-tempered. Was she always like that? I mean, even when I was here before?"

Annabelle's grin grew larger. "Oh yes, indeed. Don't you remember the time Miss Sally got the detention in high school for cheating on her math test? 'Cept she wasn't the one cheating. Someone else stuck her wid' the cheat sheet. Mr. Rudy tried to punish her at home, and she just about burned this here house down."

"Oh yes, I remember that. And you remember who it was that Sally accused passing her the sheet?" Tim remembered, unfortunately.

"Of course I do. That's when things started going downhill between Miss Sally and Miss Molly. Things only gotten worse whilst you been gone."

Tim recollected how Sally had warned Tim about getting involved with Molly back in the Pelican Inn days. Now it seemed pretty prophetic.

"I'm sure her relationship with Randy didn't help matters any between them."

"Uh uh, no, sir. Oh my, the fights this family had over those two, always at Sunday dinner, on the Lord's Day. It's why Sally mostly stopped coming over. Randy this, Molly that, Cussin' everywhere. Last Sunday, no exception."

"So I heard," Tim replied. "Hopefully tomorrow's dinner will be more civil. Think Connie will show back up?"

Annabelle shook her head. "That child's the most spoiled rotten creature on earth. Never worked a day in her life. She be run off to her friend Janie by now, tail between her skinny legs."

"I don't understand how Dad put up with her. Honestly, how many times has she been in rehab?"

"Three times, does that child no good whatsoever. Gonna' be an addict rest of her life."

Tim paused, trying to grasp what he'd learned in just the last day. He'd already been disillusioned by Sally, Connie, and Molly. Mom had an episode right before he arrived. And these were the *women,* for God's sake. He hadn't heard two sentences out of his father and didn't know squat about Randy other than he was stewing in a Georgetown jail for the weekend. The warm welcome and assurances he felt yesterday afternoon didn't seem so comforting now. Truth was his family was as screwed up as they'd ever been. Even so, he felt home, and it still felt good.

"What about you, Annabelle? I've been so concerned about my family; I haven't had the chance to talk to you personally. How is Raymond these days? And Lucy and Danielle? How old are they now?"

Annabelle smiled back at Tim. Either he didn't realize, or had forgotten, that no one else in the Culligan household other than Ruth ever asked about Annabelle's family. "Oh, you know, everyone's fine. We get along best we can. Raymond's retired now. Keeps wanting me to as well. I keep tellin' him why would I want to hang around his boring butt when I have all this excitement here to look forward to every day. Lucy and Danielle are doing just fine. Both honor students at Waccamaw — Lucy a senior, and Danielle a sophomore."

"That's great to hear. I'm really glad you and your family are doing well. Listen, I got to ask you this. From what I've been told, Randy has been living in and out of the Way for some time now. And I gather Mom and Dad really don't want him back in the house now that I'm here."

"This is so. Last Sunday really was the last straw, if you believe Judge Rudy."

"Yes, so what do you think the chances are that he'll stay away this time? I mean, it's not like there hasn't been this kind of threat before."

Annabelle shifted her feet and made some smirking noises.

"What? What are you smiling about?"

"Let's put it this way, Mr. Tim. If Mr. Randy comes back in this here house, he won't be staying long." Annabelle continued to nod her head and grin.

"And why do you say that?" Tim asked, raising his eyebrows.

"Because he'd be dead."

Annabelle excused herself from a flabbergasted Tim and went to work beginning the clean-up process. The crowd had thinned some more, but there were still at least thirty people milling around the great room and back deck. Tim spotted his father and Leroy in the corner by the bar and felt the need to find out more about his brother's situation than the mystic prophecy Annabelle had just offered. Seeing Tim approach, the two abruptly cut short their conversation.

"How are you enjoying yourself tonight, Tim?" Leroy asked. "Bet you didn't expect this much entertainment." A grin broadened over his face.

"The Culligans never disappoint, Sheriff. That's for sure. Never a dull moment at the Way. Isn't that right, Dad?"

Rudy grumbled. "What I wouldn't give for a few dull moments."

"I'm sure of it. So, tell me, what are the plans for tomorrow? I've been told I'm expected at Holy Grace for Mass. And dinner to follow here, I assume. Just as it's always been."

"That would be correct. I had hoped the whole family would be here, except, of course, for your brother. Now it looks like it'll be a somewhat smaller crowd."

"I suppose. Can I ask you about Randy? They'll release him soon on bail, I assume. What's going to happen then?"

Rudy smirked. "Your guess is as good as mine, Tim. I'll make it clear to him he is not to live here at the Way any further. Beyond that, he's a free man. He can do as he pleases — within the confines of the law, of course."

Rudy didn't appear to Tim as if he were comfortable having this conversation. Obviously, Tim had interrupted the two from some serious legal discussion. Whether it was about Randy, Tim couldn't tell. Still, he pressed on, whether out of sheer curiosity or, more likely, overwhelming anxiety.

"What about the charges he faces against Molly? Is he going to get justice for that?" Leroy and Rudy exchanged furtive glances.

Rudy wasn't about to budge. "Tim, that's a matter for the Georgetown County legal system. Neither the Sheriff nor I are at any liberty to discuss the case with anyone else. I'm sure you understand."

Tim understood perfectly. They still perceived him as an outsider. "Yes, sir, I understand. And I'm sure you can understand the concern I have for my brother's actions. I heard what went down here yesterday. What he said about me."

"That situation is also being handled by our good Sheriff here. I can assure you; you are not in any inherent danger."

Leroy stepped in to support Rudy. "Tim, Randy Culligan will not be causing any further mayhem. The situation is under complete control. As far as I'm —" suddenly, Leroy heard a disturbance at the back door entrance and looked up. Rudy and Tim looked as well. Tim heard Leroy mutter, "Oh, for the love of Christ."

The three men stood there, speechless. In a matter of seconds, everyone in the room stared at the figure who had just made his way inside the house.

"*Where's Tim?*" shouted Randy Culligan, as he stood at the entranceway, swaying back and forth, his long hair disheveled, a half empty bottle of Jack Daniels in his right hand. The room fell silent. "*Where's my brother Tim?*" echoed throughout Culligan's Way.

CHAPTER 17

Randy's sudden presence shocked everyone. A scattering of "What's he doing here?" and "I thought he was in jail," murmurs were heard around the room.

Rudy said, "Leroy, what the hell!" But Leroy was already headed towards the interloper to sort out this latest disturbance.

On the other side of the room in the kitchen, Ruth had an alternative plan. She was at the island when Randy made his appearance, talking with another of the neighbor guests. Had she gone straight towards Randy, she might have been one of the first ones there. But she had a somewhat different idea how to greet her elder son.

Ruth hustled around the granite island and made her way straight to the set of cutlery knives by the stove. Fortunately for Randy, and anyone else who may have gotten in her way, Annabelle arrived just as Ruth reached for the twelve-inch carving knife — the longest one in the set. Annabelle's eyes diverted to Ruth the instant she first saw Randy and knew exactly what Ruth was going for. As Ruth withdrew the blade from the wooden sheath holding ten knives, Annabelle wrapped her arms around her and clenched down.

"Let me *go!*" Ruth hissed at her current savior.

"Ms. Ruth, you cannot do this! Jus' put the knife back, please Ms. Ruth, *please.*"

Ruth couldn't move in the bear hug she found herself in. After a few seconds, she relaxed and slid the knife back into its slot. Annabelle let go of her arms but continued to hold her hands. Ruth looked at her with the glazed wild eyes Annabelle had seen too many times.

"Why is he here, Annabelle? What is he doing here?" They both looked over at the scene and saw Leroy having an intense discussion with Randy.

"The Sheriff gonna' take care of it, Ms. Ruth. Jus' let him do his job." The two of them watched the discussion continue, now joined by Rudy. Tim also watched from a safe distance, listening to the argument unfold.

******

"I told you, Sheriff, my lawyer came to the county jail and got Judge Kramer to set bail. Call him if you don't believe me." Randy looked almost comical, waving his arms wildly with the large bandage patch over the top of his left eye.

"And how did you get in touch with this lawyer of yours?" Leroy demanded. Rudy, who had now joined the confrontation, wanted the same information.

Randy sneered at the county's head law enforcement agent. "He just stopped by. Said he was worried about me when he couldn't reach me and, on a hunch, drove over to jail."

Rudy scoffed at the lame explanation.

"Who is he?" demanded Leroy.

Randy snickered some more. "Jerry Springfield, that's my new lawyer now that my horseshit father over there refuses to defend me anymore."

Rudy himself briefly debated going for the long carving knife. Patience, he reminded himself, patience followed by revenge. He knew Jerry was perhaps the sleaziest lawyer in the county. But he didn't believe for a second that he had just stopped by the courthouse on a Saturday evening for concern about anyone. Randy got a call out and Rudy was determined to find out who had let him make that call well before the weekend was over.

"I'd be very careful, if I were you, how you describe your family members," countered Leroy. "You're intoxicated. How did you get here?" Leroy and Rudy both noticed the sand on Randy's feet and the fact he came in the back door and not the front.

Rudy glanced over at Ruth to make sure she wasn't about to do anything rash. He saw her in the kitchen with daggers coming out of her eyes, glaring at Randy, but Annabelle was right next to her. Very close, with what looked like her arm around his wife's waist.

"I drove my boat. It's out at the beach now."

"Then I'll just arrest you for driving a water vehicle under the influence."

Randy shifted his eyes from Leroy to Rudy, then over to his mother and Annabelle. Finally, he settled on Tim, who was still silent and now stood behind Rudy.

"Hold on, Sheriff, I'm not planning on staying. I just want to have a word with QT over there."

Rudy turned around and saw Tim bristle at the hated nickname Randy had called him so often before he left. QT — Queer Tim — pronounced Cutie.

Tim stepped out from behind his father and faced his reviled brother. "Go ahead, you asshole. Say what you want and get the hell out of here." His faced flushed red as he stood opposite Randy, but faced his brother with icy determination.

"I'm putting this whole mess on you, QT," Randy spit back, pointing his finger at Tim. "It's because of you, I'm being kicked out of this house. It's *my* house, goddamn it, not yours. You think you can just waltz right back in here after ten years? You may feel safe inside this house, but let me tell you — you walk outside and you better watch your back, cuz' I'm coming after you. Mark my words I —"

"That's enough," Leroy interrupted Randy, grabbing him with two hands on his shirt and forcing him out the back door. "I've heard enough out of you."

A round of applause suddenly filled the party room. Rudy followed Leroy outside to have a last word with Randy. The scattering of guests on the deck made room for the three of them.

"This is your last chance, Randall Culligan," Rudy demanded, still livid from the interruption. "I want to know who let you make a call from jail. It's going to be much easier on you if you tell me now."

"Go to hell!" Randy's flippant reply.

"Ok Randy," Leroy broke in. "Here's the situation. You got out of jail on bail. Congratulations. You show up drunk, driving a motorized boat by your own admission. That's a felony. I could take you in right now for a breathalyzer. I'd imagine you'd blow the top off it, based on the contents remaining in your bottle there. Or I could place you under house arrest right here, but then the rest of the party would have to put up with the stench that follows you wherever you go." Leroy turned to Rudy. "Any other options on the table, Judge?"

"I'm thinking he could take a one way walk straight into the Atlantic." If only, Rudy thought.

"Ha ha. Look, I came here to see my brother." Now Randy was pleading, once again not completely seeing through a predicament he had got himself into.

"You mean you came here to threaten your brother," corrected Leroy.

"Whatever. I just want to leave the party and get on with things. I won't be causing any more trouble for you, Sheriff, I promise."

Leroy rolled his eyes. "I'll tell you what. I will not spoil the rest of the party waiting to have you arrested. But I can't allow you back in your boat in your condition. So, get your ass out onto Springs Ave, walk the hell away from here, and don't even think about coming back."

Randy looked hesitantly at Leroy, then at Rudy. "Uh, what about my boat?"

"Your boat will be right there on the beach in the morning," answered Rudy, looking out towards the john boat pulled up onto the sand. "Just don't come anywhere near this house when you get it."

******

Back inside, Annabelle had let go of Ruth, sensing the worst of the commotion was over, now that the men had taken Randy outside. Annabelle sensed a false calm. She had seen it before — like aftershocks following a major earthquake. The major damage may have passed, but the threats of further mayhem still existed. Ruth looked at what remained of their selection of homemade pies.

"Seems our pies went over nicely, Annabelle." Of the eight pies, there were only a few sections left of the apple, peach, and pecan. However, more than half of the chocolate cream pie remained untouched. "Except the chocolate one here. I wonder why?"

"I don't know, Ms. Ruth. I reckon folks just like the others better tonight."

"Hmm, yes, I suppose so. I'd hate to have this go to waste, though." Ruth stood examining the pie, her hand rubbing her chin.

Annabelle knew Ruth was contemplating something, but couldn't figure out what.

Ruth glanced outside to see the three men still arguing. Suddenly, she picked up the rest of the chocolate pie with her right hand, hid it behind her back, and marched straight to the back door.

Annabelle reacted just a couple seconds later, and she followed right behind Ruth. "Ms. Ruth! Where ya' goin' wid' that pie? Ms. Ruth!"

But Ruth was already out the back door, just as Randy was getting ready to head to the street. "Oh, Randall, one more thing before you leave." Leroy and Rudy watched as Ruth barged straight in between them.

Randy had a look of trepidation as he watched his mother approach him and shouted, "Get away from me, you schizo witch!"

Too late. Ruth brought the chocolate cream out from behind her back and, quick as a cobra strike, smashed the pie into Randy's face. A look of tranquility broke out across Ruth's face. "There now, son. Something sweet for you to remember us by."

CHAPTER 18

The rest of the party went without incident, for which each of the remaining Culligans were thankful. Annabelle stayed until after 10:00 PM, when Ruth insisted she leave the remaining cleanup until the morning. Once the final guests left, it was nearly 10:30 PM. Ruth felt exhausted, both physically and emotionally and she debated taking another Valium to calm her nerves. Her feet ached from standing almost the entire evening. She still couldn't reconcile her emotions after seeing Randy show up like he did. Thank heavens for Annabelle — again, she thought. Better a pie in the face than a blade through the chest, I suppose.

"Are you coming to bed, dear?" Ruth asked her husband. Rudy appeared lost in another world, as he had been most of the night. The one serious conversation they managed to have between them brought no resolution. He adamantly refused to tell her where he had been most of the day and snubbed any attempt from Ruth to determine the nature of the argument he had with Molly. Ruth knew he was up to something no good, but she couldn't put her finger on it — yet.

"No, I'm a bit too wound up to sleep," Rudy said. "I think I'll have a drink on the back deck." He went to the bar to pour another bourbon.

Ruth couldn't tell how many he'd had tonight. More than normal for sure, but Rudy always seemed to hold his liquor pretty well.

Overall, other than the abrupt departure of three of her children (there would certainly be much more discussion about that) and one former fiancée, Ruth was quite pleased with the party. The caterer exceeded her expectations, initial tardiness now excused. The attendance also surpassed her estimations, something she could take pride in. Ruth only hoped there wouldn't be a spread of Covid from the party. That would be a social buzzkill she could do without. With the party now behind her, she could focus her energy on Tim's recuperation.

"Ok then, goodnight." Ruth said to Rudy as he headed out the back door. She retired upstairs without a kiss or any further discussion. She took a pass on the Valium.

******

Tim also felt exhausted from the evening's activities and surprises and was breathless as he reached the top of the stairwell on the way to his bedroom. He needed to rest before his meeting with Molly on the dock at midnight. As he relaxed in his easy chair, he considered all that had taken place at his homecoming party.

Two things he couldn't get out of his mind. First was the sight of all three of his siblings unceremoniously exiting the party early, and second; the cryptic message Molly gave him. What things did he need to know about her? The fact she had broken into his sister's place of employment to steal narcotics? That would hardly be something she would need or want to tell him. Molly hadn't seen the meltdown between Sally and Connie. Nor would she know they had identified her as the thief. There had to be more than that. Maybe something to do with the argument she found herself in with his father.

Normally, Tim would be in bed getting a well-deserved long night's sleep. But not now. Looking out the window towards the ocean, he was lost in his thoughts.

He marked time, staring at his watch until 11:55 PM, then rose and tip-toed quietly downstairs. He saw Rudy on the back deck but paid him scant notice as he eased out the front door and down the steps. There wasn't a car was in sight as he crossed the empty street, a far cry from just a few hours ago.

When Tim stepped onto the marsh creek pier for the first time in almost ten years, he felt another wave of nostalgia wash over him. It was from this dock he took his first boat ride as a kid, learned to fish and crab, and watched illuminated red and orange sunsets while drinking sweet tea. It was a simple dock; a short pier extended from the road to the edge of the creek, perhaps fifty feet. At the end was a gazebo with benches on the creek and north side. A small night light cast a soft sheen over the marsh. On the south end, a ramp led down to a floating dock on the creek where the crab traps hung, and could launch small boats and kayaks.

Tim walked out to the gazebo and took a seat on the bench. No sign of Molly. Did he keep himself up only to be stood up? He'd been thinking about Molly for much of the evening since their brief conversation on the couch and the overheard exchange with Connie. His friend was a thief — how disappointing. And what was she arguing about with Dad, so badly he demanded she leave? There was much Tim didn't know about Molly, and what she had become since their relatively innocent days in high school. And what was it she so desperately needed to tell him tonight, that it had to wait until midnight?

Tim watched the road looking for Molly to arrive, then heard an outboard motor heading his way south on the creek. He turned around and saw Molly in a two-seater skiff puttering towards the dock.

"Hey there," he called down to her as she reached the dock platform, "didn't expect you to come by boat."

"Yeah, well, it's safer this way." She hopped out of her skiff and tied it to the corner post. "I didn't want to risk being followed."

"Who would follow you, Molly?" Tim descended the ramp and embraced Molly on the dock. From the soft light of the gazebo, Tim could see she had a wild look in her eyes. Like she was paranoid of something.

"Come," she pointed up to the gazebo, "let's sit up there and talk."

"Sure," he said, as they ascended the ramp.

They took seats next to each other. Molly held Tim's hands in hers as he gazed into her eyes.

"So, what's this all about?" Tim was ready for some answers.

"Oh Tim, my life is so fucked up, and just when you're returning."

Tim stayed silent, regarding her with empathy.

Molly gulped. She glanced around again and lowered her voice some more. "So, there's no other way to say this. My life is in danger. I'm going to have to disappear for a while."

Tim continued to stare at her. "Why do you say that? Does this have to do with the argument you had with my father?"

Molly hung her head. "It does, that and some other things."

Tim suspected what at least one of the 'other things' were. He let her continue.

"There are some powerful people who dislike things I've gotten involved with. It has to do with marshland development lots."

Tim looked at Molly, perplexed. This was unexpected.

"Do you know anything about Greeley Construction?"

"Nope, never heard of them." Tim focused on Molly; he had no idea where this was headed.

"Well, they're intent on turning much of the undeveloped marsh front property in the area into residential homes. But they can't, or I should say they haven't been able to get the zoning approved through DHEC — the Health and Environment Commission — until recently.

A few weeks ago, several marsh front lots in Murrells Inlet were approved for construction. I have a friend with close ties to the environmental community who said they didn't properly approve these lots. That's where your father comes in. I have sources who told me there's a kickback scheme going on between Greeley, Judge Culligan, and DHEC, to have these lots approved through back channels. I have the evidence here on my phone."

Tim slowly shook his head, now thoroughly confused. "I'm not following you. Why would my father be involved with a construction zoning dispute?"

Molly stared back at Tim with sympathy. "Tim, he's taking tainted money under the table and bribing and coercing DHEC to do something that shouldn't be happening. There's not a lot of marsh front left on the Grand Strand and developing these lots will destroy habitats of eagles, osprey, and other wildlife. I won't let that happen if I can help it."

"Ok, so why are you running away, and why are you telling me this now?"

"Because your father and Greeley know I intend to expose them. They threatened to kill me if I did. Your father threatened to kill me earlier tonight."

Tim couldn't believe his father would threaten to kill anyone, but he could see real fear well up in Molly's eyes.

"You know how powerful he was ten years ago. He's much more so now. That's why I have to disappear."

This shocked Tim. He gulped, trying to digest what Molly had just told him. He didn't have any idea what his father was involved in. But he always presumed he was on the right side of the law. This was too much to swallow. But when he saw the frantic look in Molly's eyes, he knew she wasn't joking. "Ok, Molly," he said, trying to sound reassuring, "So why are you telling me this, and what do you want from me?"

"I want you to have this, Tim," she told him, holding out her iPhone. "I can't take it with me. Everything's on it. I want you to be the one to expose your father for who he really is."

"No, Molly! I can't do that. You can't put me in the middle of all this. Really — please, I can't."

Molly pleaded, "Tim, listen to me. Just take the phone and see what's on it. I can't make you turn him in. But you need to know the truth. And I can't take the phone with me. I have to make a clean break. Whatever happens, you have the information you need right here." She handed Tim the phone. "Pass code is 1291, my birth month and year."

He didn't give it back.

"There's a friend of mine, Harvey Klinger. He's in my contacts. Get a hold of him. He can help you. I can't stay here; I don't feel safe." Molly looked around nervously, as if she were being watched — or hunted.

Tim knew she would leave soon. He felt he had to clear the table before she did. "That's not the only reason you're leaving, is it?"

"It isn't, but what are you saying?"

"Publix Pharmacy — theft of narcotics. I was upstairs earlier this evening changing my shirt after wine got spilled on it. I overheard the conversation you had with Connie."

Molly's eyes opened wide as she gasped. Then she narrowed them into slits. "I see," she replied, then looked away across the creek.

Tim felt her whole disposition change on a dime.

"Yes, that's another reason I have to disappear. There are many things you don't know about me, Tim. I think it's better if we leave them like that."

"Sally knows. She identified you on their security camera earlier today. She wanted you arrested at the party, but Keating put it off until Monday."

Molly nodded her head. "I suspected something like that. The way she looked at me at the party." She turned back towards Tim. "And what about Connie?"

"Connie?" Tim scoffed. "She and Sally had, let's say, a brief encounter. The claws came out."

"Good." Molly smirked, then paused and changed the subject. "Tim, I wanted to expose your father and Greeley tonight. But I couldn't do it. *You* deserve to do it. I know how your father treated you before you left. Tell me, has he treated you any better since you've been home?"

Tim thought about the day and a half since he'd returned. "Well, so far about the only thing positive was he hadn't kicked me out of the house. I doubt I'd have gotten even that much consideration if not for Sally and Mom."

Molly stood up and walked to the pier railing. Tim rose and followed her. "Then read the texts, Tim. Listen to the recordings. Then nail that bastard. He deserves everything that's coming to him."

Tim held Molly's hands and gazed into her eyes. "I'll do that, Molly. I promise." She was an enigma to him. A loving, caring soul, who had helped him so much and obviously still cared for him. She's taking a stand to protect the incredible natural beauty of the Lowcountry and risk her life to expose some underhanded evil to destroy it. Yet she was a thief, and probably a drug addict herself. She seemed to have a reputation as a whore. She loved him, but she had also loved Randy. How could he reconcile these things?

Tim moved closer to Molly, then embraced her. The soft curves of her body molded into his arms.

Her eyes glowed, her lips parted. "I love you, Tim. I always have."

They kissed. The passion rose in Tim. He felt on top of the world and yet he felt his world was ending. Their lips parted. "When will I see you again? How long will you be away?"

"I don't know. No time soon. I'll be in touch with Harvey. You can check with him. Go now, Tim. This is how I want to remember you. Please be safe."

Tim broke his embrace and gazed at her one last time. "You be safe. And when you get back, we'll throw *you* a welcome home party."

Molly grinned. "Ok, you do that."

Tim returned to Culligan's Way. His homecoming, and her farewell. Before he entered the house, he turned and watched Molly hang her arms on the rail of the pier, looking south down the creek towards the inlet. He heard the faint sounds of an outboard motor in the distance. Gazing up, he saw a half-moon fronting a full display of stars. He glanced once more at her phone, shook his head, then went inside.

******

Unseen by either of them, two docks to the north, under a darkened gazebo, a figure stood looking through a pair of binoculars — fuming and cursing.

CHAPTER 19

At 10:00 AM on Sunday morning, Luke and Luther McKenzie were motoring their way south through Pawleys Island creek. The brothers had a standing arrangement to go fishing each Sunday morning to stay close, as well as getting out of church duty. Their wives were none too pleased with the routine, but were helpless to change it. The McKenzie brothers were on the creek every given Sunday, regardless of time of year or the tide schedule

Although they did occasionally catch a legal flounder or two, their time together was more about the fishing, not the catching. And the smoking. They were two overweight good old boys who toed the line each workday. Luke worked at Carter's garage as a mechanic, and Luther was a short-order cook at the Litchfield Diner, where he prepared breakfast and lunch six days a week for the locals and the tourists. On Saturdays, they usually spent the afternoon watching sports on television while their wives, Betty and Joanie, busied themselves making the shopping circuit around town.

But on each Sunday morning, by 9:00 AM, the two guys would have their fishing gear loaded in Luke's pickup, headed to the Pawleys landing. They would spend the next several hours idling up and down the creek with their lines in the water, enjoying the one guilty pleasure their wives knew nothing about. One joint, shared between the two brothers; a physical and mental escape that provided the difference between a life of continuous drudgery, and one where, for a brief period, existence seemed to have real meaning. That, plus a convenient excuse to get out of church. Their religion resided on the creek.

This morning proved the best of both worlds. The weather was perfect; sunny in the low seventies with a slight onshore breeze, and the tide was just turning and heading in. That meant the best chance to catch flounder or reds. In their normal routine, they puttered down to the Pawleys inlet, about two and a half miles from the landing, then made their way back. They were usually back at their homes, sober and refreshed by noon. Today would prove to be anything but routine.

The trip out didn't differ from any other Sunday morning. Once on the creek and away from any prying eyes on the shore, Luke lit up his testimonial. Fifteen minutes later, the joint was history, and the two sat back and relaxed as Luther minded the rudder and Luke set the lines. As they moseyed on down the creek, they approached Culligan's Way.

"Big party there at the Culligan's last night," remarked Luther. "Talkin' bout it all week long at the diner. Younger son returned home from New *Yahhk*." Luther emphasized the city with a horribly false accent. Both men snorted.

"High falutin' bastards — the whole bunch, if ya' ask me," retorted Luke. "Judge thinks he owns the county; mother's crazy as a loon."

"Well, you must have the same customers I do, cuz that's the same story we hear. Rumor has it the older son got the boot."

"Worthless piece of shit, that Randy. Once tried to stiff the shop. Boss told him he didn't want to see him around ever again."

As the two brothers drifted towards the dock and looked up at the Way, they both felt the same jealous sting. "How much you think that house goes for?" asked Luke.

Luther scoffed. "Shit, beach front and marsh front with a private dock. Bet it's a minimum five bedrooms. Five mil, at least."

Luke shook his head. "Fucking rich people — make me sick."

Luther nodded his agreement. "You know what they call the place — Culligan's Way. I hear 'em at the diner — 'are ya' goin' to the party at the Way?'" he said with an exaggerated high pitched female Southern accent.

"Even that's a crock of shit. Everything in this county goes 'Culligan's Way'. Everybody knows Rudy Culligan lines his pocket every chance he gets."

"That's right, and nothin' ever proven. That's Culligan's way."

As the two drifted past the dock, they took notice of the small boat still tied to the far post.

"Wonder what's up with that?" Luke pondered. "Someone go to the party by boat and spend the night?"

"Dunno. Ain't never seen a boat docked there before." But as they coasted past the dock and looked at the creek bank, they saw something else they'd never seen before. There, or anywhere.

"Luke — what the fuck is that?" Luther cut the motor and turned the boat around the dock in towards the bank.

"Holy shit, brother, that's a body! A woman." Sure enough, both brothers gawked at the sight of the back of a woman lying face down in the mud; her blonde hair soaked and matted against the back of her dress. Her legs splayed out at an odd angle. The woman's face was completely buried in the soft pluff mud of the marsh, as were most of her arms. Luther brought the boat to a stop about ten feet away, close to the line where the tide had gone out. Both brothers continued to gape at the gruesome sight in front of them.

Finally, Luke came to his senses. "Luther. We need to call 911."

Luther just sat in his seat, stoned from the joint and gripped by stone icy fear of the dead body in front of him.

Luke pulled out his phone and made the call.

"911, what is your emergency?"

"Yes, my brother and I are on Pawleys Creek at the dock in front of the Culligan house." Luke's voice was shaky, but at least he had a voice, which was more than he could say for his brother. "We just discovered a dead body on the creek bank. A woman."

"Did you say a dead body? Are you sure she's dead?"

Luke stared at his phone, then looked at the body again. "Her face is buried in mud for cryin' out loud. Yes — she's dead!"

"And what is the address of your location?"

Luke again looked quizzically at his phone. "We are in a boat and came across the body. I don't know the address. It's the Culligan place — Culligan's Way — out near the south end of Pawleys Island. I'm sure you can find it."

"I see. We'll send someone out there right away."

"Thank you." Luke ended the call. He looked at his brother, who still hadn't stopped gawking at the body. "Luther! Snap out of it. Dock the boat over there and we'll wait on the cops."

Luther turned to Luke. His face was as white as a sheet. "I think I'm gonna' get sick." Then he promptly lost his breakfast over the side of the boat.

******

Thirty minutes later, a call on Leroy's cell interrupted his quiet Sunday morning. He and Doris were enjoying a brunch of French Toast, with bacon and strawberries, entertaining themselves with what would surely be lively gossip in the coming days about the wild welcome home party at the Culligans.

Leroy glanced at his phone — it was from Conrad Jackson, his lead deputy. This couldn't be good news. "Yeah, Conrad — what is it?"

"I'm sorry to disturb you, Sheriff, on this beautiful Sunday morning, but I'm afraid we have a disturbing development to report." Jackson paused for a second as Leroy feared the worst. "There's been a body discovered in Pawleys Creek. A woman. She's at the dock at the Culligan place."

"The *Culligan* place?" Leroy screamed into the phone. Whatever worst case scenario he might have had in mind, it wasn't this bad.

"Yes sir. Dispatch got a call at 10:10 AM from a couple of boaters on the creek. They found the victim near the creek bank, face down in the pluff mud. I notified Tony and Murrey and they're on their way here now." Murrey Kaufman was the county Medical Examiner. He'd been working with Leroy and Tony for the past ten years and Leroy considered him the best ME in the state.

"Any other details at this point? Any idea of the victim's identity?"

"No sir. We've secured the area but have not touched the body. Looks to be fairly young. Blonde hair."

Young blonde hair woman, Leroy thought and frowned. He could guess exactly who laid dead in the creek at the Culligan's dock. Molly Elmwood. "Who's at the residence? Is the Judge at home?"

"No sir," answered Conrad. "The only one home is the house servant. We're questioning her now."

Leroy looked at his watch — 10:40 AM. Of course, the Culligans weren't home. They were at church, which he knew would end at 11:15 AM. It would end earlier for them today. "I'll be there as soon as I can." Leroy ended the call.

Doris looked at him with concern. "That doesn't sound good. Any idea who it may be?"

"I got a damn good idea who it may be. Gotta run," Leroy told his wife as he headed to the bedroom to change. His mind swirled, contemplating the coming storm which lay ahead for him and his team. And the last person anyone would want at the center of a storm is Rudy Culligan. Too bad. Leroy fired off a text message to Rudy, kissed his wife on the cheek, and headed out the door.

CHAPTER 20

Tim awoke Sunday morning with his mind spinning from the events of the previous evening. Most particular of which were the last five minutes just after midnight with Molly and her cryptic warning. After he had gone back upstairs, he opened Molly's phone and quickly glanced at her text messages. After seeing long text streams from Harvey, Randy, and his Dad, Tim forwarded them to his phone, then took off his clothes and crashed. He'd read through them when he had time on Sunday.

Now, with the morning sunlight streaming in his bedroom, he could hear Annabelle already back at the Way, in the kitchen putting together a quick breakfast before they left for the 10:00 AM service at Holy Grace. He assumed Connie would be a no show.

Tim made his way downstairs and joined his parents at the table. A strained quietness settled over breakfast. Did nobody want to talk about what had transpired the night before? Rudy had the Myrtle Beach Times spread out in front of him. Ruth seemed to be lost in another world, sipping her coffee. Annabelle busied herself in the kitchen, putting away the breakfast dishes, and prepping for Sunday dinner.

Tim broke the eerie silence. "Quite a show last night."

His mother and father paused what they were doing and looked directly at him.

"Way beyond my expectations." For instance, Tim thought, I didn't expect to see my three siblings melt down and leave in disgrace.

"Yes, well," Ruth said, "Not everything went as expected. But it was lovely to see everyone come out to wish you well, dear. I'm glad your father honored us with his presence — eventually."

Rudy glared at his wife, who returned the look with narrowed eyes.

Something sure seemed amiss between them, Tim thought, and more than Dad's tardiness.

Rudy stayed silent and went back to his paper.

"The food was fantastic, Mom. And the pies were to die for. Thank you so much for everything, you too Annabelle."

"Oh, you are so welcome, Tim," answered Annabelle from the kitchen.

"So, I guess we're going to leave for the church at about 9:45 AM, if I remember correctly. I don't suppose Connie will join us?"

This got Rudy's attention. "She will not," he said without emotion.

"And Sally, will she and Steve and the kids be at church?"

Rudy shrugged, but Ruth said, "Yes, she called this morning to tell me they would all be at the service and be back here for dinner. She feels badly about how she left last night."

"As she should be," said Rudy, with a sharp edge to his tone.

"I think she wants to apologize to all of us in person. I just want us all to get along, you know." Ruth looked around to everyone in the room. "I mean, why does it always seem so hard for people in this family to just get along?" Her voice rose as the three others gave Ruth concerned looks. "And now our Tim is home — and there is so much *friction.* I just don't understand it."

Tim could see Ruth now visibly upset. She rose from the dining table and went to the kitchen to be near Annabelle. "Do you understand it, Annabelle? Do you know why this family always seems to be so upset with one another?"

Tim and Rudy quietly observed the two women.

"Folks don't always see things the same way, Ms. Ruth. God made us all different for a reason."

As Tim watched Annabelle once again calm his mother, he thought about how she probably had more wisdom in her than the entire Culligan clan combined.

When Rudy saw Ruth step back from the brink, he put his paper down and said, "Come on, dear. Let's go upstairs and get ready for church. Annabelle can finish in the kitchen. Tim, be ready to leave in fifteen minutes."

"Yes, sir." Tim quickly finished his breakfast. He prayed for a smooth day with his remaining family. Once again, he'd be sorely disappointed.

******

Holy Grace of Christ Catholic Church stood majestically alongside Waverly Drive amidst the Lowcountry's signature live oaks. The church grounds took up over five acres of landscaped beauty. A twenty-foot limestone statue of the Savior stood in the middle of a glamorous fountain, his robe draped over his outstretched arms, staring out in stony silence, beckoning his followers to enter his sanctuary.

Tim felt a wave of nostalgia flood through him, seeing the church again. He spent every Sunday morning here from the time he was five until he turned seventeen when he rebelled against the church's dogma and their dismissive attitude toward non-traditional orientations. Before they left that morning, Tim reminded his father for the second time, he would go to today's service but wasn't making any promises after that. Surely it wouldn't be a determining factor in his invitation to live at the Way.

The opulence of the place struck Tim, as he walked into the sanctuary. The early sun shone through the east-facing wall of stained-glass windows, illuminating the polished pews with broad rays of light. The massive organ covered the entire backdrop of the expansive stage, where Tim recalled performing roles in many a Christmas play and Easter reenactment. They were one of the few positives he had taken away from the years of compulsory attendance.

"Father Mulroney would like to have a word with you after the service," Rudy said, as they were about to take their seats.

Tim rolled his eyes back at his father.

"Nothing much," Rudy assured him. "Just a personal welcome, that's all. Is that too much to ask?"

Tim wiped the exasperation off his face and said, "No, sir. I'll be happy to meet the Father."

Seeing Sally's family arrive, he took a minute to greet them. Joey and Amber gave Tim big hugs, seeing their lost uncle for the first time. It gave Tim another shot of adrenaline, witnessing new family members, realizing he'd been an uncle for almost five years without ever appreciating it.

As the service began, Tim felt an amazing sense of grace. How it felt to be here, in his old place of worship, with at least most of his family — protected, loved, and missed. The problems with Randy, and Connie, and Molly temporarily put aside, he sat back to glean what goodwill he might gather from the service.

That changed about twenty minutes in when the priest began his sermon. And what subject did the good Father choose today? "Ladies and gentlemen, today I want to turn our attention to Luke 15 and the story of the return of the Prodigal Son."

Tim's mouth gaped open. Then he whispered to himself, "You have got to be kidding me."

Mulroney continued. "At its most obvious, the parable shows a parent's willingness to forgive and to embrace the child who had lashed out and who had hurt them deeply. Coming back to the father was an act of desperation for the son. He was homeless and destitute. The father stood vigil, watching for his son to return. He never gave up hope."

"Then there's the perspective of the younger son. Like him, we might have taken a long journey and realized our failings. If we had to stand before God on our own merit, we would fall short of God's laws. Forgiveness and redemption are freely offered to all who humbly seek it. Just as the father rejoiced over what was lost but then was found, we read in Luke that all of heaven rejoices over one repentant sinner."

Tim stopped listening and turned to his father with an exasperated look, then said, "Really, Dad? This isn't some coincidence?"

"Don't look at me. This is your mother's doing."

Of course, thought Tim. Who else? He turned to his right and confronted Ruth. "Mom? This is your doing?"

"Well yes, dear. It's a wonderful story, don't you agree?"

"Of course, Mom," Tim whispered back, cognizant of the other worshippers trying to listen to the sermon.

"And so timely. I made a special request just for you. It seemed so appropriate."

Perhaps, thought Tim, thinking back to the full story of the Prodigal Son. Except he didn't take half his father's inheritance. If he'd done that, he'd still be in New York. Or the fact he didn't spend the last decade wallowing in sin, or that he had returned asking for forgiveness. Of course, these were minor inconveniences to Mom. She had him right where she wanted.

Tim tried to put it out of his mind. He thought ahead towards Sunday dinner at the Way, his first in many years. Sally's family would be there. That was good. Connie probably not. He played through the events of the previous evening once more in his mind. So much turmoil, so much conflict. Dad and Molly, Mom and Randy, Sally and Connie — who knew how many more internal quarrels were in play in the world he now found himself in again. And what in blazes was on Molly's phone she was so concerned about? He'd have to spend some time this afternoon reading through the texts.

The sermon was coming to a merciful end and Tim remembered there was still the Eucharist and the Communion to follow. They were all expected to come forward to taste the 'body of Christ' and drink the 'blood of Christ'. So much metaphor, Tim recollected. It felt so over the top to him. He looked at his watch — 10:40AM. Thirty more minutes before he could breathe again.

Just then, Tim heard a buzz next to him and realized it was his Dad's cell phone. Rudy pulled the phone out of his suit jacket pocket and called up the text. Tim glanced over and could read the message, although he didn't know who had sent it.

Rudy - Get back to the Way as soon as possible. You got big trouble there.

Rudy quickly closed his phone and sat there, stewing for a few seconds. Then he abruptly rose and told Tim and Ruth, "I have to get back to the Way. Seems we have some kind of trouble over there."

Ruth shot back, "What are you talking about? We're in the middle of Mass right now. You can't just get up and leave."

"You and Tim get a ride with Sally. I have to go." Rudy turned his back without another word and moved out from the pew into the aisle. Tim and Ruth sat there shocked.

Before Rudy took three steps down the main aisle on his way out, Ruth declared, "If there's a problem at home, I'm not staying here." She rose and slid by Tim, then followed her husband out of the church.

Tim looked over his shoulder at Sally, shrugged, then rose himself and said, "Guess I'm going too. Reckon I'll see you there later." Sally sat there silently, shaking her head, dreading the worst.

CHAPTER 21

Leroy arrived at the Way five minutes before Rudy. He knew Rudy would leave the church as soon as he received his text and was closer to his home than Leroy's home in Georgetown. But with lights flashing and sirens wailing, Leroy took the South Causeway onto the island before Rudy had reached the North Causeway Road, and soon pulled up in front of Culligan's Way to see the dock area already cordoned off with yellow crime tape. Leroy exited his SUV and walked over to be greeted by his deputy.

"What do we have, Conrad?" Leroy asked as he ducked under the tape at the pier entrance. The body laid on the dock at the bottom of the ramp. His detective and ME were already examining the body.

"We just got her out of the mud and onto the dock, sir," said Conrad. "Deceased is female, around thirty, no identification on her."

"Ok, and what happened to her?" Leroy braced himself. He had seen enough dead bodies in his time. It was something he never got used to.

"Stabbed, sir, more like gutted. Wound goes right through her midsection and out her back." Conrad led Leroy to the gazebo, then down the ramp to join Tony and Murrey. The body laid face up. Leroy recognized her immediately.

"That's Molly Elmwood. She was at the party last night. Christ! Is this ever going to cause a cluster fuck!" Molly's face was partially bloated, looked to have been in the water for at least several hours. Her eyes were open — still and glazed. It looked like she had on the same clothes Leroy had seen her in at the party. Then he noticed the boat. "What's with the boat?"

"Checking the registration now, Sheriff," replied Conrad. "My guess is the victim rode the boat here last night and never returned."

"And nobody's home except the house servant, correct?"

"Yes, sir. One of my men is inside talking with her now."

Leroy looked around again. Rudy would arrive any minute now. Then the real circus would begin. "Well guys," directing his question to his detective and ME, but more so to Murrey. "What do you think?"

Tony let Murrey answer. "Leroy, we found the body over by the bank. First glance looks to have been in the water at least eight hours. But I'm guessing the tide would have exposed her sometime around sunrise this morning. Cause of death appears to be from a single knife wound entry here in the front abdomen, with an exit wound in the back by the kidney. Looks like the killer used a knife with a long, thin blade. Single stab wound. I'll have a better description of the knife when I get her back for autopsy. Same with time of death."

"I saw Molly leave the party after an argument with the Judge around 7:30 PM. Obviously she came back for something, and someone was waiting for her. Tony, what's your first take on the crime scene?"

Leroy looked at Tony, and it was clear his lead detective was going to relish every bit of this investigation. Neither Tony nor Murrey were at the party, and when Leroy mentioned the argument with Rudy, Tony's ears perked up like a basset hound to a dog whistle. Leroy bet Tony would love nothing more than to nail Rudy on complicity to murder. Or better yet, murder itself. "I'll need to go over the dock more thoroughly, Leroy, but at first glance, we have bloodstains on the floor midway from the pier entrance to the gazebo, and I found a couple drops leading to the gazebo. My guess is the stabbing took place on the pier where blood is on the floor, and the victim either fell or was pushed under the rail near the bank. Like Murrey said, she probably sank to the bottom and was underwater, stuck in the mud until the tide went out later this morning."

"Sheriff," Conrad alerted Leroy. "We got company." The four men looked up to the road and saw Rudy's Lexus pull into the carport. It appeared Ruth and Tim were with them.

"Alright," said Leroy. "Murrey, stay here and finish your work. The rest of us will get the Culligan's story. I'll take Rudy, Tony, take Tim, and Conrad, you get Ruth's story. Assuming there's no confession, meet me back here in twenty."

Rudy exited his car and marched straight across the street. Tim and Ruth were right behind him. Leroy stood at the pier entrance, waiting.

"What happened, Leroy?" Rudy burst out. "What's going on?"

Leroy waited a few seconds for all three Culligans to arrive. "There's been a murder here, Rudy, I'm sorry to say. Molly Elmwood was killed on this dock sometime last night. She was stabbed to death."

Leroy watched the family's initial reaction. Ruth gasped, covering her mouth with her right hand. Tim looked as if all the blood inside him had drained away. And Rudy stood still as a stone statue, completely emotionless.

Tim broke the silence first. "I was with her on the dock last night," he said, his voice shaking. Everyone looked at him, surprised at this unexpected early development. "Sh-she wanted to meet me here at midnight last night. She came by boat because she was afraid of being followed. Molly said her life was in danger." Rudy, Ruth, and the three law enforcement personnel all looked at Tim with astonishment. Leroy realized he didn't want any further information coming forward in this uncontrolled manner and took charge.

"Listen folks. I know this is a very traumatic morning for everyone. I'm going to need statements from all three of you, but they need to be done individually and privately. So, let's go into the house and split up. Deputy Jackson here will talk with Ruth, Detective Meacham will get Tim's story, and Rudy, you're all mine." Leroy paused. "Shall we?" he asked, showing he wanted everyone to move inside.

"Can I see her?" Tim asked. Leroy saw Tim still gawking at the body lying on the dock below.

"No, Tim," answered Leroy. "The Medical Examiner is with her now, doing his work. I can't let anybody inside the crime tape."

"Come on, Tim, Ruth," Rudy said. "Let's go inside and see if we can help the Sheriff do his job."

The six of them moved across the street and inside the house. As they entered the front door, Tony pointed to the doorbell. "See that, Sheriff? They have a Ring cam. Could be of interest."

"I'll get Rudy to call it up before we leave," Leroy said. "Conrad, why don't you take Ruth out to the back deck? Tony can talk with Tim upstairs, and I'll take the Judge's statement down here." Then he noticed Annabelle was still in the kitchen getting Sunday dinner prepared. "Miss Annabelle, I believe you've given your statement. Would you mind waiting upstairs in Mrs. Culligan's bedroom while we finish here?"

Annabelle looked over at Ruth, who nodded her approval. "Yes sir, I'll wait upstairs," then hustled up the stairwell.

The three law enforcement officers separated along with the three family members.

Conrad settled in on the back deck with Ruth. "Mrs. Culligan, this is just a preliminary statement. You are under no obligation to answer questions, but I'm sure you understand the more information we can gather this early, the quicker we can find out what happened."

Ruth sat stiffly in one of the deck rockers, while the deputy pulled up a smaller chair opposite her. "I have nothing to hide, Mr. Jackson. I'll answer any questions you have."

"I'm glad to hear that, Mrs. Culligan. Why don't you tell me in your own words what happened with Molly at the party, and what happened after that until this morning?"

Ruth took a deep breath as she recollected the events from the previous evening. "I don't know what was wrong with Molly last night. She has a history of being unpredictable, as I'm sure you know. This business that led up to Randy's arrest being just the latest. I saw her talk with Tim briefly earlier at the party. Evidently, she went upstairs after that to talk with Connie, based on the argument that happened between Connie and Sally later on."

Conrad nodded his understanding. Leroy had touched on the subject but hadn't elaborated.

"When she came back downstairs, she started arguing with my husband. I don't know what it was about, but it quickly escalated, and I had no intention of putting up with that kind of nonsense at my party. So I intervened and told her to leave immediately. I believe she said something to the effect of 'I'm not done with you,' to Rudy, and then she left. Then the argument with Connie and Sally happened, and then they left. After that, the party went fine, well, except for when Randy showed up. He didn't stay long, either. The party wound down; I believe about 10:30 PM when the last guest left. By then, the only ones in the house were Rudy, Tim, and me. Rudy took another drink out on the back deck. Tim had already retired by then and I went to bed at around a quarter after eleven. It was an exhausting day and evening. I went straight to sleep and didn't wake until this morning. I don't even remember Rudy coming to bed."

"And there was nothing out of the ordinary this morning, to your recollection?"

"No sir. Annabelle arrived at her usual Sunday morning time. We had a light breakfast before church, just Rudy, Tim, and me. Connie never came home, not that we expected her to after the scene with Sally. That's about all I can offer you, Mr. Jackson. I'm sorry it isn't more."

"It's a good start, Mrs. Culligan. I thank you for your time and input."

******

Upstairs in Tim's bedroom, he took Tony through the events of the party and Molly's request to meet him at midnight on the dock.

"I got the distinct sense Molly wasn't comfortable or welcome at the party," Tim said. "While we were sitting on the couch, some woman walked by and said 'skank' in her ear, but then disappeared into the crowd before we could tell who it was. Molly seemed very nervous and said she had to leave after taking care of some other business. She implored me, begged me to meet her on our dock at midnight — and I agreed. I was out on the back deck when the argument with Dad happened, so I don't know what was said. I didn't see her again until midnight when she arrived at the dock in a small skiff. The one that's still out there, I guess." Tim continued to summarize what Molly had told him less than twelve hours earlier, except for the kissing part. He didn't see where that had any place in this discussion. "Here," he said, reaching for Molly's phone on his dresser. "Here's her phone. Passcode is 1291."

"Thanks Tim," Tony said, taking the phone. "And have you read anything on it?"

Tim looked straight at the detective and said, "No, sir. I was too tired last night and was pretty rushed to church this morning." Technically, Tim thought, a truthful statement.

"And when you went back inside last night, Molly was still on the dock?"

"Yes sir. I glanced back once before I entered the house, and she was leaning on the rail of the pier. I guess right where she was killed." Tim paused, and again felt faint. He mustered another deep breath. "Do you think someone was lying in ambush waiting for her? I mean, there weren't any other cars around, I remember that. Oh, and I remember hearing a boat motor right before I went inside the house — very faint, sounded like it was to the south, maybe around the inlet."

Tony raised his eyebrows at hearing this. "It's possible, Tim. Lots of things are possible at this stage. But as the probable last person to see her alive, you are going to be a very important witness."

"Yes, sir, I can understand that." What he wasn't so clear about was whether the detective thought of him as an important witness or as an important suspect.

"Thank you, Tim," said Tony, finishing his notes. "That's all I need for now."

******

"Ok, Rudy, let's start at the beginning." Leroy settled into the sectional couch diagonally across from the senior county judge. "Why don't you tell me why you were late for the party?"

"Not a good place to start, Sheriff."

Leroy winced. Why did Rudy always make everything so damn difficult?

"That is a private matter and had nothing to do with Molly."

"Judge, we both recognize you have no legal responsibility to tell me anything. I'm trying to get as many facts as possible at the beginning of what will be a very trying investigation."

Rudy folded his arms and scowled.

Leroy pressed on. "Why don't you start then at the party?"

"The only thing pertinent at the party, Leroy, is the argument Molly forced upon me before I asked her to leave.

What was the argument about? I'll tell you. She attempted to extort me. That's what. About this business with Greeley Construction and these lots which were approved. The same nonsense your detective upstairs keeps sticking his nose in. Molly claimed to have facts about my involvement with the issue and demanded $100,000 in cash or she'd spill it to the media. I reminded her just how illegal, not to mention callous, it was to attempt such a foolhardy blackmail. And towards a sitting circuit judge, in his private residence, at a party she was neither invited to nor welcome at, with the County Sheriff also in attendance. But of course, this is Molly Elmwood we're talking about. I don't have to remind you of her history."

Leroy looked up from his notetaking. "You're referring to…"

"You know what I'm referring to. Besides all the turmoil she's caused around Randy, don't forget the Scottdale affair, the DUI debacle, and now we can add narcotics theft to her list of criminal activity. Apparently, now her last list."

Leroy didn't need to be reminded. He was involved in each of the previous tussles Molly had with the law. The Scottdale affair in 2015 was an ugly case of public humiliation for Chester Scottdale, CEO of Scottdale Insurance, in Myrtle Beach. Molly had seduced the poor guy, extorted his silence for $50,000, then exposed the affair anyway and extorted the wife for another $50,000 from their divorce settlement to keep a nasty drug habit of the wife secret. In the end, Molly struck a plea deal for probation and return of the funds. It cemented her reputation, however.

Two years later, she fought a DUI charge in Murrells Inlet when they found a smorgasbord of drugs and alcohol in her system after a routine traffic stop. She had accused the officer involved of trying to exchange sex with him to look the other way — which he didn't, and she served a suspended sentence after a week in the tank. Leroy knew the pending narcotic drug theft and sales would have been the most serious charges she'd face to date. In a few minutes, though, all she'd be facing was the inside of a body bag.

"Alright, Rudy, let's move on. We know she left the party following the argument. Let's go to later when the party ended. Walk me through that."

Rudy continued, "Well, let's see. I believe the last guest left around 10:30 PM. Tim and Ruth retired upstairs. I poured a drink and sat out on the back deck and was not aware Tim had gone out to the dock at midnight. However, I saw something on the beach which may be pertinent to your investigation. Not sure of the time exactly, but it was probably between 11:45 PM and midnight. Guess who comes strolling down the beach to retrieve his boat?"

Leroy looked up from his notes, surprised. "Randy got his boat last night?" He looked out the back door and, for the first time, noticed the boat wasn't there.

"He did indeed. We made eye contact, I know, but did not communicate. I didn't stop him. Simply watched him push his boat back in the water and ride off — to the south."

"To the south," repeated Leroy. He thought again about the geography of the south end of Pawleys Island. Pawleys inlet was about a half a mile south from Culligan's Way. It was the outlet of Pawleys Creek, which is where the Culligan dock resided. "Randy could have ridden to the inlet and back up the creek to your dock in less than ten minutes."

"Exactly."

Leroy thought again of the last image he had of Randy the night before. Chocolate cream pie smearing his face, he stomped off the back deck onto the beach, leaving a trail of cussing. "Do you think he had any way of knowing Molly would be at the dock at midnight?"

"Now how would I know that, Leroy? I didn't know Tim was meeting her. I suggest you find Molly's phone and Randy's as well. If they talked or texted, you might have something there."

"I'll do that, Judge, certainly. How about after midnight? Did you hear Tim come back inside? When did you go upstairs for the night?"

"I didn't, but there's one more thing that happened."

Just then, one of the other deputies who had just entered the house interrupted the conversation. "Sheriff, may I intrude for a minute? There's something you need to see out here." Deputy Jason Carlson stood at the front entrance with a serious look on his face. "Judge Culligan may want to see this as well."

Leroy and Rudy looked at each other and shrugged. They both rose and strode over to the front door. "What do you have, Jason?" Leroy asked. They both entered the front porch to find Carlson holding a pair of shoes.

"Sir, we found what appeared to be a bloody footprint at the dock entrance. We traced it back across the street and up these stairs. Here's the source." Carlson held out a pair of size 12 lace up dress shoes. He turned them over to expose a blood red smear on the front half of the right sole.

Leroy turned to Rudy. "Rudy — are these yours?"

CHAPTER 22

As the three of them stood on the front porch, Leroy watched Rudy examine the shoes, then he gazed out towards the pier. Murrey was still examining Molly on the lower dock. Two other deputies were inspecting the pier and the gazebo. It appeared like one of them had a magnifying glass out. When Leroy looked down Springs Avenue, he saw a van approaching with a large antenna on top. A few seconds later, he could make out WCXM on the side.

"There's a perfectly good explanation for this, Leroy, that I will be glad to detail for you," said Rudy, diverting Leroy's attention from the TV station's van. "But I think first you're going to want to get the media under control. Here they come now." Rudy pointed to the approaching van.

"Shit, I was hoping to have a little longer before the circus came to town. Go ahead Conrad, keep them out of our hair. Tell them I'll have a statement before we leave."

"Yes, sir. I'll take care of it." Conrad hustled down the porch steps to greet the approaching van.

Leroy turned his attention back to Rudy. "Go ahead, let's hear it."

Rudy cleared his throat.

Leroy focused all his experience to discern the honesty of what Rudy would say next.

"As I mentioned, Sheriff Keating."

Leroy bristled at the sudden formality.

"I saw Randy leave in his boat shortly before midnight. I'm guessing it might have been fifteen, maybe twenty minutes later, when I thought I heard someone scream. I remember thinking it was either a female voice shrieking or a stray cat caught in a fight with something. It came from around the front of the house, loud enough to cause alarm, so I went back through the house and out the front door, down to the pier to investigate.

I noticed the small boat on the dock, which I did not recognize. Same one that's still there now. Everything else looked normal, so I went back to the house. I took my shoes off, as we do around here, and placed them in the basket there. Then I went upstairs to bed. Tim's door was closed, and Ruth was in bed asleep. That was it until this morning. So, apparently it was Molly I heard scream. By the time I got there, she was in the mud under the water level. Looks like I must have stepped in some blood on the pier and unwittingly brought it back up here." Rudy examined Leroy intensely. "That's the truth, Leroy. And I'll swear to it."

"Very well, Rudy." Then he remembered the Ring cam they saw earlier. "I see you have a Ring cam set up here. Why don't we call up the footage from last night? That should corroborate your story and pinpoint the timeframe." And, he thought, with any luck, determine the time of any scream you say you heard.

"Good idea. That should prove my story. I don't remember ever having used it before. We've never had a reason to. But I'm sure we can figure it out."

Conrad rejoined the group after corralling the Myrtle Beach TV crew on the street. Tony also rejoined Leroy on the front porch.

"Rudy, why don't you go get what you need to call up the Ring cam footage? I need to have a chat with my men here."

Rudy looked at them both with unease.

Leroy thought it might have been the first time in his life that Rudy realized he was being treated not as the man who delivered justice, but as a man who was a suspect of the law. It didn't appear he enjoyed it in the least.

Rudy simply said, "Sure, I'll get the documents. Be right back."

With Rudy off the front porch, Leroy received a quick update. Conrad went first. "Ruth's story is she went upstairs to the master bedroom around 11:15 PM and went right to sleep. There's no reason I see not to believe her story."

Leroy concurred. "Rudy mentioned she was asleep when he finally went upstairs." Then he briefly recapped the details Rudy provided about hearing a scream and going out to the pier to investigate. He showed his detective the bloody shoe sole.

Tony's eyes just about popped out of his head. "That rat fucker!"

"Don't get ahead of yourself, Detective. Rudy's not the kind to paint himself into a corner. Let's see what the Ring cam shows. Meanwhile, we still need to finish with the body, see what else they're finding on the pier, deal with the media, find out whose boat that is, and I want those other two Culligans — Randy and Connie — found and questioned."

Tony couldn't wipe the smirk off his face.

Leroy looked at him, perplexed. "What Tony? What are you smiling about?"

"Oh, I have one other piece of evidence to go through as well." He pulled out an iPhone from his back pocket. "Molly's iPhone," he said, showing it to his colleagues. "She gave it to Tim last night. Told him she needed to disappear, that she wasn't safe, and to use it to 'nail that bastard'. Should make for some interesting reading, if I say so myself."

Leroy looked at Tony and for the first time gave serious thought to the possibility that his senior circuit judge might indeed be a rat fucking criminal.

******

After Leroy did a quick check on the status of the activities on the pier and dock, he returned to meet Rudy on the front porch.

"We can watch it on my cell phone or call it up on the computer," Rudy told Leroy. "I have the codes here."

Conrad and Jason were busy on the pier, but Tony stood next to Leroy and was eager to see the Ring cam footage himself.

"Let's view it on your PC," Leroy said.

The three of them went inside, then upstairs to Rudy's personal office. Rudy started the PC, called up the website, then followed the Ring cam instructions to load the code for his camera. As he sat in his leather reclining office chair, the two law enforcement officers standing directly behind him, Rudy fumbled with the keyboard and the mouse. Leroy could tell Rudy was nervous, something he had never really seen before.

When Rudy had the Ring cam loaded, it prompted him for a time and date range. He turned around and asked Leroy when they wanted to start viewing.

"Let's start with 11:30 PM," Leroy answered.

Rudy typed in the time frame and clicked to start. Their first disappointment came with the view the camera gave them. Evidently, the Ring cam was a much older model. The picture was a grainy black and white, and it gave a very limited peripheral scope of only the area in front of the door to the steps. That quickly doused any hope of seeing activity on the pier.

"So much for capturing the murder," said Leroy.

Rudy just grunted. With no movement on the camera, Rudy clicked on fast-forward until Tim showed at 11:56 PM.

"There's Tim, leaving right when he said he did," said Tony. The cam captured Tim walking out the door and closing it behind him. That's when the second disappointment became apparent.

"There's no sound!" Leroy declared in a huff. "Where's the audio?" No one answered. "Rudy, can you get audio on this thing?"

Rudy turned around to face Leroy with a look of sheer exasperation. "I don't know, Leroy! Does it look like I'm wearing a uniform with Geek Squad on it? How the hell would I know why there's no sound?"

Leroy simply grumbled. Now they wouldn't be able to hear Molly's alleged scream to pinpoint the time of the murder. "Ok — Tony, have the tech guys look into this. See if they can't generate some audio."

"Will do, Sheriff."

The three of them continued to watch the silent video as Rudy fast-forwarded again. The next activity occurred at 12:08 AM, when Tim reappeared and entered the front door. Then, the main event — Rudy Culligan walks out the front door at 12:13

AM, a mere five minutes after Tim reentered. Rudy made his reentrance at 12:17 AM. He removed his now blood-stained shoes and went back inside. The video remained motionless as Rudy fast-forwarded all the way until 7:30 AM when Annabelle arrived this morning. Then he closed it out and turned his seat around.

"Well, gentlemen, that's it. Looks like the murder occurred sometime between 11:56 PM and 12:13 AM last night. I hope your tech guys can figure out the audio part."

"Correction there, Judge," Tony interceded. "What I gathered from the video is we had a murder occur sometime between 11:56 PM and *12:17* AM last night."

Rudy stood up and faced the detective with rising scorn. Leroy sensed the tension, along with the implication of Tony's gut-wrenching statement.

"Sheriff Keating — I *strongly* resent the insinuation of your detective here!" Rudy's voice rose at the perceived threat. "I *did not* kill Molly Elmwood. *Period!* Now, if you have concluded your business here, I am going to ask you both to leave my house. Finish your work outside, then leave us be on this, the Lord's Day."

Rudy and Tony glared at each other, then Tony broke out into a smirk. "Yes, Sheriff. I think we're done inside for now. Let's meet the others out front."

Leroy and Tony made their way out of the office and headed downstairs, leaving Rudy in a steaming fit of rage.

CHAPTER 23

All the law enforcement officers present met on the road in front of the pier. Murrey joined the team, having just finished bagging Molly to send back to the morgue. WTLK out of Charleston had joined the WCXM crew outside the crime tape, as well as reporters from the Myrtle Beach and Charleston papers. They all anxiously awaited Leroy's statement. Back on the pier, Leroy received a brief report from Murrey and each deputy.

"Molly died of a result of a single knife wound to the abdomen," stated the ME. "Although it's possible the direct cause of death might be drowning or even suffocation since she came to rest face down in the pluff mud. What's most interesting, Sheriff, is the type of wound I found. The knife had to be both thin and long, and likely slightly curved. The entry wound is only half an inch wide, and the exit wound is not quite a quarter inch. To me, it fits the description of a fillet knife, something you might find in a tackle box, but longer. Also, a knife common in a cutlery set. We couldn't find the murder weapon on or around the dock. We searched all the area inside the crime tape."

"That's great, Murrey, a great place to start." Two things stuck in Leroy's mind when he heard fillet knife. First was Randy Culligan's tackle box, being the avid angler he was. Second was the Culligan's cutlery set. He had noticed such a set in the kitchen near the sink. Wouldn't hurt to look there. They'd certainly look in Randy's tackle box as soon as possible.

"I think I might help with the location of the murder weapon." All eyes turned to Deputy Chris Donnelly. Chris worked closely with Tony, often referred to as his gopher.

"What do you got, Chris?" asked Leroy, leading the group back on to the pier, where Chris had a kind of show and tell set up.

"Ok," he started, clearly enjoying the attention. "We can safely assume the stabbing took place here, at this point along the railing, based on the amount of blood on the deck and the location where she was discovered. Then we found three more blood droplets on the deck of the pier heading towards the gazebo."

Leroy had already known about these before he had gone inside.

"From that, we can assume the killer headed over towards the gazebo here with the bloody knife in their hands. Now, this is where it gets interesting. We found a series of three small blood drops here on this post." Chris showed the others the bloodstains on the right-side gazebo post against the creek. "If you notice, they're in a kind of arc going from lower to higher. So from that we can speculate.."

"The killer threw the knife in the creek," Leroy interrupted, finishing the deputy's sentence.

"Exactly, Sheriff." Everyone on the gazebo examined the blood drop patterns, and they all seemed to agree. "Which means our murder weapon lies at the bottom of Pawleys Creek, somewhere right out there," Chris finished, pointing out towards the quiet, still creek.

"Excellent work, Deputy, excellent!" Leroy didn't hide the excitement of such a significant lead this early in the investigation. "Conrad, how soon before we can get a dive team out there and find this thing?"

"Not today, sir. I'll make some calls and see if we can't get a team out there tomorrow."

Leroy's face contorted, irritated there would be a delay. But it is Sunday, he reminded himself. "Ok, what else do we have? Do we know whose boat this is yet?"

"No sir," answered Jason. "I called in the registration tag a few minutes ago. Should know something this afternoon."

"Ok, anything else?"

They all looked at each other. No one had anything else to add. Murrey looked like he had the body ready for removal. The ambulance was waiting on the road. Leroy looked over at the gathering media circus. It was time to face their music. He had already decided there would be no questions this morning. Only a brief statement.

"Alright then. Murrey, you have your work cut out for you this afternoon. I'll check in with you at the morgue later. Conrad, I need you to stay on guard here for the afternoon shift. Chris and Jason, go find Randy and Connie Culligan and bring them in for questioning. Tony and I will wrap up things here at the house, then we can leave the family to some privacy for the day. I don't have to tell any of you about the sensitivity of this case. I don't want to hear about *any* leaks. All information to the media goes through me. Understood?"

A smattering of yes sirs came back.

"All right, then let's get this case solved. Correctly — and quickly."

******

His officers having dispersed, Leroy walked over to the corralled media. Tony stood by his side. The cameras were rolling.

"I have a brief statement to make to you all this morning. After that I will not be taking questions. I repeat — I *will not* be taking questions at this point. I hope to have a press conference later today at the police station in Georgetown, where I will entertain questions then." Leroy looked out over the roughly one dozen reporters and journalists, then back to the serenity of the marsh and the creek, and wondered briefly how much his world had changed in just over an hour. And how much more it would change in the coming days. He took a deep breath and turned back to the media.

"Ladies and gentlemen, a murder took place on this dock last night. We have confirmed the victim's identity and will release the name pending notification of the family. The victim was stabbed to death. We estimate the time of death sometime around midnight last night. As I'm sure you know, there was a party here at the Culligan residence yesterday evening. We cannot say whether the party has any relationship to the murder. There are no eyewitnesses to the crime that we know of, but we are just beginning our investigation. That is all I have to share with you at this time. I'm going to ask all media to clear the area. This is still an active crime scene."

Leroy and Tony turned away as a cacophony of questions poured out at once. "Are any of the Culligans suspects?" "Is Tim Culligan involved?" "Is the victim male or female?" "Was the victim at the party?" "Do you have a motive yet?" "Are all the Culligans at home now"? "Do you…" Leroy didn't hear any of the other questions. He had walked back to the pier entrance to see the ambulance off.

Leroy told Tony. "I've had enough of this place for now. Let's go back to station and see what we can put together."

"Absolutely. I can't wait to see what's on Molly's phone."
******

Harvey Klinger pulled up and parked his pickup in front of the TV vans. He couldn't believe his eyes as he came upon the media circus, then saw the law enforcement vehicles beyond. He couldn't control his emotions any further. For the past four hours, he'd been a nervous wreck worrying about Molly. She was supposed to check in with him after the midnight meeting with Tim, which he had tried to talk her out of. But Molly had been insistent. After the failed extortion attempt at the party, she hadn't sent the incriminating texts out to the media. She wanted Tim to be the one. She told him she needed to disappear for a while afterwards. Molly was vague, as she often was, and even though he thought he was her best friend, it wasn't enough to receive full disclosure of her plans.

So when he dropped her off at the secluded boat launch on Litchfield beach with his two-seater skiff, she promised to get in touch with him in the morning with instructions on where to pick up the boat. Now, almost twelve hours later, with no word from Molly, all his calls went straight to voice mail, and he feared the worst.

He had no other option than to drive to the south end of Pawleys Island and see if there were any signs of her. The cluster of vehicles he saw on his approach to Culligan's Way validated his trepidation. Then a nauseating feeling struck him as an ambulance drove past with flashing lights and sirens. He knew then that something happened to Molly.

Harvey exited his truck and marched past the media, who were closing their outpost, and headed straight towards the two law officers. He was livid, after hours of fear and worry had boiled inside of him. "What happened here?" he demanded. "What happened to Molly?"

Leroy didn't recognize the intruder, but Tony did. "This area is off limits to the public, sir," Leroy told Harvey.

"I have a right to be here!" Harvey shot back. "What the fuck happened to Molly? Is she dead? Did that bastard kill her?" He pointed directly at Culligan's Way, making it clear he was accusing Rudy.

"Harvey," Tony replied. "Why are you here? Do you know something about Molly's whereabouts last night?" Both Harvey and Leroy sported surprised looks. Tony explained first to his Sheriff. "Leroy, this is Harvey Klinger. He's the source in the Greeley investigation I mentioned. He'd been a source in a previous investigation as well."

Leroy looked at Harvey with cautious suspicion. "I see. So, how do you know Molly?" It was apparent Harvey's appearance caught Leroy off guard.

"Molly is a good friend of mine. I knew she was at the party last night." Harvey looked past the two down to the dock. Then he looked Leroy directly in the eye. "I knew she came back here at midnight to see Tim. She came back here in a boat. My boat. That boat there," he stated, pointing to the skiff tied to the lower dock. "Now I want to know. Where is Molly? What happened to her?"

Leroy stated flatly, "Mr. Klinger, Molly Elmwood was murdered on this pier last night. I'm sorry to have to tell you this. This is a murder investigation, and what you have just shared with us makes you a person of interest."

Harvey was shell-shocked, hearing the confirmation of his nightmare. "How did it happen?" he sputtered out.

"Mr. Klinger, we can't divulge that information to you at this point."

Harvey glanced back and forth from the dock to the house. "You know they did it!" Harvey said, distraught, again pointing at Culligan's Way. "I don't know if that Judge did it himself, or he hired a hit on her, but I know that son of a bitch is responsible."

"Harvey," Tony responded calmly. "We're exploring all options right now. We have several good leads already. You're going to be an important piece. Do you think you can come down to the station in Georgetown and give us a statement? I know you want to sort this out as much as we do."

Harvey looked around, dazed, still not comprehending what he had just heard. "Yeah, sure, Detective, I'll be happy to. Can I get my boat back to my place first?"

Leroy shook his head at Tony. "I'll tell you what, Mr. Klinger. Right now we're not finished examining the boat for evidence. But by the time we finish with your statement, I'll be happy to get your boat back to wherever you wish."

Harvey acknowledged Leroy's offer. He had one more question, however. "Does Tim have Molly's phone?"

"He did," answered Leroy, who pulled the phone from his jacket pocket. "We have it now."

Harvey nodded his head in understanding. "Ok, I'm ready."

CHAPTER 24

While Leroy was finishing his tasks at the pier, he saw Sally's Ford Escape approach the Way. Seeing Sally, it reminded him he still had a drug theft on his agenda, even if the alleged perp was on her way to the morgue. And there was also Connie, of course — the vicious, albeit brief catfight between the two sisters last night flashed through his mind as he approached Sally in the carport.

"Good morning, Sheriff." Sally smiled and greeted Leroy.

I bet you're happy to have heard what happened here, thought Leroy. "Good morning, Sally. Do you mind if I have a word with you before you go inside?"

"Certainly. Dad texted what happened here. Such a tragedy," Sally said, the small smirk still smarting her face.

"It is, very much so. I just have a couple of questions for you."

"Go right ahead," answered Sally. The smirk now wiped away.

"We, that is me, and your parents witnessed the unfortunate scene before you left the party last night. Can I assume you went straight home afterwards — and stayed there until this morning?"

Sally looked Leroy straight in the face. "Of course. I regrettably had too much to drink at the party, and I apologize for that. I crashed as soon as I hit the bed. Steve can attest to that. Right, dear?"

"Yes," her husband replied. "We were asleep soon after we went to bed."

"And have you had any further contact with Connie since you left?"

"No sir, none. Have you?"

"We have not, yet." Leroy conceded to answer her but didn't appreciate being the one questioned. It would be her only question this morning. "Thank you, Sally. That's all I need for now."

"You're welcome, Sheriff. I know Bud will want an update on the drug theft as soon as possible." Sally turned and walked up the stairs to the Way.

Yeah, I bet he will, Leroy thought watching the elder Culligan daughter enter the front door. He walked back to the pier and found Tony waiting on him. "Come on Tony, let's get back to the station and see if we can put this puzzle together."

******

Tim sat down to the Sunday feast with mixed emotions. On one hand, the smells and the sights of dinner were everything he had expected since the day he first called Sally. Annabelle had gone above and beyond the normal fare of Mississippi style pot roast, browned potatoes with onions and carrots, rice, gravy, green beans, and biscuits. To this, she added a broccoli cheese casserole and pickled beets. Somehow, she also managed to bake a lemon pound cake. How she accomplished this in the middle of a murder investigation, Tim couldn't imagine. But he knew it ravished him just looking at it.

But the events of the morning, coupled with the information he gleaned from the messages he had forwarded from Molly's phone, left him disgusted and speechless. Tim devoted the time he had from the end of Tony's interview until he sat down for dinner to digest the messages. The texts to this Harvey Klinger fellow read like a Pat Conroy novel of deceit and abuse of power. There, in plain view, were the two sides of Molly. On one hand, a concerned citizen coordinating with her friend to protect the sensitive coastal environment from a malicious construction company's run around the law.

And then the same Molly, using blackmail and extortion to extract from his own father cash to avoid exposing the scandal. That must have been what the two were arguing about at the party. Tim had always thought of Molly as a tough cookie, but this was downright outrageous, and right inside his family's house!

And then the audio clip. She apparently plied this Jack Greeley with sex to extract incriminating information. This was one of the texts she sent to his father — perhaps the most damaging. It was hard enough listening through the sex part, Jack panting and moaning, telling Molly she meant everything to him, (what if his wife hears that part!) Then, in the afterglow, Molly prodding Jack about the marsh lots, and DHEC, and 'your ex's father smoothing over the rough spots'. The sad commentary — 'what about the poor eagles and osprey, Jack?' 'Fuck them!' the caustic reply. The papers would have a field day with that one.

So there it was, the smoking gun in Tim's hands. Also now in Sheriff Keating's hands. How would that play out? Tim told them he hadn't read the messages earlier — technically true. But soon, the Sheriff would know from Molly's phone that he had forwarded the messages to his phone. And then they'd be back, and probably none too happy.

Molly had wanted Tim to do the right thing with the incriminating evidence. Turn it in, expose his father in the media, humiliate him. Was it just because of protecting marshland lots? Did it have something more to do with Randy? Or was it something else, some deeper vendetta she held against his father? And this was her way of revenge. Have Tim do the dirty work while she disappeared, watching it all happen from a safe distance. Except it didn't work out that way, did it, Molly? They got to you first. But who? And how?

Tim had glanced through the text stream between her and his father, and then her and Randy. It didn't quite add up in his mind how Randy had the information about Greeley and had sent it to Molly. Wasn't that the day a week and a half ago, when they charged Randy with the restraining order violation? Something wasn't right there. And neither was the last message sent at 11:15 PM last night. Randy urgently needed to see Molly. Where can they meet? Molly's reply — I'll be on Culligan's pier at 12:10 AM. Don't be early. Didn't he vaguely remember hearing a boat on the creek from the south, just before he went back in the house last night? Did Randy show up after he went inside? Did he see him and Molly kissing? Did he show up and kill Molly Elmwood?

Tim shook off the all the convolutions the messages presented. He smiled at the remaining four family members at the table. The food looked and smelled amazing. He was back inside the lion's den, come hell or high water. He wasn't just involved; he was right in the thick of it. Tim recalled the old bacon and egg breakfast joke he had heard years before regarding involvement and commitment. The chicken, it went, was involved. But the pig

— well, the pig was committed. To live in Culligan's Way —
you have to be committed — in more ways than one.

CHAPTER 25

Later that afternoon, Leroy and Tony sat in the Sheriff's office looking at each other in amazement. They had earlier concluded their meeting with Harvey and were now reviewing the messages and recordings on Molly's phone. It was one bombshell after another. First, the messages between her and Rudy, including the text with the audio clip of Jack Greeley. To Leroy, it was a strange juxtaposition of humor and outrage, similar to Ruth and the rolling pin the other day. Saying 'Fuck them' to the bald eagles was tantamount to professional suicide. He might as well have said he supports euthanizing all the dogs in the shelters.

Then the texts between Molly and Harvey, confirming what Harvey had just told them, that Molly had a devious plan to seduce Jack, then blackmail Rudy. More suspicious were the texts between Molly and Randy. According to Harvey, Molly staged the incident of Randy breaking the restraining order and assault of her, in order to make it look like it was Randy who had the goods on Rudy. Seemed a bit contrived to Leroy and Tony, and it would certainly cast a different light on the assault charge. But the most concerning message of all was the last one, showing a meeting between Randy and Molly at the time and the scene of the murder. The next step was obvious.

"Have you found Randy Culligan yet?" Leroy barked into his radio.

"No sir," replied Chris. "He's not at his fish camp, but his pickup truck is there. The one guy here said Randy left in his boat before nine last night and hasn't come back since. We're tracking down a couple of other friends who might hide him. Or he may still be on the water somewhere."

"Thanks Chris, keep me posted," Leroy ordered, ending the radio call. "What do you think?" he asked, turning his attention back to Tony.

"I thank the son-of-a-bitch is hiding out in his boat. Could be tucked away in any little cove between Georgetown and Conway."

"That's what I think too. We need to flush him out. I'll call Water Patrol here and in Horry County. We'll send boats in from both directions. And put out an APB to all the marinas in the area, along with his photo. He's going to have to dock somewhere pretty soon. What else we got?"

"Connie — we picked her up about thirty minutes ago at her friend Janie's place in Surfside. They're bringing both of them in now on drug possession charges."

The drug theft, Leroy remembered. On top of all this other shit, I got that to deal with. "Good. You think there's any connection there with Molly's death?"

"Well, based on what Tim told us, and what happened at the party, you have a motive. But I'm not sure there's a plausible opportunity. I doubt Connie did anything but go to her friend in a huff and get stoned. We should know more about that soon enough."

"Yes, and speaking of Tim, we show Molly's messages forwarded to him at 12:20 AM, after the murder, when Tim went back to his room. I thought you told me he didn't read her messages."

"He did," answered Tony, now seeing the loophole. "He said he didn't read them, not that he didn't forward them."

"Which means he's probably read them by now. I'll call him and make sure he understands these messages are evidence, and he'd be breaking the law if he disburses them. So that leaves the Greeley affair." Leroy held up Molly's phone. "Where do these put things now?"

Tony smiled with a smug look on his face. "They leave Rudy hanging by the short hairs, is what I think."

"Come on Tony, you know as well as I do there isn't any hard proof here. What we need is to find the weak link at DHEC. Where do you stand on that?"

"So far, I've run into a brick wall. Last week I talked with a Robert Huntsman, who runs the department out of Columbia. He only seemed vaguely interested in the call logs from Rudy. Told me he'd look into it and get back to me. Which he hasn't. I'm thinking the stench goes right to the top. Rudy wouldn't mess around with anyone else for something this sensitive. I'm about ready to bring in a wrecking ball."

"Not yet, you're not." Leroy knew how Tony could have a short fuse. "Do we know if the calls went straight to Huntsman or not?"

"No, they went to the general department number. Could have gone anywhere from there."

"And isn't there some history with Rudy and DHEC? I seem to recall a case a few years back."

"There was. Similar to this, but a different construction company. Had to do with an alleged pollution violation. Rudy ruled for the construction company."

"And Huntsman was in charge of DHEC then, as well?"

"Not sure. I'll check on it. And consider this. Where do you think Rudy was most of the day yesterday? You told me he didn't get to the party until almost 7:00 PM. Tim said he left right after breakfast at 9:30 AM. Plenty of time to drive to Columbia, take care of business, and get back."

Leroy thought about the scenario Tony laid out. Then he shook his head. "It's plausible, but there are two problems. First, DHEC is closed on Saturday. We can check security video nearby, but I doubt he would go there when he knows we're snooping around. Plus, there's extra time unaccounted for. It's just over three hours drive to Columbia. I doubt Rudy would have hung around if he didn't need to and made a notable tardy entrance to the party. I'm thinking.."

"Huntsman's home." Tony finished Leroy's sentence. "Where he wouldn't be suspected, and where Huntsman would have access to all the DHEC files." The two cops smiled at each other. "I'll find out where Huntsman lives and see about security video nearby." Tony finished the conclusion they had both reached. "Then it will be time to put the Judge's ass on the hot skillet."

Leroy could tell Tony was far happier about the situation than he was. But he couldn't avoid his suspicion that the leads were indeed heading for a possible serious ass-frying.

******

By late afternoon, Leroy finished pulling the pieces he had together to prepare for the press conference he had called for 4:00 PM. He was ready to get home for the day, and knew he'd make some brownie points with the media by getting the circus show over before their evening broadcasts. He had his men inform the only known relative of Molly, her mother, whom they found in a run-down trailer park in Garden City. The father had been out of the picture since Molly was two, and a stepfather had been gone for about ten years. Edith Elmwood herself hadn't seen Molly in over a year and hadn't talked with her since Christmas. There seemed to be no love lost between mother and daughter. As his deputy informed Leroy when he told Edith of her daughter's demise; she scoffed, then slung a tobacco-stained wad of spit on the ground. Told the deputy Molly been having something like this coming to her for a long time. Leroy shook his head and said a quick thanks to the people in his family who cared for his well-being.

He also put Tim on ice about the messages he was privy to. Tim said he understood and confirmed that he had not lied to Tony about reading the texts. Yes, he had forwarded them to his phone the night before, but went right to sleep afterwards. He promised Leroy he would do nothing further with the incriminating texts and would certainly not be sharing them with his father.

Leroy had one of the two missing Culligan children in his custody. Connie and her friend Janie were stewing in two of his holding cells. And wouldn't you know who Connie had used her one allowed phone call to call? From what the Sargent on duty told him, Connie didn't get the response from Rudy she had hoped for. Just like Randy, Leroy thought, running to daddy to fix all their problems. Connie would spend the night in her cell, and probably suffer through some type of withdrawal. Leroy couldn't care less. They'd both be back snorting whatever by

Monday afternoon, assuming they could post bail. Leroy wasn't even sure of that.

The biggest disappointment had been Randy. The water patrols had been up and down the Waccamaw and the Great Pee Dee rivers with no sign of him. Same with the marinas — and no sight of him back at his fish camp. It was obvious to Leroy that Randy was on the run, hiding out somewhere. Problem was there were just too many places to hide a small johnboat. He could have gone south down the coast to McClellanville, where there would be hundreds of tucked away places to hide. Still, he was sure Randy would turn up eventually.

Leroy put his notes together and proceeded down the hall to the front steps of the police station. When he stepped out into the late afternoon sunshine, TV reporters and journalists swarmed around him. Several of his deputies braced the crowd back behind the loose buffers they had established on the steps.

"I have a brief statement to make," he told the hushed crowd with his booming voice. "Afterwards, I will take only a few questions. At this point in the investigation, there are many more questions than answers." Leroy assessed the crowd. They hung on every word. "Last night, between midnight and 12:30 AM, a young lady from Murrells Inlet, by the name of Molly Elmwood, was murdered on the pier of Judge Culligan's property. Molly was stabbed to death by a single stab wound. She was discovered this morning by two fishermen by the creek bank below the pier. We have several leads and people of interest, but there have been no arrests or direct suspects. We do not have the murder weapon in our possession, but we hope to have it by sometime tomorrow. That is all I have to share with you for now.

Like I said, I will take just a few questions. Yes," he said, pointing to the WCXM News reporter, Heidi Dexter.

"Sheriff, is Judge Culligan or Randy Culligan suspects at this point?"

"We have no suspects at this point. They are both persons of interest. We have talked with Judge Culligan. We are still looking for Randy Culligan."

"Sheriff," asked Judy Coleman from the Myrtle Beach Times, "Do you have a motive for Molly's murder?"

So far, so good, thought Leroy, nothing out of the ordinary. "We have several motives in play. I'm not at liberty to divulge any information about motive at this point."

"Sheriff Keating," this came from Doug Renfro from WTLK Charleston, "there have been reports of several altercations related to Molly at the welcome home party at the Culligans last night; including a drug theft from the Pawleys Island Publix, and an argument she had directly with Judge Culligan. Is there a connection between these altercations and the murder?"

Ok, now that is pushing the envelope. "We are aware of these altercations, and I have no comment about them at this point. I'll take one more question? Yes," he directed to this to Julie Reardon, the fiery redhead for the local Pawleys paper, the Coastal Observer.

"Sheriff, does Molly's murder have anything to do with the scandal involving Judge Culligan and Greeley Construction?" All the other reporters gawked at Julie. None of them were aware of this juicy addition to the mystery. Leroy looked straight at Julie. Where the hell did she get that? All he could think was

Harvey Klinger — it seemed this guy would continue to cause trouble for him.

"I have no comment on that matter. That is all for today." Leroy turned his back to the crowd, now peppering him with simultaneous questions, all falling on deaf ears. He went back inside the precinct and shut the door behind him.

CHAPTER 26

The next morning, Rudy was back in his chambers with nothing but trouble on his mind. He had one daughter chilling in a jail cell next door, one son on the lam, likely hiding out in some river shack, and a nosy sheriff and detective who already at 9:00 AM wanted to question him again. On top of that, a fuming construction executive waited outside his chambers, wanting to have a word with him. Rudy had hearings scheduled at 10:00 AM and 11:00 AM and a trial scheduled to start at 1:00 PM. He told Leroy he could meet with him after lunch before the trial. He thought better than inviting him to lunch; guessing they were past socializing for now.

Rudy sighed, then told Janice to let Jack Greeley into his chambers. He didn't even bother to rise to greet him.

"What can I do for you, Jack? This has to be quick; I have a lot on my plate today."

"Oh, I'm sure you do, Judge," Jack shot back, helping himself into the oversized leather armchair. "What with your daughter in jail, your son on the run from the law, and a pesky detective breathing down your neck, I'm sure you have a full plate."

Rudy narrowed his eyes at Jack. He already knew more than he should. But that wasn't what concerned Rudy at the moment. He knew what was coming next.

"What I want to know," Jack continued, now raising his voice, "is why I got an email this morning from DHEC rescinding the marsh lot approvals at Salt Cove?"

Rudy smirked. "Technically, Jack, those lots were never approved. They never had the proper signoffs attached to them. I would —"

"That's *bullshit,* Rudy, and you know it! We had a deal. Those lots were approved, and I paid you plenty for making it happen."

"Jack," Rudy replied, his tone dead serious. "I'm going to insist you keep your voice down, or I'll have you removed from this courthouse. Now you listen to me. Whatever you thought about those lots being approved by DHEC was premature at best, but more likely illegal. You jumped the gun, that's how this is going to go down when our Sheriff gets the facts in the case. And believe me — I'll see to that. I had nothing to do with whatever shortcuts you were trying to make in your haste to develop those lots."

Jack glared; his face grew several shades redder. Rudy could tell the pressure inside of Jack approached a boiling point.

"I suggest you contact Robert Huntsman, let him know the situation. If he can get your lots approved through the proper channels, then you'll be fine. If not, then you've got a bit of a mess on your hands. But *I'm* thinking you may have an even *bigger* mess on your hands — like, for instance, did you put someone up to kill Molly Elmwood?"

Jack shot to his feet and screamed, "That's enough out of you, Judge! I had nothing to do with Molly's death. You, on the other hand, seem to have a very close connection to what happened Saturday night. My sources tell me you had quite an argument with Molly at your party before she left. What was that all about Rudy? Did Molly threaten to spill the beans, expose your corruption in this whole mess?"

"Jack," Rudy stood up and fired back, "we're done here. And we are done — period. I don't want to see or hear from you again. Do I make myself clear?"

Jack leaned on Rudy's desk and pointed a finger at him. "Oh, I'm clear *we* are done with each other. But you are far from done with this Salt Cove scandal or with Molly's death. I'll see to that. Mark my words, Judge, I will not go down in this alone. You might think you can throw me under the bus for now, but watch out for that Mack truck right behind you. Be careful, Rudy." Jack turned and stomped out of the office without another word.

******

It was a warm sunny early spring morning when Tim ventured out to the beach for the first of what he hoped would be many beach walks. Sunday had been mentally and emotionally exhausting. Molly's death, her phone messages, the accusations about his father — it was all just too much for Tim. A tenseness had permeated the Sunday dinner. All the fresh biscuits, succulent roast and vegetables, and sweet cake couldn't cut through the uneasiness everyone felt at the table. More of the conversation was complimentary to Annabelle; how she managed to prepare this incredible feast amidst all the interruptions of the morning.

They discussed little else. Rudy asked about the Publix narcotics theft, which Sally sidelined. No one knew where Connie or Randy was, and nobody seemed to care. Sally and Steve left after dinner and then Annabelle left after cleaning the dishes. Rudy busied himself in his office and Ruth drifted off to a peaceful, mindless rest on a back porch rocker. After such a raucous beginning to his return home, Tim found the Sunday afternoon tranquility somehow discomforting. There was so much he had learned about his family in the short two days since his return, but so much more he didn't know, and wondered if he ever would — or should. In the end, Tim fell asleep on the couch watching a movie.

Now, on Monday, after a light breakfast and some simple conversation with his mother — catching up on neighbors and old high school friends — Tim was ready to begin his physical recuperation. He changed into one of his old bathing suits and a t-shirt, then strode out barefoot over the dunes and onto the beach. South, he decided, towards the inlet. He knew he wouldn't make it all the way. It was just over half a mile, but any start was a good start. He paced along the shoreline, letting the cool ocean water wash over his feet. In just a few weeks, he knew the water would be warm enough to swim in, something he had never done in New York. The Yankees may have tolerated sixty-eight-degree ocean water in the summer, but Tim had no desire to freeze on a beach that was overcrowded to begin with. Now, with only a handful of other beach-walkers scattered about, Tim had the solitude amongst nature's beauty he most cherished.

Like the first two pieces connected to a thousand-piece jigsaw puzzle, Tim began the mental process of putting the pieces of his future together. His health was his first priority. He had come to grips with his condition and its implications. He knew it would be a long slog to get back to how he needed to feel to live a normal life. These beach walks would be the remedy required for his physical rehabilitation. But despite the shocking events that unfolded since his return, Tim felt the first seed of something he never would have predicted. The possibility of not returning to New York. That maybe he might just stay here in Pawleys.

It began with the unexpected depth of warmth he received when he arrived, and further grasped at the party. From this flowed a greater understanding of how estranged his brother was from the family — and the very real likelihood Randy would never again live at the Way. As far as his father went, Tim felt neutral towards him. In some ways, it appeared he had mellowed from how he remembered him. But Rudy still came across as cold and calculating, not to mention how shamelessly he wielded his power. Tim felt relieved to have the burden Molly put on him removed. Let the Sheriff deal with what was on Molly's phone. Tim wanted no part of that, or any of the wretched affairs Rudy and Molly were involved in.

And what about Molly — murdered, and right after he had last seen her. Himself, the last person known to have seen her alive. Tim wondered if Sheriff Keating thought he may be a suspect himself. No, Leroy assured him, he was just a person of interest. Wasn't he though, a person of interest.

Standing at the water's edge, Tim took in the sight, sound, and smell of the ocean, trying to forget the events of the past few days. He loved it. Feeling his breathing beginning to labor, he looked back to see how far he'd gone — maybe a quarter of a mile. Better not push things on the first day, he thought as he turned and headed back to the Way.

Ten minutes later, winded but exhilarated, Tim arrived at the beach walkover, and as he crossed back over the dunes, he saw a man sitting in one of the rocker chairs. As he drew near the back deck, he thought this younger man, about his age, looked familiar — someone he hadn't known before but who he had just seen. As Tim walked onto the porch, the man stood up and approached him, smiling. He looked like a hippie from the sixties, with long hair straddling his shoulders, and a headband. Yes, he's the guy who showed up yesterday and had a discussion with the police.

"Tim," the man said, smiling, extending a hand to greet him, "I'm Harvey Klinger. Can we talk a bit?"

CHAPTER 27

"You were here yesterday," Tim said to Harvey as they took seats in two adjacent rockers. Before Harvey could answer, Ruth burst through the back door.

"Tim, this young man said it was urgent he talked with you. Do you know him?"

"Yes, Mom, he was one of Molly's friends. It's ok."

Ruth looked Harvey up and down, with an unapproving air. Tim thought it could have been the hair, or the beads, or maybe just the word's 'Molly's friend', but Ruth sniffed as if Harvey smelled bad and said, "I see," then turned to Tim. " Can I get you a lemonade, dear, or sweet tea? I hope you didn't overdo it on the beach."

"Lemonade would be great, Mom. Thanks."

Ruth turned and went back into the house without offering Harvey the same consideration.

"Excuse my Mom. She's usually more accommodating, but we're all a little on edge since yesterday morning."

"Not a problem at all." Harvey smiled back. "She wouldn't let me come through the house. Had to walk around the side. Don't worry, I won't be staying long."

"So, what else have you been able to find out?" Tim went right to the point. Harvey had gotten Tim's number, a feat that surprised Tim given the circumstances, and called him Sunday afternoon after he finished at the precinct. He briefly described his involvement with Molly and asked Tim if he might visit the Way in person on Monday, to which Tim agreed.

"Not much," replied Harvey. "The cops were way more interested in obtaining information than sharing it. But the key question I have, Tim, is did Molly give you her phone when you met her on Saturday night? That's what she told me she was going to do."

Tim rocked back and forth, now realizing what Harvey was after. He knew he had to be careful with the information he shared, given the trouble he had already caused for himself. But he also knew he wanted more information about Molly, and Harvey was by far the best source. "She did, but I gave it to Sheriff Keating yesterday, not by choice."

Harvey continued to rock, waited a few seconds, then prodded some more. "So, did you read what was on her phone? What she wanted you to do?"

Tim gave one more thought about whether to trust this man, then decided he needed to in order to get the answers he lacked. "Actually, I didn't have time to read them before I turned the phone over. When I left Molly on the dock, and came back inside, I was exhausted and went straight to bed. But I looked at what was in her text library and saw the message strings from my father, Randy, and yourself. So I forwarded those three strings to my phone, but never read them before the events of yesterday morning. I did, however, read through them later yesterday." Tim paused there for effect.

Harvey's eyes widened. "So, you have them on your phone now. What do they say?"

"Harvey," Tim answered with reluctance, "I'm under strict orders from the Sheriff's department not to divulge the contents of those messages. When they asked me if I had read them, I honestly answered no, but didn't divulge that I had forwarded them to my phone. They called me later and made me aware in no uncertain terms those messages were evidence in a murder investigation, and I was not to divulge them to anybody. I'm sorry."

Harvey nodded his head and stayed silent.

Ruth came back out with Tim's lemonade. "Here you go, Tim. I think you should rest for the day. You look exhausted." She glanced surreptitiously at Harvey, as if insinuating it was his fault for Tim's apparent exhaustion.

"I'm fine, Mom," Tim responded with a smile. "I'll be in for lunch after I finish with Harvey here." Ruth scoffed again in Harvey's direction and went back inside. Tim turned his attention back to his guest. "So, like I was saying, I can't let you read the actual text messages…"

"But?" Harvey's eyes widened.

"But." Tim gave him a gentle sneer. "But I see nothing wrong with discussing some things, especially if you have other things you might wish to share as well."

Harvey smiled and nodded. "I definitely can share some things you might be interested in about Molly. Let's start with Greeley Construction.

Although not exactly an environmental activist himself, Tim respected what Harvey and Molly were trying to do in stopping Greeley from their illegal manipulations and empathized with Harvey's tree-chaining episode.

"You really did that, huh?" Tim asked him. "I only heard of those things happening in California or Oregon."

"Yeah, and the thing that pissed me off the most was the bitch reporter who filmed it, didn't put it on the air that night. They're going to hear more about it now, however."

"But the thing that really bothers me about Molly," said Tim, switching subjects, "is this contradiction between her standing up for environmental justice, but at the same time committing felonies of extortion and drug theft." Tim had mentioned to Harvey what he had overheard at the party.

Harvey nodded in agreement. "First, I didn't know about the drug theft. Yes, she did drugs, too many — I wished she had stayed with just pot. And yes, I knew she had used sex as a means to an end before. But this extortion scheme to get at the Judge, your father — that was a little too much, and I told her so. Sometimes I think her entire game with Randy was nothing more than a means to extract money from Judge Culligan. You know, she had been engaged to him twice before, then broke it off because she didn't perceive the Culligans were going to be generous enough to them after they were married. I think she was angling for Rudy to put them up in a new house somewhere, and to sustain them with a substantial allowance. I assume you know that Randy's arrest the other week was all Molly's doing. Part of the extortion ploy. That was in her texts with Randy. I suppose the cops know about that now."

"Yeah, I saw that too. How long have you known Molly? I don't remember her ever being this devious when I was here before."

"I've known her for about seven years. We dated early on but stayed friends when the romance ended. She had a tough life but never gave an inch to anyone. She's duped more than a few men in her time."

Tim chuckled. "Like poor old Jack Greeley — what a sap."

"And a criminal, Tim. I don't feel sorry for him in the least. And he's going to get what's coming to him for his actions."

Tim nodded for a second, then decided. "I think I can help with that," he said and pulled out his cell phone."

Harvey smiled. "Oh yeah? What do you have?"

"I told you I couldn't share the contents of Molly's text messages with you. But there's one audio clip that pretty much nails Jack Greeley. I don't suppose it would hurt for you to listen to it."

"Not at all, Tim. I'm all ears."

Tim called up the audio clip attached to the text string she had with Rudy. It began with Molly seducing Jack in the hotel room. This soon led to a brief but intense sex interlude. They clearly heard Molly's moaning.

"That's our Molly," joked Harvey, causing both of them to laugh.

Jack's escapade ended shortly thereafter with a monumental groan, causing even more laughter. After a brief pause, allowing Jack to catch his breath, Molly questioned Jack about his dealings with the marsh lot approvals. Jack seemed at ease with himself and bragged about how he had DHEC in his back pocket, thanks to Judge Culligan, and the coast was clear for him to develop more lots.

"Oh, and by the way, I'm thinking about leaving my wife. I've had all I can take with the old bag. Thought maybe I'd set you up in a condo nearby where we could shack up."

Molly didn't respond right away. Then it was obvious she was more concerned about the environment than any love shack arrangement. "But what about the eagles and osprey, Jack? Where will they nest if you destroy their habitat?"

"Fuck them," came the caustic reply.

Harvey's eyes popped. "Did I just hear that correctly? Jack Greeley told the eagles to fuck off!"

"Pretty amazing, isn't it?" replied Tim, shaking his head.

"If that ever gets out to the press, they'll hang Jack Greeley by his balls."

"It's in the Sheriff's hands now," corrected Tim. "I can't say how they're going to handle the situation. They have a murder on their hands now, as well as the drug theft and this DHEC scandal. We'll just have to wait and see how this plays out." Tim rose from his chair. He was ready to go in for lunch. Harvey shook his hand and thanked him for the meeting.

"Tell Mrs. Culligan I appreciate her not running me off. And thank you Tim for the time and the information. I'm sure we'll meet again soon. Molly's funeral will be later this week. I'm working with the crazy mother on the details."

"Well, good luck with that. Let me know when and where it will be."

******

Harvey left the back porch and walked around the house again to his truck. Once inside, he checked his phone. He went in his photo library and called up the just recorded clip. With the volume turned up, the conversation came through loud and clear. Harvey smiled to himself, completely satisfied.

CHAPTER 28

Leroy sat in his office with Tony, mulling over the latest information in the case. He had just returned from his meeting with Rudy, which, as predicted, did not go well. Rudy had been short, and gruff — attitudes he knew the Judge often had on display — just not towards him. He's feeling the heat, Leroy thought to himself — who wouldn't. Rudy stood firm on his version of events Saturday night. He's locked into it anyway, what with the cam recording and the bloody shoe. Leroy knew Rudy was banking on further evidence coming forward to exonerate him, unless, of course, such evidence turned around and pointed the finger back at him.

Rudy offered one new piece of information. Something that surprised Leroy at first, but in hindsight, fit right into Rudy's MO. "I did some checking into DHEC," he said innocently, "after these allegations you brought to my attention last week."

Leroy sat across from Rudy thinking, did you now?

"And it turned out those marsh lots with Greeley at the Salt Cove development were *not* approved. There was some misunderstanding, some technical glitch which I'm told has been corrected. So, there are currently no marsh front lots in Salt Cove under development."

Leroy thanked Rudy for the update and ended his meeting.

Tony scoffed when he heard this. "I'll tell you exactly what happened," he began the conversation. "I did some checking myself about DHEC and this Robert Huntsman, head of the Department. Turns out he lives just outside Columbia, not five miles from the DHEC building. But he has a lake house on

Lake Murray, tucked away on the northeast end. At least a forty-five-minute drive from Columbia."

"Which, if Rudy went there, instead of DHEC, or Huntsman's home —"

"He would have been gone at least eight or nine hours. Which fits our timeline perfectly. And I'm one step ahead of you. There's a marina just down the road from Huntsman's lake house. Put a call in to them as soon as I found out about his house out there. They have a security camera, and it has a full view of the road. If we see a white Lexus sedan go down that road anytime Saturday afternoon, we'll have our Judge in a squeeze."

"Alright, I admit he'd be in a squeeze, but what does it prove? It's not a crime to take a drive out to a lake house."

"No, it's not boss." Tony chuckled. "But it sure doesn't look right. It's another piece of the puzzle. We'll need to get a hold of Huntsman soon and get his take on the whole situation."

"I agree. Let's try to set up a Facetime or a Zoom call with him. I'll try to make arrangements for this afternoon. What else we got? Any word from the dive team?"

"Not yet. They said it may take the entire afternoon to scan the area. And the tech guys came up empty getting audio on the Ring cam recording."

Leroy sighed. "I was afraid of that. It would have been so simple to pinpoint the exact time of the murder. It got me thinking though, is it even possible that Rudy could have heard a scream from the pier reach his back deck on the other side of the house? If he couldn't, his story wouldn't be as believable."

Tony thought about this for a second. "Not sure about that. It might depend on the wind direction at that time. I'll tell you what I can do. I'll check the meteorology for midnight Saturday, and when we have a close match, we can set up a rough test."

"A scream test." Leroy nodded in agreement. "I like that. Got a test screamer in mind?"

"No, but I'm sure any of our fine female employees would be happy to let one loose for the sake of justice."

"I suppose. One other avenue I thought of. I want to know who drove on to Pawleys Island before midnight on Saturday. In particular, anyone who drove on and then back off after midnight. I know there are only two ways on to the island; the North and the South Causeway. What security cameras could we look at that would show the traffic on these causeways?"

Tony thought about it for a few seconds. "I know the Walgreen at the corner of Hwy. 17 and the North Causeway will have one. On the South Causeway, I believe there's a restaurant and a gas station off 17. I'll have Chris run it down. Here's my trouble with how this is all coming together. Nobody except Tim, Harvey, and Randy knew Molly would be on that dock at midnight on Saturday. From what we heard on the messages; it would make sense to have one of Jack's guys follow Molly and knock her off. But she went by boat out of the Litchfield Beach ramp, a very secluded location. And Harvey said he didn't see anybody on the Litchfield Beach Road after he dropped her off. To me it comes down to Randy, or Rudy, if he somehow knew Molly would be returning."

Just then Leroy's radio crackled. "Sheriff, Jason here. We just found Randy Culligan. He's at the Bluefin Marina on the South Santee River. Not a happy camper, I'm afraid."

Leroy grinned at Tony. "Thanks, Jason. Bring him in. If he doesn't want to come of his own volition, then arrest the son-of-a-bitch."

"Will do Sheriff, over and out."

"Well, Detective — maybe now we'll get some answers."
******

Tony's first stop after leaving Leroy's office was to check in on Murrey downstairs in the morgue. He received a text earlier from the ME to come by when he had a chance — he had completed Molly's autopsy and there were a few items Tony may be interested in. Tony knocked on the morgue's door and let himself in.

"Got your text, Murrey. Tell me what you found."

Murrey went over to greet Tony, then proceeded to the locker holding Molly's body. "Here's a copy of the report. I just finished it after the lab results came back." He pulled the rack holding the body out from the locker. Tony caught his breath. He remembered maybe coming across Molly a time or two in the past. Now, even dead to the world, he could see how Molly possessed a raw beauty about her. No wonder she could con any red-blooded man into bed with her and persuade him to fall under her spell.

The internal exam completed; the body had been sown up. The single stabbing wound was plainly visible, much more so on her naked body. Murrey saw Tony inspecting the entry wound. "My conclusion from the stabbing wound," Murrey began, "is the same from the initial exam on the dock. Single puncture from a long, slightly curved, very sharp knife. I'm sticking with the assessment this was a ten-inch-long fillet knife. A little longer than most knives you might find in a tackle box, but not uncommon for anglers who work on larger fish.

I have the actual cause of death to be suffocation. Molly may have bled out from the stabbing, but it would have taken a while. I'm concluding she was kicked off the pier, under the railing, and fell face first into the creek, which at that point in time and location would have been about two feet deep. She sank to the bottom and into the pluff mud where she lost consciousness, then shortly thereafter suffocated. That was the end of Molly."

"So, no evidence of a struggle? No incriminating shreds of clothing or DNA under the fingernail kind of thing?"

"Afraid not, Detective. Not that I'm trying to do your job or anything, but my guess is that Molly knew her killer. She didn't try to escape, and the killer surprised her with a sudden attack."

Tony smiled. "That would also be my assessment, Detective Kaufman."

"Ok," Murrey continued with a smirk, "now for the good stuff."

Tony broadened his smile. Murrey almost never disappointed with the good stuff.

"The chemical analysis showed Molly had a cornucopia of drugs in her system. Besides THC, cocaine, and methamphetamine, she had significant levels of OxyContin and Percocet. I don't think Molly spent much time sober in her last few weeks."

Or months, or years, thought Tony. "No genuine surprise there, especially with the news of her little late night supermarket shopping spree."

"Yes, I suppose so. Now here's the second little tidbit you may find useful. Molly had a bruise around her stomach area, near to where the knife went in. This would be consistent with what she might have received immediately after the stabbing. A swift kick that knocked her off the pier."

Tony put the two pieces of information together immediately. "A kick that may have left a bloody print on the bottom of the attacker's shoe."

"Exactly."

"And we already know Judge Culligan had blood on the bottom of his shoe. And he offered a convenient alibi."

"So I heard. He could have got Molly's blood on his shoe either with this kick or by stepping in the blood accumulated on the pier floor. That would be impossible to differentiate. But if you found Molly's blood on the bottom of a shoe from another suspect, then you would have something tangible."

Tony put his hand on his chin and thought about this discovery. It was simply too early to tell whether this implicated Rudy more. But if they could find another bloody shoe, it may very well exonerate him. "Good work, Murrey. I'll pass this along to Leroy. Anything else you got?"

Murrey grinned from ear to ear. He always saved the best for last. "Oh yes. One more interesting discovery." He paused for dramatic effect.

Tony stood by with the anticipation of something big. He wasn't disappointed.

"Molly Elmwood was pregnant."

This shocked even Tony, as his mind spun rapidly to its implication. "How far along?" he asked.

"From the size of the fetus, I'd say about ten weeks. The knife went straight through the fetus. That's how I found it."

Tony shook his head at the thought of such a terrible way to end a pregnancy. Then switched his thinking to something more tangible. "So, then the question is —"

Murrey smiled, finishing the question. "Who's the daddy?"

CHAPTER 29

By the time Tony returned to his office, Randy had just arrived at the station. Twenty minutes earlier, Randy stood outside the Bluefin Marina on the South Santee River, filling his johnboat with gas and contemplating his options. He'd been on the river for a day and a half. His bottles of Jack Daniels were empty, as was the gas in his tank. His lawyer had left at least a dozen messages on his phone, as had the Sheriff's department. He didn't want to return to the Waccamaw fish camp yet — he was still smarting from the fight he had with Benny on Saturday morning. But he had to eat, and he certainly wasn't going to show up at Culligan's Way. There was food at the fish camp, as well as his pickup truck. As with many times before, eventually, he had to face reality.

When Randy pulled into the marina, the shopkeeper, Rufus Dressler, recognized him immediately, having seen him there plenty of times before for gas and supplies. Today, Rufus identified the elder Culligan son as the same person on the wanted poster which hung on the wall behind the cash register. He dialed 911, and the cops were on their way before Randy even started pumping. Rufus made sure his loaded 38 Special was in easy reach, in case Randy caused any trouble.

But trouble found Randy first. He went inside to pay for gas and a pack of Camels and looked behind Rufus to see his mug shot grinning back at him. At that same moment, he heard police sirens closing in. In a panic, Randy raced out of the store without paying (another charge they'd tack on later) and made a run for his boat. He didn't make it. Two of Leroy's deputies cut him off before Randy could step on to the dock. A brief scuffle ensued before they made Randy an offer he couldn't refuse. He could accompany the deputies to the precinct without handcuffs for questioning, or he could take the same ride with his hands cuffed behind his back under arrest. Leroy told his deputies under no circumstance were they to let him know about Molly's murder. If he had to be arrested, Leroy was sure they would think of something. However, the cuffs weren't needed. Randy's memory from the last arrest only three days ago was still fresh on his mind. They rode to Georgetown in silence.

When they arrived at the station, Leroy and Tony were waiting for him. Randy asked to call his lawyer and was told if need be, he could, but right now they simply wanted some background information on a breaking case. Randy shrugged and agreed, and now sat in the windowless room with the two law enforcement agents.

"Randy, we appreciate you coming in today for questioning," said Leroy. "Let's begin with where you've been for the last day and a half."

Randy darted his eyes back and forth between the two interrogators. "I was on my boat, alone, minding my own business."

"Why didn't you go back to your fish camp on the Waccamaw?" asked Tony.

"I had an altercation with my friend Benny. I didn't wish to be around him this weekend."

Leroy and Tony nodded at each other. That part added up. "Where were you at midnight on Saturday night after the party at the Culligans?" asked Leroy.

Randy looked at them cautiously. Again, he nervously glanced between Leroy and Tony. "I went back to the beach at the Way a little before midnight that night. I know you told me to wait until the morning, but I had nowhere else to go that night. I .. I wasn't myself. Guess I was depressed."

Leroy rolled his eyes. "Ok, so I asked you, where were you at midnight?"

"I just told you I was on my boat!"

Now Leroy wanted to slap him. "*Where* Randy? *Where* were you on your boat?"

Randy replied with all innocence, "I was sitting in my seat."

Leroy lost his patience. He reached across the table and slapped Randy square across the side of his face. "Try again, you nitwit!"

"Ok, ok. Jeez. I drove down the coast to the Santee River. Been in and around there ever since."

Tony looked at Leroy and nodded, now having caught Randy in a lie. "You're lying, Randy. You didn't go straight down the coast, did you? Where did you go first?"

Randy's expression changed to a devious look. Whatever was in his mind that thought he could fool the Sheriff and his detective, he gave it one more try. "I told you, I went straight down the coast, past Georgetown to the Santee."

"That's bullshit, Randy, and you know it. Show it to him, Sheriff."

Leroy took out Molly's phone, called up the text and showed it to Randy. "You want to change your story now?"

Randy looked at the phone and the text message he had exchanged with Molly. "That's Molly's phone. What are you two doing with it?"

The two cops looked keenly at their suspect. He wasn't hooked up to a lie detector yet, but from their experience, they knew what to expect next. His response would tell them what they were looking for.

"Molly Elmwood was murdered after midnight Saturday at the Culligan's dock. You were there. Start telling us the truth!" Tony demanded.

Randy stared blankly back at the two. Tony would tell Leroy much later that, in all honesty, Randy's first impression of the news seemed to be one of genuine surprise, not feigned surprise. But then, with a man of Randy's dubious background, you could never tell for sure.

"What? Murdered? She's dead?" Randy paused, trying to digest the shocking news. "How?" he asked next.

"Before we get to that," Leroy broke in, "let's go back to what happened after you retrieved your boat on the beach in back of the Culligan house." He intentionally didn't say 'your' house. If it ever was, he doubted it would be any longer.

Randy collected himself, now seeing the potential serious trouble he was in. "Ok," he began slowly, "I sent Molly that text, some time after you asked me to leave the house. I had intended to speak with her at the party, but I didn't see her there — and, well, you know, other things happened. So she replied to meet me at the dock at 12:10 AM, not early, which I found a little strange but, I mean I was just glad she would meet me. I needed to clear the air about the problem the other week. That's all I wanted to do; I swear it."

So, I rode into the inlet and around to our dock. I think it was maybe a little later, maybe 12:20 AM. and she wasn't there. No one was there. I remember seeing a little two-seat skiff tied up on the dock. I didn't recognize it from anywhere, so I hung around a few minutes, but the place was quiet and she wasn't anywhere to be seen, so I left, maybe ten minutes later. Then I rode down to South Santee, where I've been until you picked me up. That's the truth, Sheriff, I'll swear to it."

Leroy and Tony looked at each other, then back at Randy. "Ok, Randy," said Leroy. "That's all we're going to need for now. Your free to go. But let me make myself clear. I don't want to find out you've run off somewhere. That would look terrible for you. I suggest you go back to your Waccamaw fish camp where we can find you if we need to and stay off the water. Do what ever it is you do there. We'll be in touch with you shortly."

The two rose to show the interview was over. "Wait, what about Molly?" Randy cried out. "What happened to her? How was she killed? Do you know who did it? Was it my father?"

Leroy was just about to let Randy go without another word until Randy mentioned Rudy. Tony's ears perked up. Leroy took the bait. "Now why would you suspect Judge Culligan killed Molly?"

"I got my reasons," retorted Randy.

"I'm listening."

"I'm not saying anything about that without my lawyer present."

Now he's going to lawyer up, thought Leroy. "Have it your way, Randy. We can easily arrange that."

CHAPTER 30

Later that afternoon, Tony caught back up with Leroy in his office. "I just sent you an email with some interesting video footage," Tony told him, taking a seat across from his desk. "What's the latest from your end?"

"Well, not too much, I'm afraid. I've been stewing over what Randy knows about Rudy. Does he have something on him or is he just blowing smoke?" Leroy opened his email and saw the message from his detective.

"And what price do you think he's going to want us to pay for the information? We're not at that bridge yet though, Leroy."

"I mean, I don't think Randy has any idea about the Greeley affair. Remember, Molly deleted the text she made up on his phone. And they weren't exactly on speaking terms as of late. You're right, we'll see if it amounts to anything. But I have Randy's DNA sample. He'll be first up to bat for the title of Molly's baby's daddy. And I received word from the dive team. They came up empty-handed today, but they want to give it one more try tomorrow, expand the area some. So, what do we have here?" Leroy saw three video files. The first one labeled 'Lake Murray', then 'North Causeway' and 'South Causeway'. "These look interesting," he said as he clicked on the first one.

Tony came around to Leroy's side of the desk and looked over his shoulder as he narrated. "Well," described Tony, "this is outside the Dockside Marina, down the road from Robert Huntsman's lake house. And there's our judge." With the video date/time stamp showing 4/3 1:38 PM, it showed a white Lexus L450 driving past the marina. The video then skipped ahead to

3:13 PM and showed the same sedan going in the opposite direction. "So that confirms our timeline of where Rudy spent his Saturday before the party."

"Yes, and I've left a voice mail for Huntsman and haven't heard back. We don't seem to have a very cooperative department head on our hands. Plus, from what Rudy told me earlier today, approval for the Salt Cove lots in question was rescinded. Looks like Rudy is going to hang Jack Greeley out to dry."

"Don't be too sure about that, Leroy. We need to talk to Huntsman. And then we need to get Greeley in here to see what he'll spill to us. What's our option if Huntsman stonewalls us?"

Leroy looked back over his shoulder at his detective. Tony was always pushing the envelope. Leroy knew going over Huntsman's head would cost him political capital. Something he was loath to do, especially with going against Judge Culligan. "Tony, I won't push things in that direction. Let's see where the other leads take us first. Now," he continued, opening the North Causeway video clip, "what do we have here?"

"Ok," said Tony, switching gears. "This is the Walgreen security camera facing the North Causeway. I have all the traffic between 11:30 PM Saturday night and 12:45 AM. There are eight cars and trucks that went onto the North Causeway from Highway 17 before midnight. Now, some of them may not have crossed the bridge, but that's ok. The camera is too far from the road to make out any license plate numbers or make a positive ID on the driver."

Leroy watched each of the eight vehicles drive down the road past the camera. "Alright, what's next?"

"So, we watched the footage until 12:45 AM and did not see any vehicles exiting Pawleys Island. That's it for the North Causeway. Now open the South Causeway. This is where things get interesting."

Leroy opened the third video and saw a view from the canopy of a gas station pump. "Ok, so what am I looking at here?"

"This is the view from the Circle K station pump, next to the Raw Bar restaurant at the head of the South Causeway. Same time frame, 11:30 PM to 12:45 AM. We see fifteen cars driving south on the causeway before midnight. Again, some, if not most, did not cross the bridge. But after the murder, from 12:10 AM to 12:45 AM, there is only one car that came down the South Causeway headed back to the mainland. And it's the same car that went on the island from the North Causeway."

Leroy could feel the hair stand up on the back of his neck. He sensed he was about to witness something very significant.

"Here she is now. And even better, she cut through the gas station parking lot as a shortcut to get back on 17 heading north."

Leroy watched as a black Ford Escape appeared and drove right by the pump camera. The car was clearly visible, as was the driver and the license plate.

Tony stopped the video at this point. "That's our vehicle of interest. We just need to ID the plate and find out who she is."

Leroy stared at the screen, speechless. For a second, his mouth opened without a sound. Then he groaned. "Oh, my fucking Jesus!"

Tony looked at his boss, astonished. "Boss, you know who she is?"

Leroy turned and stared at Tony dead in the eyes. "You bet I do. That's Sally Hobart. Sally *Culligan* Hobart. Rudy's elder daughter."

******

Meanwhile, the younger Culligan daughter sat in her jail cell, suffering from detox shakes. Connie had spent a miserable sleepless Sunday night, the first night she didn't have her usual fix of pot and OxyContin in weeks. Then she couldn't keep the jailhouse breakfast down. She spent the rest of Monday in a depressed funk, thinking only of when her father would bail her out so she could get her next fix. The fact that she only had three more OxyContins, and no cash, didn't faze her one bit. The thought of going back to rehab never entered her mind. Neither did the legal mess she had put herself in. All she could think about was getting high.

After the revelation on the Circle K security video, Leroy hatched a new plan to kill two birds with one stone. He told Tony to give him thirty minutes and then meet him out front. They and Connie were going to take a ride up to Pawleys Island to pay a visit to her sister, then head out to Culligan's Way. First, Leroy had to clear things with his DA, then make a call to Rudy and explain what was about to happen.

When he arrived at Connie's jail cell, he found was a sniveling mess. From the looks of the poor girl, she couldn't get to rehab soon enough. With any luck, Leroy figured she'd be there by dinner.

Connie looked up from her cell cot when Leroy appeared. "Am I free to go now, Sheriff?" she asked hopefully.

"You'll be leaving here, Connie, but you won't be having any freedom for a while." Leroy entered the cell and sat down next to Connie.

"What do you mean?"

"Let me explain to you what's going to happen next, young lady. I've talked with the DA and your father, and they have agreed to this plan. So, before I lay it out to you, I want to make sure you understand what you'd be facing should you not agree to it. We have you in possession of a controlled substance, stolen narcotics. But that's nothing compared to a charge of aiding and abetting a grand larceny."

"I told you, Sheriff, I had nothing to do with that!" Connie groaned.

"Be quiet child and listen to me. Don't interrupt me again. The first thing you need to know is that your partner in crime, Molly Elmwood, is dead. She was murdered late Saturday night on the pier by your house."

This put a pin in Connie, as she gaped back at Leroy in surprised silence.

"Now, we don't believe her murder has anything to do with this drug theft from Publix, but you are going to help us in the investigation, as I'll explain to you later."

Connie sat still; she was all ears now.

Leroy continued, "Now don't even begin to tell me you weren't involved with the drug theft. Your brother, Tim, overheard the conversation you had with Molly in your bedroom at the party. The one where you argued about being gouged on the OxyContin price, and where you were told you were well paid for stealing the keys to Publix from Sally. We have that on record. Tim told this to Sally, and that's what prompted the fight you had with her. Since then, we have a record from Ace Hardware, two days before the first theft of three key copies made, and video evidence of you making the purchase. That puts you on very thin ice. Are you with me so far?"

Connie nodded her head. It was clear she was stunned by the information overload.

"Good. Publix has already filed charges. But now their thief is dead. That leaves only you as an accomplice. Your father and I both agree you need help more than you need punishment. And, with your consent, that's what's going to happen. But not before you make some apologies. I am going to charge you with the crime I alluded to, to which you will plead no contest. We'll see to it you get a deferred sentence of community service after a successful completion of a stay in rehab. Probation and a period of negative drug testing will then keep you out of prison. Do you understand this?"

Leroy could tell that reality now dawned on Connie. She would not be going home to get high; she would face a long period of sobriety. It could be in jail or back in rehab. It was this reality that was so sobering.

"I.. I think so. It doesn't appear I have any choice in the matter."

"Oh, no Connie — you have a choice. You can choose to stay here in jail, fight a losing battle in court, which won't be much of a battle because you have no funds and Judge Culligan has already told me he will not pay for any such defense. Then, after your public defender loses your case, you can spend three to five years at the woman's penitentiary up in Columbia. That's your choice, Connie. Is that what you want to do?"

"No sir." Reality now bit even harder.

"Good, then let's get started. Your father is waiting for you."

******

Ten minutes later, Leroy knocked on Rudy's chambers door.

"Come in," he barked.

Leroy and Connie made their way into the chambers. Connie looked down at her feet, unable to make eye contact.

Leroy broke the silence. "Judge, your daughter has agreed to the terms we discussed. When we're done here, Connie will appear at the Pawleys Publix, where I believe her sister and the GM will be glad to hear what she has to say. A rep from the Center of Hope rehab center will meet her at the Way after that. I'll forward the proper paperwork on to the required parties."

Rudy understood it was now between the father and the daughter. Both were in an awkward position, and the silence proved it.

Finally, Rudy broke the impasse. "Connie, what do have to say for yourself?"

Connie hadn't looked up since she entered the chambers. But Rudy could tell she was crying.

When she finally looked up at her father, her face appeared soaked with tears. "I'm so sorry, Daddy, I am so sorry. Please, I promise to get better this time. I *promise.*" Then she broke down again and was speechless.

Rudy had heard enough. Whether it was a grieving victim's mother, an apologetic defendant, a long line of plaintiffs robbed of their wealth, their health, or their sense of self-worth, or in this case, his youngest daughter — Rudy had seen and heard every kind of emotional breakdown. He understood, and to an extent empathized with many, but in the end, he saw crying as weak. And he had no tolerance for weakness in his position of authority.

"That's enough, child," he answered, as if Connie was a delicate eight-year-old and not a twenty-four-year-old grown spoiled woman. "Look at me."

Connie wiped the tears and snot off her face with the sleeve of her shirt and turned her head towards her father. She shuddered when she met his eyes.

Rudy calmly walked around the side of his massive desk and took Connie in his arms. They hugged for a full minute while Connie continued to heave sobs into his chest. Finally, Rudy lifted her chin with his finger and said, "Never again, Connie. Do you understand me? This will *never, ever,* happen again. Will you swear to it?"

"I swear to it, Daddy. I do, I really do. Never again." The sobs returned.

Rudy had heard enough. "Thank you, Leroy, for taking this on. I'll catch up with you again in the morning." The meeting concluded.

"You're welcome, Judge. I'll talk to you later. Come on, Connie, let's get you home."

CHAPTER 31

Twenty-five minutes later, Leroy's Sheriff SUV and Tony's cruiser were parked outside the Pawleys Island Publix. Bud had been notified and he told Sally the cops were coming to discuss the robbery, so don't go anywhere. Leroy didn't tell Bud he also had a much more important topic to discuss with his assistant manager. Also unknown to Sally was that another of Leroy's deputies was on their way to Publix to impound Sally's Ford Escape for a thorough inspection once the interview had concluded.

By the time they were ready to go inside, Connie had stabilized her emotions somewhat, but it was clear to Leroy the face to face with her sister was something Connie did not look forward to. Leroy told her it would be a quick meeting, and if she made it through the meeting with her father, she could make it through this one. He assured her he'd be right by her side, and nothing would get out of hand.

The first stop, once inside, was Bud's office. Bud rose from his desk and greeted Leroy, then invited both of them to sit down.

"Mr. Wright, as I discussed over the phone, we are here to wrap up the robbery of your pharmacy. As you know, the perpetrator, Molly Elmwood, was found murdered yesterday morning outside the Culligan's home in Pawleys Island. So, obviously there will be no charges against her. Her accomplice is sitting beside me. Your charges against her were recorded and I am here to inform you that Miss Culligan has agreed to plead no contest to the aiding and abetting charge."

This caught Bud by surprise. "Excuse me, Sheriff, I did not agree to allow a plea bargain for this criminal here."

Leroy chuckled. "Mr. Wright, it doesn't work that way, sir. The District Attorney has the last word in what pleas she may or may not accept. Here, she accepted the no contest plea in exchange for community service, mandatory successful rehab, and consequent drug testing, probation, and an apology. That's why we're here today, sir. In addition, we're processing the materials found in Miss Elmwood's apartment and will return a portion of the narcotics that were stolen. This should happen within the next couple of days. If you would like to sue to regain the remaining value of the drugs lost, that is your prerogative."

Bud crossed his arms to show he wasn't happy. Leroy didn't know he almost never wore a different expression. "So, no prison time, then?"

"No sir. Connie is here to apologize to you and Sally. Then I need to talk with Sally alone for a minute, and then we'll be on our way."

"Very well then," Bud stared straight at Connie, indicating she was free to talk.

Connie shivered. "M..Mr. Wr..Wright, sir, I am deeply sorry for the trouble I have caused you and Sally and Publix. I have promised to get sober and stay sober and never get into trouble again. I hope you can forgive me, sir."

Leroy was glad to hear the apology without tears this time. Two down, one to go.

Bud had clearly heard enough. "Very well then," he told both his visitors. Finish your business with Sally and be on your way. I need to get back to work."

Leroy and Connie rose and left Bud's office, then walked two doors down and knocked on Sally's office. "Come in," she answered. "Have a seat," she said without looking up as they both entered the small office. Sally exited the computer file she had been working on and looked up at Connie, completely expressionless.

Leroy could tell, behind her eyes, Sally fumed. "Connie expressed her apology to Bud, Sally. She'll have her say here, then we have some other business to discuss."

Sally broke her glare and looked at Leroy, somewhat surprised. Then she turned her attention back to Connie. "Go ahead, say what you want to say. Don't ask me to forgive you, though."

Leroy rolled his eyes. She definitely got her hard edge from her father. And her mother, he supposed. While Connie spit out another tear stained, hesitant apology, Leroy looked straight at Sally, who never broke her death-stare at her younger sister. When Connie finished, Tony and Chris were waiting outside the door. Leroy handed Connie off to his deputy, then he and Tony took seats back in Sally's office and closed the door.

Now Sally's expression changed from a glower to one of surprise tinged with a dose of anxiety. "What's this all about, Sheriff?"

"Sally, this is Detective Meacham. He's the lead investigator on the Elmwood murder." He gauged Sally's reaction.

"Ok," she responded slowly, shaking Tony's hand. "I already gave you my story, Sheriff. I went home from the party and went to bed."

"Yes, we know that. Now, I'm going to give you an opportunity to change your story to one that more closely fits the truth." Leroy caught the slight change in Sally's facial expression. The one that ever so slightly shifted from confusion to fear.

"I don't know what you're talking about," she replied, again with a grain of trepidation mixed in. "Why don't you enlighten me?"

Leroy looked over at Tony. "Detective, please enlighten our suspect." Sally's mouth opened slightly when she heard herself referred to as a suspect.

"Gladly, Sheriff." He already had the photo of Sally in her car at the gas station by the South Causeway, along with the date and time stamp, called up on his phone. "Sally, can you confirm this is you?"

He handed the phone to Sally, who gasped. Now her expression more resembled the proverbial deer in the headlight. "Where did you get this?" she asked.

"I'm sorry, Sally," responded Tony, "but we're the ones asking the questions here. And we'd like an answer."

Sally stared at Leroy and Tony, dumbfounded.

Leroy could tell Sally was trying to determine in her mind what the least offensive thing she could say would be.

"Yes," she answered without emotion. "Yes, that's me, in my car, driving back home after midnight Saturday night."

Leroy nodded his head. Now we're getting somewhere.

Tony took his phone and sat back down. "Alright then, so let's hear your latest story of why you went back on to the island and were there at the time of Molly's murder."

"No!" Sally answered, clearly startled. "No, I wasn't there at the time of the murder. I swear it, Sheriff. Let me explain."

Leroy and Tony sat silently with their arms folded.

"Ok," Sally gulped and took a deep breath. "I did go back to the island shortly before midnight, by the North Causeway. I knew Molly was going to be there on the pier at midnight, with Tim, because I overheard part of the conversation between Tim and Molly earlier at the party. I didn't want Molly anywhere near Tim. He's so vulnerable now." Sally looked at the two officers for any sympathy but found none. "So, when Steve and I went to bed after my abrupt exit, I couldn't sleep. I just couldn't let it go. I felt I needed to confront Molly about the drug theft, and other things she, you know, has caused trouble with our family."

Tony raised an eyebrow and jotted down a note.

"So, I got out of bed without waking Steve, and drove back on the island. But I didn't want to confront Molly when she was there with Tim. I parked two houses down and watched them from a neighbor's pier, with binoculars. When they kissed, I was furious."

"Excuse me!" Leroy interrupted. "They *kissed*?"

"Yeah, they kissed. They had a thing back in high school. They worked together at the Pelican Inn for a summer."

Tony wrote more notes.

"And then Tim left and went back inside. But I froze. For one second of clarity, I didn't let my emotions get the best of me. I remember flashing a scene in my mind — what a fight with Molly would be like. Nothing good could have come from it, and probably something terrible would have happened to either, or both of us. So, I left. You might say I chickened out. I got back in my car and turned around and left. Came back on the South Causeway and cut across the gas station. That's where you got my picture there. But when I left, Molly was still standing on the pier, looking south, like she was waiting for someone else. I know this doesn't look good for me, Sheriff Keating, but I swear it's the truth."

Leroy looked down and shook his head. More unexpected developments with another Culligan. When he looked up, Sally anxiously awaited his response. "And Steve never knew you were gone?"

"No, he was sound asleep when I left and was still asleep when I slipped back into bed. You can imagine how I felt when we arrived back at the Way for dinner yesterday."

"Yeah, I bet. Tony, what do you think?"

"Sally, did you see or hear anything else from the Culligan pier before you left? Anyone coming out of the house?"

"No, I didn't see anyone coming out of the house."

"Did you hear anything? A boat on the creek?"

"No sir. I didn't hear or see anything. Molly was facing the other way; she never knew I was there."

"Ok, Sally, we've heard your explanation. We're going to impound your Escape for evidence. If you would give us the key, we should have it back to you by the end of tomorrow."

"Is that really necessary, Sheriff?" Sally protested.

"It is," reprimanded Leroy, clearly irritated. "And if we find one drop of blood in that car, you can expect to be arrested. You already lied to us once. You better hope you didn't just lie to us again. We'll be in touch with you soon."

Sally reluctantly removed the Ford key from her key ring and handed it to Leroy. "Please do," she meekly replied. As the two law enforcement agents left her office, Sally collapsed in her chair, shellshocked and dazed.

*****

Tim, Ruth and Anabelle were waiting outside Culligan's Way when the two patrol vehicles pulled into the carport. Connie feared the worst when she exited and faced her mother, having been on the receiving end of her wrath many times before. But as she saw Ruth approach with a look which appeared to have more empathy than scorn, Connie eased her anxiety and let her mother embrace her.

"Connie dear," Ruth began after she released her daughter. "How are you feeling? Did they treat you alright in that nasty jail?" Ruth cast a sideways glance towards Leroy. She would have a word with him before he left concerning his truly reprehensible decision to keep her obviously ailing daughter overnight in a jail cell meant for common criminals.

"Sure, Mom," Connie replied, relieved to sense Ruth's support. "It was just like the Ritz."

"Humph," Ruth muttered back. "The Ritz don't have rats." This time, she looked directly at Leroy, daring him to disagree.

Leroy grimaced and shook his head. "Neither do our cells, Mrs. Culligan. I assure you; Connie was well taken care of. But she needs help." He looked around, somewhat disappointed the van for Center of Hope hadn't arrived yet. "Center of Hope should be here any minute. In the meantime, I'd like to get our one item of business taken care of and then we'll be on our way."

"Of course, Sheriff. We wouldn't want to stand in the way of our wonderful law enforcement. Connie, come inside when you're finished. I have something for you before you leave."

Tim and Annabelle took turns giving Connie hugs and assurances. "I feel so bad for you, Connie," said Tim. "I know you're going to come through this in flying colors."

Connie grinned back at her brother. "I hope so. I hope it will be different from the black and blue I feel now. I can't believe I have to leave so soon after you got home. I'm so sorry about what happened at your party. And everything else." Connie's emotions got the better of her as she started crying all over again. Tim went in for another hug.

When it was Annabelle's turn, Connie looked at her long-time housekeeper and friend and simply said, "I'm sorry, Annabelle," as they embraced.

"You be fine, child," Annabelle answered in her unique voice, containing both sternness and comfort. "They take good care of you where you're going. You come back to us in one piece, you hear?"

Connie heard. "I will, Annabelle. I promise." She turned to Leroy and Tony. "I guess I'm ready."

"Alright then. Tony, take Connie to the spot on the pier and wait for my signal. Mrs. Culligan, let's go out to the back deck and show me where you saw Rudy late Saturday night."

Connie and Tony crossed the street to the pier as the others made their way up the stairs to the front entrance. All four dutifully removed their shoes before entering the house. Ruth, Tim, and Leroy made their way out to the back deck, while Annabelle tended to her chores in the kitchen.

Once outside, Ruth pointed to the lounge chair closest to the beach access gate. "That's where I saw the old fool before I went to bed."

"Thank you, Mrs. Culligan." Leroy went to the lounge and took a seat. Tim and Ruth took seats in two of the back deck rockers. Leroy closed his eyes and tried to picture himself as Rudy sipping his bourbon after midnight Saturday, unaware of anything which would disturb the tranquility of the evening. He called into his radio, "In position, Tony — you all set?"

"Ten four, Sheriff. We're ready to rock and roll," came the radio response.

"Ok, turn the radio off and let her rip."

"Radio off." Leroy turned his radio off as well.

Back on the pier, Tony gave Connie a last instruction. "One scream now, girl. As loud as you can make it."

Connie nodded and drew a deep breath. She summoned all the emotion bottled up inside her — her angst, her addiction, her fear, and her unrestrained anger at the world and everything about it that had put her in this position and screamed as loud as she could.

On the back deck, the three listeners looked at each other with widened eyes. Leroy nodded his head and turned the radio back on. "We got it, Tony, loud and clear. You can head back to the station. I'll be along in a few minutes." Leroy turned to Ruth and Tim. "Mrs. Culligan, if you would excuse us for a minute. I need to have a word with Tim." Leroy watched Ruth stare curiously at him. He knew she felt entitled to take part in the conversation. "Privately," he added.

Ruth's expression changed to resignation. "As you wish, Sheriff," she replied and went back inside.

Tim turned to Leroy. "What is it Sheriff?" Leroy could tell his voiced tinged with anxiety.

"Tim, we just found out there was another witness to your conversation with Molly the other night."

This caught Tim by surprise. "You did? And who was that?"

"Your sister, Sally," Leroy replied calmly, watching Tim for any signs of foreknowledge.

"Wow! I didn't know that. I thought she said she went straight home after her, um, her exit from the party."

"She said that. But then changed her story after we saw her car on security tape outside the island just after midnight." Leroy knew what would come next.

"So, then, did she see who killed Molly?" he asked hopefully.

"She did not. Her statement stated she went to back to the island to confront Molly after overhearing the conversation between you and Molly at the party arranging the late-night meeting. She parked two houses down and watched you both from another pier. When she saw you leave, she got cold feet and turned around without a confrontation. She claims she did not see the murder, even though it happened soon afterwards." Leroy studied Tim's reaction, which seemed to be genuine shock.

"I'm stunned, Sheriff. I had no idea."

"Yes, well, so were we. She also told us something else which was left out of your statement, Tim. She said she saw you two kissing right before you left. Is that true?"

Tim gulped as a pale look came over his face. He took a deep breath. Leroy could tell he was shaking. "Yes," Tim said, looking down, as if ashamed of himself. "Yes, we did. We were quite close back in my high school days. We worked together at the Pelican Inn for two summers. I'm not sure if you were aware of this. So, yes, we kissed, briefly. That had nothing to do with her murder. That's why I didn't tell you earlier." Tim grimaced at the way he just sounded. Leroy picked up on it.

"Tim, it's not your call to determine what is relevant or not in our investigation. When we asked for a complete accounting of your time on the pier, that's what we expected. Now, is there anything else relevant that you're not telling us?"

Tim gazed at the Sheriff. Leroy saw he was clearly stunned by the rebuke. "No sir," he said hesitatingly. "No sir, there isn't."

"I hope not, Tim. I surely hope not."

CHAPTER 32

Tuesday morning began hopefully for Leroy. He had high expectations the dive team would find the murder weapon today. He also looked forward to the final autopsy and the DNA results from Molly's poor unborn fetus. Plus, he now had Connie taken care of and Sally's car in impound, with the results due back later in the day. This was all shattered, however, by an early morning phone call from WCXM News, which came in on the landline at 6:15 AM.

Doris picked up the phone, and said, "Just a minute," then handed the receiver to Leroy as he sat at the breakfast table, moving around his eggs and toast. She took a seat and listened in to his side of the call.

"Hello, who is this?" Leroy answered, then shut his eyes tight. "And how did you get this number?" Another pause. "The *White Pages?* They don't print White Pages anymore." Leroy shook his head back and forth. "Ok, so they do still have them. What do you want?" Doris watched her husband's face slowly contort into a grimace, then a frown, then finally an explosion of rage. *"What did you say?"* he shouted into the phone. "Where did you get this information?" Pause. "Oh, of course you can't reveal your source. I know damn well where you got your source. And you can bet your ass I'll be having a talk with Sheriff Shepard this morning." Doris knew Lawrence Shepard, the Horry County Sheriff in charge of the Myrtle Beach metro area, had a good relationship with Leroy. She continued to listen with mounting concern. "You media people have got to respect the boundaries of the law." One more pause, then "Yes, I'll be watching. Good day." Leroy put the receiver down and pushed aside his breakfast plate. He had lost his appetite.

"And what, pray tell, was that all about?" asked Doris.

Leroy pinched his nose and shook his head. "Channel 12 is about to run a news story about the Greeley case from a source they never should have been able to get. But first I need to run down the street and get a copy of the Times." Leroy rose and went to the bedroom to retrieve his wallet and keys. On the way out the door, he told his wife, "You know Doris, sometimes this job just isn't worth it." Doris watched in stunned silence as her husband stormed out the front door.

******

If Leroy was having an awful morning, it was nothing compared to Jack Greeley's. Jack still smarted from the news of Molly's death, once again having to face the reality of spending life with his nagging wife. He fumed at Rudy's about face regarding the Salt Cove lot permits. More damage control needed to be done there, including having to stoop to directly begging Robert Huntsman at DHEC to approve the two lots where trees had already been removed. At least they hadn't started pouring concrete yet. He regretted this whole affair with Rudy and DHEC. Served him right getting a sitting county judge involved in the dirty politics of government environmental policy. But he wasn't done with Rudy yet. Jack still had a few cards up his sleeve.

Those cards turned out to be jokers when he opened his front door to retrieve his usual morning version of the Myrtle Beach Times. He planned on a casual read over a simple breakfast of coffee, Cheerios, milk and bananas — he was trying to cut back on the days he went to the diner for bacon, ham, grits and eggs — doctor's orders and whatnot. Instead, the most shocking headline he had ever seen in his life assaulted him. In bold two-inch tall letters above the fold, the eye-catching caption read:

GREELEY CONSTRUCTION TO OUR BALD EAGLES — F U

A sub-heading declared: **Secret sex tape of murdered Murrells Inlet woman incriminates local construction CEO and Georgetown County judge in a pay for permit scheme.**

Jack thought he was going to have a coronary. "What the holy fuck!" he screamed at the paper now shaking in his hands, then staggered back to the kitchen table and collapsed in his chair.

His wife, Karen, looked at him with interest. "What is it, dear? What does the paper say?"

Jack ignored her as he speed-read through the article. Every few seconds he'd moan, "Oh no, oh no, oh shit." Then he got to the juicy part. The part where he was suddenly glad Molly Elmwood was dead, because if she wasn't, he would have gone straight over to her place and strangled her.

And there was Karen, looking over his shoulder, increasingly concerned by the subject of the article. The paper quoted word for word the conversation Jack now so regretted having in bed with Molly, the one where he called his wife the old bag.

Jack quickly closed the paper and looked at the clock — 6:28 AM. He had to see if this nuclear weapon was going to be on the 6:30 AM News. "It's a smear piece, Karen. That's all it is.

Probably one of my competitors trying to make me look bad." Jack went to the living room and turned on the TV. He felt like a cornered rat. There was no way he could keep Karen from reading the article, and if they played that tape on the news. Oh my God, he thought. I am so screwed.

"What's this about a sex tape with you and another woman? Don't ignore me, Jack!"

While Jack ignored his wife, he quickly weighed the consequences of WCXM playing the tape on air for them both to hear against the uncertainty he'd have if he didn't. He decided he simply had to know. So at 6:30 AM on the dot, Jack sat down alongside his soon to be ex-wife and witnessed the final act of his own Passion Play.

"Good morning, everyone," spoke the sparkling, white-toothed newscaster with wavy, curled blonde hair, "I'm Katie Underwood and this is the WCXM Morning News."

"God," groaned Jack to himself. "She even looks like Molly."

"News broke early this morning of a strange new twist in the Molly Elmwood murder investigation. If you recall from our previous reporting, police found Molly murdered outside the home of Georgetown County Judge Rudolph Culligan on Sunday morning. Now, just two days later, WCXM has received an audiotape of a secret recording between Molly and Jack Greeley of Greeley Construction out of Myrtle Beach. From the tape, it appears Molly and Jack were involved romantically, and Molly questions Jack about controversial marsh lot permits in the Murrells Inlet Salt Cove development. Jack has some unkind words regarding our natural wildlife, then promptly implicates

Judge Culligan in a pay for permit scheme, also involving the South Carolina Department of Health and Environmental Control. But before we get to the content of the tape, our onsite reporter, Heidi Dexter, has an update on the Salt Cove controversy when Greeley Construction destroyed two ancient live oak trees on the marsh front. Heidi."

"Thank you Katie. WCXM received exclusive footage of a scene which played out during the first stages of the marsh front development in Salt Cove. Here we see environmental activist Harvey Klinger chaining himself to one of the live oak trees in a futile attempt to save the tree and stop the construction, which he claimed did not have proper clearance to develop."

Jack and Karen watched in silent awe as the tape showed Harvey pitching a fit, as they released his chains with a large set of bolt-cutters. The clip went into his brief description of the unauthorized permits and ended with his skinny ass hauled into a Horry County cruiser. Jack remembered being informed of the incident last week and was relieved the clip didn't make it on the news then. Now, it just added fuel to the fire.

"So now, Heidi," Katie asked with great interest, "it appears that Mr. Klinger's protest may have had some merit to it."

"That's right, Katie." Heidi now sported a pouty look, a prelude to the first of the two-part bombshell. "And the sad fact which Mr. Klinger pointed out is that the particular tree taken down had been a long-time home to a bald eagle family."

"Which makes the accusation in the audio tape even more disturbing," quipped Katie, now in full eagle defense mode.

"I'm afraid so," lamented the same reporter who, five days earlier, bemoaned the station's decision not to air her piece much more than the plight of a couple birds. Still, "But I'm happy to report that they have temporarily halted construction in Salt Cove until this controversy is settled. Back to you, Katie."

"Thank you, Heidi. Now, as I mentioned earlier, the audio tape obtained by WCXM between the now murdered Molly Elmwood and the President of Greeley Construction, Jack Greeley. As a warning, this tape contains graphic detail. Viewer discretion is advised."

Jack braced himself for what he was about to hear, as the screen cut to split photo images of Molly and Jack. It began right at the end of the interlude. Molly moaned. Jack groaned as he climaxed. Molly whispered how wonderful he was. Jack panted, trying to catch his breath.

Karen was not impressed. "Were you having sex with this woman?" she yelled at him.

"It would appear so," admitted the scoundrel.

Karen remained seated and stewed while the tape continued. And there was Jack, tongue now loosened sufficiently, spilling his guts about how Molly's ex's father, Judge Culligan had paved the way for the lots to be approved. How the kickbacks would pay dividends in the long haul.

"But what about the eagles and the ospreys?" Molly asked.

"'Bleep' them," played the edited tape. In the living room, Jack shook his head now recalling the newspaper heading. A brief silence followed, then Jack heard himself again. "Listen Molly, I was thinking about setting you up in a condo here in Myrtle Beach, much nicer than this place you're in now. I should be able to join you pretty soon. I've got to get away from that old bag."

The audio clip ended, and the screen went back to Katie, sitting there with a disgusted look on her face. "Unbelievable," she said, shaking her head, knowing full well she just witnessed media gold. "Mrs. Greeley, I sincerely hope you're not tuning in to this." Mrs. Greeley had indeed tuned out, but not before she dumped the rest of her coffee over her cheating husband's head, then stomped off to her bedroom to call her lawyer.

"So," Katie asked the audience. "Is there a connection between Greeley Construction and the murder of Molly Elmwood? Was Molly silenced for exposing the scheme? What did Judge Culligan do, and how were these lots approved? We have reached out to Jack Greeley, Judge Culligan, DHEC, and the Georgetown County Sheriff's office and we hope to hear from them later today. Be sure to tune in to the WCXM Evening News at 5:00 PM to get the latest on this breaking story."

Katie flashed her glittering smile to the camera once more and the newscast cut to a commercial. Jack sat alone on his couch, both now stained with black coffee, and wondered just how it all went so south, so fast.

CHAPTER 33

Rudy soon joined the list of men entangled by the media's tentacles. He met his as he approached the courthouse steps just after 8:00 AM. Not one to read the morning newspaper or watch any local news, such things were beneath the dignity of his position, Rudy stepped into a hornet's nest as soon as the circus gathered around the courthouse front steps saw him approach. They instantly bombarded him with questions regarding Greeley, Molly, and DHEC. What was his opinion of the sex tape released? Does he support our local wildlife? How much money was he paid in kickbacks? All hurled at him simultaneously to his bewilderment and as he pushed his way through the throng of microphones. Rudy could only mutter "no comment" over and over until he managed to enter the building, where he promptly stormed to his chambers and barked at Janice to get Sheriff Keating on the line.

After a minute, Janice reported Leroy was currently unavailable, but she had left a message for him to contact the Judge as soon as possible. Rudy's call to Leroy's cell went straight to voice mail, where he left another urgent message. He sat stewing in his office for another minute, trying to make sense of what was going on. He ordered Janice to go to the lobby and get him a copy of the Times, then picked up the phone and dialed Jack's cell phone.

Jack answered on the third ring, clearly upset. "What do you want?" he snarled, recognizing the incoming number.

"Jack, what the hell is going on? I was just assaulted by the media outside the courthouse."

Rudy could hear Jack snicker on the other end. "So," he replied, "you haven't seen the news this morning, have you?"

"I have not. Although I have this sinking feeling I wouldn't like what I see. Care to enlighten me?"

"Enlighten *you?*" Jack exploded. "You bastard! Why don't you enlighten me about how the media got hold of a sex tape Molly secretly recorded of us in bed together. The contents of which are all over the news this morning — print and TV — you motherfucker!"

Rudy stared at the phone in disbelief. "I know nothing about a sex tape, Jack. I sincerely hope you didn't mention my name in any of this."

Jack began laughing. Not an amusing laugh, but more like the laugh of a patient in an insane asylum who just played a practical joke on his nurse. "Heh, heh," Jack's laughter calmed a bit. "Your name is all over it, Judge. Elicit payments, kickbacks, interference in government policy. Read the Times today, Judge, when you can break away from your busy schedule. Oh, and don't call me back. Our lawyers can do the talking from here." Jack hung up on Rudy.

Rudy sat stunned in his chambers, unable to piece together the bits of information he just received.

Janice came back with the paper and an anxious look on her face. "I'm so sorry, Judge," she said. "I'm sure this is all a misunderstanding." She laid the newspaper on Rudy's desk and turned to leave.

"Thank you Janice, I'm sure it is," he replied while staring at the headline. In particular, the sub-headline with his title splashed for all the Grand Strand to see. "Janice," he called to her before she left his chambers. "Please hold all my calls, except for Sheriff Keating."

Janice gave her boss a weak smile. "I'll do that, Judge." And she quietly closed the door behind her.

Rudy read the entire article. Halfway through, he had to break and take one of his special high blood pressure pills. The ones he only took when he thought he'd blow out at any instant, like, for example, this instant. Then he deliberated — slowly, thoughtfully, thoroughly — just the way they trained him to do, the way he had done all these many years. Except this time he wasn't considering some common criminal's guilt or innocence. He was worried about his own skin — and how he was going to go about saving it.

******

Leroy dreaded the meeting he had to have at Culligan's Way. He felt sorry for Tim, getting mixed up in all this drama so soon after he arrived home. But it pissed him off Tim would be so careless with the evidence he had copied into his phone. Leroy couldn't bring himself to believe Tim would just hand over the evidence to the media. He didn't know who leaked the tape, but he was sure as hell going to find out — and make sure they leaked nothing else. Leroy cursed himself for not confiscating Tim's phone on Sunday when he had the chance. He left instructions with Tony to get hold of someone at DHEC and get a statement, and to track down Harvey Klinger and see if he was behind any of this mischief.

As he pulled his cruiser onto Springs Ave, for the third consecutive day, Leroy pondered what lay in store for the rest of the day, now that he had a media storm to put out, besides all the other activity already planned. And sure enough, there was the circus, camped out in front of the Way, waiting to pounce. Leroy parked on the other side of the crime tape and first checked on the dive team, who were just getting set up for their second and final day of searching for the murder weapon.

Sensing their good fortune to be in the right place at the right time, the reporters jumped at the chance to get a comment from Leroy as he exited his SUV. They strained at the crime tape as he approached to give a statement. Amid the cacophony of questions cast his way, Leroy simply held up his arms to show he wanted the hyenas to shut up. They did, as if they were musicians of an orchestra responding to their maestro. Leroy looked over the microphones and eager faces and thought for a brief second, this had to be the most bizarre case he had ever been involved with. He took a deep breath.

"All right, all right, I know y'all are chomping at the bit to get some comment about the story on the news this morning. So, I'll make a brief statement and will not be taking questions at this time. Should new information become available, there may or may not be a press conference at the station later today.

The taped recording which was in the paper and on the news this morning was illegally obtained leaked evidence. We are currently tracking down the source of this leak. The information on the tape is not proof of anything and may or may not be used in any court case. I am not at this point going to make any conjecture or speculation about the content heard on the tape. We are working with the Horry County Sheriff's department on the matter concerning Greeley Construction. I am also expecting a statement from DHEC out of Columbia sometime today regarding the permitting of lots in Salt Cove. That is all I have for you now. I will not be taking any questions at this point."

Leroy turned his back on the media crunch as a torrent of questions poured forth. He ducked back under the crime tape and made his way over to the pier to check on the dive team. "Every day another shit show," he muttered to himself, wondering how many more of these days he would have to endure before life returned to normal in his typically sanguine beach community. The dive team assured him they would finish mapping the area of the creek within throwing distance of the dock, probably by one or two o'clock.

Satisfied with the operation in the creek, Leroy lumbered up the front steps of the Way to face Tim, and most likely Ruth as well. He didn't see Anabelle's car and figured she had the day off. Leroy rang the doorbell and removed his shoes. Ruth answered promptly, as Leroy figured she'd been eyeing him ever since he arrived.

"Come in, Sheriff, please come in and tell us what in tarnation is going on out there." Leroy could tell immediately that Ruth was in no mood for chit-chat, which was fine. Neither was he.

"Thank you, Mrs. Culligan. Yes, there's been quite a disturbance this morning. I'm here to explain and to talk with Tim here. Seems he might be at the center of it." Leroy looked over towards Tim, standing behind Ruth. It looked like all the blood had drained from his face.

"Tim?" asked Ruth, with a puzzled look on her face. "What on earth would Tim have to do with your problems here?"

Leroy extended his arm. "Come, both of you. Let's sit at the table and have an honest discussion." Leroy knew there was no way in hell he was going to exclude Ruth from his questioning. It'll serve her well, he thought. Knock her down a peg or two. The three of them made their way to the dining table.

"Can I get you anything to drink, Sheriff Keating? We have coffee and tea Keurigs, and I have some sweet tea in the fridge."

"I'm fine, Mrs. Culligan. But thank you," Leroy declined.

"Tim and I were getting ready to go on a beach walk, so you came at a good time. I assume this has something to do with what was in the papers this morning?" Ruth tersely asked.

Tim looked up. The look on his face changed from anxiety to perplexity. "What was in the papers this morning, Mom?" he asked.

"Here Tim," Leroy laid the copy of the Times he had brought with him down on the dining table. "I assume you haven't seen this yet. And you have Mrs. Culligan?"

"No," Ruth answered, "but I've received three calls from friends in the past hour about this horrific smear piece the Times ran. I thought that outfit held themselves to higher standards than tabloid trash."

Ruth and Tim read the headline. Ruth gasped. Tim closed his eyes and shook his head.

"Would you like to take a minute and read the entire article, Mrs. Culligan? Tim doesn't need to. I believe he already knows what's in it. Don't you Tim?"

Leroy and Ruth both looked at Tim, who at first appeared speechless. "Um, well yes," he said timidly. "I'm afraid I do."

Now Ruth looked completely confused. "I don't understand," she replied.

Leroy could see her jaw clench, anticipating bad news. He knew the next part would hurt. Oh well, he thought, just rip the bandage off. "Well," he began, addressing them both. "It seems the Myrtle Beach Times and WCXM News received an audio clip last night from an unknown source. A clip that was secretly recorded by Molly Elmwood in bed with Jack Greeley, the president of Greeley Construction. The contents of the tape, as listed in the newspaper article and played on this morning's newscast, casts allegations of bribery and interference in government environmental policy between Greeley Construction, Judge Culligan, and the Department of Health and Environmental Control, regarding approval of marsh lot permits in the Salt Cove development." Leroy paused for a second to gauge their reactions.

"So I heard," huffed Ruth, her arms now crossed. "As if anything that came out of that woman's mouth could be believed." Leroy could tell the implications now had hit Tim like a two by four over the head. Ruth continued, "And how does this involve Tim?"

"That's what I came here to find out, Mrs. Culligan. We knew the tape was on Molly's phone. It was in Tim's possession when we first arrived here Sunday morning. Seems Molly and Tim were out on the dock shortly before she was murdered, and she had given Tim her phone for safekeeping."

Ruth sat at the table, thunderstruck. The silence was deafening. Finally Ruth asked Tim, "Is this true, son? You had Molly's phone with you before she was killed?"

"Yes, Mom," Tim muttered reluctantly, still trying to wrap his head around the news leak. "Molly told me at the party she wanted to meet me on the pier at midnight that night. She arrived by boat, and we talked some. She told me she had to flee because her life was in danger, and she gave me her phone to do the right thing. I took the phone and went back inside and went straight to bed. I never looked at what was on the phone, but I forwarded some text messages to my phone before we went to church on Sunday. After Sheriff Keating took Molly's phone, I read through the messages. They're pretty damaging, if you wish to believe them."

"That's all correct, Tim," replied Leroy, "but you left out one other part we discovered later."

"And what's that?" asked Tim.

"That you and Molly kissed, just before you came back inside."

Leroy saw Tim roll his eyes as if to say, thanks for the reminder. Ruth had heard enough. She stood from the table and demanded, "That's just a bunch of hooey! Tim and Molly were not involved. Isn't that correct, Tim?"

Tim pursed his lips as his face turned a deeper shade of red. He wasn't happy with the information revealed so far and knew the worst was still yet to come. "Actually, Mom, that's true too."

This infuriated Ruth. "Who told you that, Sheriff?" she demanded, glowering with her arms crossed.

"See, that's the thing Mrs. Culligan." Leroy spoke in as serious a tone as he could. "In my line of work, we don't divulge sources. And when we ask someone connected to a case who has sensitive information not to share it, we expect them to do just that. Which brings me to the real reason for my visit today." Leroy directed his question to Tim. "Who did you share that audio clip with?"

Ruth suddenly intervened, raising her hands in protest. "I beg your pardon, Sheriff. How dare you make such an accusation towards Tim."

"Mrs. Culligan." Leroy had to bite his tongue not to bark at Ruth to back off. Maybe he shouldn't have let her sit in. He swallowed hard to bite back the bile. "This is between Tim and me. I would appreciate it if you let me finish my interview." It still came out pretty stern.

Both Leroy and Ruth now turned their attention back to Tim, who sported a sheepishly guilty expression on his face. He bit his lip, trying to determine how to best respond. "It must have been Harvey Klinger."

"What!" Ruth cried out. "That creepy man who was here yesterday?"

"Mom, please. Let me talk to the Sheriff." Tim said, exasperated in having to deal with this shocking fresh development and his emotional mother at the same time.

Leroy could clearly see a storm brewing inside her head. He needed to finish his business here as soon as possible and let them sort it out themselves.

"Yes," continued Tim. "Harvey Klinger came by to see me yesterday. We sat out back for a while after I came back from a beach walk. Seemed he was also a close friend of Molly. I didn't give him any of the sensitive information on her phone. I swear it, Sheriff. Most of the stuff we talked about he already knew. In fact, he knew much more about what was happening with this Greeley thing. But ..." Tim paused.

Leroy and Ruth both moved their heads in, hanging on what Tim would say next. "But what, Tim?" asked Ruth, now quite concerned.

"But I played the clip to him. He must have secretly recorded it. I promise you I divulged nothing to the media. Now I see it was a mistake. I'm very sorry."

Seeing Tim consumed with guilt was more than Ruth could take. She shot up from her seat and demanded to Leroy, "I have heard quite enough this morning. You have disturbed my household and my son beyond reason. I'm asking you to leave this instant."

Leroy stood as well, but he wasn't quite ready to leave. "Mrs. Culligan, I'm going to leave as soon as I conclude my business here. And I do not appreciate being talked down to like this. Need I remind you; I have purposely not followed up with the rolling pin assault from last Friday. A little less cooperation might find you facing a charge yourself. Is that what you really want?"

Ruth stood still, her mouth open, appalled by the insinuated threat. "Finish your business then and leave us be," she said curtly. She gave an exacerbated sigh. "Of all the God forsaken things, I just never ..." Ruth trailed off, then turned and walked away towards the kitchen. She had clearly heard enough.

"I apologize to you, Sheriff, for what I did and for mother. Is there anything I can do to make things right?"

"Well, Tim, the cat's out of the bag now. But to avoid any further chance of leaks, I'm going to ask for you to hand over your phone. We'll clear it of any confidential information, and I'll give it to your father to bring home tonight."

"Very well then," Tim replied, then handed Leroy his phone.

His task now completed; Leroy couldn't get out of the place soon enough. He walked past Ruth in the kitchen on his way to the door. "I'll let myself out, Mrs. Culligan. Thank you and Tim for your cooperation. We'll be in touch if we need anything else. Good day now." Leroy glanced once more at Ruth. She glared silently at him. It looked to Leroy like she could melt down at any second. Get me out of this freaking nuthouse, was all he could think to himself as he exited Culligan's Way.

As soon as Leroy left the house, Ruth said to Tim, "Come on son, let's go on our beach walk. There are some things I need to tell you."

CHAPTER 34

Jack wasn't about to take his humiliation lying down. After Karen huffed out of the house to see her lawyer about beginning divorce proceedings, Jack changed his coffee-soaked shirt and called his own lawyer to meet him at his office in thirty minutes. Leonard Baxley and his firm Baxley and Sons had been Greeley's legal representation ever since Jack founded the company in 1997. Although they didn't have a perfect record, what law firm did in the construction business, Baxley had won many more scuffles than they lost, and Jack owed Leonard far more for their services than he would ever pay for their still stratospheric fees.

Today, however, he needed Leonard's help, not so much as a business defense, but to save his own neck. Leonard told Jack he had already read the Times and not to worry, he'd be at Jack's office waiting for him. When Jack arrived at his office just down the street from the Boardwalk, the media was also there waiting for him. Never friendly, this morning they were more like a pack of hyenas smelling blood. At least a dozen of them congregated outside the front door, TV cameras rolling, microphones stuck as close to his face as they could manage, all screaming at him for his comments after the morning's bombshell.

Believe me, my comments would not be fit to air, he thought as he wrestled his way through the throng to get into the building. He muttered, "No comment," several times with his head down, then opened the door to the safety of the glass walled modern lobby.

Amy Smythe, his long-time loyal receptionist, and secretary was the first to greet him. "Mr. Baxley is waiting for you, sir. I'm so sorry for all of this," she said with awkwardness, as if it were her fault.

"Thank you, Amy. Everything is going to be fine. My apologies for the mess outside. Please hold all my calls and let me know when Mr. Folger arrives."

"Yes, sir. I'll do that."

Jack greeted Leonard and ushered him into his corner office. Beyond the pulled shades were panoramic views of the Myrtle Beach Ferris Wheel and Boardwalk, framed by a long row of pastel colored high-rise beach condos.

"Come in and have a seat, Leonard." It was never Len or Lenny, always Leonard. "Thank you for coming in on such a short notice. It's been a morning. Did you watch the CXM News as well?"

"Not a problem at all, Jack. Yes, I did. I would plan to file a protest, but I somehow feel Judge Culligan will deal with it in a more direct fashion."

"More about him later. Can I get you anything to drink before we begin?"

"I'm fine, Jack. How's Karen taking it?" Leonard eased himself into one of Jack's leather guest chairs.

Jack chuckled back. "Well, right after she threw her cup of coffee on me, she took off to see her divorce attorney. But that's another problem which can wait. What are we going to do about our situation?"

"Well, that depends." Leonard gave Jack a wry smile. "Why don't you tell me the story from your perspective and then we'll map out a plan."

"Sounds fair. Well, you know the problems I've had with DHEC getting my lots approved for residential construction. After the last fiasco, I needed to take a more, let's say, assertive approach. So, I called in a favor from Rudy Culligan and he greased the wheels with that dickhead Huntsman at DHEC for the Salt Cove marsh front lots. I got two of them approved, with a promise to add more. Then I meet up with this blonde bitch from Murrells Inlet and, well, you know, one thing led to another. Next thing I know she winds up dead at the Culligan's party and now this tape suddenly appears in the media. Rudy tells me he's out of it and I'm on my own to deal with DHEC. Lots of unanswered questions which I intend to get to the bottom of. But first, I need your help. That's it in a nutshell."

Jack watched as Leonard took it all in. Leonard nodded when he understood and frowned when he didn't. "Alright Jack," he finally replied. "Now I need to know what went on above the table and what didn't. Don't blow me with "favors" and "greased wheels". What transpired, how much, and how was it delivered? These are the important facts."

Jack took a deep breath. He knew attorney client privilege would protect him. It just unnerved him anytime he had to sit and tell his lawyer how he broke the law. "Of course, Leonard. That's what you need to know. So, I gave Rudy a hundred grand. Cash. Withdrawn from my Grand Caymen account, safely transported here via my connection with DHL in Miami. I hand-delivered it to Rudy's chambers two weeks ago. Rudy gave fifty grand to

Robert Huntsman at DHEC. Can't say how they washed their money, but no one is going to trace it to me. As soon as I got word they approved the first two lots, my guys went to work. Obviously, being seduced and having my tongue loosened wasn't in the plans. And of all the goddamn bitches, she was Culligan's son's ex-fiancé." Jack watched Leonard chortle. This wasn't the first time he'd been caught by the short hairs, but it certainly was playing out to be the worst.

"Ok then," Leonard began, his tone now serious, "this is what we're going to do."

Fifteen minutes later, their plan now mapped out, the two boldly walked out the front door and faced the media crunch. The hyenas leapt to attention, their microphones crowding in on the two businessmen. Leonard stood solid as a statue, his 6'4" frame exquisitely draped by his gray Armani suit. Jack took his position at Leonard's side, arms crossed over his barrel chest, a scowl on his face. He didn't have to say a word.

"Ladies and gentlemen of the media," Leonard began his defense with a booming baritone voice. "I have a brief statement to make regarding my client, Jack Greeley, and the outrageous slander you all have subjected him to this morning. Jack Greeley is an innocent man. He has done nothing improper in his legal and just pursuit of expanding his construction business. I am sure you have all read and seen the news this morning of the secretly recorded tape from the unfortunately now deceased woman, a Miss Molly Elmwood. The first assertion I want to make to you all is that this tape was not only illegally recorded, but it was also illegally transferred to the media, and there is no way will it be allowed as evidence should there be any kind of trial. You all should know better.

To the Myrtle Beach Times — your long-respected establishment is now reduced to tabloid trash, the Grand Strand's National Enquirer." Leonard's voice deepened further with resentment-tinged sarcasm. "And WCXM — shame on you putting this garbage on the air. You make Jerry Springer look like the Gospel Hour. My client and I are reviewing the genuine possibility of suing these two organizations for character assassination and damage to Greeley's reputation.

I repeat, my client has done nothing wrong. Greeley applied to have the lots in question approved. DHEC approved them but has now rescinded them. We were not told why. This is a question you will need to ask DHEC. Greeley has incurred the costs involved. My client will not be making any further statements on this issue, and I will not be taking questions. That is all."

Leonard and Jack made a quick about face and reentered the office building as a surge of questions poured forth, none of which they would either hear or answer.

******

Once back inside, Jack saw Ian Folger waiting for him in the lobby. He bid his attorney goodbye after thanking him again for his bang-up job facing down the mob outside. Then he invited Ian into his office.

Ian Folger's official title was Private Investigator, and Jack certainly used him as such, as he needed him today. He also worked as Greeley's head of security; their strongman, keeping Jack a proper and safe distance between himself and certain unpleasantries such as unruly unions, nosy HOAs, and the occasional crooked cop — all hazards that came with the territory. Today's mission was straight PI work, and Jack knew he could depend on Ian.

"Quite a headline this morning, Jack." Ian opened the conversation. "Not to mention that audio on the news. Did you really only last the ten seconds they played, or did she somehow start recording it mid-fuck?" Ian laughed at his own joke. Jack didn't.

"You're fucking hilarious, Ian. I've got genuine problems here and you're cracking jokes."

"Indeed you do, my friend. Seems like you've been a busy boy bribing judges. That's a new low for you, Jack. Even by your standards."

"Thanks again, asshole. And look where it's got me."

"And how's the wife taking this? Not lying down, I suppose."

"She's divorcing me, for your information. But that's not what I need help with."

"I'm all ears, Jack. Lay it on me."

Jack laid back in his seat and cracked his knuckles. A sly grin came over his face, one the Grinch would be proud of. "I want back at that Judge," he said with a snarl. "Rudy Culligan has been sticking his nose and his dick in all kinds of places it didn't belong for years now. And he always gets away with it. I'm sure he believes this little squall will be no different. I want you to make sure it *is* different this time, Ian. I'll make sure it will be well worth your while."

Ian grinned at the possibilities. "Getting dirt on the most powerful judge on the South Carolina coast can be rather dicey, Jack. What do you have for me to start with?"

"Well, what I'd really like to find out is if Rudy had a direct or even indirect role in Molly's death. I bet something happened at that party between the two of them. Then find out how that tape got from Molly to the media. Lean on that crazy son of his, Randy — Molly's ex-fiancé. Squeeze that dickhead at DHEC, Robert Huntsman. I don't know Ian, take your pick, but I want dirt on that Judge. I'm out a hundred grand and look what I have to show for it. A media nightmare, a legal thornbush, two leveled lots I can't touch, and a pending divorce."

"And you're out your hottie mistress," Ian jested.

Jack didn't know whether to laugh or cry. "Yeah," he said, appreciating Ian's sense of humor. "She was a good lay; I'll admit to that. But if I knew what she was doing, I'd have snuffed her out right on that motel bed. Oh well, water under the bridge now. Here's the number for my new burner phone. Keep me up to date. I want to know everything you find out."

Jack's desk phone buzzed. "Yes, Amy, what is it?"

"Sir, there's a detective from the MBPD here to see you."

"Thank you, Amy." Jack rolled his eyes. "Tell him I'll be out in a minute." Jack turned his attention back to Ian. "See what kind of day I'm having? Now I'll show the cops what it means to lawyer up."

"I'm sure you'll do fine, Jack. I'll get started on this right away."

"Thanks Ian, I know I can count on you. Don't forget, I want to see that judge hanging by his balls."

CHAPTER 35

Leroy sat in his office, organizing his material while he waited for Tony to come by. He had left a message with Janice at Rudy's chambers that he could not meet with the Judge before Rudy was due in court at 10:30 AM. Janice informed Leroy that Rudy was tied up with court business until 4:00 PM. Leroy told her to tell Rudy he'd come by his chambers then.

Meanwhile, he had recovered from the shock of the morning news debacle and the pejorative attitude he received from Ruth at Culligan's Way. He just got off the phone with the South Carolina Attorney General, Alex Winston, who was suddenly taking a curious interest in the shenanigans going on in Georgetown County, having had a copy of the Times thrust in front of him earlier that morning. Leroy notified Winston he was making good progress on the murder case, and Sheriff Shepard in Horry County was pursuing the Greeley angle this morning.

"What about Judge Culligan?" the AG asked.

"What about him?" Leroy answered with caution.

"How deep is he involved, Leroy? What do you have on him? Lord knows I find it more than a little discomforting to wake up and find one of my judges caught up in a bribery scandal."

"And a murder investigation," Leroy reminded him.

"Well, doesn't that just put a cherry on top of it."

"Mr. Attorney General, Judge Culligan is a person of interest in the murder which took place on his property late Saturday night. He is not currently a suspect, but we have not ruled him out just yet. I'm hoping to get more information today which will help narrow down our list of suspects. Right now, we don't have any direct connection between the murder and the bribery case, other than the owner of the leaked audio clip is also the murder victim. Now, I'd like your help in one other angle of the scandal."

"Name it, Leroy. How can I assist?"

"We're getting stonewalled at DHEC. The Director, Robert Huntsman has yet to respond to any of our many attempts to contact him. We know the marsh lots in question were suspiciously approved, then, suddenly they're rescinded. We need their side of the story, but of course, I have no jurisdiction over a state department."

"Consider it done. I'll place a call as soon as we're through here. Anything else?"

"Ask Huntsman why Judge Culligan made a four-and-a-half-hour trip to his lake house on Lake Murray during the day on Saturday. Right now, that is confidential information. We just found out late yesterday. We have security footage of Rudy's Lexus coming and going from a marina just down the road."

Winston paused on the line. It was clear to Leroy this hit a nerve with the AG. "I see," he replied. "Is there anything else I should know about?"

"Not at this time, Mr. Attorney General. I very much appreciate your help in this sensitive matter."

"Any time, Leroy. You let me know if there's any other way my office can be of help. Right now I have a couple of important phone calls to make. We'll talk again soon. Goodbye."

"Goodbye, sir." Leroy hung up his phone and smiled to himself. He'd finally get some action on DHEC. As far as Rudy was concerned, he knew he'd be pissed at having his own county sheriff go over his head. Tough shit, he should have thought about that before he got up to his neck in a mess of his own making.

******

"Hey boss. Are you ready?"

Leroy looked up to see Tony knocking on his door. "Yeah, Tony, come on in. Had a pleasant chat with the AG a few minutes ago. He's taking an interest in our situation."

"Well, that's some good news." Tony took a seat in one of Leroy's guest chairs. "Is he going to help with DHEC? I'm still getting nothing out of Huntsman."

"Yes, that, and I believe he's going to make our judge quite uncomfortable this morning." Leroy watched Tony grin from ear to ear, knowing he'd be happy to hear that. "I'm meeting with Rudy at 4:00 PM this afternoon. Hopefully, we'll have some more evidence collected by then. So, let's go over everything and see where we're at. I have Tim's phone here. The lab will clean it today."

"And Chris is trying to track down Harvey. I'm sure they'll find something illegal on him and bring him in for a good once over."

"Make sure I know when that happens. I want a word with that creep myself. What about Sally's car?"

"Guys should complete their inspection around noon. They'll let us know immediately."

"That leaves the dive team. They told me an hour ago, no later than 2:00 PM. So, let's focus on the murder. Who's on the list? I need motive and opportunity. Shouldn't be a long one.

Let's start with opportunity. Who either knew Molly would be at the dock at midnight, or would be close enough to the dock at midnight? We know the party was over, so only the Culligans were home."

"Right," Tony agreed. "We know Harvey knew she'd be there. But there's no motive, and from what we've seen and heard from him, I believe we can rule him out. I also believe no one followed Molly on the boat that night."

"Yes, I agree. Then we have Tim, the last person we know to be with her alive. But also no motive. I think we can rule him out."

"Agreed. Now for the family who had motive; Connie, Rudy, Randy, and Sally."

"Yes. I think we can rule Connie out. We both saw her yesterday. No way could she have come back to the Way at midnight. Plus, she didn't know Molly was coming back."

"Right. So, first Rudy — plenty of motive. We don't know what they were arguing about at the party, but it was enough to draw everyone's attention and have her booted."

Leroy recollected the events leading up to Molly's departure. "I wasn't near them when they were arguing. By the time I realized what was happening, they were escorting Molly out. If we believe Rudy's story, that would be the end of his involvement. How would he have known Molly would return?"

"Same way Sally did. He could have overheard the conversation between Molly and Tim. Or someone else did and told Rudy."

"I agree it's possible. But it's a stretch. The bloody shoe and the Ring cam times don't support or undermine the case against him. Gut feeling though, I don't think Rudy would have done this."

"Pardon me, Sheriff, if I respectfully disagree with that opinion."

"Noted. A reminder Detective — don't let personal grudges cloud your reasoning. That leaves the other two Culligan kids as lead suspects. Both had motive and both were at the scene at or near the time of the murder. Take Sally first."

Tony flipped back through his notes. "Sally Hobart, 32-year-old married female, no record I'm aware of. Motive — she took the narcotic theft very personally, as you alluded to in her behavior at the party. Revenge is always a powerful motive. She was at the scene at least moments before the murder. She lied to us once already. Do you think she's still lying?"

"Honestly, Tony, I do. I don't believe she turned and left before the murder. But whether she's the actual murderer, my gut tells me no. I don't think she has it in her to be a cold-blooded killer. I think she witnessed the murder and then left, and is covering for the killer, most likely another member of the family."

"I agree. Of course, the examination of her vehicle might lead us to a different conclusion."

"Let me check here a second." Leroy went to his computer and clicked on his email, then shook his head. "No, no report on the car yet. Then that leaves Randy. Both motive and proximity to the murder. The man's a worthless piece of shit. But did he kill his ex-fiancé? What exactly would have been his motive?"

"Any number of things. She set him up to be arrested. No telling what other cons she had going on involving him. Or how about this for motive? He idles up to the dock, thinking he would have an honest chat with Molly, only to find her kissing his hated younger brother. The one who shows up suddenly after ten years away. Randy feels Tim is the main reason he's being driven from the house."

"Hmm," pondered Leroy, "I can see that. But there's still no hard evidence."

"Find the knife," Tony coolly replied.

"Sure, find the knife, with any luck, today. So, that's a cast full for you. Who am I leaving out — Ruth."

"Ruth," echoed Tony. "No direct motive, and according to her, never knew the whole thing happened. But…" Tony trailed off, nodding his head, then broke out in a grin that grew into a belly laugh.

"But what?" demanded Leroy. "What the hell is so funny?"

"Ruth Culligan," Tony stated, trying to control his laughter. "The only one in the family actually convicted of attempted murder." Tony continued to giggle.

Leroy failed to see the humor in any of it. He pounded his fist on his desk as his face contorted in anger. "Fucking Culligans!"

CHAPTER 36

Ruth stayed quiet after Leroy left. Tim could only imagine what nugget of insanity his mother may choose to unburden herself from. He dressed in another old baggy pair of swim trunks from his high-school days, still loose around the waist, and a ragged t-shirt, also a leftover. He grimaced at the slack in the trunks as he tied the pull strings tight. Tim weighed himself each morning since he returned. As of Tuesday, he had gained three pounds. A good start, he thought, but still a long way to go.

He was waiting for his mother when she walked down the stairs. To Tim, she was the essence of middle-aged beauty. She wore a pair of trim knee-length cotton shorts, a loose-fitting flower print shirt and a wide-brimmed hat. When she smiled at Tim, her bright blue eyes looked like the furthest thing in the world from crazy. But he knew better.

"Are you ready?" Ruth asked, walking past Tim towards the back door. She even had a bounce in her step.

"Sure am, Mom."

Ruth reached out to hold his hand as they made their way over the beach access. Once on the beach, Ruth directed them south towards the pier.

"How far did you go yesterday?" she asked. They were barefoot, feeling the cool ocean water lap gently on their feet.

"Not far. Maybe a quarter mile. How far do you usually go?"

Ruth smiled back at Tim. Whatever was bothering her twenty minutes ago sure wasn't now. He didn't remember ever seeing Ruth so happy. "Oh, I can go as far as the Pawleys pier and back. That's almost a four-mile round trip. We'll just go as far as you feel comfortable." They walked a few more paces. "I just love the beach in April. Everything is in bloom. It's not too cold, not too hot."

"Plenty of pollen, though." Another memory resurfaced. Southern pollen season, and how he suffered through it each spring, compounding his asthma.

"Is it bothering you, son?" Ruth asked with concern.

"I'll be alright. Always have my inhaler nearby. Wouldn't hurt to get some Claritin though. I forgot how much worse it is down here than up north."

"I'll make a note to have Annabelle pick some up tomorrow."

They walked hand in hand some more at a leisurely pace. Tim paid close attention to his breathing and also wondered when Ruth would change to a more serious subject. He was in no hurry. They practically had the beach to themselves. No one was even within shouting distance. The sky was a bright azure blue and for the second day in a row, Tim felt his senses brimming to the max, and the feeling of being truly home washed through him.

They had reached the point where he turned around yesterday, but Tim felt better today, so he continued further. Ruth stayed quiet. Tim could tell she was putting her thoughts together. He knew she knew what she wanted to tell him. Probably just figuring out how.

After a few more minutes, Tim told Ruth, "Mom, we've gone further than I went yesterday. I think maybe we should turn around now."

Ruth smiled back. "Of course, dear. But first, let's have a seat up by the dunes. We can talk there."

******

The two took a seat on a slope of sand just below some newly rooted sea oats shooting out of the dunes, which made up the berm on the end of the island. They sat for a minute looking peacefully out over the ocean. Ruth seemed to continue to be lost in thought. Tim knew she'd begin when she was ready. He gazed south, down the last few beach homes before the inlet, girding himself for what his mother would tell him.

"I'm not well, Tim," Ruth began. "You know that, right?"

Tim turned and looked into his mother's eyes. "I know of the issues you dealt with before I left. They've not brought me up to speed about what's happened since. But I heard about what happened with Randy on Friday and saw what happened at the party with him. Why don't you tell me in your own words?"

Ruth took a deep breath. "Yes, well now, let me see. Where do I begin? My doctor, well, my psychiatrist, Dr. Freedman, she's had me on this medicine for most of the past fifteen years or so. Risperdal. Supposed to help with my mood swings and other things. And I have to say, mostly, it has done me good. That, and of course Annabelle being around to keep me straight. Only when I forget to take a dose or two, things could get a little wiggy for me."

Tim nodded that he understood. He could only imagine what wiggy meant to his mother.

"But lately — well, it seems it hasn't had the same effect on me. I mean, what I'm trying to say, Tim, is there are demons that lurk inside me. And they can tell me to do horrible things. I regret that I've done some terrible things in my past. I did a bad thing last Friday with your brother. And the Sheriff there to see it all, my goodness. Anyway, the medication normally helps keep these demons at bay. It's like they knock on my door, but I don't have to answer. But a few months ago, I well, it's like I was unable to not answer the door. And it's a scary thing, let me tell you. Dr. Freedman said she had already increased my dosage twice over the years, and I'm at the maximum dose they allow."

Tim listened. He couldn't recall his mother ever opening up this much to him. "Does Dad know about this?"

Ruth gave him a cursory glance, then scoffed. "Your father wouldn't know what to make of it. I try not to bother him with details. Anabelle knows. Maybe Connie knows a bit. I'm not sure."

"So what does this Dr. Freedman advise you to do?"

"Not much, I'm afraid. Maintain a healthy lifestyle, you know — diet, sleep, exercise, that sort of thing. But medically not much. She said eventually, I may need to be institutionalized, but I should still be a long way from that. Thing is, I can't go back to Charleston. I don't want to go into the reasons, but I simply couldn't. I'd rather be dead."

Tim wondered many things at that moment, but it wasn't the right time to prod any more than he felt he had to. "I'm sorry to hear that, Mom. Really I am."

"Something happened about a month ago," Ruth continued, changing the subject. "Something happened at one of our Sunday dinners. It was very disturbing to me." Ruth paused.

Tim reckoned she was trying to figure out how to tell him what happened without revealing too much. "I'm listening, Mom. What happened at dinner?"

Ruth broke eye contact and gazed out over the water. It seemed to Tim she was talking to the seagulls. Maybe she was. "It was a warm day in late February. Randy and Molly came to dinner. They came by boat, I remember that. They docked it at the pier. This would have been just before they broke off their engagement for the second time. It was the last time I saw Molly until the party last Saturday.

Anyway, they got into a terrible fight at dinner. I don't understand why people have to fight at dinner. It's so impolite. They said terrible things about each other. Accusing each other of lying and cheating, and abuse, and oh, the language they used. Your father insisted they leave, but they kept on arguing. Then Molly turned her anger toward me. Told me it was all my fault. Blamed me for every problem she ever had. Said she never felt welcome in my house, which was a bald face lie. She even brought your name up. Told me it was my fault you 'turned out the way he did.' Everyone was shocked to hear your name come up, Tim. It hadn't in such a long time. I stood from the table and went to her. Then…" Ruth brought the palms of her hand up to her face. "Just as I closed my hands around her skinny throat and smothered every bit of life right out of her, your father and Annabelle came up from behind and wrestled me away."

Tim's eyes bulged as he gulped. He let his mother finish.

"The demon knocked on my door that day. And I let him in. I let him in, and it felt both hideous and exhilarating. Does that make any sense to you? I know it sounds crazy."

"No, it doesn't. It's your condition, your illness. I'm thankful they were there for you then."

"Oh," she chortled. "There have been other times as well." Ruth sighed and looked back at Tim, searching for empathy.

Tim reached over and took her hand.

"I'm very thankful for Anabelle."

"We all are, Mom. We all are." He took a deep breath. He had to ask the question. "Mom, tell me the truth. Did you kill Molly? You can tell me. I swear I'll never let on."

Ruth stared at her son, silent and shocked.

Tim peered into her eyes, searching for a sign of truth, or sanity, or anything. For a moment he didn't know what lurked behind her eyes.

Then it seemed a light came on from within. "Heavens no," she responded, seemingly offended by the accusation. "I was like you, in bed asleep, just like I told the Sheriff. Although to be honest with you, son, I'll not shed a tear for that wicked woman. But no, I did not kill her."

"Ok, Mom. I believe you. I'm sorry I asked."

"Here's the thing, Tim. I can't rely on Annabelle to always be there for me. And now, with Connie gone, I don't have her either. I need your help, son. I need you to be there for me, to guide me, to protect me. You know I'm here for you. Your coming home has been the best thing that has happened to me in a very long time, maybe ever. We need to help each other. Protect each other. Can we do that, son?"

"Of course, Mom," said Tim, relieved to be off the murder subject. Why did he need to bring it up? He didn't know, it just came out. "We'll help each other — for sure."

The two looked out at the ocean. Tim felt a sense of peace come over him again. Like yesterday, but even stronger now. His stomach rumbled. "Come on, let's head back. I'm ready for lunch." Tim helped Ruth to her feet. She smiled back at him, and they walked back to Culligan's Way. Protection, he thought. That's what we both need the most. They would give it to each other. In many ways, they always have.

CHAPTER 37

Sally sat at her office desk paralyzed with fear. She couldn't work, she couldn't even think straight. All she could imagine was what the Georgetown County police were going to find in her Ford Escape, and what would happen to her if they found what they were looking for — blood. The last thing Sheriff Keating said to her yesterday kept ringing in her ears. "If we find one drop of blood, I'm going to have you arrested."

And what if they did? Her entire world would crash down on her. She would lose her job. She may lose Steve and the kids. She may even go to jail. Why did she have to go back to that pier? Why couldn't she have just left well enough alone? Now the police have her on record as lying to them. If they found out she lied again, she'd be finished.

Last night was horrendous. She had to admit to Steve what happened. At first, he was empathetic. He came by and picked her up after her shift, as she requested, full of concern.

"Why did the police impound your car?" he had asked.

So, she told him. And things went downhill from there.

"What do you mean you went back to the Way at midnight?"

And she told him.

"What did you think you were going to do to her?" His voice rose along with his incredulity. "Why did you lie to the police the first time?" Now his tone had anger in it. Finally, "And did you lie to them again? What did you see?"

She looked at him in the car, trembling as they approached their home. "No, nothing," she lied again.

As they pulled into their driveway, his last words to her, "You better hope not," were relayed with pure disgust.

They hadn't talked since. All she could do last night was prepare a simple dinner and make small talk with the kids. Steve excused himself right after the meal and disappeared into his study, leaving her to deal with all her anxiety by herself.

Then this morning, the same silent treatment. She couldn't recall ever seeing her husband this upset and distant. But then again, she had never in her life been caught lying to the police. Steve was kind of a stickler about those things. Why wasn't she?

Through it all, the same concern stayed lodged in her mind, like some splinter buried in your finger you couldn't get out. What would they find in her car? Sally racked her brain for what might be possible. Joey had a bloody nose a couple of weeks ago when she picked him up from soccer practice. Could any of it have found its way onto the front seat, where he got in? And Amber scraped her knee at school. What about that? But even if they found blood, it wouldn't match Molly's, right? But what if they couldn't tell?

Sally was still in her funk when she heard a knock on her door. She looked up surprised, then relaxed when she saw it was Linda, thankfully not Bud.

"Hi, Sally, do you have a minute?"

"Sure, Linda, come in." Surely, Sally thought, there's not another problem in the pharmacy.

"Thanks." Linda entered Sally's office and took a seat. She didn't look concerned, but a worried look came over her face when she saw Sally. "Are you ok?" Linda asked.

"Oh, I'm fine." Sally pasted a fake smile on her face. "Just have some issues going on at home. What's up?" Sally knew word had gotten around that the police impounded her car yesterday and figured Linda could put two and two together. At least she wasn't one to pry.

Linda's expression switched back to her smiley face. "I just wanted to let you know we have the final numbers on the narcotics losses after counting the returns we received this morning. Here are the results." Linda handed Sally a printout. The four narcotics were listed with the totals stolen, returned, and unaccounted for each one. A quick glance looked as if they recovered about half the drugs.

"That's great, Linda. Have you shown this to Bud?"

"No." Linda paused. "Not yet." Sally could see Linda's reluctance written on her face. "I was wondering if you might. I think he's still mad at me."

Sally shook her head. "No, he isn't," she said, trying to sound reassuring. "You know Bud, he's always mad at something." Linda wasn't taking the bait. She's terrified of him, Sally thought. "Ok, Linda. I'll give him the report."

"Oh, thank you Sally, thank you so much!" Relief broke out on Linda's face. "I'll let you get back to what you were doing. Thank you again so much." Linda rose and left the office.

"Great, yes, get back to what I was doing," Sally said out loud to no one. "And you think you have problems?" Sally buried her head in her arms on the desk and closed her eyes. Why is this happening to me? she thought. This can only end up as bad, or worse. Or I could just tell the whole truth. What's worse than worse? Worst. Not an option.

After another minute of destitute anxiety, Sally's phone rang, snapping her out of her trance. "Hello," she answered with trepidation.

"Sally, this is Detective Tony Meacham with the Georgetown County Sheriff's Department. We met yesterday."

Sally gulped. "Yes, Detective. Have you finished with my car yet?"

"We have, Sally. I'm glad to tell you it was clean. You can pick it up at your convenience. You are no longer a suspect in Molly Elmwood's murder. However, you are still a person of interest, and we ask that you keep yourself available in case we have any further questions."

Sally was shell-shocked. She couldn't believe what she just heard. She barely got out, "Thank you, Detective. Thank you very much. Goodbye." Sally hung up the phone and collapsed on her desk, the tears of relief flowing freely into her arms. She couldn't stop crying for five full minutes.

******

Leroy busied himself with some paperwork, nervously waiting to hear news from his outside sources. Tony had gone to the impound lot to check on the status of Sally's car. Chris radioed in that he had found Harvey Klinger at his pad with a room full of pot. Harvey didn't put up a fight and was on his way in right now. Chris described the look on his face as smug. Murrey emailed that the fetus DNA results would be ready by the end of the day. Leroy replied to please let him know ASAP.

That left the dive team as the last piece of news Leroy waited to hear from. He knew the marsh lot investigation was out of his hands now. Conrad told him a short time ago that Jack

Greeley had lawyered up and not to expect any new information from Horry County. That left Huntsman at DHEC. Leroy hoped he'd hear from either Huntsman himself, or at least an update from the AG. And of course there was Rudy, stuck in the middle. They'd be meeting at 4:00 PM, about four hours from now.

Leroy ate a quick bag lunch at his desk as he pondered the two cases. The pressure was on to make some kind of arrest. At this point, he had three Culligan family members as suspects, but no hard evidence to go on. He told the press he'd issue another public statement by 4:30 PM today. Hopefully, he'd have something more substantial to report than what he had now.

As soon as he finished his lunch, Tony called and told him Sally's car was clean. He just called Sally to inform her. "Alright then," Leroy told his detective. "Circle back around here when you can. Chris ought to be back with Harvey pretty soon."

"Will do, boss. Let me grab a quick bite and I'll be by in about half an hour."

Leroy tried to go back to his paperwork but couldn't concentrate. Too many balls up in the air. He went to take a walk in the courtyard between the station and the courthouse. Once outside, he reviewed his suspects again. He couldn't trust any of them. Nothing could be believed that came out of Randy's mouth. Leroy witnessed that too many times. Even with Sally ruled out as a suspect, he still believed she hadn't told him everything she knew or saw. And Rudy — well, Rudy knew his way around the law better than anyone. Harvey and Molly may have messed things up for him a little, but he just couldn't see Judge Rudolph Culligan going down with any ship he sailed on.

Leroy's cell rang. It was Jason at the Culligan pier. "Yeah, Jason, what do you got?"

"We have a knife, Sheriff. A long fillet knife, just like we were looking for."

Leroy closed his eyes and bit his lip. "Eureka", exploded in his mind. He took a deep breath before responding, "That's great news, Jason. Fantastic. Bring it on in. Can't wait to get a look at it."

"I can text you a pic of it right now. You're gonna love what it has inscribed on the handle."

Leroy wasn't expecting this. "Oh really? What does it say?"

"Got the initials RJC. Bet that means something to you."

Leroy couldn't believe this stoke of good fortune. "You better believe it does. Randall Jennings Culligan. Bring it straight in, Jason. Can't wait to inspect it."

Leroy ended the call and headed back to the office, but not before he texted Tony.

"Get back here ASAP. We have a knife."

Tony responded immediately, "On my way."

As soon as Leroy was back at his desk, he opened the text he received from Jason. Attached were several pics of the knife. Like he was told, the knife looked to be about ten inches long, and it had an ivory looking handle. A close up of the handle illustrated Randy's initials in capital letters carved into it.

Tony knocked and entered the office. "Let's see what you got," he said, noticing Leroy focused on the phone.

Leroy handed Tony the phone with the pics showing. "I believe, Detective, that what we have here is a murder weapon. And it belongs to our now lead suspect."

Tony nodded his head in approval. "You're sure of that? What's the J?"

"Jennings, Randy's middle name, also Ruth's maiden name. The reason I know this is because just a few days ago I looked at Randy's arrest document. Full name right at the top. I have no doubt this is Randy's fishing knife, or that it's the murder weapon. And I have very little doubt now that Randy killed Molly. How about you?"

"I'm with you there, Sheriff. No doubt in my mind."

"Good, as soon as the knife gets back here and we get it processed, let's drive out to that fishing camp and bring that son-of-a-bitch in."

"Nothing would make my day more."

CHAPTER 38

Leroy couldn't have been happier as he pulled into the fish camp and saw Randy's pickup truck outside one of several trailers. Off by the dock, he also noticed Randy's johnboat tied up. That meant the rascal should be inside, most likely drunk and stoned, watching TV. He was. In fact, he was smoking a joint when the two law enforcement men burst through the door. To Leroy, the place stunk to high heaven; a mix of stale beer, stale cigarettes, skunkweed pot, and old fried fish along with a side of BO. The place looked like it hadn't been cleaned in, well, forever.

Randy didn't even try to get up when he saw Leroy and Tony, guns drawn, come towards him. It wasn't as if he could have made it to the door. He just sat on the couch with a dumbfounded look on his face.

"Randall Culligan, you are under arrest for the murder of Molly Elmwood. You have the right to remain silent. Anything you say, can and will be used against you in a court of law."

This time, instead of trying to run, or wail, Randy just laid on his beaten down couch and stared at his arrestors. Leroy figured he was simply too stoned and too stunned to put up much of a fight. After they cuffed and escorted him out to the cruiser, Randy slurred to Leroy, "I told you before, Sheriff, I never saw Molly that night. I didn't do nothing."

"Let him sleep it off in his cell," Leroy told Tony. "He wouldn't be able to dial his lawyer if he wanted to in this condition."

Tony nodded his agreement.

Once back at the station, with their perp dumped in a cell, the two headed over to the lab and discussed the knife with the lead technician, Sylvia Harrelson. Sylvia had been with the department for four years now, a bright young graduate of USC Columbia in Criminal Justice. She had a knack for finding obscure details in evidence, and she was as sharp with the technological tools at her disposal as anyone. As Leroy and Tony entered the lab, Sylvia was deeply involved in looking at the knife with a magnifying glass.

"What do you see there, Miss Harrelson?" asked Leroy. He knew Sylvia was fine working on a first name basis, but Leroy liked to at least start out formally. It also looked better in front of Tony.

Sylvia looked up from her examination. She set her long brunette hair in a ponytail, accenting the sharp features of her nose, cheeks, and brown eyes. "I was hoping to see blood, Sheriff Keating." Even if Leroy felt comfortable on a first name basis with the lab tech, she wasn't. Being white, attractive, single, and thirty-years younger prevented her from even the slightest hint of being too casual.

"Which was going to be my first question. Have you found any blood? There wasn't anything obvious to us when it came in."

"No, there wouldn't be, being underwater for at least two whole days. But what I'm trying to see, is if any seeped down between the handle and the blade. That would be the only chance. If there is any, we'll have to think about slicing into the handle to get to it. But that would also mean at least some destructive testing on the evidence."

Leroy looked at Tony. "What do you think? What's the plan with the knife?"

Tony put his hand to his chin and said, "That's tricky, Leroy. The knife is going to be a crucial piece of evidence. Having a blood match to Molly would be the final piece of the puzzle. But we don't want to destroy the knife to get to it." He turned to Sylvia. "How much damage to the knife if we cut into it, Sylvia?"

Sylvia looked at the two inquisitive lawmen and grinned. "I can't do a good enough job here. There's a fab shop in town I could use. If they're careful, they should be able to cut about a quarter inch around the base of the blade. I'm sure the blade goes deeper into the handle. It looks to be a pretty high-quality knife."

Satisfied with the answer provided, Leroy told her, "Sounds good, Sylvia. Arrange to have it sent out tomorrow. I'll take it off your hands for now. I have a couple of Culligans I'd like to show it to later today."

******

It was getting on towards the end of the afternoon. Leroy felt much better than he had in the morning when he was so rudely greeted by the news in the paper and on TV. He still had to deal with the media at 4:30 PM, but he was much more confident, based on the newly gained information he had received during the day. The two most consequential of which were the arrest of Randy Culligan, thus putting the murder suspect speculation to rest, and the result of the phone call he had with AG Winston.

Winston called Leroy shortly after Leroy returned from the lab and told him he had talked with both Robert Huntsman and Judge Culligan. Leroy sat back in his office recliner and listened with interest. He had been speculating in his mind all day about what kind of cockamamie story he'd get from the top. He was pretty sure it wouldn't have anything to do with the truth, and he wasn't disappointed.

Disappointment, however, was certainly on the mind of the AG, mostly for political reasons. "I had to catch some heat from the Governor over this," he said outright, as if it was Leroy's fault this whole affair came to light. He supposed it was in part, by not controlling Molly's phone like he should have. But once Winston got that off his chest, he delved into his more interesting findings. Chief amongst them was Huntsman's assertion that the permitting process for the Salt Cove marsh lots had been hacked.

Leroy just about choked when he heard that. "Hacked, sir? Hacked how?"

"We don't know at this point. Huntsman suspects Greeley hired a hacker after he couldn't get his lots approved appropriately."

"Ohhh Kayy. And Judge Culligan?"

"Yes, I spoke with Rudy as well. He admits being in contact with Huntsman at DHEC. He told me he owed Jack Greeley a favor, some home improvement or something at his beach home. So, he asked if, perhaps, Huntsman could approve these lots, no strings attached."

"No strings attached," Leroy repeated. "And do you believe him, sir?"

Winston paused on the other end. Leroy held his breath. Finally Winston said, "I do, Leroy. And you need to as well. I understand you have a suspect detained for the Elmwood murder, the Judge's son it seems. Rudy didn't seem too upset by that. Find out how Greeley hacked into DHEC's files, and you should be in a good place. A much better place than you found yourself in this morning."

"I'll do that, sir," Leroy dutifully answered.

"Very well. Keep me abreast if there are any further developments. That is all."

"I will, sir. Goodbye." Now he knew exactly where he stood. Won't Rudy be pleased.

After a few minutes of stewing, Leroy realized it was all for the best. The odds of finding anyone hacking into DHEC's files were less than a snow cone's chance lasting ten minutes on a South Carolina beach in August. The media might not get their scapegoat, but in the end, everyone could breathe a little easier.

Leroy got some much-neglected paperwork done, and when he looked at his watch, it was almost 4:15 PM. He'd have to get his thoughts together for his meeting with Rudy. Just then, his door knocked, and he saw Murrey appear at the door. Leroy had forgotten about the autopsy, with everything else going on.

"Come in, Murrey. I forgot about the report. I assume you have some news for me?"

Murrey entered the office and took a seat. "I certainly do, Sheriff, and it's not what you might be expecting."

Leroy eyed his ME. Why is he looking at me with that shit-eating grin? he wondered. "So, I can assume you have a match to the father of Molly's baby then. It's Randy?"

"Oh, we have a match alright, and it has Randy's DNA. But Randy is not the father."

Leroy's face contorted in confusion. "I don't understand. If the fetus has DNA that matches Randy's, doesn't that make Randy the father?"

"Well, it would if the DNA of the fetus had fifty percent of Molly's DNA and fifty percent of Randy's DNA. But it doesn't. The DNA of the fetus has only a twenty-five percent match to Randy. Which means..." Murrey paused for effect.

Leroy still looked confused. "Which means a sibling? That would only be Tim. That's not possible."

"Not a sibling, my dear Sheriff. You need to back up a generation."

Now the cards were on the table. Leroy's expression changed from perplexity to astonishment. "No!" he shouted out, slapping his hand on his forehead. "You have got to be kidding me. Rudy is the father?"

"It's a medical certainty, Leroy. The only other possibility would be a brother of Rudy's. But I don't believe he has any brothers."

"No, he doesn't. He has two sisters, that's all." Leroy's mind swirled as the implications of this development ran through his head like a freight train. "This is very classified information, Murrey," he said, returning to the reality of the situation. "I'm sure you can understand why."

"Of course, Leroy. The only people who know are you and me."

"Make sure it stays that way. For now, at least."

"Of course, Sheriff. I'm going to complete the autopsy, but I won't publish it until you let me know how you want to handle it."

"Thanks Murrey, and thanks for doing such a great job with the autopsy. I'll let you know."

CHAPTER 39

By 3:30 PM, Randy had sobered up enough to understand the pickle he was in and was ready to make his call. This time, he had the wherewithal to contact his lawyer instead of his father. Jerry Springfield told Randy he'd be there in ten minutes; he was in his law office just down the street. Jerry immediately called Leroy and demanded to know why his client was being subjected to the continued harassment of Georgetown County law enforcement, and that he hoped they had better evidence this time than the sham charges slapped on his client last Friday.

Leroy told Jerry the case against Randy was solid, and he would arrange a meeting as soon as he could get here. Then he called Tony and told him to meet him in the interrogation room in ten minutes. Jerry would be there. Leroy heard Tony moan on the other end.

The three were waiting for Leroy when he came to the room. Jerry, Tony, and Leroy shook hands and exchanged pleasantries. Leroy utterly detested Jerry Springfield, Tony even more so. Jerry was the epitome of every sleazy defense lawyer. His dark straight hair was slicked back, like some reincarnation of Elvis Presley. His tall lanky body fit tightly in a glossy, striped, grey suit; the tie, some psychedelic pattern of color tied into a perfect knot. He even sounded like Elvis when he spoke. Leroy never knew if this was natural, or an act. He thought everything about Jerry was an act.

"Shall we, gentlemen?" Leroy motioned the other three to enter the room as he unlocked it. Randy had yet to say a word. He stood by the side, handcuffed; still disheveled, appearing somewhat less than fully coherent. Leroy had the knife in a plastic evidence bag.

Once the four sat around the small rectangular table, Jerry reminded Randy not to answer questions unless he approved. Then he told Leroy, "Alright Sheriff, show us what you got."

"Jerry, before I get to the physical evidence here, I'll briefly cover the facts we know and what Mr. Culligan has already admitted to. After his disturbing and uncalled for appearance at the Culligan party last Saturday night, he texted Molly and asked to meet with her. She texted back and agreed for him to come to the pier at their home after midnight. "Not before 12:10 AM" to be exact. We know Randy returned to retrieve his boat on the beach at Culligan's Way before midnight. According to Randy, he drove his boat through the inlet and around to the pier near the time mentioned. He claims he did not see Molly at all but saw the skiff she had taken to the pier. Our contention is Randy saw Molly at the pier, in fact, he saw her and Tim kissing. This enraged Randy, and right after Tim went back inside, Randy docked his boat, took his fishing knife out, went up the pier, and killed Molly in a fit of rage. He then kicked her body over the side of the pier, into the shallow water on the creek bank, threw the knife into the creek and left the scene." Leroy sat back to let Jerry digest what he had laid out.

"And what you have there," Jerry asked tentatively, "is what you believe to be the murder weapon?"

"It is," Leroy stated flatly. He put on a pair of latex gloves and removed the knife from the bag. "I'll ask you not to touch the knife. We're still processing it for evidence." Leroy laid the knife on the table, with the monogrammed etching face up. Everyone stared at it. Leroy watched Randy for his first reaction. Randy gulped. "So Randy, tell us. Is this your knife, with the RJC initials on it?"

Randy looked at Jerry, seeking advice. Jerry frowned as he continued to examine the knife. Finally he nodded to Randy and said, "Go ahead, Randy. Is this your knife?"

Randy licked his lips, contemplating what to say. "It is," he answered without emotion.

"And can you explain why we found it in Pawleys Creek outside of Culligan's Way?" Leroy asked.

Randy looked skittishly between Jerry and Leroy.

Jerry shook his head.

"No, I can't," he replied.

"When was the last time you saw this knife, Randy?" Leroy continued the questioning.

This time Jerry nodded.

"I don't know. I keep it in my tackle box, along with another smaller fillet knife. I only used this one for bigger fish; Redfish, Mackerel, that sort of thing. I doubt I've used it since last fall."

"That's fine, Randy. Does anybody else know you have this knife? Would anybody else have a reason to take this knife?"

Jerry butted in. "I think my client made it clear he doesn't know why his knife is not in his tackle box where it belongs. Look, I'm going to ask we take a break for the day so I can converse with Randy and get more background on the case. From what I saw and read in the news this morning, our murder victim had her hands full of juicy mischief with Greeley Construction and Judge Culligan. I'm sure there's a connection between that scandal and the murder which does not involve my client. And I fully intend to find out what it is." Jerry rose, as did the other three. "I'll touch base with you tomorrow. Randy, I'm sure our good Sheriff here will not see fit to have you released tonight. We'll get you out on bail first thing in the morning."

"We'll see about that, Jerry. But thanks for coming in on such short notice. We'll be in touch."

Jerry turned and left the room while Leroy and Tony escorted Randy back to his cell. As they were walking back to Leroy's office, Tony told him, "That guy really makes me sick."

"Who? Jerry or Randy?"

Tony laughed. "Well, both of them. I was talking about Jerry."

"Yeah, me too," retorted Leroy, "but don't let the sleaze factor fool you. Jerry Springfield is a damn good lawyer. I just hope our case is rock solid. We'll schedule a meeting with Gina in the morning. She'll set us straight if it isn't. But right now, I have a meeting with Judge Culligan and then the press."

Tony laughed. "Well, good luck with both. I'm glad I don't have to deal with either of them."

"I'll be glad to switch if you'd like,"

"No thanks, boss. They're all yours."

******

"Come in," Leroy heard Rudy bark when he knocked on his chambers door.

Leroy entered and gave Rudy a broad grin. It wasn't returned. "Good afternoon, Judge. I take it you've had a productive day."

"Apparently not as productive as yours has been. Have a seat, Leroy. We have some important things to discuss."

"Oh, that we do." Leroy took a seat in the oversized armchair. "How shall we begin? Don't forget, I have a 4:30 PM press conference out front. I'm sure your name will come up." Leroy smirked. Careful how you poke the bear, he reminded himself again.

"I'll start things off. First, let me express my disappointment in how you put me on ice this morning. I expected a little more consideration from you."

Well, that sure sets the tone, Leroy thought, the smirk now completely wiped off his face. "I'm here now," he said without emotion.

"Yes. I see that. So, now, tell me, have you found the source of this preposterous leak that splattered all over the media this morning like diarrhea from a loose diaper?"

"We have, Your Honor." Pleasantries now put aside; Leroy pulled no punches. "It turned out to be your son."

"Randy! That son-of-a-bitch."

"No, Judge. Your other son. Tim."

This caught Rudy off guard. He sat at his desk stunned by the news, looking stone-faced at Leroy. Finally, he took a deep breath calmly said, "Please explain."

"Rudy, I'm going to share some confidential information with you. As we're both aware, there's been too much information released already." Leroy paused. Rudy kept his same silent, rigid expression. "Molly gave Tim her cell phone when they met on the pier Saturday night. She told him she felt her life was in danger and wanted Tim to 'do the right thing' with it.

When we took Molly's phone on Sunday, we were unaware that Tim had already forwarded several text messages to his own phone. Then we learned this morning, this character Harvey Klinger, the same guy who chained himself to the tree in Salt Cove, was in cahoots with Molly on whatever scheme they had planned. He paid an unannounced visit to the Way yesterday and had a discussion with Tim about Molly and what they were up to. Apparently, he got Tim to play the clip of Molly and Jack in bed, which she had secretly recorded, then Harvey also secretly recorded it from Tim. Obviously, then, he went to the press last night. Their plan all along."

Rudy listened to it all until Leroy finished. He pinched his nose and shook his head. "And where is this Harvey Klinger now?"

"We have him in lockup, at least for the night — on drug charges. There wasn't anything else of interest on his phone. And here," Leroy pulled Tim's phone out of his jacket pocket. "Here's Tim's phone. We removed all of Molly's texts from it. I told him this morning I would give it to you to give back to him." Leroy handed the phone to Rudy.

"And what about these other texts? What were on them?"

"Judge, I'm not at liberty to discuss any further evidence than what I just shared. I assume you know we arrested Randy this afternoon for murder." Leroy watched Rudy keenly. He knew how the Judge hated not being in control of a conversation. And he certainly wasn't in control of this one.

Rudy narrowed his eyes before he replied. "I have been appraised, yes. You found his fishing knife in the creek, did you? The one with his initials engraved?"

"That's the one."

"Humph," Rudy snorted out. "I gave that knife to him on his twelfth birthday. Not one bit of gratitude out of him. Not then, not ever. So, is the case against him solid?"

"We wouldn't have arrested him if it wasn't."

"And I assume Springfield is his lawyer."

"He is."

"And am I now off your list of suspects?"

Leroy wondered if there wasn't a slight tinge of sarcasm in his voice. "You were never on a list of suspects, Judge. You still are a person of interest, however." Leroy felt like he was in the middle of some verbal jousting match. He reminded himself to choose his words carefully.

"I see. I also understand you impounded Sally's car. What was that all about?"

Leroy could see Rudy was clearly fishing. He already knew a lot. He wouldn't be getting more. "Again Rudy, I'm not at liberty to discuss that."

"So then, clearly she's also a person of interest, as is Tim. Jesus, Leroy," Rudy's voice rose in anger, "is my whole damn family, people of interest in that fucking whore's murder?"

Leroy let the hurtful words fall. He took another deep breath, then replied. "Connie isn't."

"Well, isn't that just lovely. And what about my wife?"

"As of now, no." By now, the tension in the room was as thick as peanut butter. The two men glared at each other. Leroy needed to move on. "I need to change the subject, Rudy. I know we both talked with AG Winston today. I need to make sure we're on the same page with this Greeley problem before I go in front of the press in a few minutes." Leroy stopped there to give Rudy the opportunity to frame his answer the way he wanted to.

"I believe the Attorney General made it clear how he wanted this presented."

More jousting. "Which exonerates you and DHEC and makes Greeley the lone bad guy."

"Quite a succinct summary, Leroy. I certainly hope you're on board with it."

"My obligation, Judge, is to uphold the law."

"Your obligation, Sheriff, is to follow the evidence and arrest the lawbreakers. Now, what evidence do you have, other than an illegally obtained audio clip from a deranged extortion seeking woman, which you know damn well will not hold up in court? As I told the AG, I was in contact with Huntsman. Yes, I travelled to his lake house last Saturday to ensure our privacy. His permit sites had been hacked, and we needed to ensure that no further harm was done. The investigation of the hack is in Horry County's jurisdiction. Your hands are clean, Leroy. You're free to focus on the murder case. I suggest you do just that."

Leroy had heard enough. It was clear that Rudy and Winston had hatched their plan to cover their sensitive asses and throw Greeley under the bus. He had one last point to make. "Your point is clear, Judge. Now I know where we all stand. But let me make something else clear to you. This murder case will go to trial. I hope they find Randy guilty as I am sure you are as well. But you know Jerry Springfield. He is going to do everything in his power to shed shade on our case. And that will undoubtedly drag in Greeley, DHEC, and possibly yourself into it. Plus, whatever else he can get his grubby hands on."

"I'm quite aware how defense attorneys behave, Leroy. Now, if there isn't anything else, I believe you have a press conference to prepare for. I'd appreciate you keeping me in the loop tomorrow on Randy's status." Rudy rose and came around to see Leroy to the door. He put his hand on the Sheriff's shoulder and smiled. "It's nothing personal, Leroy. It's just how business is done."

"I understand. Good day Judge." Leroy left the chambers shaking his head. "How business is done," he muttered derisively, heading back to his office. Then he thought, it ain't nothing but monkey business. Wait until he finds out he was the father of Molly's baby. Then that fat gorilla's going to end up looking like a chimp in the zoo.

CHAPTER 40

As he drove back to Culligan's Way Tuesday evening, Rudy pondered his predicament. It was Annabelle's day off, so it would be just leftovers for dinner. Him, and Ruth, and Tim. Looked like it was going to be just the three of them for a while now.

He stayed in his chambers until the media disbursed after Leroy's press conference, which Rudy caught on his private TV. Leroy played his part to the tee. Nothing to see here, he conveyed in the most basic of terms. Go talk to Sheriff Lawrence in Horry County. They have jurisdiction on the DHEC hack. Neither Judge Culligan nor DHEC is under any suspicion. Molly's recording is being treated as neither legal nor credible. End of story. Leroy diverted a few nosy questions, and the conference was over. Rudy used a back entrance to leave the courthouse undisturbed, where his Lexus was waiting on him.

As he drove over the Waccamaw River bridge out of Georgetown, the lowering sun cast a shimmering light over Winyah Bay and the vast stretch of Lowcountry marsh grass surrounding it. The early evening view always seemed to soothe him. It satisfied him, how the day's events turned out after such a disastrous beginning. He owed the Attorney General a big-time favor now for bailing him out. He already had a few ideas about how he might thank Winston. Even Jack Greeley should be able to squirm out of his mess with fairly minor damage. Jack wouldn't have his precious lots to build on, at least in Salt Cove, but there'd be plenty of other sites he could go after once the smoke clears. Horry County could look for a hack against DHEC until the cows came home, and they'd find nothing. Rudy felt certain Jack had hid his the money trail end from ever seeing the light of day, and he knew his own transfers were plenty safe. The only remote chance of being caught would be if the FBI got dragged into it somehow and started sniffing out offshore accounts. He felt certain Winston wouldn't let that happen.

With the marsh lot scandal now in good hands, Rudy turned his deliberation to Molly's murder, and what may lie in store there. Finding Randy's knife was certainly a stroke of good fortune. What are the freaking odds, he thought, laughing at the incredible coincidence? Talk about killing two birds with one stone. The biggest problem Rudy thought he'd have on his plate, once he learned about Tim's return, was what to do with Randy. He knew the arrest last Friday was only a temporary measure. Kicking him out of the house for good was another issue altogether. After all, he and Ruth had been trying to do just that since 2008, when Randy turned eighteen. And assuming they found his son guilty, then his biggest problem from last week will be solved, for a long, long time, maybe forever. Rudy smirked, knowing the death of Molly and her fetus was tantamount to multiple homicide in South Carolina, which carried the death penalty.

Rudy wondered what Jerry Springfield might offer as a defense. Overcoming the evidence at hand — Randy at the scene near the time of the murder, plus the knife in the creek, plus various motives available, would be a high wall to climb. Jerry would have to plant reasonable doubt in the minds of the jurors. For that, he would need some plausible explanation how someone else could have done it. But who?

Tim was the last person known to have seen her alive, but there was certainly no motive there and no way he could access the knife. Rudy's mind switched to Ruth. Was there any way possible she could have killed Molly? The animosity was certainly there. He saw it plain as day at the party, not to mention the debacle at the dinner in February. But how could she have gotten hold of Randy's knife? And how could she have made it to the dock and back in such a tight time frame without being detected? That seemed to be too much of a stretch. And what about Sally's car being impounded? Leroy wasn't giving anything away there. He'd have to make some discreet inquiries. After the drug theft fiasco at the party, Sally would certainly have a motive. Could she have come back to the Way at midnight Saturday? Is that why they wanted to search her car?

Who else did that leave as possible suspects? Just himself. And what did they have on him? The bloody shoe? Easily explained, although the timing could be problematic. Access to the knife? Jerry could plant doubt by saying he took the knife from Randy's boat while it was on the beach. Could the jury believe that? And what about motive? Rudy didn't know what else was on Molly's phone, but the prosecution probably knew she was trying to extort him with the marsh lot scandal. Jerry could use that. But there was one other motive they didn't have. One other way Molly tried to extort him, that blew his lid off at the party. And it was a secret. A secret that would never see the light of day. Molly's baby. If that news came out, things could indeed get sticky for him. Sticky indeed, in more ways than one.

Before he knew it, Rudy arrived home to Culligan's Way. Dinner with just his wife and son. Three potential murder suspects, if Jerry Springfield had his way. Ought to make for some interesting conversation.

******

Rudy attempted to kiss Ruth as he entered the Way, but she turned her cheek instead. Not a good start, he thought, and immediately went to pour himself a bourbon. "How was your day dear?" he asked when finished, turning back towards the kitchen where he took a seat in one of the bar chairs on the island. Tim also sat on the island, while Ruth was busy heating leftovers from Tupperware containers. As was the norm for Tuesdays, without Annabelle, the remaining contents from Sunday's dinner were to be finished. Ruth hated throwing food away. "I understand Sheriff Keating paid the two of you a visit this morning."

Ruth paused her preparation and turned to face her husband. Her icy glare sent a shiver down his spine. Tim played the interested bystander, for now. "Yes, he did," began Ruth, "and I'm going to say this just once. I did not appreciate the accusations he made towards myself and Tim. I do not appreciate all the disturbances we have had to deal with around here the last three days. And I certainly did not appreciate our good name being splattered all over the news as tabloid trash for all the world to see this morning."

Rudy evaluated his wife's concerns. He assumed she had either watched or been informed about the morning's news bombasts. Yet concern about her elder son's arrest didn't make the top of the list. It didn't appear to make any list. "I understand completely, Ruth," Rudy responded, as soothing as he could, "and I feel the same way. Did either of you catch Sheriff Keating's news conference this afternoon at 4:30 PM?"

"I did, Dad," said Tim. Ruth had turned her back on them again. "Looks as if things will work out for you after all."

"We'll see. I'm sure the announcement of your brother's arrest pleased you as well."

"I didn't shed any tears, if that's what you mean."

"And you Ruth? What do you think about Randy's arrest?"

Ruth turned around again, still wearing a scowl. "I hope he rots in prison." She then resumed putting the leftovers together.

Rudy smirked, then turned his attention back to Tim. "Oh, Tim, here's your cell phone." Rudy pulled out Tim's phone and handed it to him. "I know you're under strict orders not to divulge any more material that was on it. But —"

"Dad, really, I can't talk about it at all."

"Very well, I understand. But you can talk about things that were not on her phone. Like the discussion you had with Molly at the party and out on the dock."

"I'd rather not. But there really isn't anything to add. Molly obviously had it in for you, and she feared for her life. For good reason, it turns out."

"Her death had nothing to do with what was on her phone. Assuming your brother killed her, it was for very different reasons."

"If you say so, Dad. Please, I *really* don't want to discuss this anymore."

Ruth abruptly turned around again. "And I don't want to hear any more about it either," she shouted. "At all!"

Rudy sipped his bourbon. "Very well then. The subject is closed."

Silence ensued as Ruth set the table and brought the reheated dinner over. Rudy downed the rest of his drink and moved to the dining table. The three took their seats, and after a short blessing, served themselves. "Mom and I took a walk on the beach after the Sheriff left this morning," Tim offered as a new direction from the offending subject. Ruth looked over with concern. "I walked further than I did on Monday."

Rudy eyed them both again, wondering what they had been discussing between themselves. Certainly more than he'd be getting at the dinner table. "That's good, son. I'm glad to hear it." Rudy dug into heaping portions of roast, potatoes, carrots, and a couple of leftover biscuits — not as good as right out of the oven, but still pretty tasty. He let things rest on the legal problems the family faced. In between bites, he looked up and saw Ruth staring him down. He noticed that Ruth wasn't eating. "What? What is it?" he demanded of his wife.

Tim looked up to see his parents glaring at each other from across the table.

"There's something not right with you," Ruth declared. "Something you're not telling me."

Rudy scoffed. "I thought we were not talking about the case anymore."

"I didn't say it has anything to do with the case."

"Then what is it?" Rudy asked, perturbed.

Tim glanced between his two parents.

Rudy watched Ruth with a modicum of apprehension. He knew from past experience, about Ruth's uncanny ability to have a kind of sixth sense. That was why he was always so careful anytime he strayed from the straight and narrow. What was she on to this time, he sat there wondering? It could have been any of several things. One in particular.

"I don't know. But I have a bad feeling."

"Ruth, honey, you've been under a lot of stress. It was a stressful day, been a stressful week, for crying out loud." He ate some more, noticing again Ruth had yet to touch her plate. Rudy glanced over at Tim, who shrugged his shoulders and shook his head. "Perhaps a Valium would do you good after dinner, dear."

"Oh, you'd like that, wouldn't you?" Ruth shot back. "Drug the old woman, get her mind off of everything that's gone to *shit* in this house!"

"Ruth!" Rudy screamed out, not believing his wife had just swore. This almost never happened. "How dare you curse in the home!"

"Mom?" Tim asked with concern. "Are you alright?"

Ruth set her silverware down on the dining table hard enough to cause the two men to jump in their seats. Ruth was definitely not alright. "I don't know what it is, Rudy. I don't know. But I'm going to find out. And when I do, I'll tell you this. Justice *will* be served. And I will serve it cold."

That was enough to send a chill down Rudy's spine.

Ruth rose suddenly, left the table, and went directly up the stairs to her bedroom.

CHAPTER 41

Jerry was at home in his study, late Tuesday afternoon, going over the notes he obtained from the Sheriff's department. Besides pics of the knife, Leroy forwarded to Jerry some texts from Molly's phone and the pics of the blood found on the dock. He promised Jerry more as each piece of evidence was processed and would make the discovery fully accessible no later than Friday.

Earlier, Jerry had another brief meeting with Randy and promised him he believed in his innocence, and with any luck, he should be able to avoid a trial. Privately, Jerry had his doubts. He knew Randy Culligan to be one of the least credible people in the county, and the surfacing of the presumed murder weapon with his clients' initials on it would prove way beyond problematic. It could be a death sentence. Still, given the media firestorm of the morning, connecting the Culligans with Molly, anything was possible. He made that clear to the media, who had turned to his attention after Leroy finished his press conference. Jerry soaked up the attention up like a sponge.

When Jerry's cell rang, he didn't recognize the number, and picked up on the third ring.

"Jerry Springfield here."

"Jerry, Ian Folger. Long time buddy. How have you been?"

Ian Folger, Jerry thought. Greeley's fix it man. What were the odds? "Ian, good to hear from you. I had a hunch you might call on me," Jerry lied. "Quite the news story this morning. Bet your boss was none too happy."

"He's not. And what about you? Representing my boss's mistress's killer. Quite a coup. I caught both news conferences this afternoon."

"Alleged killer, Ian. Randy stands by his innocence."

"Right, Jerry. And I stand by my virginity. I wish you the best of luck."

"What can I do for you, Ian? I got a lot on my plate right now."

"Of course. As I mentioned, my boss is none too happy with how things went down this morning. He blames Judge Culligan most of all. Thinks he threw Jack under the proverbial bus."

"Wouldn't argue that."

"Yes, well, Jack wants revenge. Told me cost is not an issue. He wants dirt on Rudy. Now I believe you're going to come into some very interesting findings during your discovery. Anything we could use against that judge would be highly valuable information, if you catch my drift."

Jerry caught it in an instant. "And just how valuable might this information be?"

"Five figures at least," Ian said without hesitation. "Very good home improvement rates in this environment."

Jerry thought it over. Not for long, though. "I'll see what I can do, Ian. I'm promised discovery by Friday. We'll touch base then. Thanks for the call."

"And thank you, Jerry."

Jerry ended the call and thought about how nice a newly installed built in hot tub on his back deck would look — and feel.

******

The next morning at 9:00 AM, Leroy, Tony, and Gina met in Gina's office. Gina Slocum was a polished prosecutor with twenty years of experience under her belt. She was known for being a tough but fair DA without even a whiff of ethical impurity around her. Rudy liked to call her a goody-two shoes behind her back. To her face, she was always DA Slocum. Brunette and petite, Gina always wore business suits which showed her physical fitness, class, and exuded her determination.

The three took seats at the conference table in her expansive office. Tony had prepared a PowerPoint presentation with a timeline of events at the pier, and pics of the other evidence. The autopsy report sat in the middle of the table.

"So," Gina began, "we have Stevenson as our judge and Randy's hearing in an hour. What are we asking for there?"

"I'm fine with house arrest, Gina," offered Leroy. "As long as it's not at Culligan's Way."

"Where else does he live?"

"He stays in a trailer at a fish camp on the other side of the Waccamaw River. That's where we arrested him. Fine with me if he hangs out there until the trial. Place stinks to high heaven."

"Alright. Are we expecting Jerry to ask for a change in venue, given the closeness of Judge Culligan to the case?"

"He might, but my guess is it plays into his hand. Rudy polarizes the demographic. Jerry only needs one dissenter. And even if he did request one, I don't think Stevenson would grant it."

"I agree," concurred Gina. "He'd have to show a good reason he couldn't get an impartial jury. Ok, let's go to the evidence. Two keys — the knife and the timeline. I understand

Sylvia sent the knife to a local fab shop to get a blood sample. Where do we stand on that?"

"Should have it back tomorrow sometime," Tony answered. "No guarantees, but it's worth a shot. There's not any other evidence on the knife that directly links it to the murder. But the circumstantial implication is pretty —"

"Overwhelming," Gina finished his sentence. "I don't think we'll have any problem convincing a jury that was the knife that killed Molly and got tossed in the creek immediately afterwards. The only question in my mind is, could someone else have come into possession of the knife?"

"Gina," Leroy broke in. "We believe Jerry is going to try to put reasonable doubt in the minds of the jury by making plausible cases that either Rudy or Sally could have killed Molly. And tying the knife to either of them is going to be a stretch."

"Maybe, maybe not," interrupted Tony.

"Please explain," Gina asked.

"I still have some doubts Rudy didn't do it. And if I have doubts, the jury may as well. Here's my theory. Like Sally, Rudy somehow either overheard or got wind of the conversation between Molly and Tim about their clandestine meeting at midnight. Then Rudy and Molly get into an argument leading to Molly being thrown from the party. We know Molly tried to extort Rudy about the marsh lot exposure. Perhaps she also meant to extort him about the pregnancy. Rudy has to eliminate the threat. Randy was forced to vacate the house, then leaves his boat on the beach. This gives Rudy the chance to grab the knife he knows will tie to Randy, then commit the murder right after he sees Tim return to the house."

The other two listened closely and thought for a second. "It's plausible, Tony," countered Gina, "but on cross-examination, it's full of holes. Just for starters; could he really have also overheard the conversation? How would he know Molly would still be at the dock after Tim came back, and how could he have known Randy was coming back? Also, if he went to the beach and back out the front door, there'd be sand tracked through the house. I could go on if need be."

"Ok," Leroy broke in. "What about Sally? I still don't believe she's telling the whole truth. Look at the timeline. We know she's at the scene two docks down when Tim leaves to go back in the house, 12:07 AM. Molly is murdered sometime between then and 12:17 AM when Rudy reenters the house, more likely 12:13 AM when he goes out of the house, if he didn't do it himself. Sally is caught on tape at the gas station at 12:19 AM. The station is just under four miles from the pier. Even going 25 mph all the way there, she should have been there before 12:19 AM, if she left when she said she did. If she stayed a few minutes longer and witnessed the murder, she's covering for someone. Or she murdered Molly herself. I just don't know how she could have gotten that knife."

"Exactly, Leroy," Gina rejoined. "It all goes back to the knife. But I do agree she may have stayed and witnessed, and then is now covering up. Do you think she'd cover for Randy?"

The other two looked at Gina and both shook their heads. "Hard to imagine, Gina," said Leroy. "Why would anyone? But it is her brother."

"I don't see where Jerry has a reasonable defense," Gina stated in conclusion. "We should be able to poke enough holes in anything he throws up to keep reasonable doubt out of the jury's mind. Agreed?"

"Agreed," they both said.

"What about the autopsy, Gina? How do we handle that?"

Gina grinned back and opened the autopsy report again to the last page. DNA match to the prior generation of Randy Culligan. Paternity is determined to be Judge Rudolph Culligan. "We don't," she stated bluntly. "If Jerry wants to use it, it's Rudy who'll be held out to dry — not us."

Tony and Leroy couldn't agree more.

CHAPTER 42

Less than two hours later, they released Randy from detention, sporting a brand-new ankle bracelet, courtesy of the Georgetown County Correctional facility. Jerry had bail arranged and gave Randy instruction for how he was to spend the next few weeks. Basically, on the couch in his trailer at the fish camp, watching TV. Jerry told Randy he could drink anything and as much as he wanted, as long as he didn't try to go anywhere more than ¼ mile from the trailer, at which point both he and the Sheriff's department would get a nasty alarm on their phones. Jerry warned Randy just how unpleasant that would be for both of them, but mainly for Randy. For all Jerry cared, Randy could drink himself to death before the trial began.

At the hearing, Randy submitted his not guilty plea, bail was set, and they arranged the home arrest details. Judge Stevenson received assurances from both sides they would have sufficient time to prepare. A brief attempt by Jerry to change venues went nowhere. Jerry wanted to know when discovery would happen, and Gina told him she was waiting on one last report, which she expected Thursday. Jerry would get his hands on the evidence of the case on Friday morning.

Stevenson appealed to the lawyers if there were any way they could avoid a trial with a plea bargain. Both shook their heads. Randy shook his vehemently.

"No way," declared Jerry. "My client is innocent."

"The prosecution stands by their case, Your Honor," countered Gina.

"Very well," announced Stevenson after he sighed. He had read the autopsy report, and knew his esteemed colleague and senior judge would be sucked into this mess — one way or another.

Stevenson gaveled the hearing to a close. A trial between Randall Culligan and the State of South Carolina in the case of the murder of Miss Molly Elmwood would begin in three weeks, on Wednesday, May 5. May justice be served.

******

On Thursday afternoon, shortly before 3:00 PM, Leroy received a text from Sylvia.

The DNA report from the knife just came back. Can you meet me in the lab?

Leroy replied he'd be there in ten minutes, then called Tony and told him to meet him there. He was excited to be at the end of the evidence collection. It meant the final handoff between him and Gina. And won't he be happy to wipe this case off his slate. He couldn't believe it hadn't even been a week since Tim arrived back at Culligan's Way and Randy was arrested for the first time. The image of Ruth's rolling pin slamming into Randy's face would be forever etched in his mind.

Leroy knew he would take the stand once the trial started. He also knew Jerry Springfield would try to drag the Greeley fiasco, as it became known throughout the station, into the murder trial. Depending on how much rope Stevenson gave Jerry would determine how messy things got for him, as well as Rudy. Rudy told him just that morning he considered the matter closed and added he still hoped Horry County would find the source of the hack. With his hands clean from Greeley, and Randy on ice,

Rudy seemed in as good a mood as Leroy had seen him in weeks. That would change when the autopsy report saw the light of day.

Leroy greeted Tony and Sylvia in the lab. Sylvia handed Leroy the knife in an evidence bag and a report.

"So," he asked, "what's the verdict? Did they get enough blood to run the DNA?"

Sylvia smiled. "They did, just enough. And they did a super job on the knife. See for yourself."

Tony carefully undid the bag and removed the knife. At the base of the blade, not 1/8" wide and 1/16" deep was a machined-out notch. The rest of the knife was in perfect condition. "They sure did," commented Tony, nodding his head.

Leroy opened the two-page report and immediately scanned down to the conclusion. It stated there were two very different types of blood found in the notch. One marine, one human. Upon the polymerase chain reaction spectrometric testing, the marine sample matched one from the mackerel family. The human DNA sample was a dead match to Molly.

Leroy and Tony smiled at each other. "One-part mackerel, one part Molly," quipped Leroy.

"Yeah, and all murder," answered Tony. Leroy couldn't agree more.

******

The next morning Leroy, Gina, and Jerry met in Gina's office to hand over the discovery evidence. To Leroy, Jerry looked like a kid in a candy store, with wide-open eyes, and a sense of wonderment in his face. The physical evidence was fairly limited; the knife, a couple of blood samples from the dock, and Rudy's bloody shoe — kept by Leroy at Tony's insistence.

Gina had the main bulk of evidence packaged into a neat
PowerPoint presentation. The video portions included the Ring
cam videos and Sally's car at the gas station. Statements of Tim,
Ruth, Sally, Rudy, Randy, and Harvey were included as well.
Then the inspection report of Sally's vehicle and the DNA report
of the knife were detailed. A minute-to-minute timeline around
the murder timeframe put everything in perspective. Finally, the
autopsy report finished the PowerPoint.

Gina and Leroy both watched Jerry's expressions as they
went through the evidence, trying to pick up on which items
caught his attention more than others. Jerry seemed most
interested in Rudy's and Sally's statements, as well as Rudy's
shoe. The reason was obvious to both Leroy and Gina. It was
through Rudy and Sally where Jerry would try to cast reasonable
doubt to the jury.

At the very end of the autopsy report, Jerry learned of the
bombshell finding. His eyes popped wide open. "Are you kidding
me!" he shouted out, unable to keep himself from laughing at the
revelation of Molly's baby's father. "Rudy? And Molly?"

"I wouldn't read too much into it," Gina told Jerry. "You
can use it if you must. But don't forget, you still have to practice
law in Rudy's court."

"Oh yeah, right," chortled Jerry. "As if Rudy ever cut me a
break defending my clients."

"Still," continued Gina, "I would tread lightly if I were
you."

"Concern noted, Gina, but I'll decide how best to defend
my client. I appreciate the discovery items listed. But what about

the Greeley affair? I don't see any documents related to that here."

Gina and Leroy looked at each other and frowned. "Jerry," Gina cautiously began her answer. "Greeley is not on trial here. Randy Culligan is. We don't see any relationship between Greeley and Molly's murder. So there's no discovery for it."

"What! Are you joking? Molly was trying to extort Rudy because of Greeley. And you're telling me there's no connection between the two? Give me a break."

"What we're saying, Jerry," Gina's voice deepened with irritation. "Is that there is no *evidence* connecting Greeley and Molly's murder. This is a discovery meeting, to share evidence. You understand that, don't you?"

"Oh, I understand it alright. I guess I'll have to do my own legwork to show the connection."

"Which you are free to do. Don't forget, discovery goes both ways. And Judge Stevenson will not allow hearsay as evidence in his courtroom."

Leroy could tell the omission of all Greeley related matters had gotten under Jerry's skin. But he couldn't resist adding a little fuel to the fire. "Or smoke, or mirrors," he added curtly.

Jerry had pressed matters as far as he needed for now. "Very well then," he said, rising to his feet. "Send me the PowerPoint, Gina. I appreciate what you've found. I'll be in touch." He shook both Gina's and Leroy's hand and marched out the door.

When he left, Gina turned to Leroy and said, "Was that really necessary, Sheriff?"

Leroy smirked and replied, "Necessary, no, but he deserved it." Gina just shook her head.

******

As soon as he got back to his office, Jerry placed a call to Ian Folger's burner phone. The disclosure of Rudy as the father of the poor impaled fetus was going to be a gold mine of possibilities for Ian, and Jack, and in due course, himself. He could already see himself on his expansive new deck, in his brand new built-in hot tub.

And it wasn't just the paternity result that had Jerry giddy with excitement. Rudy Culligan had been a pain in his side ever since Jerry started his practice in Georgetown eight years ago. Rudy made it clear on many occasions in his not-so-subtle way that he didn't care for Jerry as a lawyer, or as a human being. Jerry got the impression Rudy thought he was a sleazy ambulance chasing, defense lawyer with low levels of morals, and high levels of obstinacy. He didn't like Jerry's hair, his accent, his clothes, or his choice of clients. Jerry would tell those around him he didn't care, but in reality, he knew he was as insecure as a four-year-old who just wet the bed. Jerry had long wanted payback to Judge Rudolph Culligan. Now he had his chance.

"Ian, Jerry here," Jerry said, happy Ian answered on the first ring.

"I know that, Jerry. You're the only one who has this number. What's up?"

"I believe I have something very juicy for you and your boss. I just got back from discovery in the murder case, and I got a first look at Molly's autopsy report." Jerry paused to increase the suspense.

"Yes, and —"

"Well, it seems that when Molly was killed, she was ten weeks pregnant. The knife went straight though the tiny fetus."

"You're breaking my heart, Jerry. Get to the point."

"And — they did a DNA test on the fetus. Long story short, Judge Culligan was the daddy."

Jerry heard silence for a few seconds, then, "Now that is something I wasn't expecting. I can use that for sure. Got any suggestions?"

"I do, as a matter of fact. Are you familiar with the wife, Ruth Culligan?"

"Can't say I am."

"Well, she's crazy as batshit on fruitcake. Last time she caught Rudy cheating, she put rat poison in his pimento cheese. Almost killed him then. So —"

"Ha! Yes. I see where you're going. We get this autopsy to her personal attention, then let the chips fall where they may."

"Exactly my thoughts. I'll get a copy of the report printed out. Where can I meet you?"

After a couple seconds, Ian responded, "Meet me on the Murrells Inlet boardwalk, outside The Crab Shack, 2:00 PM."

"I'll be there, Ian, thanks." After Jerry ended the call, he went straight to his PC and printed out the autopsy, all the while thinking how nice that hot tub was going to feel.

CHAPTER 43

Things calmed down in Culligan's Way over the next several days. After the first weeks' worth of drama, Tim was more than pleased for the place to return to the calm he had expected when he arrived. With Randy on house arrest at the fish camp, Connie corralled in rehab, and his father keeping to himself when not at court, Tim settled into somewhat of a set schedule. Annabelle took great pleasure cooking him a homemade full breakfast each morning, and he had adjusted into a routine of breakfast, a beach walk, normally with his mother, then some reading, followed by lunch, then a nap — usually a long one on the original Pawleys Island hammock which hung in the southeast corner of the veranda. After he woke, normally by around 3:00 PM, he would continue to read and rest until dinner, when his father returned home. Evenings usually found Tim watching Netflix, or on occasion, driving to the mainland to visit Sally.

In a week's time, he had already found he could add a quarter mile to his morning walk, and each afternoon he seemed to find himself more rested than the previous day's nap. He mentioned the peacefulness that seemed to settle over Culligan's Way to Sally when he visited her home the following Monday after dinner. How Mom, and Annabelle, and even Dad seemed less tense and more personable than he noticed the previous week, Molly's murder aside.

"It's Randy," Sally assured him. "And a bit Connie. Even when Randy wasn't staying at the Way, he'd show up unannounced and disrupt whatever passed for peace in that house. It was always like a walking time bomb when he was around. And with Connie, she'd spend hours, days even so stoned no one could talk with her. Then she'd get on some kick and bitch like a she-devil. This is the first time I believe neither of them was in the house. Enjoy it while it lasts."

"What about the murder trial? Do you think he's guilty?"

Sally looked at her brother with a sly grin. "Do I think he's guilty, or do I think he'll be convicted?"

Tim looked stunned for a moment. "Well, both I guess."

"Let me tell you something about justice in dear old Dad's courthouse. Convictions can be based more on who you know than whether you're guilty. In Randy's case, he might know many people around here, but he doesn't realize most of them hate him, which doesn't bode well for our brother. Bottom line, I think he's toast."

Tim tried to digest what Sally had just fed him. "Let me ask you the same question in another way. Do you think Dad is going to intervene on his behalf?"

Sally grinned again. "Now you're thinking like a Culligan. Honestly, I don't think so. I know someone who absolutely will not be pulling for him — Mom. If Dad intervenes, he's going to face the wrath of Ruth. We'll see soon enough. But my hunch is you'll be back in New York well before you see Randy Culligan show his face at the Way again."

Tim smiled as he noted his sister's acerbic response. It gave him a peace of mind he had only dreamed of not long ago.

******

On Tuesday morning, Tim was getting ready for his daily beach walk with his mother. Annabelle once again had her regular Tuesday day off and the Way was as quiet as ever. As he strode downstairs in his bathing suit and ragged t-shirt, Tim noticed Ruth slumped over the dining table, studying some document. When she heard him coming down the steps, she shot a look up towards him and quickly turned over the documents.

"Are you ready, Mom?" he asked, noting Ruth's unusual behavior.

Ruth stared at Tim with blank eyes.

He thought his mother was seeing straight through him, as if he wasn't even there.

"I'm — I'm not feeling right this morning, son. Go on ahead without me. I apologize." Ruth's sentence drifted off on the last word. She was in another world.

"Are you ok, Mom?" Tim asked, now very much concerned. "What are you looking at there?"

Now Ruth returned to her stark reality. She shot an icy look at Tim. "It's nothing of your concern, Tim. Please, if you let me be, I'll be fine." Ruth returned to staring at the document in front of her, shutting Tim out from her world.

Tim knew better than to push his mother too far. "Alright then. I'll be on the beach for a bit. You're sure you're ok by yourself?"

Ruth never acknowledged Tim, she just kept gaping at the papers in front of her.

Tim let himself out the back door and walked towards the crossover.

******

Twenty minutes earlier, after their breakfast had been cleared and Tim was upstairs, Ruth had gone out front to retrieve the mail, which always arrived by 10:00 AM each morning. Among a few pieces of junk and a bill, there was a large yellow envelope marked as confidential to the attention of Ruth Culligan. Ruth examined the envelope curiously, noting there wasn't a return address or a postmark. It appeared to have been placed in her mailbox and not delivered by the post office. She returned to the house and sat down at the dining table to open it.

The title of the document immediately sent a shiver down her spine. Final Autopsy Report on Molly Elmwood, the bold heading declared to a shocked Ruth. Why did this come to my attention in a package without a return address? she wondered. Ruth skimmed through the three-page report to see if there may be something the sender wanted to point out. And at the end of the report, there it was. Circled with a black Sharpy pen and highlighted in yellow, Ruth read the words which would send her world upside down. The DNA analysis on the fetus of Molly Elmwood has determined that paternity belongs to Judge Rudolph Culligan. Ruth stared blankly at the document as she reread it over and over. She took a few minutes to read the entire document. Stunned by the news that Molly had been pregnant to begin with, she reeled from the revelation of Rudy's infidelity.

When Tim came downstairs, Ruth was in no condition to take a walk. She needed time to digest, time to comprehend, and time to plan. After she sent him out to the beach by himself, Ruth reread the autopsy one last time, then set it down. She could feel her mind slip from a delicate balance of sanity into madness. This time, she took no action to stop it. She felt the rage brewing inside of her, the betrayal she could never reconcile, and the need to take revenge overwhelm her psyche. She had a plan alright. Oh, did she ever have a plan.

Realizing she had maybe fifteen minutes left to herself before Tim returned from his walk, Ruth went straight to work. She first checked Rudy's bourbon supply. As she remembered seeing from the day before, the latest bottle of Woodford Reserve had only a couple of inches left in the bottom. It had been full before the party, but between Randy and Rudy, most of the high-quality brown elixir had been consumed. It was just what Ruth needed for her plot. She grabbed a plastic bag, went upstairs and started with her own medicine cabinet. A bottle of Ambien she kept for insomnia was almost full, having just been refilled for sixty tablets. She examined her meds of Risperdal and decided they would be a waste. Same with the Valium. She didn't need them for this purpose and wasn't about to waste her special pills.

Placing the drugs in the bag, Ruth moved on to Rudy's side of the bathroom. He had his high blood pressure medication, his cholesterol meds and a bottle of Percocet he kept for when his phlebitis acted up. Such a wuss, Ruth thought, placing the pills in the bag. The man had absolutely no tolerance for pain. He'll be plenty painless before long.

Next, she went across the hall to Connie's room. Ruth was certain there wouldn't be anything other than over-the-counter pills in her medicine cabinet, but that was alright. She knew where Connie hid the good stuff — in the back corner of the third drawer from the top of her Queen Anne dresser, right under her silk panties.

Ruth had long known about her younger daughter's drug habit and hiding places. She supposed she facilitated it by not calling her out. Ruth reasoned in her own convoluted manner that Connie dealt with her demons similar to how she dealt with her own. Ruth took a moment and pondered Connie's latest crisis. Connie chose her drugs by her own volition, as opposed to Ruth's strict prescriptions. Either way, the Culligan women had mental challenges above and beyond what society prescribed as normal. Ruth wasn't sure exactly how Sally stayed above the fray of it all.

Ruth found four and a half pills in all. Three were Oxycontins. Probably the drugs from Molly's final sale. The other pill and a half had no markings. Curiously, there was a razor blade inside the stash wrapped in a kerchief. Apparently, it was used to slice off portions of the unmarked pills. Whatever, mused Ruth. I'll add them to my witch's brew.

Satisfied with the accumulated stash of drugs, Ruth returned to the kitchen and set to work preparing her concoction. She brought the bourbon bottle over to the island and carefully dumped all the pills she had collected onto the large cutting board. Then she took out the rolling pin, smiling at the still visible faded blood stain on the one end, and gently pulverized the collection of pills. There were probably over a hundred pills in all, and in less than five minutes Ruth had herself a small pile of crushed narcotics. Gratified with the good work she had accomplished; she took out a funnel they kept in the miscellaneous drawer and placed it in the mouth of the bourbon bottle. Then she scooped the pill powder and deposited it all into the bourbon. She placed the top on and shook the bottle to get as much of the powder into solution as she could.

Ruth examined the bottle again and said to herself, "I'll need to reshake it before the old buzzard gets his cocktail tonight." Thinking things over, Ruth felt there was something else she could do for a topper. Then it came to her. She opened the cabinet below the sink and pulled out a bottle of bleach. Just for kicks, she thought slyly, as she added an ounce to the bottle. Damn swill smells like bleach to begin with. He'll never know the difference. She then gave the whiskey one final shake and returned it to the bar. Ruth didn't blink an eye as she made her way out the back door, then took a seat in a rocker and waited for Tim to return.

CHAPTER 44

Rudy arrived home that evening in his usual grumpy mood. Whatever was ill on his mind as he walked through the door would be nothing compared to what he was about to face. As he pulled into the carport, Ruth made her way to the bar and gave the bourbon bottle one last good shake. She could tell at least some of the powdered concoction lay on the bottom of the bottle and wanted to make sure Rudy got the maximum effect. Ruth didn't have a clue what exactly that would be, but whatever it was, in her mind, it was roundly justified.

Ruth knew Rudy would want dinner as soon as he finished his regular cocktail. Tim was helping in the kitchen in Annabelle's absence. It was the usual Tuesday fare of leftovers from Sunday, this time the remaining pork loin roast along with roasted potatoes, green beans, and a broccoli casserole. Tim was busy getting the Tupperware trays ready to reheat and didn't notice his mother making a side trip to the bar. Nor did he pay any attention to the large yellow envelope sitting on the dining table at his father's normal position.

Ruth greeted Rudy at the front door, but without the normal kiss. "There's something I need to show you," she told him curtly. "Get your drink and come over to the table."

Rudy grumbled, "What is it this time, Ruth? Seems every time Annabelle isn't here to lead you around like a lost puppy, something runs amuck."

Ruth never heard a word. She took a seat at her usual place at the table next to Rudy. She glanced back and forth between him fixing his drink and the envelope on the table. When Rudy finished pouring, he took his normal first sip. Ruth held her breath. Rudy didn't seem to notice anything amiss, and he came over with his drink in his hand. Sitting at the table, he looked at the envelope in front of him.

"What's this?" he griped and opened the top.

"Just read it," Ruth replied, staring at the whiskey glass.

When Rudy saw the heading on the report, he became outraged. "What the hell is this? Where did you get this?" He took another sip, a bigger one. This time he looked at the glass oddly, but then turned his attention back to the autopsy report.

"Are you blind? Can you not read?" answered Ruth, who girded herself for what would happen next.

Rudy ignored her as he skimmed over the report. When he arrived at the third page with the circled and highlighted revelation, he screamed, "What! That's outrageous!" He turned to Ruth with an icy glare and demanded, "I asked you where you got this report. Now answer me."

"It came in the mail this morning. With no return address. Now you answer me. What was going on between you and Molly, you scumbag!"

Rudy was speechless. His faced flushed red as his temper grew to a boil. However, instead of more vitriol pouring out of his mouth, he decided he needed the full impact of his cocktail first. He drained the tainted bourbon in one last gulp and Ruth immediately knew something wasn't right. She watched as Rudy first seemed to have difficulty focusing his eyes. He stood to his feet and muttered, "What did you…" but before he completed his sentence, Rudy keeled over and crashed to the floor like a mighty bull elephant shot down in the Serengeti.

By this time, Tim became alerted to the confrontation at the dining table and was on his way over when he saw his father collapse on the floor. "Mom! What happened?"

Ruth sat her in her seat, rigid as stone, not saying a word. She tried to open her mouth but couldn't speak.

Tim rushed to his father and turned him over. Rudy had foam coming out of his mouth and was unconscious. Tim kneeled over his chest and tried to listen to a heartbeat. "I don't think he's breathing, Mom!" he cried out. "Call 911." Tim panicked when he saw Rudy's eyes roll back in his head. He straddled his father's wide chest and began doing compressions. "Mom!" he screamed, "Call 911, *now!*"

Ruth finally blinked and regained a sense of reality. "Oh, my goodness. Oh my goodness, what have I done?" She looked around to find her phone and saw it sitting on the island. The sight of her husband laying still on the floor and her son giving CPR sent a shock wave through her. Ruth reached for the phone and dialed 911. After she finished the call, she went over to where Tim lay straddled over Rudy. "Will he live, Tim, will he?"

Just then Rudy coughed and let out a slow moan. Tim stopped his compressions and stood up. "Looks like he will, Mom. The ambulance should be here in a couple of minutes." They both looked at the sight of the county's senior circuit court judge, laying prostrate on the floor, groaning. Tim turned his attention back to Ruth. "Ok, Mom. You want to tell me what this is all about?"

Ruth hung her head, then shook it slowly. "I didn't want to kill him. I just wanted to make him sick."

"But why, Mom? Why did you want to hurt him?"

Ruth turned her head to the envelope and report on the table. "There," she showed for him to see. "That damn report on that witch."

Tim bristled at his mother swearing, then picked up the report. He quickly scanned it and went to the highlighted section. When it sank into him what had happened, he closed his eyes and shook his head. "Aw geez, Mom," he said, turning his attention back to Ruth, "Not again."

******

Two hours later, the remaining three free Culligans gathered in the waiting room of the Georgetown Medical Center hospital, anxiously awaiting word of Rudy's condition. Ruth was beside herself and could not be consoled, despite Sally's and Tim's best efforts. Thirty minutes earlier, Ruth gave the ER on-call doctor her best estimate of what she had placed in Rudy's whiskey along with how much bourbon was in the bottle to begin with. The ER doc pressed her if she missed anything, because the extreme reaction Rudy had had did not reconcile with the amount of drugs he would have consumed. Ruth described the pill and a half taken from Connie's drawer, which she could not identify. "We'll know when we get the labs back soon, Mrs. Culligan," Ruth was told. "Thank you for your help."

What the ER doctor hadn't told Ruth or any of the other Culligans was that they had contacted the Sheriff's office and someone would be at the hospital soon to investigate. That someone turned out to be Sheriff Keating. When Leroy appeared in the waiting room, Tim initially thought he was there for Rudy's support. That changed when he requested a private meeting with just Ruth and Tim. Tim brought the copy of the autopsy report with him when the three of them sat down at a small conference table the hospital provided.

"You need to see this," Tim told Leroy, handing him the report. "It was sent to Mom this morning by mail. But look on the envelope, no return address and no postmark. Somebody placed it in the mailbox."

Tim saw Leroy do a double-take when he opened the yellow envelope and saw the autopsy report. "*This* was hand delivered to your mailbox?"

"And look at the end of the report. Whoever did this clearly wanted to get under Mom's skin."

Leroy went to the last page and saw the highlighted results. He gawked. "This report is highly confidential, and constitutes a serious breach of protocol. My sincere apology to you, Mrs. Culligan."

"So, do you know who leaked this?" Tim asked.

"I have a pretty good idea, Tim, but I'm not at liberty to discuss it with either of you. Now Mrs. Culligan, I'm going to have to take a statement from you. Can you tell me what you did to make Judge Culligan sick?"

Tim was stunned by the direct line of questioning and took offense to it. "You don't have to answer him, Mom," he interrupted. "He knows that." Tim shot a sideways glare at Leroy. "I think you may want a lawyer with you before you say anything to the Sheriff here."

Ruth observed Tim, then Leroy.

Tim crossed his fingers that his Mom would understand her rights and the jeopardy she might place herself in.

"Sheriff Keating, sir," Ruth began, "I believe I will take Tim up on his advice and hold off any statement until I have my lawyer present."

Tim let out a sigh of relief. He knew Leroy had no choice but to consent.

"Very well, Mrs. Culligan. You are under no obligation to answer any questions at this point. I may insist you come to the station along with your attorney, but I'll wait until the morning. I will hang around here, however, until the lab tests are complete. You're free to rejoin Sally in the waiting area."

As Tim and Ruth returned to join Sally, Leroy had a brief discussion with the nurse on call and took a seat at the other end of the room. Moments later, the ER doctor came into the waiting area.

"Mrs. Culligan?" he asked to the room.

"Yes," Ruth shot up, anticipation caught in her breath. "That's me."

"I'm Dr. Brighton, the ER doctor on call tonight. Judge Culligan is awake and doing fine. You can come see him now."

"Oh, thank goodness!" Ruth cried out, nearly collapsing in Sally and Tim's arms. The three followed Dr. Brighton down the corridor into Rudy's private room. He was sitting up in his bed when he saw his family enter, followed by his doctor. "Rudy, oh Rudy," Ruth said, rushing to his bedside. "I am so sorry for this. I'm so —" Ruth buried herself into Rudy's chest and cried uncontrollably. Tim and Sally stood to the side and watched their mother make peace with the man whom they had both thought tried to kill two hours earlier.

Rudy held Ruth in a big bear hug and let her cry herself out. "It's ok, Ruth honey. I'm alright, I'm going to be fine," he said in as soothing a voice as his children had ever heard come out of his mouth.

"Rudy," Ruth said when she had finally gained her composure. "I didn't mean to harm you. I only wanted to make you a little sick, after seeing that dreadful report. Please, do you believe me?"

"I do, Ruth. I understand. And I'm very sorry you had to see that report. I have only myself to blame."

Now Tim eyed Sally, astounded. Did he really just hear what their father had said?

"But I did this to you. I could have killed you. They're going to want to send me back to Charleston, Rudy, I know it. Sheriff Keating is already wanting to know what I did to you. He's out in the waiting room now, waiting on the lab results."

"Is he now?" Rudy grumbled, sounding more like his normal self. "You let me take care of that, darling. And don't worry. No one is going to send you away again."

Ruth started crying again. "I can't go back Rudy, I can't. I'd kill myself first. I'm so sorry, I'm so sorry." Rudy let Ruth cry herself out again. When Ruth was finished, it was as if someone turned a hose off. She dried her eyes and sat up straight on the side of the bed, then looked at everyone around who had been watching her. "What are y'all looking at? Haven't you ever seen a woman upset before? Lord have mercy." Ruth turned her attention to the doctor. "Well doctor, what can you tell us? Do you know what made my husband so sick?"

Dr. Brighton looked around the room waiting on a signal from someone other than the unstable woman on the bed to let him know it was safe to begin. "Go ahead, Doctor," Rudy signaled he was ready to hear what he had to say. Everyone turned their attention to Dr. Brighton.

"Judge, you're a very lucky man to be here. I have a laundry list of substances that tested positive in your body, but none of them were at levels that would have been mortally toxic. Except for the Fentanyl. You had potentially fatal levels of Fentanyl in your system. In fact, I'm told your son, Tim, gave you chest compressions soon after you were afflicted. It most likely saved your life." Dr. Brighton paused here for Rudy to give a well deserved thank you to Tim, which he did after he thoroughly digested the news for a few seconds.

"My thanks to you, Tim. I truly appreciate it."

Tim smiled, hearing what had to have been the first words of gratitude he had ever received from his father. "My pleasure, Dad. It was the least I could do."

Dr. Brighton continued. "As far as the other substances we found in your system, there was Ambien, Amlodipine, Percocet, Oxycodone, and Bleach. None were at levels that would have harmed you seriously.

Rudy stared blankly at Ruth beside him. "Bleach, dear — seriously?" Ruth simply shrugged.

"However, as I'm sure you are aware, Fentanyl is an extremely potent drug. As well as highly illegal. I'm going to have to turn the lab report over to the Sheriff's department. I'm told an officer is outside waiting for it now."

"Um, ahem," Rudy loudly cleared his throat. "Yes, Dr. Brighton, about that. Could I have a minute with you alone please? Ruth, kids, please wait outside while I have a private word with the doctor here." Staying wasn't an option. Ruth, Sally, and Tim quickly left the room to the doctor and Rudy.

As soon as Rudy and Brighton were alone in the room, Rudy got straight to the point. "You're Dr. Bruce Brighton, I assume."

"That's correct, Judge. What is this about?"

"Well Bruce, I believe you have a pending malpractice suit currently in our system. Something to do with an AFIB patient who crashed in the ER because of an incorrect injection under your supervision."

Dr. Brighton bristled at Rudy's ascertain. "It was an allegedly improper amount of a drug to bring the patient's heart rate down. Nothing was proven and I have every intention of clearing my name."

"And I'm sure you do, doctor, absolutely. But your legal fees have been quite staggering and I'm sure your malpractice insurance rates have, let's say, ballooned. Yes?"

"What are you getting at, Judge? Let's hear it."

"What I'm getting at, sir, is that we are both in a situation where we could help each other out immensely. I cannot let the Georgetown PD get a hold of these lab results. It will incriminate my wife and she is in no condition to be sent back to Charleston Arlington, let alone prison. You heard what she said. She means it. You, on the other hand, would stand to benefit nicely should your malpractice suit, let's say — disappeared."

Dr. Brighton rubbed his hand over his chin as he pondered the possibilities. "Ok, Judge. I'm game. What exactly would you like for me to do?"

Rudy broke into a broad grin. He had what he felt was a very easy and sure-fire plan. "You see Dr. Brighton, I have another daughter, Connie, who is currently in rehab for drug addiction. I'm sure the Fentanyl which made its way into my system came from her stash. It seems last week, after I made it clear she had no choice but to enter rehab, she got her revenge on me by placing one of her Fentanyl pills into my Amlodipine blood pressure bottle. I take a blood pressure pill each evening before dinner. The Fentanyl pill looks very similar to the Amlodipine. Once she placed it in the bottle without my knowledge, I was playing Russian Roulette each evening. Tonight my luck ran out. So, change your lab report to show only the Fentanyl in my system. As you said, it was enough to nearly kill me. Connie will take the fall, but I'll deal with that once she's out of rehab. If you make that change, Dr. Brighton, I will promise you your malpractice suit will find its way into the trash can."

Brighton looked at Rudy earnestly, then smiled. "Judge Culligan — we have a deal.

CHAPTER 45

The next morning, Rudy anxiously waited in his chambers for Leroy to come by. He had a 10:00 AM hearing and Leroy promised him he'd be by before then. Now, at 9:45 AM, Rudy wondered if Leroy was again, putting him on ice.

Rudy had been an uncharacteristically nervous wreck ever since he hatched his plan with Dr. Brighton. At first, it seemed perfect. Save Ruth from any legal risk and cover for Connie. Nothing left for Leroy to prosecute. But, as the evening unfolded, it became apparent that the plan was fraught with danger, with all possible incriminating fingers pointing at him.

The first problem was the doctored lab report. It wasn't just Dr. Brighton who had seen the initial report. The lab tech who ran the tests and the lab supervisor were also aware of the multitude of drugs in his system. Brighton assured Rudy there should be no problem in keeping the old report from seeing the light of day.

"Should?" Rudy asked with more than minor concern.

"It's under control, Judge. Trust me." Rudy had more trust in used car salesmen than most doctors he knew, including this one.

Then there was Connie. The call he made to Circle of Hope didn't exactly go as planned. First, Connie denied having any Fentanyl to begin with. When Rudy assured her she did, Connie balked at playing the scapegoat.

"You can't do this to me, Dad," she had screamed on the phone. Rudy got the feeling things weren't going as smoothly at rehab as he was led to believe. "You have to get me out of this place. I'm going crazy here. Now you want to pin attempted murder on me? You can't do this!"

Rudy assured her in no uncertain terms that he could, and if she didn't play along, she'd find herself in more trouble than she could ever imagine. "You think you have it rough there?" he scolded his younger daughter. "Try the woman's penitentiary in Columbia on for size. You give the Sheriff the story I'm feeding you and I'll get you out as soon as I can. I promise you that." Connie reluctantly agreed, but how much could Rudy trust his drug addicted daughter? He just couldn't say.

Finally, there was Leroy. Thank goodness Tim intervened and kept Ruth from divulging information at the hospital. Between that and the chest compressions Tim provided, Rudy realized he owed his son much more than a simple thank you. He put it on his mental agenda to come up with something more meaningful.

Now, Rudy was running out of time and patience. He was about to page Janice to ask if she knew where Sheriff Keating was when Leroy knocked on his chambers door.

"Good morning, Rudy. Sorry I'm running a little late," Leroy offered his apology.

"That's fine, Leroy. Thanks for coming in. Please have a seat."

Leroy removed his hat and slid into Rudy's cushy leather armchair.

"I only have a few minutes. Where do things stand with you this morning?"

"Rudy, I've got two more felonies staring me straight in the face with your mug right in the middle of them both. I want

Ruth and Tim to come in and give a statement. Bring your attorney if need be. You were poisoned with a potentially lethal dose of Fentanyl last night according to the lab report I received. All signs point to Ruth, given the timing of her receiving the stolen autopsy report. I'll also need that report with the highlights as evidence for the second felony."

"I'll be glad to be of help to you, in both cases. As far as the unfortunate poisoning last night, I believe I've gotten to the bottom of it, and it has nothing to do with Ruth."

Leroy's face contorted in surprise. "It doesn't? Please explain."

"Yes, well, this has to do with Connie. Apparently, she stashed a Fentanyl pill in her drawer, which wasn't discovered when we sent her to Circle of Hope last week. When I talked to her last night, she admitted placing the pill in with my Amlodipine blood pressure medicine bottle, which I take each day when I get home before dinner. A bit of family revenge, I'm afraid, although she didn't know it could have almost killed me. It was only a matter of time before I took the tainted pill, which is what happened last night. You can follow up with her if you wish, but I'm hoping to keep this within the family. I hope you understand the sensitivity here, Leroy."

Leroy slowly shook his head. "So, you're telling me what happened to you last night was a random pill in your normal meds and has nothing to do with the autopsy report, which mysteriously shows up the same day. And your wife, who I remind you previously tried to poison you after an affair was exposed, had nothing to do with this. That's one *big* coincident."

Rudy smiled and nodded. "That's right, Leroy — one big coincident. Which leads to our second problem of the morning, this one not a coincident. You know who leaked that autopsy report, right?"

"I have my suspicion."

"Come on, Leroy. You know as well as I do, the only people with access to that report are you, Gina's staff, and that scumbag Springfield. Now, why do you suppose anyone would risk their job to expose something like that — to my wife, no less?"

"I don't know, Rudy, why don't you enlighten me?"

"I'll be glad to. Who amongst them has an ax to grind with me? Only one, Leroy — Springfield. I could give you a laundry list of his perceived slights against me. I don't like him, I admit it. But I've always treated him with respect in my courtroom. Now, when he gets something in his greedy, slimy hands he thinks he can use against me, he skirts the law and drags my wife into it. That's beyond the pale. Odds are he's in cahoots with one of Greeley's goons. Pin that leak on Springfield, Leroy." Rudy's voice rose in anger. "And when you do, I want that son-of-a-bitch disbarred from ever practicing law in this county again!"

"One step at a time, Rudy. Your suspicion is noted, and I do share it with you. I know you need to get to your hearing. After I get the report and speak with Ruth and Tim, I'll have a discussion with Jerry."

"You do that, Leroy, and please keep me abreast." Rudy stood up and moved around from his desk and patted Leroy on the shoulder. "I know you always do the right thing."

******

"Come in," Jerry said when he heard the knock on his office door. "Sheriff Keating, to what do I owe this surprise?" Jerry quickly closed the web page he was on — www.hottubsforbabes.com.

Leroy entered Jerry's office and looked around. The sleaze practically hung all around him. Tacky wall paneling, a garish desk, signed pictures of Jerry sporting massive smiles with various football and basketball coaches, placed in gaudy looking frames hung every which way on most of the available wall space. And then there was Jerry, the reincarnation of Elvis himself, with the ridiculously long sideburns and an equally large sequined collared shirt. How in the hell, thought Leroy, did this man ever pass the bar?

"I have something for you to look at, Jerry," Leroy said as firmly as possible, making it clear this wasn't a social visit. He plopped the yellow envelope addressed to Ruth on Jerry's desk. If this surprised Jerry, he didn't show it.

"And what exactly do we have here? Let's see, an envelope addressed to Ruth Culligan, no return address and does not appear to be postmarked." Jerry opened the envelope and pulled out the report. He looked up at Leroy and saw a very humorless sheriff. Jerry flipped through the three-page report and froze at the end, staring at the inflammatory highlighted section. "What's this all about? Why are you showing me this? Surely you don't think I —"

"Had something to do with this?" Leroy shouted. "That's exactly what I think."

Jerry shot to his feet. "How dare you make such an accusation. What proof do you have?"

Leroy reached over and retrieved the report and envelope. "Proof Jerry? You're asking me for proof? Tell me, who else would have leaked something like this? You think it's one of my staff? You think it's someone on Gina's team? Huh Jerry? You think maybe I leaked it!" Leroy stood just to the other side of Jerry's desk, not three feet from his face. Jerry put up a good front, but Leroy could tell he was quaking in his fake rattlesnake boots.

"Leroy, I swear, I don't know what you're talking about. No, I don't think anyone on your side leaked this. But I didn't either. And if you don't have any proof, then I suggest you stop harassing me and go find out who did."

Leroy took a step back and lowered his voice a notch. "I'll do that, Jerry. In fact, I'll start right now. Since you're the lead suspect in my new most pressing priority, Detective Meacham is outside waiting to have a more detailed discussion with you. He'll want to see your phone records, web traffic, and everywhere your bony ass has been in the last four days since you first laid eyes on this report. I hear of any trouble; I'll haul your ass in front of Judge Stevenson in a heartbeat. Do I make myself clear, Jerry?" Leroy's eyes bore a hole straight into Jerry's stunned face. But Jerry didn't blink.

"Crystal," Jerry tersely replied.

"Very well then." Leroy turned, then opened the door. "Tony, he's all yours."

CHAPTER 46

Three weeks later, the trial of the State of South Carolina vs. Randall Culligan was set to begin. After the Fentanyl incident had passed, things calmed down in Culligan's Way. Tim continued his slow recovery, now able to walk completely to the inlet and back without breathing complications. His goal was to make it the nearly two miles north to the pier by the end of the summer. Ruth kept to herself mostly, confiding in Annabelle during the day and showing a renewed affection for Rudy in the evening. Rudy minded not in the least. The memories of having his stomach pumped, and the various aftereffects of his spiked cocktail were never far from his thoughts. Both Culligan parents realized they had hurt each other and were making extra efforts to forgive and be kind to each other.

Connie was scheduled to be released from Circle of Hope by the end of the week. She pleaded no contest to the accidental poisoning charge. So, there were no further legal avenues for Leroy to pursue. Connie accepted a two-year probation and community service in lieu of any prison time. All the Culligans were looking forward to Connie's return and a Mother's Day celebration that Sunday at the Way.

That is, all the Culligans except Randy. The defendant spent his time confined to his fish camp trailer and the immediate vicinity around it. He mostly stayed drunk and stoned, reaching an understanding with Benny to keep him supplied in exchange for the steady flow of bass and croppie Randy pulled in from the river dock each day. When he wasn't fishing, Randy watched a lot of television, in particular crime dramas, crime documentaries, and a heavy dose of Judge Judy. He had several on-site discussions with Jerry regarding his defense strategy. Randy's part was simple. Do nothing, say nothing. He would plead the fifth when the prosecution called him to the stand, and not a word would be spoken otherwise — especially to the media. Jerry seriously considered placing an actual muzzle on his client for the entire trial if not for the visual effect it would have on the jury. Many in the community would have thought it perfect, including, as Jerry found out, many in the jury pool.

Potential juror after juror admitted under oath that they not only knew who Randy was, but wouldn't believe a word that came out of his mouth. In the end, Jerry and Gina found twelve county residents who didn't have a preopinion of the defendant. Jerry would make sure the only words they would hear from his client would be him taking his constitutional right not to hang himself in front of everyone.

As far as Jerry's other preparations went, nothing seemed to go his way. Presiding Judge Marcus Stevenson made it clear early on he would not be led astray by Jerry's attempts to link Molly's murder to the Greeley fiasco. Stevenson denied Jerry's request to have Jack Greeley, or anyone at DHEC, testify and wouldn't allow any evidence linked to that case in this trial. He gave Jerry leeway only to allow the contents of Molly's phone as evidence, and would allow Rudy to testify. But he made it clear he would confine Judge Culligan's testimony to the narrow boundaries of the events of the night of the murder.

Twice, an apoplectic Jerry threatened to walk out of the trial altogether, hurling accusations of cronyism and a miscarriage of justice at the presiding judge. This earned him a formal rebuke and a threat of further punishment if Jerry didn't get his ass in line and stick to the facts of the case. Stevenson knew all about the leaked autopsy, and like Rudy, would love to see proof Jerry was the source of the disclosure. But in the past three weeks, Leroy and Tony had come up empty-handed in the pursuit of finding who leaked the report. For Jerry's part, at least he had the temperament to hold off having Jack install his hot tub. Even he could see how the optics would have been less than optimal.

Still, Jerry felt they stacked the cards against him. He knew his only hope of getting Randy off was convincing the jury there was some connection between Greeley, Rudy, and DHEC to Molly's murder. With Stevenson's rulings, this was going to be extremely difficult. As the trial date drew near, Jerry's hope of sticking it to Rudy looked to be more like a pipe dream.

******

On the morning of May 5, the three available Culligans, as well as Sally and Steve, entered the Georgetown County courthouse together and took their seats in Judge Stevenson's courtroom. The media was out in full force, dubbing it the Lowcountry trial of the century. Leroy had made sure security was locked down tight. A few dozen spectators, the ones who had stood in line since four in the morning, were allowed in, along with three court reporters. Everyone else in the media circus would have to wait outside. Jerry gave them a dose of his hot air, assuring the throng of his client's innocence. Gina gave the media a terse statement, assuring that justice would be properly served.

Inside, Rudy surveyed the jury, seeing them together for the first time. It was comprised of four black men, all older than fifty, and two black women, even older. There were three white women, they were younger, thirties and forties perhaps, an elderly white male and a much younger white male. Rudy didn't recognize any of them, but they looked to be a fair-minded bunch. The only one he thought might have trouble convicting was the younger white male. It was the one concession Gina made during the selection process. Rudy could only hope it wouldn't be a fatal one.

After Marcus went over the ground rules for his courtroom, Gina was ready to kick things off. Jerry and Randy sat stiff at the defense table. Jerry toned things down a bit with a grey suit and not quite over the top bright orange tie. Randy also had on a dark grey suit and plain blue tie. They cut his hair as short as Rudy had ever seen it, and at least at first glance, Randy appeared to be sober. He also looked scared to death.

Gina stepped out onto the courtroom floor and addressed the jury, dressed in a conservative formfitting grey pencil skirt and white blouse. "Ladies and gentlemen of the jury. Thank you for your time and dedication to this very important exercise of justice. Your role in determining guilt and innocence is a cornerstone of our freedom and democracy. It is precisely because we live in a country where there is liberty and justice for all, that we are free to begin with. You and I, and everyone in this courtroom, value our freedom more than anything else in our lives. But if we wish to enjoy our freedoms, we must also have a fair and balanced justice system. We all must face consequences for our actions. Randy Culligan, who stands on trial in front of you today, must face the consequences for his actions. You all, as an impartial jury, have been selected to make the determination whether it was Randy who murdered Molly Elmwood in cold blood just after midnight on April 4.

You will hear testimony over the next two days about Randy's relationship with Molly. She was his ex-finance. Their relationship was fraught with argument and disagreement. Randy had only the previous week been arrested for sexual assault of Molly. You will hear testimony from the Culligan family and others about the events that led up to her murder. What happened at the party at Culligan's Way earlier that night? What happened between Tim Culligan and Molly on the pier shortly before she was killed? You will hear and see hard evidence that clearly points to Randy being in the crime's vicinity at the time of the murder.

Molly had feared for her life that evening. She was looking to disappear after her late-night meeting. We don't know why. We will never know why. But we know this. Molly was killed in a very narrow time frame shortly after midnight on April 4. We know that Molly was stabbed to death with a long fillet knife which not only belonged to Randy Culligan but was kept in his tackle box, which stayed in his boat. The same boat Randy was in when he went to the Culligan pier for a late-night rendezvous with his estranged fiancé.

There were no witnesses to the murder. Tim had just returned to his home after his meeting with Molly. So there is speculation — on both sides. You will hear plenty of debate over what might have happened or could have happened. Your job, ladies and gentlemen of the jury, is to determine what *did* happen. And when you have made this determination, unanimously, speaking with one powerful voice, you will have fulfilled your obligation as a citizen of this great country to dispense justice as justice deserves. I am confident in your ability to do exactly this. Thank you."

When Gina took her seat, Jerry rose, soaking in the spotlight he so relished. "Ladies and gentlemen of the jury. I will beg to differ with my esteemed colleague, Ms. Slocum, on the job which sits in front of you today. Your job here is *not* to determine if my client, Randy Culligan, is innocent or not. It is your responsibility to decide whether Randy is guilty beyond a reasonable doubt. It's as simple as that. Is there reasonable doubt that Randy killed Molly Elmwood? I would profess that yes, there certainly is. Randy did not want to see Molly dead. Randy loved Molly. On the night of Molly's murder, Randy was hoping to patch things up between them. This despite Molly's own underhandedness at dragging Randy into her web of lies and deceit. I will show this to you in her phone records.

You will see that, although Randy was near the Culligan pier the night Molly was murdered, he was not at the scene until after someone callously tossed over her over the side of the pier. There are no witnesses that we know of currently. But there are other suspects to this murder. Members of the Culligan family who not only had a motive to see Molly dead, but also had the means and the opportunity. And you will hear from these family members, under oath, and you, the jury, will decide if indeed, there is a reasonable belief that someone other than my client killed Molly Elmwood.

My client and I have decided for Randy not to provide testimony in this trial. He will exercise his fifth amendment rights. I can only say that we did not make this decision lightly, and it has no bearing on his innocence or guilt. We simply made it in the best interest of my client. Randy has given his statement earlier to the police, and this will be his testimony.

So, members of the jury, keep an open mind when you hear the evidence. And keep your ears open as well. Ask yourself what sounds truthful and what doesn't. What seems reasonable and what doesn't. And, most importantly, what could have happened on that pier shortly after midnight on April 4? I yield to the prosecution."

Marcus turned to Gina and said, "Very well. Ms. Slocum, you may call your first witness."

Gina stood up and made her way around the prosecution table. "Thank you, Your Honor. The prosecution calls Timothy Culligan."

CHAPTER 47

Tim knew he'd be first in the box and dreaded every minute. Gina had coached him through what to expect and Rudy gave him a good dose of support at home. He had nothing to worry about, Gina told him, as long as he stuck to the truth. Jerry would try to trip him up, catch him in a contradiction or two, or just try to rattle him on the stand. Be prepared to explain forwarding Molly's texts without telling the police. It was wrong, and you regretted it. Stick to your story, her last advice; use simple answers in as few of words as possible. The jury needs to empathize with you, so your credibility is crucial.

Once on the stand, Gina threw Tim a series of softball questions to build trust with the jury. Tim eloquently described his Covid diagnosis, his need to return to Culligan's Way, and his warm welcome home. Soon they were at the party when Molly entered the scene.

"Tim, tell us how you felt when you saw Molly at the door."

Tim gulped. It was one thing to think about Molly and the trial, but now to be actually talking about her sent a chill down his spine. "I was very pleased to see her. I'd been thinking about her ever since I got back on the island. We had a lot of good times back before I left."

"You were very close friends with her, then?"

"Yes, we had worked together for two summers at the Pelican Inn. This was long before she was involved with Randy."

"And tell us about the conversation you had with her at the party."

"Well, she was very glad to see me, but also seemed extremely nervous, on edge. We sat on the couch, on one end of the sectional, and she told me she couldn't stay long, that she had to leave after taking care of some other business, and that she needed to see me at midnight on the pier. She wouldn't tell me why."

"And was there anyone nearby who could have overheard you?"

"No, I mean, not that I was paying any attention. I found out later that Sally had, but I didn't know it at the time."

"How about your father?"

"No, Molly made a point of sitting as far away from him as she could. I remember he was over by the bar, well out of conversation range. Plus, the party was pretty noisy by then."

"Ok, Tim, now let's jump ahead to your brother's appearance. Take us through that."

Tim looked around the courtroom, then focused on his brother. He looked so different from the last and only time he saw him at the party. Today he looked almost human. Hair cut short, groomed, sober. Nothing like then. "Well, obviously, no one was expecting to see him that night. I remember he looked like a crazed animal bursting through the back door, screaming my name. Wild-eyed, drunk, obnoxious. I remember thinking the only thing changed from what I remembered him as before was he had put on some weight. Anyway, he threatened me, told me it was all my fault what had happened to him and that he was 'coming after me.' Then he left shortly afterwards."

"So you perceived him as drunk, disorderly, and a threat."
"I did."

"Good, now let's go to midnight when you met Molly on the pier. I'm going to ask the jury to refer to the timeline shown on the display set up here." Gina pointed to the large foam core presented on an easel for the jury to refer to. Listed on the display were the known timeline of events from the Ring cam footage around the time of the murder.

11:56 PM — Tim Culligan exits the front door

12:08 AM — Tim Culligan reenters the home

12:13 AM — Judge Culligan exits the front door

12:17 AM — Judge Culligan reenters the home

"Well, I came out right around midnight and walked out to wait for her at the gazebo. I thought she would drive up, but then I heard a boat and saw her pull up to the dock. She got out, we embraced, and went back to the gazebo. I remember how paranoid she looked, how she told me her life was in danger because of what she found out about Greeley Construction and how my dad was involved. Then she told me she had to disappear and needed to give me her phone, with incriminating evidence on it. At first I didn't want it, but then she insisted. She said goodbye to me then, like she needed me to leave. I hugged her again, and she kissed me. So, I took her phone and went back to the house. When I looked back, she was still on the pier, as if she were waiting for someone else."

"Objection, Your Honor," Jerry blurted out. "The witness could not know why Molly was still on the pier."

"Sustained," Marcus declared. "Son, just tell us what you know."

"Yes sir, so," Tim lost his train of thought, then regained it. "So, the last I saw of Molly, she was still standing on the pier, leaning on the railing. Then, just as I was about to take my shoes off and reenter the house, I remember hearing another outboard on the creek. I thought nothing of it at the time, but I remember hearing it on the south end."

"Thank you, Tim. Anything else happen that night? Did you hear anything inside or outside the house?"

"No, I was exhausted. I went straight to bed and was asleep in no time."

"And how about the next morning? Take us through that."

"Well, I remember coming down for breakfast. We had some discussion about the party and then we went to church. I forwarded some of the text messages from Molly's phone to mine. Not all, just the ones from Randy, my father and Harvey Klinger. I didn't have time to read or listen to any of them until later."

"Later, being after you returned and learned Molly was dead."

"That's correct."

"And then you turned Molly's phone over to Sheriff Keating."

"Yes, that's right."

"Tell the court, Tim, why you didn't mention the texts you had copied to your phone at that time?"

Tim paused. He knew she would ask him this question. Gina had told him it was better to answer it from her than Springfield. Once he gave an honest answer in his testimony, she would shield him in cross-examination. Tim took a deep breath.

"I honestly can't tell you why. I was still shell-shocked by the news of Molly's death. I guess I just froze, didn't think it through. I mean I wasn't trying to protect anyone, or to warn anyone either. After the police left, I was able to see what was on the phone. I didn't think it through, and I regret not telling the Sheriff at the time what I had done."

"Thank you, Tim. I know that's hard to admit, especially under oath." Gina turned to Marcus. "That's all I have for Tim." Then to Jerry, "Your witness."

******

Jerry rose and leisurely strode to the witness stand. "Tim, would it be fair to say you hate your brother?"

Tim's heart rate shot up. He tried to take a deep breath and found it difficult to inhale a sufficient amount of oxygen. He gulped, then he looked over at Randy and once again felt nothing but contempt. "Yes sir, I believe I can say that I hate my brother."

"I don't blame you, Tim," Jerry said empathetically. "I mean, your brother had treated you poorly from what I have learned, before you left for New York. And from what I've gathered, he made a poor impression once again at your party. My client feels badly about that. He wishes he had made more of an effort to welcome you back."

Tim almost threw up in his mouth when he heard this. When he looked at Randy, his brother broke into an obviously fake wide smile.

Jerry continued. "And since you have admitted hating your brother, I don't suppose it would be a stretch to say you hope they convict him of Molly's murder."

Tim didn't take the bait. "I only hope justice is served."

"But Tim, having Randy convicted would solve so many problems for you, would it not? And if he were acquitted, it might create a whole new set of problems. Isn't that right?"

"Objection Your Honor," Gina interjected. "Counsel is leading the witness."

"Sustained. Mr. Springfield, restate the question."

"My apology, Your Honor. Tim, how would you feel if Randy were acquitted?"

Tim's eyes darted from Gina to the jury as he pondered his reply. "If they acquit my brother, I will accept the reality and deal with it. My family will support me."

"Hmm, yes, I would suppose so. But it would be so much better for you if my client was convicted. So much so, I contest, that you would perjure yourself here today to ensure that indeed happens."

"*Objection!*" Gina shot back.

"Withdrawn," Jerry instantly replied. "All right, Tim, one last question. Let's go to the pier after midnight. It's 12:08 AM, the family's Ring cam has you returning to the front porch. You stated you heard a boat motor from the south end of the creek. We know Judge Culligan returned with a bloody shoe at 12:17 AM. So my question, Tim, is how far away would you estimate the boat you heard was from the Culligan dock?"

All eyes in the courtroom focused on Tim. Both lawyers knew the placement of Randy at that time was critical. "I honestly can't say. I mean, I barely remember hearing it at all. I couldn't tell you which way it was going. Best guess, it was near the inlet."

"And how long would a boat from there take to reach the pier?"

"Well, of course it depends on how fast it was going. Assuming it was Randy's johnboat, I'd say as soon as three minutes or as long as seven to ten."

"Randy's statement says he saw no one when he arrived at the pier. Molly would have been dead, and your father had already come and gone. If he took ten minutes from the time you heard the boat, then he would have missed the murder. Is that correct?"

"If he took that long. If he got there in three, he'd have had plenty of time to kill her."

Jerry took a long look at Tim, then Gina, then the jury. "Except that he didn't. I'm going to say this one more time, Tim." Jerry stared at the jury bench with as much intensity as he could muster. "You have every reason to lie, and no reason to tell the truth."

"Objection Your Honor. Really!"

"The jury will disregard counsel's last statement," Marcus stated, glaring at Jerry.

"Withdrawn, Your Honor. I have no further questions for this witness."

CHAPTER 48

Marcus called the two lawyers to his bench, clearly pissed off. "Is this how it's going to be, Jerry? Because if you keep this up, I'm going to hogtie you like a pig on a spit. You understand what I'm telling you, Counselor?"

Jerry looked at Marcus, astounded. "I'll make every effort, Your Honor to exercise restraint," Jerry lied. "I can't help it if emotions are running high. My client's life is at stake."

"Spare me the drama, Jerry. Your future practicing law in this county is also at stake. So button it up."

Jerry tucked his tail between his legs and returned to his table.

Gina announced, "The prosecution calls Murrey Freedman." Gina's plan was to set the tone with Tim. He did exactly that. She next wanted to get the autopsy out of the way early on. Then she planned to let Rudy tell his tale. Then Ruth, then Leroy would finish with the knife and all other manners that needed winding up. She left Sally and Harvey to be defense witnesses.

Murrey took the stand and stated his oath. After formalities, Gina got right down to business. "So the wound to the victim matches the fillet knife we have identified as the murder weapon?"

"Yes, it's a perfect match in both length and width."

"And was this a fatal wound, Mr. Freedman?"

"No, we determined the cause of death to be suffocation. The victim fell face down in the pluff mud. She was in too much shock to move, and she didn't."

"And you also determined that Molly was pregnant." Gina glanced over at Rudy. She saw him gird himself for the revelation. "Why would you have determined this?"

Murrey spoke without emotion. "Because the knife wound went straight through the fetus. Molly was about ten weeks pregnant. The fetus was only one and a half inches long. Had the wound been slightly off, we may have missed it." A murmur went through the gallery.

"And the Sheriff's department determined to run a DNA test on the fetus, is that correct?"

"Yes, it is. We all assumed it would have shown Randy as the father."

"But it didn't. However, the test results *could* identify the father. Tell the court what they found."

Murrey glanced over at Rudy. He sure hoped Gina knew what she was doing. He took a deep breath and said, "The father of Molly's fetus was determined to be Judge Culligan." The entire courtroom erupted in gasps and whispers as all eyes turned to Rudy. Rudy sat motionless with his head down.

"Thank you, Mr. Freedman, we'll be hearing from Judge Culligan a bit later. Let's turn our attention to the blood found on the pier. They confirmed it to be Molly's, correct?"

"That is correct."

"And the blood found on the gazebo, three spots as seen here." Gina held up a picture of the blood found on the gazebo post to the jury. "These were determined to be consistent with the killer throwing the knife into the creek, where we found it two days later?"

"Yes, that is what we determined."

"How long would you conclude it would take the killer to dock a boat, then climb the ramp?"

"Objection, Your Honor. It has not been determined that the killer arrived by boat."

"Sustained."

"Let me rephrase then." Gina glanced over at Jerry as if to say, two can play this game. "How long in your estimation would it take for the killer to enter the pier, either by boat or by foot, kill Molly, kick her off the pier, toss the knife in the creek, and get away?"

Murry knew she would ask him this question, and he had his response ready. "My estimation is it could have taken as little as two minutes, as long as four, assuming there wasn't an argument beforehand."

"Two to four minutes," Gina repeated, "with a five-minute gap between the time Tim returned to the house and Judge Culligan exited the front door. Plenty of time for Randy to show up, dock his boat, and kill Molly Elmwood. Thank you, Mr. Freedman. Your witness."

******

Jerry rose and walked over to the witness box. "Mr. Freedman, why did you believe it was important to determine the father of Molly's baby?"

Murrey paused for a second, formulating an answer. "Well, Mr. Springfield, first, it wasn't my decision to run the DNA test. You would have to ask Sheriff Keating that."

"Wouldn't it make sense that perhaps the child's father wouldn't want Molly to have his baby, so much so that he would kill Molly to prevent her pregnancy from coming to term?"

"Objection, Your Honor. Leading the witness."

"Sustained." Marcus glared at Jerry again.

"Mr. Freedman," Jerry switched gears, "Let's talk about the blood found on the pier. Do you think it would be possible for the killer to stab Molly, kick her over the side, and throw the knife, now dripping in blood, into the creek, while getting no blood on themselves, their clothes, or their shoes?"

Murrey thought it over for a few seconds. "I would say it's possible, but not likely."

"And yet in the police investigation of my client, not one drop of blood was found on him, or on any of his clothes or shoes — including the articles he wore the night of the murder. How can you explain this?"

"Like I said, it's possible no blood was transferred. I suppose the killer also could have washed their clothes or cleaned their shoes."

"Mr. Freedman," Jerry chuckled. "You obviously haven't seen my client's living quarters at his fish camp. It's safe to say there isn't a washing machine in sight. So, I would contend to the jury that the reason none of Molly's blood was found on my client was because he wasn't there in the first place to kill Miss Elmwood. One final question, Mr. Freedman, the blood drops on the gazebo post. You measured them at between five feet two inches and five feet six inches from the floor. Now, my client is six feet tall. I would imagine a normal throwing motion like this." Jerry demonstrated a throwing motion like a pitcher throwing a baseball, stopping at the point of release. "Would have left the blood drops higher. Would you agree with this?"

"It's possible, certainly."

"And a more likely scenario would have been for a shorter person to have made the same throw to have left the blood where it was found. Do you agree with this?"

"Again, sir, it's possible. I would say it also would depend on the location the killer was at the time of release, in other words how close they were to the post, and whether they threw it overhand like you showed, or more of a sidearm motion."

"Oh really," Jerry laughed out loud. "So are you suggesting my client is a side armer?"

"I'm not suggesting anything of the kind, sir. I was simply explaining the how the blood could have appeared on the post."

"So, unless my client is some kind of side winder pitcher, he is too tall to have left the blood stains where they ended up. That, ladies and gentlemen of the jury, is what you will need to decide. No further questions, Your Honor."

CHAPTER 49

"Prosecution requests a ten-minute recess, Your Honor," Gina asked Marcus. Gina and her team, along with Leroy and Rudy, exited to a side conference room and huddled around a table.

"I'm going to pass on you as the next witness, Judge. I don't like Jerry's attack methods, and I want to be sure I have the last word when you're on the stand. That alright with you?"

"I was thinking the same thing, Gina," Rudy responded. "I know he's going to put all kinds of shade on me, so I'd be more comfortable with you following on cross."

"Good. That will leave just Ruth and Leroy for us today. Tomorrow, we'll deal with you, Harvey, and Sally."

"Are you concerned about Harvey?" asked Leroy.

"A little," answered Gina. "You said he's a bit of a wild card. But from what you've told me, he mainly wants justice for Molly."

"I have complete faith in you, Gina," assured Leroy. "Whatever smoke Jerry generates tomorrow; I know you will clear away."

"And Sally, you're sure Sally will not change her tune again?"

Leroy looked at Rudy and shrugged. "You tell me Rudy. She's your daughter."

"Sally's going to play ball with us. I have no doubt."

"She needs to," stated Gina. "Or we could be in serious trouble."

******

"The prosecution calls Ruth Culligan," announced Gina after discussing the change in witnesses with Marcus and Jerry. Jerry looked at Gina with surprise when she made the request. It was obvious he had relished taking on Rudy next. Now he'd have to wait another day.

Ruth took the stand and pasted a serious look on her face. She knew when it came to Jerry's turn, her patience and composure would both be tested.

"Mrs. Culligan," Gina began, "your son, the defendant, and Miss Elmwood had a rocky relationship for some time. I believe they were engaged to be married twice, the second time ending just a couple of months ago. Can you tell the court your understanding of why they broke the engagement again?"

Ruth cleared her throat, then began. "Both of them were abusive narcissists. They both tried to use each other for their own gain, and everyone around them. Judge Culligan and I tried our best to make things work out for Randy. He constantly refused to give us the only thing we asked out of him. Respect and the behavior of any decent human being. Molly was no different. As to why they broke their engagement again, I don't know exactly why, but it happened shortly after Molly's last Sunday dinner with us back in February."

"And Mrs. Culligan, would you take us through what happened at that dinner?"

Ruth's expression grew more serious. "It started with Molly throwing around accusations against Randy, telling him he wasn't fit to be her husband. He was a worthless drunk who couldn't support himself on his own, never mind a family. All of which is true. Randy followed this by accusing Molly of having affairs and was nothing but a gold-digging slut trying to steal his family's wealth. Also true. Things devolved from there. Molly dragged my husband and myself into the argument, accusing us of all kinds of horrible acts. Awful things were said. I can't remember them all. But before my husband put an end to the dinner and expelled both of them from our home, Randy threatened Molly. I clearly remember him doing that."

"And what exactly did Randy tell Molly, Mrs. Culligan?"

Ruth addressed her attention directly at Randy. She calmly said, "He told her, 'I'm going to kill you, you fucking whore slut.' They both went their separate ways after that. It was the last I saw or heard from Molly until the party." Ruth glanced over to the jury and saw at least half of them with their mouth open.

"Now, Mrs. Culligan," Gina continued after pausing a second to let Ruth's last statement sink in. "Let's jump ahead to Tim's party. What did you witness Molly doing when she was there?"

"Well, obviously, I wasn't happy to see her. Although it didn't surprise me because I knew she was friends with Tim from before. I kept a close eye on her. She had a conversation with Tim on the couch. Then she went upstairs for a few minutes. After that, she got into an argument with my husband. I watched for a minute from across the room, but when they began shouting at each other, I intervened and demanded she leave the party immediately. She did. I didn't know she would come back later that night."

"And Mrs. Culligan. Take us through your activity after the party ended."

"Like I told the Sheriff the next morning. I retired upstairs at about 11:15 PM. Tim had gone up a little earlier and Rudy was on the back deck drinking. I was exhausted from the long day and evening. I went to sleep right away and didn't wake until 7:00 AM the next morning."

"Thank you, Mrs. Culligan. Your witness."

******

Jerry rose and approached Ruth. Ruth glared at him, seeming to dare him to cross a line.

"Mrs. Culligan, you've struggled with mental illness for much of your life. Tell the court what you have been diagnosed with and what medications you're currently on."

"Objection, Your Honor," Gina wasted no time confronting Jerry. "Mrs. Culligan's medical history is not relevant to this trial."

Marcus paused for a second to consider. "I'll allow it but keep it brief, Mr. Springfield."

Ruth looked to the Judge, then back to Jerry. "I have a bi-polar condition, and a type of schizophrenia — I forget the name of it, and some OCD. I'm taking Risperdal, and sometimes I take Valium."

"And Mrs. Culligan, you also have a history of violent outbursts. In fact, four times in the past you have been committed to the Charleston Arlington Mental Health Institute, twice of which involved attacks on your own son, Randy."

"I'm sorry to say, but yes, this is true."

"In fact, Mrs. Culligan, just the day before Tim's welcome home party, you assaulted Randy yet again with a rolling pin. Hit him right above the left eye, needing four stitches."

"Objection, Your Honor," Gina intervened, "Is this going somewhere relevant?"

"Mr. Springfield, please make your point and move on."

"Yes, Your Honor. My point, Mrs. Culligan, is that you are a woman who is prone to violence. A woman who is capable of violence and who has a violent past with members of your own family. Now tell me, Mrs. Culligan, how you felt about Molly Elmwood when she left the party that night?"

"I was disgusted with her."

"You were disgusted. May I suggest you were so disgusted; you could have been violent to her had you had the chance?"

Ruth looked over to Gina. She didn't object here. Ruth showed signs of distress. This was what she feared the most. "No. No, I would not have been violent to her, even if I had the chance."

"Oh, I'm not sure about that Mrs. Culligan. I'm not sure of that at all. So, let's see. You stated you went to bed by 11:15 PM and did not know Molly had returned at midnight and was on the pier with Tim. But, if you were awake, you could have been out on your bedroom balcony with a clear view of the pier. Isn't that correct?"

"Objection, Your Honor! Speculation."

"I'm going to allow it. Finish your line of questioning, Mr. Springfield."

Ruth looked squarely at Jerry. Her face quivered as she formed an answer. "Yes, *if* I were awake, and *if* I were on my balcony, I could have seen them from there."

"And if you saw Molly and Tim kissing, that would have made you very upset. Isn't that correct?"

"Again, *if* I saw them, then yes, I would have been upset."

"And I would suggest, Mrs. Culligan, that you would have been so upset that you could have gone straight downstairs, and out to the pier, and stabbed Molly Elmwood to death."

"Objection, Your Honor, please!"

"Sustained. That's quite enough Mr. Springfield."

"That is all I have for this witness."

However, Ruth wasn't finished yet. She stared at Jerry, possessed. "I *could* have done those things, Counselor. Just like you *could* have been a lawyer with a shred of decency, instead of the donkey's ass you turned out to be."

A smattering of laughter was heard throughout the courtroom as Ruth returned to her seat.

CHAPTER 50

Leroy took his turn next on the witness stand. He'd been looking forward to it ever since he arrested Randy in his stink hole of a trailer three weeks earlier. Leroy was ready for anything Jerry had to throw at him and was confident Gina and Marcus would steer the discussion clear of any potential landmines. He felt the real minefield lay ahead for Rudy the next day. The text message he just received from Tony, who had slipped out of the courtroom, also encouraged him.

Might have something on our yellow envelope case. Catch up later.

He didn't know what it meant, but if Tony could pin something on Jerry leaking the autopsy report — well, that would be the icing on the cake.

The bailiff swore Leroy in, and Gina methodically led him through the history of his office's involvement with Randy and Molly. Randy had rolled up no less than eight DUI offenses, two for disorderly conduct, and one assault with a deadly weapon — a brawl at the fish camp that left a 'buddy' stabbed in the shoulder. Molly's rap sheet was less lengthy; the insurance attempted con, two DUI's, and a couple misdemeanor drug charges. Her most serious violation, the Publix narcotic theft, would never make the official list.

He was then questioned about the arrest of Randy before the party. Was there some arrangement with Judge Culligan to have Randy conveniently missing from the party? "Just doing my job," Leroy calmly answered, glaring at Jerry. It wouldn't be so easy on the cross.

"Ok, Sheriff, then take us through the party. Did you know when Molly came in?"

"No, but I saw her and Tim talking on the couch."

"And do you know where Judge Culligan was at the time?"

"I did. He was over at the bar, well out of earshot, talking to me."

"So there was no way Judge Culligan could have overheard the arrangement for Tim to meet Molly at midnight, unlike his sister Sally."

"That would be correct."

"How about when Judge Culligan and Molly were arguing? Did you overhear any part of that conversation?"

"I did not. I believe I was out on the back porch. When I heard a commotion from inside the house, I went back in and saw Molly leaving."

"And did you ask Judge Culligan what had transpired?"

"I did, but he shook it off. 'Molly being Molly' is what he said."

"Now, Sheriff, we've heard Tim's testimony when Randy arrived at the party. Is there anything else you would like to add or change?"

Leroy thought it over for a second. "I believe Tim didn't do enough to explain how belligerent Randy was."

"And you told him to leave his boat on the beach and pick it up the next morning when he was sober."

"That's correct."

"Which he didn't."

"Evidently not."

"Ok, Sheriff, take us through the next morning, when you arrived at the scene." Leroy went through the morning's events, from the first look at the body, to the Ring cam videos, to Rudy, Tim, and Ruth's initial statements, then to the blood evidence on the dock. When he finished, Gina asked, "At what point, Sheriff, did Randy become your lead suspect?"

Leroy looked straight at Randy when he answered. "I would say it was when we reviewed Molly's texts back at the station that afternoon. When we realized he was in the pier's vicinity at the time of the murder."

"And you were looking for him, then?"

"Yes, we had a search underway on the rivers in the area. At that time it was just for questioning."

"Now Sheriff, please tell the court how it was you concluded that Randy was the one and only prime suspect."

"Well, once we retrieved the knife and identified it as Randy's, it was pretty simple. We knew only four people had knowledge of Molly being at the dock; Harvey Klinger, who was Molly's friend and confident, Tim, Randy, and, as we found out later, Sally Hobart. We ruled out Tim quickly, as he had no motive and had no access to the knife. We also ruled out Sally after we questioned her and examined her car. Although there was a motive there, Molly had stolen from Sally's place of employment, Sally has no record of violence and also did not have knowledge of Randy's knife. I believe we'll hear more from Sally tomorrow. We also ruled out Judge Culligan. We don't believe he had knowledge of either Molly being at the pier or of Randy's knife. We confirmed his version of hearing a scream at around 12:10 AM as a distinct possibility. That left Randy. No one else, to our best understanding of the events, had the motive, the accessibility to the crime scene, and accessibility to the murder weapon. Thus, we believe Randy Culligan is guilty of the murder of Molly Elmwood."

"Thank you, Sheriff Keating." Gina turned to Jerry and smiled. "Your witness."

******

Jerry rose and approached Leroy. "Sheriff Keating, would it be safe to say you and Judge Culligan are friends?"

Leroy narrowed his eyes. "It would. The Judge and I go back many years."

"And would it also be correct to say that you have, in the past, done favors for Judge Culligan?"

"I'm not following you, Counselor. Please clarify," Leroy answered without humor.

"Clarify what a favor is, Sheriff? I'm sure you know what I mean; a courtesy, an indulgence, an act of goodwill."

"I like to think I do many people these things."

"Including Judge Culligan."

"Yes, including Judge Culligan."

"And would you say shortly before Tim's welcome home party, you did Judge Culligan the favor of arresting my client? Not only arresting him, but arranging for bail to be postponed until Monday so that he would not be present and cause a scene at this party?

Leroy scoffed. "He still did exactly that."

"Please answer the question, Sheriff."

Leroy glanced over at Gina, who looked back and slowly shook her head. "No, Counselor, I would not consider that a

favor, as you defined it. I had sufficient evidence to consider
Randy a threat to Molly and acted accordingly. As far as the bail
went, we arraigned Randy in front of Judge Kramer. You'd have
to ask him."

"Yes, yes, I might do that. And Sheriff Keating, would
you say you did a favor to Judge Culligan when you removed
him from your list of suspects? This despite finding blood on the
Judge's shoe, that he removed immediately after Molly was
murdered."

"Objection, Your Honor." Gina had heard enough.
"Counsel is badgering the witness. There's no evidence that
Judge Culligan returned to the house immediately after the
murder."

"Sustained. Mr. Springfield, I'm asking you nicely this
time to tone it down."

"Very well, Your Honor. Let's say shortly after Molly was
murdered."

"The answer to your question, Counselor, is no. I
explained to Ms. Slocum why we removed Judge Culligan from
the list of suspects."

"But Sheriff. I hate to tell you how to do your job, but…"

"Then *don't!*" Leroy loudly interrupted. Now he was
glowering at Jerry.

"If I may finish my question, please, sir. I would expect,
given the circumstances, given that Judge Culligan had both the
motive and the proximity to murder Molly Elmwood, that you
would have searched for other plausible explanations. The Judge
claimed he heard a scream at around 12:10 AM. He leaves the
house two minutes later and returns five minutes after that with a

bloody shoe. Only two pieces of information are missing. Did Judge Culligan indeed have knowledge of Molly's midnight return? And did he have access to Randy's knife?

I contend the answer to both questions is yes. And as the supervising law enforcement professional, I would have expected both of these possibilities to have been investigated further. Someone else at the party could have easily overheard Molly's and Tim's conversation about the midnight rendezvous. We find out later that sister Sally did. Did someone else hear and let Judge Culligan in on it? And what about that knife? There were over two hours between the time Randy left the party and the meeting at the pier. Judge Culligan could have easily gone to the boat to grab the knife, knowing full well how neatly that would frame his son."

"Objection, Your Honor! Counsel is grandstanding here."

"Are you quite finished, Mr. Springfield?"

"I just want an answer to my question. Did the Sheriff not investigate these possibilities because he didn't do a thorough job? Or was he doing yet another *favor* for our Judge here?"

Leroy peeked a look over to Rudy. It appeared to him that Rudy could have happily torn Jerry apart one limb at a time. Leroy simply answered, "There was no favor. Your contentions are simply not credible. Our investigation was complete, thorough, and accurate. I resent any implication otherwise."

"Yes, Sheriff, I imagine you do. And I *resent* my client being held out to hang, when the genuine possibility that someone else committed this brutal murder is sitting in this courtroom, scot free. No further questions."

Silence permeated the courtroom. Finally Gina told Marcus, "We have no further witnesses, Your Honor. The prosecution rests."

Marcus gaveled the trial to an end for the day. "Court is in recess until 10 AM tomorrow morning.

CHAPTER 51

Later that afternoon, Rudy and Leroy sat around the small conference table in Leroy's office, mulling over the day's events. Earlier, Rudy had organized a private lunch in the backroom of a Front Street restaurant, where he tried to put a positive face and spin of the proceedings to Ruth, Tim, Sally, and Gina. Gina assured the Culligans that the trial was still in their favor, regardless of the points Jerry had made. She mentioned, and Rudy confirmed, that Jerry certainly had made no points with Marcus. Ruth didn't seem to agree, and she voiced her disappointment that Marcus had overruled any of Gina's objections.

Now, with the rest of the family resting at home, Rudy could speak openly to Leroy.

"I expect I'll be subject to more of the same medicine tomorrow that you received today," lamented Rudy. "I had hoped Marcus would have cracked down a bit more than he did."

"I'm afraid so, Rudy. I expect Jerry will unload both barrels on you, including pushing the Greeley affair as much as he can."

"Humph," Rudy growled. "Marcus assured me that wouldn't get out of hand. After today, I'm not so sure."

"And what about Sally? He's not exactly going to treat her with kid gloves either, you know."

"Sally's tough. I'm not worried about her."

"Then what is it, Judge? Something's got you concerned."

Rudy stroked his mustache over and over, something he often did when stressed. "It's just Jerry. The man has a way of getting under your skin."

Leroy chuckled. "Well, that's why he's a defense lawyer."

"That's why he's a first-class asshole!" Rudy shot back. "You mentioned you thought Tony had some kind of lead on the autopsy leak. Where does that stand?"

"Haven't heard. He should be back any time."

As if on cue, Tony knocked on the door and entered the office. "Hey boss," he said, smiling. "Judge," he turned and addressed Rudy politely, though Rudy could tell he was less thrilled to share the news with him. "I think I got the goods on Jerry." Now Rudy's attitude suddenly improved.

"That so?" Leroy asked. "We were just talking about the louse. Come, have a seat."

Tony took a seat and took out his phone. He was grinning from ear to ear. "Ok," he began, "so I went back to the hours after the evidence discovery, when Jerry first got his hands on the autopsy report. We haven't been able to place his whereabouts until 3:00 PM that afternoon when he had a court appearance, leaving about two and a half hours open. A couple of weeks ago, I had a conversation with his secretary, Hannah. She was pretty tight-lipped discussing her boss, so we talked about some lighter subjects. Turns out she's kind of a beach bum and has the hots for one of your beach patrol dudes — Hank — tall, dark-haired, very tan. You know who I'm talking about?"

"I do," Leroy answered slowly. "I've met Hannah. Isn't she married?"

"She is." Tony grinned. "So what?"

Leroy rolled his eyes. "Continue."

"So, I talk to Hank and said maybe he could flirt a little with this Hannah. I mean, she's no slouch on the beach, you know. I told Hannah that if I could arrange a discreet meeting one day when Hank was on duty on Litchfield Beach, where Hannah likes to go, could she maybe share some information about Jerry's whereabouts that afternoon?" Now Tony had Rudy's and Leroy's undivided attention. "She says, 'you do that for me, and I'll play along.' Well, turns out Hank and Hannah had a friendly talk on the beach this past Monday. Having another one tomorrow, in fact. When I went to see her this morning, she's all smiles, thanking me etc. etc. Then she informs me Jerry likes to go up to the Crab Trap in Murrells Inlet for lunch when he's meeting someone down from Myrtle Beach. Why don't you check there? So, I go and see the manager at the joint and he says, 'yeah, sure, the Elvis guy, comes in every so often.' Can I see the security footage from April 16? Well," Tony punched up a video clip on his phone. "Here's Jerry entering the Crab Trap with —"

"A fucking yellow envelope!" Rudy jumped out of his seat.

"Wait," cautioned Tony, "It gets better. So, Jerry has his lunch, crab cakes, and pays with cash. That's why we couldn't trace him that day on credit card records. Then he leaves and hangs out on the boardwalk right outside." Tony switched to another clip. "And look who shows up." They all watched the next clip of a burly bald man appear next to Jerry. The two have a quick conversation and the man leaves with the envelope.

"And who the hell is that? Do you know him?" demanded Rudy.

Tony broadened his grin as he addressed the other two. "At first, no. But after a little research, our new owner of that mysterious yellow envelope is none other than Ian Folger, head of security for Greeley Construction."

"That Motherfucker!" screamed Rudy. "That's payback for the —" then Rudy realized who he was talking to. "uh what I mean to say is, Jack was very upset — with me — for his perceived slight in that little marsh lot problem. Tell me Leroy, did Horry County ever find out how Greeley hacked into the DHEC computers?"

Leroy slapped Rudy on the back and laughed. "No Judge, they seemed to have hit a dead end there."

Rudy looked directly at Tony. "Detective Meacham, whatever has happened in the past between us, I want to say how grateful I am for this fine piece of investigative work. I believe I owe you one."

"It's my pleasure, Judge Culligan. And I will remember to ask for that favor one day. Leroy, what do you want to do with this bit of evidence?"

"I'm on it like stink on shit." Leroy punched in a number on his cell. "Marcus, Leroy here. My detective and I would like to come by in a minute and show you something I think you will find very interesting." He paused for a second. "Thank you, sir. We're heading that way now." Leroy grabbed the yellow envelope from his desk drawer and headed out the door behind Rudy. "I hope you're feeling better about things now, Rudy. I'll see you in court tomorrow. Good luck."

"Thank you Leroy. Now I'm truly looking forward to it."

CHAPTER 52

The sight of a sitting senior circuit court judge taking a seat in a witness box, giving testimony in a murder trial, was something no one in Georgetown County had ever seen. But there was Rudy, dressed in a grey striped suit and silver tie, looking ready to relish a good fight. So was Jerry, who'd been waiting for this day as long as he could remember. This was his big chance, to make a name for himself, and to put the whammy on the judge who had ridiculed him so many ways on so many occasions.

To Jerry, Marcus seemed edgy this morning. The presiding judge gave both lawyers more caution about the legal boundaries he would allow. But all of Marcus's attention seemed to be focused on Jerry. Jerry blew it off, thinking it was just because he was in *their* sandbox now. And he was getting ready to kick some of that sand in a certain pain in the ass's eyes.

After swearing Rudy in, Jerry went straight at him. "Judge Culligan, you also don't care for your son Randy very much, do you?"

"I do not."

"And it's safe to say you would be happy to see Randy convicted of this crime."

"Is that a question?"

"Would you, sir, be happy to see your son convicted for the murder of his ex-fiancée?"

"I wish to see justice done. That is why I'm a judge."

"I see. And what about our victim? How did you feel about Molly Elmwood?"

"I didn't like her."

"You didn't like her. Did you hate her?"

"I hated some things she did. The way she treated Randy occasionally. Stealing narcotics. But as a person, no sir. I don't *hate* anyone."

"But I imagine you hated Molly for trying to extort you for money, holding the incriminating video of her and Jack Greeley as ransom."

Rudy glanced over to Gina to see if she would object, but she shook her head. "That didn't happen."

This caught Jerry off guard. "What's that, Judge? What didn't happen?"

"Molly did not try to extort me for money."

"So you're denying the statement by Harvey Klinger stating otherwise. Tell me, Judge, what did you and Molly argue about at the party?"

"I had heard from her earlier about her misunderstanding with the Greeley / DHEC dispute. I wanted to set the record straight for her."

"You mean the dispute where you illegally coerced DHEC into approving marsh lots in exchange for kickbacks from Greeley construction?"

"Objection, Your Honor. Nothing but slander."

"Sustained. Mr. Springfield, you're on thin ice here."

"Allegedly, Your Honor, my apologies. Now Judge Culligan, if you were simply as you say, 'setting the record straight', about a 'misunderstanding', I wouldn't have thought it would have led to such an argument that caused Miss Elmwood to be asked to leave. Tell the court why you were so upset with Molly."

"Molly never liked to take no for an answer."

"I see. Well, let me paint a different picture for you how that argument went down. Molly attempted to extort you to the sum of $100,000 at the party. This was per the statement of what Molly told Harvey she would do. And she threatened to expose you in the media should you refuse. You, Judge Culligan, aren't the only one who doesn't like to take no for an answer, but you had another plan all right, to keep Molly from exposing you."

"Objection, Your Honor. Counsel is off on another fishing expedition."

"Mr. Springfield, ask the witness a question."

"Did you, Judge Culligan, have a plan to keep Molly from exposing you in the media?"

"I did not!" Rudy roared back.

"Molly told Tim she was running for her life because she was afraid of what you would do to her. She had to have a good reason to do something that drastic. What reason is that Judge Culligan?"

"I don't know what went through her mind."

"But she did indeed have a good reason to fear for her life. Because there *was* a plan in place, sir. A plan which resulted in her being stabbed to death on the pier after midnight and framing your son, whom you can't stand, in the process!"

"Objection!" Gina shouted.

"Sustained." Marcus glared at Jerry. "Counselor, this is your last chance."

Jerry ignored him. "Judge Culligan, Miss Elmwood's autopsy report concluded she was pregnant at the time of her murder and that you were the father of her child. Would you tell the court how that came to be?"

"We had sex."

"I gather that, Judge. Please explain the circumstances of how you had sex with a woman, who was at the time, engaged to your son."

"Objection Your Honor. What relevance is this?"

"Overruled, I'll allow this one."

Rudy looked back at Marcus and mouthed 'thanks a lot', then took a deep breath. "It was one time only, about three months ago. Molly came to my chambers to discuss how things were going badly with Randy. She wanted to know more about restraining orders and whatnot. Her true intent was to seduce me, which I'm ashamed to say, she was successful at. Now I can see she intended to get pregnant and later file a paternity suit against me. I assure you it had nothing to do with what happened to her."

"So you say Judge, so you say. Alright then, let's go back to the end of the party. Your statement has you on the back deck at around 11:30 PM, after Tim and Mrs. Culligan had gone upstairs."

"That is correct."

"And you claim you saw Randy come back to retrieve his boat shortly after that?"

"I did."

"And did you know that the murder weapon, Randy's fishing knife, was in his boat?"

"I didn't know it. I assumed that's where he kept it."

"And did he keep his tackle box on the boat locked?"

"I have no idea."

"And assuming it wasn't locked, you would have had every opportunity to retrieve this knife from the time you went out on the back deck, knowing no one would have seen you, but before Randy came back."

"Objection, Your Honor. Fishing again."

"Sustained." Marcus shook his head and pointed a finger at Jerry.

"Now Judge," Jerry ignored Marcus again, and moved right along, "You claim you heard a noise like a scream from the front of the house shortly after midnight and went to check it out. Ring cam shows you leaving the front door at 12:08 AM. Tell the court how long it was from the time you heard the scream until you walked out the front door?"

"I would guess no more than two minutes."

"And did you hear an outboard motor on the creek?"

"I heard nothing when I went out on the pier."

"How is that possible, Judge Culligan? If Randy had come by boat, killed Molly at say 12:06 AM and escaped immediately afterwards, how is it possible you would not have heard his boat?"

"I can't explain why. I did not hear a boat."

"Oh, there's a simple explanation for this, Judge. It's because Randy had not even come to the dock at 12:06 AM, or 12:08 AM, or even 12:17 AM when you returned to the front door and took off your bloody shoe. Would you say that would be a reasonable explanation, Judge?"

"I would say that could be one explanation, not *the* explanation. It's entirely possible Randy had left the scene and was out of sight before I came outside."

"And I would counter it was not possible at all. One last question, Judge Culligan. After you stabbed Molly Elmwood to death and deposited your bloody shoe on the front porch, did you get a good night's sleep?"

"Objection, Your Honor."

"Sustained." Marcus sighed.

"I did, Counselor. Which is more than you'll get tonight."

******

After surviving Jerry's antics, Rudy was ready for a few layups. Gina started out with a glittering testimonial of Rudy's service to the community, and the leadership he had shown the county for over thirty years.

Jerry yawned at his table, thinking more about Rudy's veiled threat than paying attention to Gina's cross.

She then reiterated to the jury that Rudy's explanation of the events at and after the party were sound. There was no knife stolen from Randy's boat, there was no plan or vendetta to get back at Molly, and there was plenty of time for Randy to get away after killing Molly without Rudy hearing his boat.

On further thought, Rudy testified, since he hadn't looked at his watch during the entire midnight sequence, it may have been over two minutes from the time he had heard the scream to the time he walked out the front door.

"I remember first wondering what the sound was. A woman, or a feral cat or fox in a fight — didn't know. Then I waited to see if it would sound again. Once I got up, I didn't exactly race to the front door. So maybe four or even five minutes passed."

"Judge Culligan," Gina was ready to switch gears, "Let's go back to the Sunday dinner five weeks before the murder; when Molly and Randy fought in front of the family and Randy threatened to kill Molly. What happened after he made the threat?"

"Well, I kicked them both out of the house. Molly left the house in a tizzy, saying she would never come back there again. That news was well received. Randy, not so much. I knew he'd be back soon enough. A couple days later he showed back at the Way, as if nothing had happened."

"And you had a discussion with him then, correct?"

"Yes, I reminded him he had threatened to kill Molly in front of the family, and if he didn't make amends to us, it might come back and bite him in the butt."

"And did he — make amends to anyone?"

"Not to my knowledge, no. Certainly not to Ruth or myself."

"And Judge, let's jump ahead to the phone call you received from Randy after his arrest before the party. He wanted you to get him out of jail, is that correct?"

"Yes, heh heh," Rudy chuckled softly. "Any reasonable person would have used the allotted call to contact their lawyer. One more example of how Ruth and I were nothing but enablers for a sick narcissist."

"And what else did Randy say on that call?"

Rudy's tone grew serious. "He told me Molly made up the accusations, but he didn't know why. Then, when he finished also blaming me, and blaming Tim, and blaming Ruth, he told me again that when he got out of jail, he was going to kill Molly and then she'd never cause any trouble with anyone ever again. I advised him against any such foolishness." Rudy glanced at the jury. He had them in his pocket — lock, stock, and barrel.

"No further questions, Your Honor."

CHAPTER 53

Upon further contemplation, Jerry decided against calling Harvey Klinger as a witness. After a discussion with Harvey the week before, Jerry realized that although Harvey was no fan of Rudy, he wasn't exactly going to stick his neck out for Randy. He wanted justice served, and in Harvey's mind, Randy was guilty. Jerry thought whatever good may have come from Harvey's testimony, Gina would make things look even worse for his client. They had Harvey's statement. Jerry let it sit with that.

So, Jerry called his last witness, Sally Hobart, to the stand. Rudy's cross had rocked his confidence somewhat, but he still felt he landed some good punches and had at least a decent chance with the jury. Especially with the young white kid, who looked a lot like another drunk stoner. It just takes one to hang a jury, he kept reminding Randy. He may be our best, or only chance.

Although calling Sally as a defense witness involved some risk, Jerry felt he had to take it. Little did he realize how difficult it was going to be to find any character witnesses to bolster his client. It was, in fact, impossible. He couldn't find even a single person willing to take the stand and defend or support Randy. When he asked Randy why this was the case, Randy's caustic reply was 'the world is full of assholes.' And yet here he was, defending the world's biggest one.

So that left two potential hostile witnesses for his defense case. Both of them key to instilling doubt in the jury. Rudy lived up to his billing alright. Even with Gina's objections, Jerry knew the jury heard enough evidence and supposition to cast at least a modicum of doubt in their minds. He hoped for the same with Sally. The way Jerry viewed Sally, she would either stick to her statement of not witnessing the murder, wherein he could cast doubt she was hiding her own guilt. Or she may even, in his wildest fantasy, change her story and implicate her father as the actual killer.

After Sally described her relationship with her family, her job, and the identification of Molly as the narcotics thief, Jerry arrived at the party.

"Mrs. Hobart, please tell the court how you felt when you first saw Molly at Tim's party."

"I wasn't happy to see her, of course. But I had the feeling she would make an appearance, knowing how she was a friend of Tim's from before."

"And had you planned on confronting her about the drug theft at the party?"

"I wasn't sure. This was before Tim told me about Connie's involvement."

"And how, Mrs. Hobart, did you overhear Tim and Molly's discussion on the couch?"

"Well, I kept a close eye on her after she came in the house. When I saw them sit on the couch, I wanted to try to eavesdrop some, out of sight, but within earshot."

"And that's when you overheard the midnight rendezvous plan?"

"That's right."

"And did you decide you were going to confront Molly at that time?"

"No, that wasn't until later, after I got home."

"You were quite upset with Connie and Molly after learning what they both did."

"Yes, I was. I don't always do a good job of controlling my anger. I didn't at the party."

"And tell me, Mrs. Hobart, what did you hope to accomplish going back to the Culligan pier at midnight?"

Sally took a deep breath. She hated reliving this scene, but knew she had to. "I, uh, I rightly didn't know. I remember asking myself just that driving there. What did I hope to accomplish? I told myself to just take it as it goes."

"And you parked out of sight two houses down, by another pier, and watched them. Could you hear what they were saying?"

"I could not."

"But you saw them kiss on the pier?"

"Yes, I did."

"And tell the court, Mrs. Hobart, what you did after Tim left the pier."

"I, um, I saw Molly was still standing on the pier. She wasn't leaving right away." Sally's voice shook. "Then I heard what sounded like a boat motor come from south of the pier. So I didn't go right over to her. I stayed and watched."

Jerry didn't expect this, but wasn't surprised either. "Tell the court then, Mrs. Hobart, what you did next."

Sally's whole lower jaw was quivering wildly. Her eyes skirted back and forth between the jury and Randy. Then, as if a light switched off, Sally changed her voice. When she spoke, it came out as something throaty and raucous in tone. "I did nothing. I watched my brother Randy pull his boat up to the dock and tie it off. He reached in his tackle box for something. I couldn't tell what. Then he marched up the ramp and, without hesitation, stabbed Molly in the gut."

The courtroom erupted. Randy jumped to his feet and screamed, "You lying bitch! You're a goddamn lying bitch!" Jerry was dumbstruck. He couldn't believe what he just heard. The jury and spectators burst into a cacophony of shock and disbelief. Marcus began to gavel the courtroom to order. Randy was apoplectic. He kept pointing at Sally and continued calling her a liar and that she was dead meat.

"Order! Order in this courtroom!" bellowed Marcus, banging his gavel repeatedly on his desk. Gina and the rest of the Culligans watched it all with smiles on their faces. Jerry finally got his wits about him and addressed Sally, even before order was restored and with Randy at his side continuing the verbal harassment of his sister.

"Mrs. Hobart," Jerry tried to talk above his client's screaming and the continued noise all around him. "Mrs. Hobart, that is not what happened, and you know it!"

Marcus kept hammering his gavel home and called for order. Randy still wouldn't shut up. Finally, Marcus told the bailiff, "Get him out of here. Now!" The bailiff and two uniformed cops grabbed Randy by both arms and hauled him out of court. He never stopped his string of accusations, even as he disappeared in the hallway.

By now, the courtroom had quieted down, and order finally restored. Jerry stood there, shaken to the core. When Marcus allowed him to continue, it was obvious Jerry was off his game. "Mrs. Hobart, you are now stating under oath that you, in fact, gave not one, but two false and misleading statements to the police. How on earth can anyone believe you now?"

Sally, who had kept her composure throughout the eruption, said flatly, "I am under oath now, Counselor. I decided to tell the truth here now in court."

"You realize they can charge you with purposely giving false statements to the police."

"I do. They can charge me if they want to."

Jerry looked around the courtroom. He was in a daze and didn't know which direction to go. After a few more speechless seconds, Marcus asked, "Mr. Springfield, do you have any further questions for this witness?"

Jerry finally addressed Sally and asked, "Is there anything else you wish to add to your fabricated story, Mrs. Hobart?"

"Yes," she replied right away. "I want to state that the events happened exactly as the prosecution laid them out. Randy stabbed Molly, then kicked her under the pier. He walked to the gazebo and threw the knife into the creek, then jumped in his boat and took off back towards the inlet. I went back to my car and left the scene before my father came out the front door."

Jerry tried to swallow. He was still in shock. "And why, Mrs. Hobart," he stopped to cough, then clear his throat, "why did you not tell this story to the police?"

"The first time, I simply did not want to get involved. The second time, after they detected my car, I suppose I was trying to protect Randy from a life in prison. In the end, I just couldn't lie again. So I told the truth."

"Except you did lie again, Mrs. Hobart. You lied and now you might send an innocent man to prison and perhaps even his execution."

"Objection, Your Honor."

"Sustained."

Jerry was at the end of his rope. "No further questions, Your Honor. The defense rests."

"Ms. Slocum, your witness."

"The prosecution has no questions for this witness."

"Then we'll proceed to closing statements."

******

The closing arguments were anti-climactic. Sally's testimony clearly rattled Jerry and with Randy not even by his side, he gave a mealy mouth, washed down version of how the jury still needed to consider the reasonable doubt which had to exist in three different Culligan suspects. Sally could not possibly be telling the truth because she had lied two previous times before. And what about Judge Culligan not hearing the boat on his way back into the house and what about — Jerry lost his train of thought. It didn't matter. The jury had stopped listening to his dribble.

Gina gave an impassioned speech about the clarity of the testimony and the evidence provided and how the jury must do their supreme duty and convict the defendant. Not twenty minutes after Sally's shocking testimony, the trial ended, and the jury retired. Gina asked Rudy if they wanted to grab a lunch with the family while the jury deliberated.

"No," he told her. "I don't want to miss the verdict. I have a feeling it won't be long. It's 11:00 AM now. Let's give it to 12:30 PM at least."

They didn't even have to wait until noon. When the bailiff went to get Marcus in his chambers, Marcus knew what the verdict would be. They brought Randy back out, this time in handcuffs, and stood him next to Jerry as the foreman prepared to read the verdict. Jerry hoped against hope that somehow he had convinced all twelve of them to embrace his reasonable doubt theory. Randy was already thinking about his appeal with a much more competent lawyer.

When Marcus asked the jury if they had reached a unanimous verdict, the foreman said, "Yes, Your Honor, we have."

"In the case of the State of South Carolina vs. Randall Culligan, do you find the defendant guilty or not guilty?"

"Guilty, Your Honor."

"I find the defendant guilty of first-degree double murder. He shall be incarcerated in the Georgetown County detention center until sentencing. Court is dismissed." Marcus gaveled the trial to an end. They hauled Randy off without another word.

Rudy found out later that one of the jail cell guards who watched over Randy during the closing statements made it crystal clear to Randy that if he so much as uttered a peep during the verdict, he wouldn't be able to sit for a week. For once in his life, Randy showed some discretion.

As the crowd dispersed, Gina and Rudy went over to give Jerry their condolences. Sort of.

"You put up a spirited defense, Jerry," Gina told the defense counselor.

"Yeah, well thanks. They stacked the cards against me, I'm afraid," he tersely replied, scowling at Rudy.

"Yes, well, speaking of the cards you did play, you may have overdone one of them."

"Whatever are you talking about?" he asked.

Gina diverted his attention to Marcus, who was staring directly at Jerry. "Jerry!" demanded Marcus. "My chambers — now!"

CHAPTER 54

Later that afternoon, Tim and Sally were walking along the beach. Sally had the rest of the day off and planned to spend the afternoon and evening at Culligan's Way. It was the start of a new life for the whole family. The stress of the trial was behind them now, and the realization of Randy behind bars for a long, long time gave the entire family a peace of mind they hadn't had in years — ever, in Tim's mind. He couldn't think of a time at the Way when he wasn't tormented in some manner or fashion by his older brother.

Sally also pondered the broader implications for Tim and the family. "So, now that you don't have to worry about Randy anymore, have you given any more consideration to staying at the Way permanently?"

Tim kicked at the waves lapping the shore. They were headed north, towards the pier. A few days ago, Tim and Ruth made it a mile from the Way, more than halfway to the pier. His recovery had made considerable progress. Not only did he have more endurance, but his breathing had eased some as well. His feelings of being truly home had only grown. He hadn't told anyone yet of his plan to stay indefinitely in Pawleys.

Tim made an inquiry at the Reynolds Dance Studio in Georgetown, on Monday, and they had showed interest in hiring him once he regained most of his strength. "You're like a celebrity here, Tim." Kim Reynolds, the owner, told him. "We'd love to have you on board."

Perhaps now was as good a time as any to break the news. And, of course, Sally deserved to be first. He owed her so much. "Actually Sal, I have."

"You have what? Thought about it?"

"No, I've decided to stay indefinitely at the Way. I have a lead at the Reynolds Dance Studio, the same place I went to in High School. They'll let me come teach the kids after I've regained more strength."

Sally looked at her brother in awe. "Oh my God, Tim! That is so wonderful to hear. Have you told Mom yet?"

"No, I haven't. But now, with the trial behind us, well, I wanted to tell you first."

Sally lunged at Tim and gave him an enormous hug. "That is unbelievable good news." Tim hugged her back, much tighter than he had when he first saw his sister at the airport five weeks earlier. When Sally broke the hug, she took a step back and looked at Tim more carefully. "It seems to me you've already gained back a lot of strength. And you've gained weight. How much have you put on?"

Tim looked down and rubbed his belly. He realized there was actually some meat on his bones now. "Ten pounds since I arrived. I'm at 150 now. Thank you, Annabelle."

"Oh yes. And she's not done yet. What weight do you want to be?"

"Well, I was 155 before I got sick. Any more after that and I really will get fat. Can't have fat dancers, you know."

"And what about New York? Have you settled your rent yet or the other obligations you mentioned?"

"No, I haven't, and I need to. The rest of the rent is due by the end of May. I really didn't want to ask Mom and Dad for money, but I'm afraid I'm going to have to. Or maybe just ask for a loan. My friend Brian will take care of getting rid of the furniture. I told him he can keep whatever he makes selling the stuff. Other than that, I believe I'm done with New York. It's amazing to me I don't miss it more. In fact, I don't miss it at all."

"This place will do that to you."

The two continued to walk along the shore, taking in the late spring sunshine and warm ocean breeze. They turned around a little past the spot Tim had reached on Monday. About half the way back, Tim noticed a broken bottle washed up on the beach. "Can you believe this?" he stated, picking up the jagged glass. "Who brings a beer bottle on the beach and doesn't put it in the trash?"

"Unfortunately, New Yorkers don't have a monopoly on being inconsiderate."

"It would appear not. Or maybe it was just one of those transplants."

"Like you, Tim?"

"No, Ma'am, I was just a wanderer for ten years. But now, I believe I've found my way home."

******

When the two arrived back to the Way, Sally took a seat on a back porch rocker.

Tim said, "I'm going to throw this bottle away and I'll be right back up."

"Ok. Then are you going to tell Mom and Annabelle what we talked about?"

"I believe I will," he called back, bounding down the side steps from the back porch that led to the narrow backyard behind the carport. Tim had intended to cut through the carport to the street side where the garbage can they used for pickup was located. But when he entered the carport from the beach side, he noticed a smaller plastic trash can over in the corner with a lid on it. He'd never taken notice of a garbage can there before. It was next to the door that led to the stairwell that led up to the back corner of the great room. The stairwell was enclosed and hardly ever used. Most people who didn't know about it thought the door in the corner of the great room was a closet. Ruth had long ago discouraged its use in order to limit the number of ways to track dirt and sand into the house.

Tim went over to the trash can and removed the lid. But when he was about to throw the broken bottle in the can, he saw a pair of house slippers at the bottom. He instantly recognized them as his mother's. Tim reached in and removed the shoes, then was shocked to see one of them covered with dried blood. "What in the hell?" Tim said out loud. The one shoe had blood stained both on the top side and the bottom sole. He placed the bottle in the trash and set the two slipper shoes on the floor. Then he went back outside and called to his sister, "Sally, come down here. I need to show you something."

A minute later, Sally made her way down the back porch stairs and saw Tim standing beside the trash can. "What's up?" she asked.

"Look at this. What do you suppose these are?"

When Sally picked up and examined the blood-stained slipper, her face went white. She turned to Tim and, with her hand over her mouth, said, "Holy Shit! I can't believe she did that!"

"You can't believe *who* did *what*?"

Sally turned to Tim and said seriously, "Tim. There's something I need to tell you.

CHAPTER 55

Ten Weeks Earlier.

Ruth wasn't thrilled when Randy told her Molly would be at the Way for Sunday dinner that day. She was coming off another one of her spells again. Something she noticed was happening more frequently. It wasn't the medication. She'd been on the current dosage of Risperdal for almost a year now, but in the last month or so, Ruth noticed several times the feeling of overall dread come over her for no reason at all. It happened again last night. Was it something about Rudy that was different? He seemed to be in a strange mood when he returned home on Friday. Like he was trying to avoid her through the evening. When she tried to ask him if something was wrong, he dismissed her derisively. Not a good way to build her confidence.

Randy and Molly were at the Way when she and Rudy and Sally returned from church that Sunday and there was already tension in the air. Ruth knew something rotten was up as soon as she saw Annabelle in the kitchen, motioning for her to come over.

"What is it, Annabelle? Did something happen when we were at church?"

"Why is that evil woman here, Ms. Ruth? Why can't she just stay away from us?"

"What happened, Annabelle? Tell me."

"Those two been fightin' like cats and dogs, Ms. Ruth. The whole time you been at church. Why can't she leave us in peace? And on a Sunday, Lord have mercy."

Ruth peered over to where Randy, Molly, and Connie were all laying on the sectional, each one engrossed with their phones. "What in blazes have you two been fighting about?" Ruth demanded. They ignored her, so she ratcheted her voice up a notch. "Did you hear me Randy, Molly? What's been going on here?"

Molly cut her eyes over to Ruth but said nothing.

Randy glanced over at his mother and said, "Nothing of your concern, Mother. Go back to the kitchen." Then, under his breath, "Where you belong."

But Ruth heard him. And her circuit breaker tripped. "Where I belong!" she shrieked, now heading straight towards him. "Where I belong? Is that where you think I belong, you no good piece of crap? I'll tell you where you belong — face down in the bottom of a garbage can. And I'm going to put you there right now!"

Just before Ruth reached the couch, Sally shot in front of her mother and blocked her path. "That won't be necessary, Mom." Annabelle hustled over to help. Rudy sat in his recliner, breaking his attention from the Sunday Post and Courier to assess the situation.

"Ms. Ruth, let's take a break for a few minutes, shall we? Sally, why don't you sit with your mother upstairs while I finish dinner?"

"Good idea, Annabelle. Come on, Mom. Let's go upstairs and have a chat."

Ruth calmed for a second and regained her senses. "Yes, yes dear. That will be fine."

As Sally led Ruth toward the staircase, she turned and silently mouthed to Randy, "Fuck You." Randy shot her the bird, then went back to looking at his phone. A minute later, Rudy declared he was going upstairs to check on Ruth. Annabelle returned to her duties in the kitchen.

When the three were upstairs, Connie whispered to Molly, "Psst — now's our chance." Molly sprang to her feet and went over to the kitchen and started apologizing to Annabelle. When she had Annabelle sufficiently occupied, with her back to the front of the house, Connie went to the small secretary table by the stairwell where Sally had placed her purse. Checking once more to the kitchen, she took out an extensive set of keys, and after a quick examination, removed three of them. She quickly replaced the keys in the purse and nodded to Molly. Molly ended her brief discussion and returned to the couch. Randy watched it all unfold with mild interest. He knew about their plan and was in for a cut himself.

After about fifteen minutes, Ruth, Rudy, and Sally returned downstairs after Annabelle declared dinner was ready. As they prepared to take their seats at the table, Rudy pointed a finger at Randy and warned him about any further impolite conversation. Randy simply said, "Humph" and sat down. Connie was about to take her normal seat next to Rudy, who always sat at the end, and opposite Ruth, but Molly slipped into the seat ahead of her.

"Hey," Connie objected, "that's where I sit."

"Sit somewhere else, you little brat," Molly hissed at her. Connie shrugged and moved down a seat.

Annabelle brought the platters to the table, and Rudy began to say Grace. Just as he was about to finish, his eyes opened wide, and he forced out a cough. No one could tell that Molly had just reached under the table and grabbed Rudy's balls — they all had their eyes closed. Rudy stumbled through the rest of the Grace.

"Are you alright, dear?" Ruth asked with concern.

Rudy cleared his throat again and cut his eyes at Molly. "Yes, yes, I'm fine. Excuse me for that."

Molly giggled like a schoolgirl.

Dinner started out fine, but soon, chaos once again reared its ugly head. It began when Molly rubbed her leg against Rudy's. This time Rudy called her out.

"Do you have a problem sitting still, Miss Elmwood?" Everyone at the table stopped eating and looked at Molly.

Embarrassed by the sudden attention, Molly drew out a long, "Nooooo."

Things might have been left at that had Randy not contributed, "She can't keep her ass still for five minutes. What's the matter dear? Do you need to hump?"

"Randy!" Ruth shouted out. "How dare you speak like that at our Sunday dinner."

Molly retorted, "Fuck You! Asshole."

Rudy dropped his silverware and shouted, "That's enough out of both of you. You can leave the table now!"

But neither of them were going anywhere. Like a spark igniting a fuel-soaked conflagration, Randy and Molly both started screaming obscenities at each other, up to and including a blunt death threat to his soon to be former fiancée. Rudy kept trying to restore order, but this wasn't court, and he wouldn't have succeeded even if it were. After a couple of deranged minutes, the combatants seemed to exhaust themselves. But Molly wasn't finished. She turned her ire on Ruth.

"This is all your fault, you mean bitch. You've never welcomed me in this house or in this family. You drive Rudy and Randy nuts with your batshit antics. It's probably your fault Tim turned out the way he did."

And that's when Ruth's final circuit breaker snapped. When she heard Tim's name brought up in a such a dismissive fashion, the last fuse that connected her to sanity blew, and she lunged at Molly. Launched herself, actually; flew right across the table with her arms outstretched, then on the way down, secured her fingers around Molly's throat. As Ruth crashed full body onto the dining table, sending food, plates, and silverware everywhere, she held tight to Molly's windpipe and clamped down with everything she had.

It didn't last long, however. In a moment, Rudy was on top of Ruth and extracted her hands from Molly's throat. Annabelle appeared seconds later. Dinner had come to a sudden end.

******

Everyone in the room was sufficiently stunned by the event. They all retreated away from the dining table, except for Ruth, whom Annabelle comforted. Rudy barked he wanted Molly and Randy out of the house immediately.

"Come on, Connie," Molly said. "Let's get out of here. We have an errand to run."

"Oh yes, that's right." She jumped up and grabbed her purse. "Be back in a bit, Mom. Hope you feel better."

Randy took the hint and headed out the back door. "I'll be on the beach, away from you nut jobs."

After a few minutes cleaning up the mess that was left, including the pieces of Ruth's favorite serving platter which met its fate when she crashed onto the table, Ruth told Annabelle to stop what she was doing. "Go with Sally and find me another serving platter, please. TJ Maxx is open this afternoon."

Annabelle looked oddly at Ruth, then at Sally, and shrugged.

"Mom, we can get a new platter any time," replied Sally. "We don't have to go now."

"I wish to have some quiet time. *Now.*" Ruth raised her voice to show her insistence.

Sally wasn't about to argue with her mother after what had already transpired. "Ok — Annabelle, let's go. We'll be back shortly." Sally pulled her keys out of her purse, not realizing her three work keys were missing.

Ruth then looked at Rudy, the only one left in the house. "I need some quiet time down here, Rudy. Don't you have something to do on the computer upstairs?"

Also, not one to argue with his wife on an episode, Rudy said, "Yes, indeed I do, dear. How much time do you need?"

"Don't be sly with me. I'll let you know." Rudy made a hasty exit up the stairs.

Now, finally alone, Ruth began what she had in mind. She went out the front door, down the stairs, and walked across the street to the pier, where she made her way down the ramp, onto the dock, and carefully stepped into Randy's johnboat. Ruth opened the built-in tackle box and had no problem finding what she was looking for — Randy's long fishing fillet knife. The one with his initials carved into it. Ruth tucked it in her apron, closed the tackle box, and made her way back to the house.

Once inside, after carefully checking that no one was downstairs, she opened the utility drawer in the kitchen island. It was basically a junk drawer with all kinds of miscellaneous stuff in it, including some random mismatched knives. Looking around once more, Ruth placed the fillet knife all the way in the back of the drawer. She smiled to herself and said softly, "The next time you pull a stunt like that, bitch, I'll be ready for you."

CHAPTER 56

On the night of Tim's party, Ruth was full of merriment and frivolity. She couldn't remember a recent time where she felt so alive with good feelings, lightheartedness, and joy. The Way was playing host to the party of the year. The Culligan home was a beacon for all who made up serious society in Pawleys Island and the surrounding area. Randy was locked away, at least for the weekend, perhaps longer than that, and Tim was once again the center of attention, not only of the party, but in Ruth's life.

Only one fly buzzed around the ointment which could mar her perfectly planned event — Molly Elmwood. Ruth knew she may very well make an appearance, even without an invitation. Tim had asked about her a couple of times and even if he hadn't been in contact with her, Ruth knew Molly had ways of knowing what was happening around town. She'd be there alright. Ruth prayed things wouldn't get out of hand.

Those prayers wouldn't get answered, however. After Molly arrived, dressed like a whore, of course, Ruth kept a close eye on her when she had a conversation with Tim on the couch. Ruth was talking with Agnes Gallagher, also not a Molly fan, after what Molly had done to her son Alex a few years back. Agnes told Ruth to excuse her for a minute. She wanted to pass along a message to Molly. Agnes walked up behind the couch where Molly sat, then bent over and said something briefly in her ear. Molly shot her a look, then watched Agnes return to Ruth's side.

"What did you say to her?" Ruth asked.

"Skank," replied Agnes. "That's all I needed to say."

"Sums her up, doesn't it?"

"What do you think she wants with Tim?"

"If it's anything more than just catching up, she's going to have a surprise waiting for her."

Agnes looked at Ruth suspiciously, but didn't pursue the matter any further.

It wasn't long after Molly returned from her disappearance upstairs when she started getting into it with Rudy. It was the last straw for Ruth. She felt the demon boil up inside of her. She marched over and butted right in between the two of them.

"I want you out of my house this instant. No one invited you, and you have disrupted the party. Leave now!"

Rudy stood there, speechless and stunned. Molly looked around to see several guests looking straight at her, none of them happy with what they were witnessing. Molly took the cue and said tersely, "Fine, I wasn't planning on staying." She glared and pointed at Rudy and told him, "Don't you forget what I told you." Then she turned her back on Ruth and marched right past her without another word. Once she was out the door, the party returned to normal.

"And what was all that about?" Ruth demanded of her husband.

"Just some comments about Randy," Rudy lied. Ruth let it be at that.

When Randy made his appearance, the demon rose to the surface again. Thank goodness for Annabelle, once more, Ruth thought. Things could have gotten a bit bloody and wouldn't that have just spoiled the party?

By 11:15 PM, the party was over, and Ruth was exhausted. Tim had retired upstairs, and Rudy went out back with more of his bourbon to do whatever he does by himself. Ruth went upstairs herself, but as tired as she was, sleep was elusive. Shortly before midnight, she got out of bed and went out on to the bedroom balcony. The night was still warm, and a slight offshore breeze blew in from over the creek. Then, to her surprise, she saw Tim walk across the street and onto the pier. A minute later, she heard a small boat motor coming from the north and soon dock at the pier. Ruth's blood boiled when she saw Molly exit the boat and walk up the ramp.

Molly embraced Tim, and they talked. Ruth was seething, as she tried to imagine what they were talking about and why that loathsome creature had returned to her home to disrupt her son. When she saw them kiss, it was the last straw, and Ruth suddenly remembered the fishing knife in her utility draw. Without a moment's hesitation, she quickly and quietly descended the stairs, still in her nightgown and house slippers. Rudy was out back, looking out over the ocean, paying no attention to the inside of the house.

Cognizant of what she was about to do, and remembering the Ring cam at the front door, Ruth went to the side entrance door, the one no one ever used, and stepped down to the carport. Tim was just then making his way back to the house, so Ruth hid close to the stairwell door until Tim had reentered the house. Then Ruth crossed the street, glad to see Molly not heading straight back to her boat. She held the knife close to her side and out of sight.

When she entered the pier, Molly turned and looked shocked to see Ruth approach.

"What you do want, you crazy witch?"

"Just this!" Ruth took the knife out from behind her and plunged it into Molly's midsection to the hilt. Molly let out one bloodcurdling scream, then dropped to deck.

"Now you won't be bothering my family anymore." Ruth kicked Molly a few times, squeezing her under the bottom rail, where she splashed into the creek. Ruth looked down and saw her right slipper covered in blood on the top and also on the bottom, where she gave Molly the boot. "Now look what you've done, you stupid bitch," she cursed. "You ruined my good slippers."

Not wasting another second, Ruth removed her prized house shoes, then walked to the gazebo and hurled the knife as far as she could into the creek. She took a deep breath, then returned to the carport, depositing the slippers into the trash can by the carport stairwell. Then she returned to the house, cringing from walking in with dirty feet. Rudy wasn't out back, but yet Ruth didn't see him inside either. When she went upstairs, Rudy still wasn't there. She washed her feet and slipped back into bed. Rudy joined her minutes later with no comment, but Ruth never heard him. She was asleep as soon as her head hit the pillow.

******

"So you saw the whole thing!" Tim couldn't believe the story Sally just told him. They had gone to the back deck to talk, but not until after Tim found a plastic bag and tied the bloody slippers up, then placed it in the main garbage can. The trash would go out in the morning, and the lone remaining piece of evidence tying his mother to the murder of Molly Elmwood would lie undetected for perpetuity in a Georgetown County landfill.

"I did," replied Sally. "It was the most incredible thing I'd ever seen in my life. Sad part is, I was happy to see it. She deserved it. Whatever she was in your past, she had changed for the worse. And it wasn't just Randy, although he surely didn't help. She was just white trash in our eyes, and that's what she'll always be."

"So you lied to the police and in court three times."

"I did what I had to do, Tim. I did it for Mom, I did it for you, I did it for us all. We all have a much brighter future ahead of us now."

Tim rocked back and forth. He glanced inside the house and saw Ruth and Annabelle busy in the kitchen, preparing yet another fantastic meal. "You know, I asked Mom about it a few weeks ago on one of our beach walks. She confided in me how she had struggled with the demons inside of her. She mentioned a dinner back in late February where she went after Molly. Told me she tried to choke her."

"Oh yes! I remember that well. In fact, come to think of it, it was when Molly mentioned your name, when Mom lost it. I know Molly left with a bruise on her throat that day."

Tim shook his head. He didn't know what he was getting into when he came back to Culligan's Way. "When I asked her point-blank if she killed Molly, she gave me an empty stare for a second or two. I couldn't tell what was going through her head. Then she blinked and denied it. I never thought about it again."

"Mom will be fine," Sally assured her brother. "It was people like Randy and Molly in her life that stirred up the demons. They're both out of the picture now."

"And there's Dad, of course."

"Ha! Well, of course, there's always dear old Dad."

Tim and Sally rocked some more in silence. Finally Tim said, "So there's one more secret Culligan's Way will hold forever, I suppose. My lips are sealed."

Sally laughed. "They better be Tim! Pinky swear?"

Tim remembered how the two would 'pinky swear' secrets when they were younger. "Absolutely! And this time we really need to mean it."

Tim and Sally both licked their little finger and hooked them together. They smiled knowingly at each other, recollecting the good old days.

"I'm mouse quiet, Tim."

"Church mouse quiet — me too." They both laughed again. "Connie's coming home on Sunday. Are you ready for that?"

Sally rocked and thought silently. Finally she said, "Yes, yes I am. I'm able to forgive now. I'll tell her that. It's going to be a wonderful Mother's Day this year. I'm really looking forward to it. We all are. Do have a gift bought yet?"

"No, I didn't know what to get her. But now I think I do."

"And I have a pretty good idea what that's going to be."

Tim smiled and nodded his head.

CHAPTER 57

It was Mother's Day Sunday and Ruth looked forward to it more than any Mother's Day she could remember. Randy was the furthest thing from her mind. Connie was coming home from rehab, and by all accounts, she had come through in flying colors. Rudy would pick her up in Myrtle Beach directly from church while the rest of the family prepared another feast for the ages. It may not be a homecoming on the scale of Tim's triumphant return, and it was far from Connie's first return from rehab, but to Ruth, this time felt special. To have her two youngest living in Culligan's Way again, without the hassles and chaos her addiction always seemed to bring, was extra special to Ruth. Randy's absence made it even more extraordinary.

Ruth and Annabelle pulled out all the stops for the day's celebration. A twelve-pound standing rib roast slowly cooked in the oven. Annabelle would shortly prepare roasted potatoes and onions, bacon wrapped asparagus, farm fresh green beans, and homemade Parker House rolls. For cold sides there was a seven-layer salad — one of Ruth's summer specialties, three bean salad, and an assortment of fresh fruits. Tim couldn't believe how great the house smelled when he returned from service. To his surprise, the church was even growing on him, something his mother and father truly appreciated.

Ruth, Annabelle, Tim, along with Sally, Steve, and the kids anxiously awaited Rudy's return with Connie. When the Lexus pulled into the driveway, they all hustled down the front steps to greet her. Tim recalled his own return, just over a month earlier. He couldn't believe it hadn't been longer. When he had his turn to hug his sister, after Ruth and Annabelle, he could tell immediately how much Connie had improved physically. Her eyes shone bright blue, her skin glowed and her brown hair radiated brilliantly. She was always the looker in the family when she could actually hold herself together.

When Tim finished, Sally was the last of the Culligans to greet Connie. Everyone held their breath, recalling the ugliness the last time the two were together. But Sally was true to her word and welcomed her sister with open arms.

"Welcome home, Connie," Sally said. "You look great."

"Thank you, Sally. It's great to be home. I'm sorry for what I put everybody through."

"And I'm sorry for how I reacted at the party. And I forgive you for what happened. It all turned out well in the end."

"I'm so glad to hear that. I heard you were the hit of the trial."

"I'd say she knocked it out of the park," Tim contributed to hearty laughter.

"Come on, y'all," declared Ruth. "Annabelle has a feast like no other waiting on us." Rudy grabbed Connie's one suitcase and they all headed back up the stairs.

******

When dinner finished, with everyone stuffed to the brim, Annabelle announced that her homemade apple pies will have to wait until the Mother's Day gifts were given out. The whole family gathered around the sectional with the gifts laid out on the large, square glass coffee table. Sally went first, opening a couple of cute homemade cards from Joey and Amber, then a gold necklace from Steve.

"Oooh," Sally cooed with delight. "I must have been a very good mommy this year."

"You have stood out from all the rest," declared her husband, meaning only the best.

Not to be outdone, Rudy offered his present next. Ruth looked around coyly as she opened the small box to find a diamond tennis bracelet inside. "Oh, Rudy," Ruth gasped. "You shouldn't have." She held out her arm and let Rudy fasten it on her wrist. "It's absolutely gorgeous. You are truly the greatest husband a woman could ever want."

"I'd be nothing without you, Ruth. You know that."

Ruth smiled and nodded.

Sally followed next with an updated framed portrait of her, Steve, and the kids. Ruth gushed with delight, telling her she had the perfect spot for it.

"I'm sorry, Mom. I didn't have time to get you anything," announced Connie. Ruth looked at her youngest daughter with eyes full of empathy. "Connie darling, you know the greatest gift I could have received today was your return and your health. I am so grateful for that." Connie looked moved to tears and went over to give Ruth another hug.

That just left Tim. Ruth pulled the final wrapped package from the table, a shoe box size gift. When she opened it, her eyes lit up with delight. "A new pair of house slippers!" She looked at Tim curiously. "My old pair went missing a few weeks ago. I don't know what happened to them. I've been wearing these old second hands and been meaning to get a new pair. How thoughtful of you, Tim."

"I thought you'd enjoy them, Mom. I'm happy I could help." Tim looked over at Sally, who suppressed a laugh.

Ruth caught it, however. "What is it, you two? What's so funny?"

"It's nothing, Mom, really. We just —" Tim couldn't think of how to finish his sentence.

"We just always know what's best for you, Mom," Sally came to his rescue. "And we're always looking out for you. You know that, right?"

"Of course, dear, and I'm so very grateful for everything you've done for me." Ruth smiled at Sally and Tim so subtly sly, that they both knew she knew exactly what they meant.

******

It is said that inside a woman's heart hides a deep ocean of secrets. For Ruth Culligan, the secrets of Culligan's Way knew no bounds. "This is a special place," Tim remembered his mother telling him on one of their beach walks. "Culligan's Way is more than just a home, Tim. It's where your heart lies. All the memories, the activities, the conversations — everything that has taken place here is bound together to define who we are — who we really are. But it's not just the things we do together. To me, this place, this home, this beach — it knows more about me than any person alive. Only Culligan's Way knows where all my secrets are buried. And that is the way it will always be. I can take solace in that."

Tim smiled and told his mother he understood exactly what she meant. Ever since he returned, he had felt this seminal pull the home exerted on him. Like as if he had some kind of silent, invisible pact with the place that only he could identify. It was his safe place, his shelter from the outside world, and the place which held the family together. Despite all of its secrets. Perhaps because of them. Tim knew in his heart that the secrets of Culligan's Way were meant to be buried, and buried forever they would stay.

ACKNOWLEDGEMENT

I wish to thank my first readers Margaret, Jim, and Emma. Thank you again, Melinda, for a fantastic cover. Thank you to Wendy and Olivia for giving me the opportunity to promote my work. What you do for your authors and your readers is amazing. And a special thank you to my friends in our local chapter of SCWA. Your feedback and help have taught me so much and have made me a much better writer. So to Kathleen, Tibby, Becky, Camile, Annette, Richard, Barbara, Nicki, Madison, Robert, and Anica, I look forward to many more sessions of your help and guidance.

ABOUT THE AUTHOR

Culligan's Way is Marvin Levine's fourth novel and his second in print. Like his previous novel, A Trail of Vengeance, Culligan's Way is set in his hometown of Pawleys Island, South Carolina. Retired now four years after his career in Manufacturing, Marvin has settled into the beach life with his wife Margaret. He enjoys biking and kayaking when he isn't travelling to visit his three children and five grandchildren.

Made in the USA
Columbia, SC
07 July 2023